NEW WRITING 6

New Writing 6 is the sixth volume of an annual anthology which promotes the best in contemporary literature. It brings together some of our most formidable talent, placing new names alongside more established ones, and includes poetry, essays, short stories and extracts from novels in progress. Distinctive, innovative and entertaining, it is essential reading for all those interested in British writing today. *New Writing 6* is published by Vintage, in association with the British Council.

A. S. Byatt's first novel, *The Shadow of the Sun*, appeared in 1964 and was followed by *The Game* (1967), *The Virgin in the Garden* (1978), *Still Life* (1985), *Possession* (1990, winner of the Booker Prize for Fiction) and *Angels and Insects* (1992). She has published three collections of stories, *Sugar and Other Stories* (1987), *The Matisse Stories* (1994) and *The Djinn in the Nightingale's Eye* (1994). A volume of critical essays, *Passions of the Mind*, appeared in 1991, and her most recent novel, *Babel Tower*, in 1996.

Peter Porter was born in Australia in 1929 and has lived in London since 1951. He has published thirteen collections of poetry and collaborated with the painter, Arthur Boyd, on four books of poems and pictures. He is also a reviewer of literature and music in journals and for the BBC. After his *Collected Poems* (1983), his recent publications include *The Automatic Oracle* (1987), *Possible Worlds* (1989) and *The Chair of Babel* (1992).

New Writing 6

edited by

A. S. BYATT
and
PETER PORTER

V

VINTAGE
in association with
The British Council

Published by Vintage 1997

2 4 6 8 10 9 7 5 3 1

Vintage
Random House, 20 Vauxhall Bridge Road, London SW1V 2SA

Random House Australia (Pty) Limited
20 Alfred Street, Milsons Point, Sydney
New South Wales 2061, Australia

Random House New Zealand Limited
18 Poland Road, Glenfield,
Auckland 10, New Zealand

Random House South Africa (Pty) Limited
Endulini, 5A Jubilee Road, Parktown 2193, South Africa

Random House UK Limited Reg. No. 954009

A CIP catalogue record for this book
is available from the British Library

ISBN 0099545519

Papers used by Random House UK Ltd are natural,
recyclable products made from wood grown in
sustainable forests. The manufacturing processes
conform to the environmental regulations of the
country of origin

Typeset by Palimpsest Book Production Limited,
Polmont, Stirlingshire
Printed and bound in Great Britain by
The Guernsey Press Co. Ltd., Guernsey, Channel Islands

PREFACE

New Writing 6 is the sixth volume of an annual anthology founded in 1992 to provide an outlet for new short stories, work in progress, poetry and essays by established and new writers working in Britain or in the English language. The book is intended primarily as a forum for British writers, and the main object is to present a multi-faceted picture of modern Britain; contributions from English-language writers of non-British nationality will occasionally be accepted if they contribute to this aim. It was designed by the British Council's Literature Department to respond to the strong interest in the newest British writing not only within Britain but especially overseas, where access to fresh developments is often difficult. The aim is that, over the years, and through changing editorships, it will provide a stimulating, variegated, useful and reasonably reliable guide to the cultural and especially the literary scene in Britain during the 1990s.

New Writing 7, edited by Carmen Callil and Craig Raine, will appear in March 1998, and *New Writing* 8, edited by Tibor Fischer and Lawrence Norfolk, in March 1999. Though some work is commissioned, submissions of unpublished material for consideration (stories, poetry, essays, literary interviews and sections from forthcoming works of fiction) are welcome. Two copies of submissions should be sent: they should be double-spaced, with page numbers (*no* staples), and accompanied by a stamped addressed envelope for the return of the material, if it cannot be used. They should be sent to

New Writing
Literature Department,
The British Council,
11 Portland Place,
London W1N 4EJ

The deadline for *New Writing 7* is 18 April.

CONTENTS

CONTENTS

CONTENTS

INTRODUCTION

WRITERS ARE NOTORIOUSLY the victims of their own minds. Wherever they go, they tend to interpret what they see in terms of metaphor. While reading manuscripts as one of the editors of this collection of *New Writing*, I kept being reminded of what I was up to by everyday experiences. My favourite jogging of the imagination occurred in a confectionery shop, itself a place of semi-illicit pleasures, perhaps as attractive and personal as any book. In front of me were set out rows of bins containing dozens of different sorts of lollies, sweets, chocolates, nut-and-biscuit derivatives, all under a grand heading, *Pick 'n' Mix*. You took your bag up to be weighed and paid an overall rate for what you'd gathered. Just like an anthology, I thought.

But perhaps the parallel is not exact. A. S. Byatt and I have done the picking and the mixing, and hundreds of writers from Britain have provided the sweetmeats and delights for us to choose from. It is the mixing which I am particularly attracted to. Writing is too much given to ghettoising. People who like fiction may seldom bother with poetry. Journalists of ideas, politics and science may be too busy to attend to short stories or to novels. Many writers are naturally outside any straitjacket of genre. All this we have tried to break down in this anthology. The unclassifiable can feel at home, whatever its nature.

For instance, we have a fantasy about British fiction of the past hundred or so years, written from the point of view of its creations and not of their creators. Proust and Joyce meet one night in Paris, and talk about more interesting things than their stomachs, as they ought to have done and which irresponsibly they did not. An island which might well exist is given a history which it certainly couldn't have had. Character and archetype are weighed in the balance. And all this is what the supermarket packagers refer to as 'added at no extra cost' – over and above the many stories and poems we have gathered together in just over five hundred pages.

Creativity is always having its temperature taken. Writing is apparently continuously in crisis. In my experience it is only authors' bank balances which are seriously endangered. The impulse to write is unstoppable and produces, fountainlike, a constant flow of fine work. *New Writing 6* is a biopsy, if not quite a distillation, of the millions of words written in Britain or by British writers during the past twelve to eighteen months. The editors leave it to their readers to spot trends and to deplore tendencies. They have already had proven to them that, whether it be innovative or traditional, writing in Britain today is richly endowed with imagination and is multifarious in form.

Peter Porter

Louis de Bernières

A NIGHT OFF FOR
PRUDENTE DE MORAES

PRUDENTE DE MORAES paused briefly to glance down with satisfaction at the freshly gleaming leather of his shoes. He had just had them buffed up by a barefoot and bedraggled fellow with a Bahian accent, paying him more than was strictly necessary, and therefore a feeling of virtue and beneficence was spreading in his stomach as though he had swallowed a fine glass of *aguardente* with one stylish tip of the chin. It was good to be wearing casual dress, walking as slowly as he liked in the early evening, listening to the crash of the waves and watching the plumes of spray.

He strolled along the Avenida Vieira Souto, dawdling to watch the interminable games of volleyball played by the golden-skinned young men. Just now and then one might see a boy practising fancy tricks with a football, and one would wonder at the elegance and precision of it all. Prudente reflected that often the most beautiful things were those that were intrinsically the most useless.

He stopped at a kiosk and asked for an *água de coco*, merely for the pleasure of witnessing the attendant ritual, smiling to himself and chinking the change in his pocket as the man delved into his frigidaire to retrieve a large coconut. He lopped off the end with a machete, so that it would stand on a table if required, and then, with three deft twists of the wrist and three smart blows, he removed a triangle of the outer pith from the other end, through which he inserted a couple of straws. 'The reason,' mused Prudente, 'that he does

1

it with such swiftness and precision, is that he wants me to be impressed. What vain creatures we are.'

He took the coconut and sat at the white plastic table, sucking the cold coconut milk into his mouth, and feeling it insinuating its soft liquid tentacles around the contents of his stomach. He had not often had *água de coco* since he was a little boy, having graduated to beer, but now he resolved to do so more often. Sometimes it was a good idea to reclaim one's past, even if only in the smallest ways. He looked up at the digital clock that had been sponsored by McDonald's, and bathed in the luxurious feeling of having an entire evening to waste.

Prudente decided to take off his shoes and socks, and go down to the edge of the waves. It was a good twenty-eight degrees, but the clouds had prevented the sun from baking the sand directly, and anyway there was a trick to walking on hot sand, which was to keep going and not to think about it.

He wove between the volleyball games, and down to the long flat strip where there seemed to be nobody who was not young and exquisitely beautiful. He felt wistful when he saw the flat stomachs and well-defined pectoral muscles of the young men, and even more wistful when he saw that every one of the young girls was a teenager. Most of them wore the kind of bikini bottoms known popularly as 'dental floss' because they had no real seat to them, but only an exiguous fillet that disappeared between the cheeks.

His eyes roved over hundreds of heartbreakingly brown-buttocked lolitas laid out in rows on their towels, soaking up the sun, and soaking up the longing of the males who watched them from behind the cool privacy of their sunglasses. It was a beach full of narcissists, he realised, and then reflected with a flash of honesty that the only reason that he himself was not a narcissist these days, was that he no longer had very much to be vain about. He watched two men floundering comically in the prodigious waves. One was tall and angular, the other short and spherical. Few of the locals were swimming, because the coastguard's red flag was flying, and from their puce faces and eccentric behaviour, Prudente rightly inferred

2

that the two bathers were Englishmen. He watched them being bowled over by the waves every time his eyes needed to be refreshed after having seen yet another fabulous but untouchable girl patrol past him like a panther, or flow by with the loose-limbed elegance of a gazelle.

He was about to leave Ipanema beach when he became aware that a spectacular sunset was developing over the sea by São Conrado. Normally a mist rose on the horizon, obscuring the sunset altogether, but today the clouds and the ocean's vapour had left a space for the sun to display itself, so that it was sinking at a sedate but visible speed, growing ever larger and more splendid. It was incandescent and fluorescent, with a colour that struck him more as artificial than as natural. Streaks of vermilion and scarlet spread horizontally, and Prudente wished idly that there might be some orange and black. Orange and black sunsets were his particular favourite, because their savagery made them less sentimental. He loved beauty as much as any man else, but he was not unduly sentimental, and he liked his beauty to be slaked with just a touch of terror.

He realised that the sun was going to sink at precisely the mid-point between the rocks out to sea and the headland, as if it had been aiming deliberately at the most aesthetically pleasing configuration of land and sea. Prudente looked up at the peaks known as 'The Two Brothers', and reflected once again that they looked more like two ill-matched woman's breasts. Come to think of it, the Sugar Loaf was somewhat breast-shaped too. He watched the lights begin to go on in the *favela* above São Conrado, the pinpricks of light oscillating in the hot air like distant stars. He remembered when the *favela* had been nothing but sheets of tin and lumps of timber held together with wires and beachcombed lengths of rope. Now they were built of bricks, but they still seemed to disgorge the same plague of thieves and rogues that they always had.

Prudente did not want to spoil the sunset by ruminating upon intractable social problems, however, and like many others had long ago come only to the conclusion that radical cures were required. He turned his attention back to the natural glory of what was happening in the west. The sun was now half drowned, and was throwing out thick and undulating plumes of scarlet fire. They had become like the locks of a woman imagined by an artist who was thinking of a wild goddess, or was attempting to epitomise a passion such as grief, or vengeance, or desire.

Prudente noticed that an odd thing was occurring. The crowds of young *Cariocas* had risen to their feet, and were facing the west, entranced by the dying moments of the sun. He watched the volleyballers, the footballers, the seekers of suntans, the young heartbreakers of both sexes, the dedicated narcissists who had just become absorbed in something even more beautiful than themselves, and felt profoundly stirred. There must be something naturally wonderful within the human heart, an impulse that opened it to the ineffable, the sublime, and the marvellous. He rose to his feet and stood among the crowd, sensing sympathetically the waves of unanimous spiritual awe that sparked in the charged air between them.

The sun slipped to the rim of the earth, a final ball of red light flared briefly like a ruby at the outer edge of the sea, and then it was gone. Spontaneously the throng of *Cariocas* burst into applause, congratulating the sun and the sea upon the finest possible performance, as if the whole world had become a theatre and the human race the spectator to its virtuosity. The sky darkened to violet-blue, but still the people stood silent, as if awaiting a curtain-call. A cool gust of wind blew in off the southern Atlantic, and a sigh passed through the crowd. Without a word, Rio de Janeiro's throng of beautiful young sybarites leaned down, picked up their beach paraphernalia, and walked quietly away towards the Avenida Vieira Souto. They would take a final *guaraná* perhaps, a final Coca-Cola, a final *água de coco* from one of the kiosks, and then be off home before the thieves came down from the slums.

Prudente had been deeply stirred by the whole experience, not merely by the extraordinary splendour of the sunset, but also by the unexpected manner in which it had seized the hearts of so many people simultaneously. Chills had run down his spine, and his own sigh had joined the sussuration of the crowd at the final moment of the sun's descent. He would have felt the same if he had caught a glimpse of the Virgin herself, or seen St Sebastian ride through the city with his incorruptible body full of arrows. He went to a bar in the Rua Visconde de Piraja, and ordered a *caipirinha*.

He watched the barman crushing the ice by whacking it with a spoon, and observed him slicing the limes, putting in the sugar, and finally pouring the spirit. He took the glass and braced himself for the impact; the first gulp was always a shock to the system, no matter how many times one had drunk it before in one's life. It was that strange combination of sweet, bitter, and sour. Prudente never drank more than two at one sitting, because it had a most insidious way of making one drunk; one might suffer double-vision, for example, whilst remaining otherwise clear-headed.

Prudente drank his two *caipirinhas* over a period of one hour, engaged in conversation with a fat and intoxicated security man who rather tediously insisted upon showing him his pistol, and then wandered out into the night. It was humid, a trickle of sweat began to slip down his temple, and he wiped his mouth with the back of his sleeve. He decided that he would walk down the Rua Garcia d'Avila to the lagoon, so that he could look at the Christ, floodlit at the top of the Corcovado mountain. It was a sight of which he could never tire, for sometimes the top of the mountain would be enclosed in mist, and the gigantic Christ would glow gold, as if coming in glory upon the clouds at the resurrection of the dead. Equally one could imagine that the Christ was an angel, perhaps Michael or Gabriel, and Prudente wondered how many crimes had been prevented by a thief or a murderer looking up at the last moment, and being reminded of the omnipresence, justice, and beauty of God. Sometimes Prudente wondered how anyone could do wrong in Rio, with the Christ resplendent in the sky at night.

Prudente knew that it was foolish to wander these streets unaccompanied, and without urgency or purpose in his stride.

He realised with wry honesty that he did not live up to his name at times such as this, and therefore he was not altogether surprised when an arm went around his shoulder, and the barrel of a gun was stuck into his ribs. He knew immediately that he was being robbed, but, strangely enough, he also realised that he could not be bothered to be alarmed.

'Senhor,' said the robber, walking along with him with his arm around his shoulder in apparent friendship, 'you are richer than me, and I am very poor. If you give me your money and your watch, you will come to no harm.'

'How do you know that I am richer than you?' demanded Prudente, with an edge of irritation in his voice, 'and if you're so poor, how come you can afford to buy a gun?'

'I stole it,' replied the man, offended at the suggestion that he was lying about being poor.

'Then you probably haven't got any bullets, have you?'

'Of course I have bullets.'

'Prove it. Go on, fire into the air or something, and then I'll believe you. Otherwise I give you nothing.'

'If I fire it, everyone will come running.'

'If you don't fire it, I must assume either that you don't have any bullets, or that it's a replica.'

The thief sucked his teeth in irritation, and poked the gun a little harder into Prudente's ribs. 'Come on, cut the chatter. Hand over.'

Prudente continued both to be calm and to be surprised at how calm he was. He changed tack. 'Do you know how boring you are?'

'Boring?'

'Yes. Very boring. Today I had a day off work, I had my shoes polished, I walked on the beach, I saw a beautiful sunset, I had a couple of *caipirinhas*. I was happy, and then you have to come along and disturb my peace of mind when I was only going to have a look at the Christ. It's boring. Look, I'll show you how boring you are.' Prudente reached into his trouser pocket and produced a sheaf of cruzados. 'Have a look at those, I keep them specially for muggers.'

The thief looked down at them and said, 'They're out of date. You can't use cruzados any more.'

'Precisely, but in the dark a thief just takes them and runs, and looks at them later. I've been mugged four times, and now I carry a little wad of cruzados. And look at this . . .' Prudente reached into his shirt pocket and brought out a rectangle of plastic, '. . . this is an expired credit card that I carry for the same reason.' He drew himself up to his full height and inhaled as if with exasperation. 'That is how boring you are. You and your kind are so inevitable that I don't even care about it.'

The robber appeared both crestfallen and insulted. He avoided Prudente's reproachful and disdainful glance, and said, 'Nonetheless, hand over the cash, and your watch.'

Prudente held up his left wrist. 'Plastic watch,' he announced, with a glee that was almost malicious, 'resale value nil. What a shame.' There was a long pause as the two men looked at each other, and then Prudente said, 'Are you poor and hungry?'

'Yes. Why else would I do this?'

'Because you're a lazy son of a bitch who won't get a real job? Because you have no sense of morality? Because you like the excitement? Who knows?'

'I am poor and hungry,' insisted the thief.

'You have nice clothes. Nice shoes. A nice gold tooth.'

'Nonetheless, I am poor and hungry. Not everything is as it seems.'

'So you don't like to do bad things?'

Prudente felt the barrel of the gun prod with less intensity into his ribs. 'Of course not,' replied the robber at last.

'Come and have dinner with me,' proposed Prudente. 'I have an evening off, and if you are so hungry, then you can have a free meal on me, without doing anything bad.'

The robber eyed him suspiciously. 'I think I'll just go home,' he said at length.

'No, no, no, come on, I invite you. Be my guest. I'd like the company. What's your favourite meal?'

'*Feijoada*.'

'Ah, me too, but I don't know anyone who serves it in the evening. By the middle of the afternoon there's nothing left.

I'll take you to a *churrasco* house, perhaps, and we can have a *picanha*. How about that?'

'What's the catch?' asked the thief, finally putting the gun into the waistband of his trousers.

'We've got to go and look at the Christ first.'

'One false move and I shoot,' warned the thief, who had watched a great many Westerns on the television, and had picked up one or two of the most time-honoured clichés.

Together the two men walked down to the lagoon. A row of white egrets perched upon a jetty, recuperating from a hard day's fishing, and one man with a torch was paddling in the shallows, hoping to attract a fish or two to the pool of light that he was casting upon the water. In his right hand he held a machete with which to despatch his victims. High above, the statue of Christ shone in glory above the clouds, its arms outspread in a gesture that was both a crucifixion and an embrace.

'I come here when I need to think, to have a little consolation,' said Prudente.

'I like it too,' said the thief.

'Where are you from? You don't have a *carioca* accent.'

'I'm from Salvador. I love it, but to be honest, there's no future up there. Rio's where the money is.'

'And São Paulo.'

'São Paulo's OK. Brasilia's just one big traffic jam.'

'You're right there. Come on, let's go and eat. We can try Luna's or "Paz e Amor".'

'I've never been to a proper restaurant,' said the thief, 'you'll have to tell me what to do.'

In 'Paz e Amor' Prudente watched with satisfaction as his guest chewed with enthusiasm upon the medallions of rare beef. Juice trickled down their chins, and they clinked glasses at every gulp. Prudente had chosen first a bottle of Concha y Toro from Chile, and then a bottle of Brazilian Forestier. 'We Brazilians make good wine,' he observed, 'but we've forgotten to tell anyone. All the more for us, eh?'

The dish of *picanha* was large enough for four people, but the two of them managed to demolish it nonetheless, with the aid of copious draughts of mineral water, and fine swigs of the red wine. Prudente instructed his guest upon the art of attracting the waiter's attention, and explained that you always get better service if you say 'thank you' a great deal. 'What's your favourite football team?' he asked.

'Flamengo. What's yours?'

'What a coincidence. Mine's Flamengo too. Did you see the game last week?'

'I heard about it. Did you see it?'

'It was fantastic.'

'I heard it was. I couldn't get in, so I went and had a drink.'

Prudente attracted the waiter with a snap of his fingers, and said, 'Two cognacs. Have you got the one with the ginger in it?'

'*Macieira*, sir?'

'That's the one.'

Prudente showed the thief how to warm the glass in his hands so that the vapour would rise up and be trapped in the glass. He showed him how to sniff it. The thief inhaled deeply, a slow smile spreading across his face. '*Nossa Senhora!* I could get drunk on that alone,' he said.

'Have you heard the rumour about the police executing people like you?' asked Prudente.

'People like me?'

'Thieves, armed robbers, that sort of thing. They say that the cops are so fed up with lawlessness that they're taking the law into their own hands.'

The thief looked at him reproachfully, as though resentful of being named for what he was. 'I heard it was the police who killed all those street children on the steps of the Candelária.'

'I don't think the police kill children,' said Prudente, 'but I heard they were killing people like you. Somebody found a corpse on the Corcovado recently. Apparently they only do it in their spare time, when they're out of uniform. That's dedication for you, eh?'

The thief regarded him, a small glow of fear alight in

9

his eyes. 'Don't talk like this,' he said, 'it gives me the creeps.'

'Hey, I bought you a meal. You're OK with me. By the way, was I right in thinking that you didn't have any bullets? Too expensive, eh? Or is the gun a replica?'

'I've got bullets,' said the thief, 'I just don't like to kill anyone. It's bad enough when someone like you keeps reminding me that I'm a thief, but I'm not a murderer. I hope I never sink to that.'

They sat in companionable silence, sipping their cognac, and feeling the *picanha* lie in their stomachs with the mildly uncomfortable weight of a small cannonball. 'I've got to go to the men's,' said the thief, 'keep an eye on my things.'

'That's OK, I've got to make a phone call. Do you want me to order some coffee? Do you like it pure, or with sugar?'

After the thief had gone, Prudente took his mobile phone from his jacket, stabbed at the buttons, and talked for a few moments into the receiver. He put it down as the thief reappeared, and let it lie on the table, as if to indicate 'You could have stolen this.'

'Do you mind if I look at your gun?' asked Prudente, 'I have an interest in them.'

'In a restaurant?' protested the thief. 'Certainly not.'

'Oh go on. Just pass it under the cloth. Take the bullets out first if you want. Is it a nice one?'

'Browning automatic, 9mm. It's a sweetie.'

'Let's have a look.'

The thief thought about it, and then removed the weapon from inside his jacket. He withdrew the ammunition clip, and passed the weapon under the tablecloth. Prudente hefted its weight in his hands, and said, 'I prefer a .38 revolver. I mean, with automatics you can't ever be sure that they're not going to jam, and if that happens in a tight spot, you're done for.'

'I know.' The thief leaned forward confidentially. 'I bet you'll never guess where I got it from.'

'You said you'd stolen it.'

'I bought it from one of the soldiers at the Copacabana Fort.'

'*Nossa Senhora*!' exclaimed Prudente, 'I heard that such things happened, but I didn't think it was true.'

'They're all in it,' said the thief, bitterly. 'Police, politicians, the army, you name it.'

'I don't know why you're so disgusted,' said Prudente. 'You're a thief yourself.'

The thief looked at him wearily. 'As you keep reminding me.'

Prudente reached inside his jacket and withdrew a pair of panatellas. 'Cigar?' he asked. 'It goes well with the cognac and coffee. A good way to end the evening happily.'

The thief accepted the cigar and blew out his cheeks. 'I'm stuffed,' he said. 'Tomorrow I'll be shitting pure blood, like a vampire.'

The two men watched with interest as a Military Police vehicle disappeared slowly around the corner. 'They're up to something,' observed the thief, 'you can always tell. When the sirens are going, you know that they're just trying to get home quickly. It's when they're creeping about that you know something's up.'

'You're probably right,' said Prudente, nodding his head, and blowing a thick cloud of blue aromatic smoke into the air above the thief's head.

'Nice cigar,' said the thief.

'I'm going to pay the bill,' said Prudente de Moraes. 'It's time we were off. It's been a great evening. After an inauspicious beginning to our acquaintance, I am beginning to feel that I have almost made a friend.'

'You've been very kind,' said the thief, 'a true Christian.' He hung his head, and a choke came into his voice. 'I didn't deserve to be treated so well, after what I tried to do.'

As they walked off together, Prudente put his arm through that of his new friend, and they matched step as they considered the beauty and calm of the evening. 'Did you know,' asked Prudente, 'that in the northern hemisphere they see a completely different set of stars? I've often thought of that as a metaphor for something, but I don't know what.'

'It makes you think,' said the thief, and at that moment

11

the two men became aware that ahead of them, walking towards them, were four very large men walking in line abreast. 'Better cross the street,' said the thief, 'better be on the safe side.'

'It's too late now,' replied Prudente de Moraes. 'All we can do is look strong and confident, and keep going as if we know exactly what's what.'

'Maybe we should invite them to dinner,' said the thief, with a small and very nervous laugh.

'It's OK,' said Prudente, 'I think I know these characters. Friends of mine.'

'That's a relief. I thought we were done for.'

Prudente called out to the men, who were now within a few paces, 'Hey, Vargas, Francisco, Bartolomeo, Paulo, how's things? Good to see you. What a coincidence. Let me introduce you to my friend.'

They shook hands all round, the thief revealing that his name was Luis Ribeiro.

'We've had a great evening,' said Prudente, 'you'll find that Luis is good company.'

The thief eyed the four men, and grew suspicious. They all had neatly brushed hair, broad shoulders, bulky jackets, freshly shaved faces, and very shiny shoes. It did not seem quite right.

'This is him, is it?' asked one of the men, and Prudente nodded.

The thief howled and protested as he was dragged towards the Military Police car, forced up against it, disarmed, searched, and handcuffed. One of the men briefly inspected the thief's Browning automatic, and handed it to Prudente. The thief was pushed into the vehicle, and Prudente leaned in through the window. The thief was shaking with fear, whimpering, almost unable to speak.

'Don't take it too badly,' said Prudente, soothingly, 'you've had the traditional meal, the traditional smoke, even a chance to repent. We've had a great time. I would shake your hand and wish you well, but I can't because of the handcuffs. It's a pity.' He reached out his hand, and patted the thief comfortingly upon the shoulder, '*Adeus.*' To the four men he said, 'Good night, boys. Go carefully.'

'Good night, Sergeant,' they chorused in reply, and Prudente de Moraes watched the car pull away from the kerb and head towards the Túnel Rebouças. A twinge of regret tugged at his heart, and he set off back towards Ipanema beach, where he bought a can of *guaraná*, sat on the steps, looked up at the Southern Cross, and listened to the sea.

Dorothy Nimmo

GOODWIFE

I live in her skin. I look out from her eye-sockets.
I have made her bed, I have slept with her husband.
I knead her bread, I spit on the heel of her iron
and hear it sizzle. I stoke her fire. I slip my hands
into her rubber gloves and plunge them in hot water.
I prune her roses. My feet are heavy in her boots.
I have carried her children.
                                            She wraps herself up warm
but I am always cold. She eats but I am always
hungry. She confesses but I am not forgiven.

Hares dance in the furrows, owls haunt the barn, no swifts
nest in the rafters and we have no luck with parsley.
All the yard cats are black, not a white hair on them
and all our children are barren.

MY FATHER'S SHADOW

At Seascale our shoes were full of sand.
Daddy emptied them out in the front porch
and we went up the stairs like good girls
and pulled the quilts over our heads as
the rocks dragged the darksilk sea back
over the wet ridged sand
again and again and the sea was lovely really.

Mother said, It's not cold really,
you'll get used to it but I was frightened.
Daddy said, She'll go in when she's ready.

14

He found a hollow in the sand
and something sweet in his pocket.

I wouldn't have chosen to grow up
quite this way, to be quite so far out,
to become so used to the cold
that now I can even lie down in the snow
and imagine it is warm, imagine
I am in the warm sand
in the shadow of my father.

LEFT RIGHT

If you had your time again what
would you choose? If we were playing
Oranges and Lemons would you pick
oranges? Lemons? Would you pick me?
If you picked me would I be your
better half? If there was only half
of me would that be better? Would
you take left or right? If there was only
one left would you take it? Would you
see me right? If I couldn't take it
would you give me the other?
If you were the other would I
be the one? Would I be all right?
Or would I be left?

If it's half-time do you feel like
a right lemon? When you have sucked
the juice will there be anything left?
How much of this can you take?

How much time have you left? If
you had your time over again
do you think you would get it right?

LAST WORDS

Perhaps we could all agree to avoid the word
filigree. Do any of you still remember
those pierced silver dishes filled with Turkish delight,
grapes or nuts set among folded napery
(and that word too should be avoided). What would we lose
if that image was no longer available?

How do we feel about stipple? Are we happy
with pock? Patina? Lambent? These words are under threat,
their future uncertain but how would we describe
the interlocking rings of raindrops on water?
The distant sound of tennis on summer evenings?
The richly weathered surface of garden bronzes?

I would like to apply for a licence for pock,
stipple, shard, patina, lambent, filigree.
I feel under an obligation to keep them
alive when so much is endangered. Could they be
recycled? Tigree, stippent, lambock, stopple, filipat.
It might be kinder to let them go quietly.

Faraway a pock-a-pock-a and the evening sky
stippled, lambent. The long high note of filigree
screams thinly for the last time gree! gree! and falls
apart and the fragments go fluttering across
the moon. Ock lam ipp ent sha . . . sha . . . sha . . .
whispering into the silence.

Ruth Padel
THE YAKS

. . . and never tell you

how I'll never see
or partly see

the yaks
descending the tree-line,

first as spots on flat
emerald, then their own buttocks

lurching above them at sunset
under the felt-sacks

of salt, fur, charcoal,
down to the Tsang-Po river.

Piebald yaks, dun, sable, ginger –

their amber and vanilla
steaming eyes

finding the way home as I never will
through the fat tufts

(something something) . . .
steady the tilt

of their horns
over creamcurds of froth

in the rapids – this fallout
of infamous rocks.

Look. Lean out and touch them –
there in the pale-face fjord

where girls on the bank
still tugging their shoes off

yodel an evening
song to a bamboo flute.

Exactly this song
for a faraway lover.

Michael Hulse

CAPUT MORTUUM

An apple orchard, meadows and a river,
a raft at a mooring where children are swimming,
an ancient ash, the sawmill and the bridge,
and at the heart the home of all our colours –

tin pails of white lead paste, and silver mica
from China, and zinc oxide from Peru,
Carrara dust, pozzuoli, burnt sienna,
red ochre, aniline, Verona green,

dammar resin, madder lake, campeachy,
bone black, indigo and dragon's blood,
Dutch pink and gallnuts, dried black mallow flowers,
kamala, berberis root and walnut shells,

and dark in the stillness a man with a mortar and pestle,
cracking the lapis lazuli apart,
grinding the purest in the pulverisette,
a second grinding, then a sifting,

binding the powder with turpentine resin
and heated beeswax, letting it draw for a day,
then straining it in a linen bag
in a bucket of lukewarm water,

colour coming in a tide,
filling fifty pails, returning
to the first to pour the water off
and dry the sediment and sift again –

this, I think as I gaze beyond the river where the children
  swim,
beyond to where the sky consoles
with old familiar colours of our physics and our souls,
this in our stillness is our purest blue.

Penelope Fitzgerald

DESIDERATUS

JACK DIGBY'S MOTHER never gave him anything. Perhaps, as a poor woman, she had nothing to give, or perhaps she was not sure how to divide anything between the nine children. His godmother, Mrs Piercy, the poulterer's wife, did give him something, a keepsake, in the form of a gilt medal. The date on it was September the 12th, 1663, which happened to be Jack's birthday, although by the time she gave it him he was eleven years old. On the back there was the figure of an angel and a motto, *Desideratus*, which, perhaps didn't fit the case too well, since Mrs Digby could have done with fewer, rather than more, children. However, it had taken the godmother's fancy.

Jack thanked her, and she advised him to stow it away safely, out of reach of the other children. Jack was amazed that she should think anywhere was out of the reach of his little sisters. 'You should have had it earlier, when you were born,' said Mrs Piercy, 'but those were hard times.' Jack told her that he was very glad to have something of which he could say, This is my own, and she answered, though not with much conviction, that he mustn't set too much importance on earthly possessions.

He kept the medal with him always, only transferring it, as the year went by, from his summer to his winter breeches. But anything you carry about with you in your pocket you are bound to lose sooner or later. Jack had an errand to do in Hending, but there was nothing on the road that day, neither horse nor cart, no hope of cadging a lift, so after waiting for an hour or so he began to walk over by the hill path.

After about a mile the hill slopes away sharply towards Watching, which is not a village and never was, only a single great house standing among its outbuildings almost at the bottom of the valley. Jack stopped there for a while to look down at the smoke from the chimneys and to calculate, as anyone might have done, the number of dinners that were being cooked there that day.

If he dropped or lost his keepsake he did not know it at the time, for as is commonly the case he didn't miss it until he got home again. Then he went through his pockets, but the shining medal was gone and he could only repeat, 'I had it when I started out.' His brothers and sisters were of no help at all. They had seen nothing. What brother or sister likes being asked such questions?

The winter frosts began and at Michaelmas Jack had the day off school and thought, I had better try going that way again. He halted, as before, at the highest point, to look down at the great house and its chimneys, and then at the ice under his feet, for all the brooks, ponds, and runnels were frozen on every side of him, all hard as bone. In a little hole or depression just to the left hand of the path, something no bigger than a small puddle, but deep, and by now set thick with greenish ice as clear as glass, he saw, through the transparency of the ice, at the depth of perhaps twelve inches, the keepsake that Mrs Piercy had given him.

He had nothing in his hand to break the ice. Well then, Jack Digby, jump on it, but that got him nowhere, seeing that his wretched pair of boots were soaked right through. 'I'll wait until the ice has gone,' he thought. 'The season is turning, we'll get a thaw in a day or two.'

On the next Sunday, by which time the thaw had set in, he was up there again, and made straight for the little hole or declivity, and found nothing. It was empty, after that short time, of ice and even of water. And because the idea of recovering the keepsake had occupied his whole mind that day, the disappointment made him feel lost, like a stranger to the country. Then he noticed that there was an earthenware pipe laid straight down the side of the hill, by way of a drain, and that this must very likely have carried off the water from his hole, and everything in it. No mystery as to where it led, it joined another pipe with a wider bore, and so down, I suppose, to the stableyards, thought Jack. His Desideratus had been washed down there, he was as sure of that now as if he'd seen it go.

Jack had never been anywhere near the house before, and did not care to knock at the great kitchen doors for fear of being taken for a beggar. The yards were empty. Either the horses had been taken out to work now that the ground was softer or else – which was hard to believe – there were no horses at Watching. He went back to the kitchen wing and tried knocking at a smallish side entrance. A man came out dressed in a black gown, and stood there peering and trembling.

'Why don't you take off your cap to me?' he asked.

Jack took it off, and held it behind his back, as though it belonged to someone else.

'That is better. Who do you think I am?'

'No offence, sir,' Jack replied, 'but you look like an old schoolmaster.'

'I am a schoolmaster, that is, I am tutor to this great house. If you have a question to ask, you may ask it of me.'

With one foot still on the step, Jack related the story of his godmother's keepsake.

'Very good,' said the tutor, 'you have told me enough. Now I am going to test your memory. You will agree that this is not only necessary, but just.'

'I can't see that it has anything to do with my matter,' said Jack.

'Oh, but you tell me that you dropped this-or-that in such-and-such a place, and in that way lost what had been given to you. How can I tell that you have truthfully remembered all this? You know that when I came to the door you did not remember to take your cap off.'

'But that – '

'You mean that was only lack of decent manners, and shows that you come from a family without self-respect. Now, let us test your memory. Do you know the Scriptures?'

Jack said that he did, and the tutor asked him what happened, in the fourth chapter of the Book of Job, to Eliphaz the Temanite, when a vision came to him in the depth of the night.

'A spirit passed before his face, sir, and the hair of his flesh stood up.'

'The hair of his flesh stood up,' the tutor repeated. 'And now, have they taught you any Latin?' Jack said that he knew the word that had been on his medal, and that it was *Desideratus*, meaning long wished-for.

'That is not an exact translation,' said the tutor. Jack thought, he talks for talking's sake.

'Have you many to teach, sir, in this house?' he asked, but the tutor half-closed his eyes and said, 'None, none at all. God has not blessed Mr Jonas or either of his late wives with children. Mr Jonas has not multiplied.'

If that is so, Jack thought, this schoolmaster can't have much work to do. But now at last here was somebody with more sense, a house-keeperish-looking woman, come to see why the side-door was open and letting cold air into the passages. 'What does the boy want?' she asked.

'He says he is in search of something that belongs to him.'

'You might have told him to come in, then, and given him a glass of wine in the kitchen,' she said, less out of kindness than to put the tutor in his place. 'He would have been glad of that, I daresay.'

Jack told her at once that at home they never touched wine. 'That's a pity,' said the housekeeper. 'Children who are too strictly prohibited generally turn out drunkards.' There's no pleasing these people, Jack thought.

His whole story had to be gone through again, and then again when they got among the servants in one of the pantries. Yet really there was almost nothing to tell, the only remarkable point being that he should have seen the keepsake clearly through almost a foot of ice. Still nothing was said as to its being found in any of the yards or ponds.

Among all the to-ing and fro-ing another servant came in, the man who attended on the master, Mr Jonas, himself. His arrival caused a kind of disquiet, as though he were a foreigner. The master, he said, had got word that there was a farm-boy, or a schoolboy, in the kitchens, come for something that he thought was his property.

'But all this is not for Mr Jonas' notice,' cried the tutor. 'It's a story of child's stuff, a child's mischance, not at all fitting for him to look into.'

The man repeated that the master wanted to see the boy.

The other part of the house, the greater part, where Mr Jonas lived, was much quieter, the abode of gentry. In the main hall Mr Jonas himself stood with his back to the fire. Jack had never before been alone or dreamed of being alone with such a person. What a pickle, he thought, my godmother, Mrs Piercy, has brought me into.

'I daresay you would rather have a sum of money,' said Mr Jonas, not loudly, 'than whatever it is that you have lost.'

Jack was seized by a painful doubt. To be honest, if it was to be a large sum of money, he would rather have that than anything. But Mr Jonas went on, 'However, you had better understand me more precisely. Come with me.' And he led the way, without even looking round to see that he was followed.

At the foot of the wide staircase Jack called out from behind, 'I think, sir, I won't go any further. What I lost can't be here.'

'It's poor-spirited to say "I won't go any further",' said Mr Jonas.

Was it possible that on these dark upper floors no one else was living, no one was sleeping? They were like a sepulchre, or a barn at the end of winter. Through the tall passages, over uneven floors, Mr Jonas, walking ahead, carried a candle in its candlestick in each hand, the flames pointing straight upwards. I am very far from home, thought Jack. Then, padding along behind the master of the house, and still twisting his cap in one hand, he saw in dismay that the candle flames were blown over to the left, and a door was open to the right.

'Am I to go in there with you, sir?'

'Are you afraid to go into a room?'

Inside it was dark and in fact the room probably never got much light, the window was so high up. There was a glazed jug and basin, which reflected the candles, and a large bed which had no curtains, or perhaps, in spite of the cold, they had been drawn back. There seemed to be neither quilts nor bedding, but a boy was lying there in a linen gown, with his back towards Jack, who saw that he had red or reddish hair, much the same colour as his own.

'You may go near him, and see him more clearly,' Mr Jonas said. 'His arm is hanging down, what do you make of that?'

'I think it hangs oddly, sir.'

He remembered what the tutor had told him, that Mr Jonas had not multiplied his kind, and asked, 'What is his name, sir?' To this he got no answer.

Mr Jonas gestured to him to move nearer, and said, 'You may take his hand.'

'No, sir, I can't do that.'

'Why not? You must touch other children very often. Wherever you live, you must sleep the Lord knows how many in a bed.'

'Only three in a bed at ours,' Jack muttered.

'Then touch, touch.'

'No, sir, no, I can't touch the skin of him!'

Mr Jonas set down his candles, went to the bed, took the boy's wrist and turned it, so that the fingers opened. From the open fingers he took Jack's medal, and gave it back to him.

'Was it warm or cold?' they asked him later. Jack told them that it was cold. Cold as ice? Perhaps not quite as cold as that.

'You have what you came for,' said Mr Jonas. 'You have taken back what was yours. Note that I don't deny it was yours.'

He did not move again, but stood looking down at the

whiteish heap on the bed. Jack was more afraid of staying than going, although he had no idea how to find his way through the house, and was lucky to come upon a back staircase which ended not where he had come in but among the sculleries, where he managed to draw back the double bolts and get out into the fresh air.

'Did the boy move,' they asked him, 'when the medal was taken away from him?' But by this time Jack was making up the answers as he went along. He preferred, on the whole, not to think much about Watching. It struck him, though, that he had been through a good deal to get back his godmother's present, and he quite often wondered how much money Mr Jonas would in fact have offered him, if he had had the sense to accept it. Anyone who has ever been poor – even if not as poor as Jack Digby – will sympathise with him in this matter.

Paul Magrs

THE 1971 TUBE JOURNEYS

EROS WAS SO fucking skinny. Looked like you could just reach up, grab him in one careless fist, snap him off his world-famous podium.

All these streets were small. David was showing me round, bit by bit, the days he could get off. The days we could get free to explore. Wander round together. Did we look as if we were together?

At Greenwich he pointed to the buildings twinned either side of the river. Queen Victoria's tits. There was a tunnel between, under the Thames, pitch dark. He stroked the hair out of his eyes with both hands. When he was twelve or so, him and his mates rode their bikes – Chippys, Tomahawks, Budgies – through the misted-up tunnel at full pelt. They screamed out in warning to anyone who might be down there.

He would have been such a *boy*. I imagined him being such a *boy*.

He still did such boyish things. *Star Trek*. Sometimes two episodes a night, after work. Not while I was there, mind. Internetting. Pot-holing and climbing at weekends. There was a yellow and purple spongy inside-out rubber suit in his bathroom.

When I arrived, whenever I arrived, I lined up my usual things on his dirty, dusty basin. Armani aftershave, deodorant, balm, all that. Grin wryly at the purple and yellow suit clumped inside out, a fagged-out *doppelgänger*, beside the bath. His second skin. I never asked him to do anything sexy with it or in it. Somehow that never came up. I think he would have been shocked – or worse, mystified. His suit was beyond the pale. Or beyond my pale, at least. The self I never saw. Our relationship didn't fully exist anywhere but his bed. It never became a wholly extant, living, life-devotable thing, until we were on his bed-settee, all our feet off his floor, palpitating madly in each other's fists.

'I'm sorry, baby, but it frightens me here.'

He sat up in bed and rubbed his eyes. He looked at me through the dark. 'You what?'

'Your flat. The noise. I've been in the bathroom and it sounds like *Reservoir Dogs* going on next door. Or downstairs, or some fucking place.'

I sat down heavily on the bed-settee beside him. That night I had a throat virus coming on. In the next few weeks I'd be back and forth to the doctors. My tonsils were beginning to swell up like lychees. I had a hangover, too. All the drink I'd drunk in Soho, urging on the germs. I was a mess. And now all this frightening noise.

He clicked the lamp on. 'I know. I can't fucking sleep either.'

Gloomily we listened.

Downstairs: the snooker club, dark in the daytime, dusty windows, metal gratings the colour of dry blood. Tonight the floor pounded with techno and shouting. You could hear it much worse in the bathroom. Someone screaming threats and beating someone else about.

'I'm going to go and say something,' he said grimly, hoisting himself up.

'You what? You can't. That's mad.'

'What can I do? Let them walk all over me?'

I lay down. Thinking if I lay down, he'd have to lie down. If I closed my eyes, he'd have to close his. The night would slip away. Noise would blank out.

Shrieks. Laughter. Breaking glass.

Shut the fuck up, he whispered.

This is just the kind of thing, I whispered, just the kind of thing that makes me nervous as hell. I remembered him getting up in the middle of the night, the first night I ever visited him and he screamed 'Shut the fuck up!' at the wall. He was standing in the corner of his room. He claimed that the man above the newsagents next door was doing carpentry at three in the morning. He was planning to refit his poky shop. I never heard it.

'It terrifies me,' I whispered now, as if to myself. 'I grew up on our estate, remember.'

'And I did on a terrace in the East End.'

Was that meant to make me feel safer?

I snuggled into his armpit. It was acrid and homely. I was used to him. Three months into our do. Did he mean to make me feel safer? Sometimes. Just then, I think, he was simmering and listening to the snooker hall downstairs.

It came up from the floor.

He had so little floorspace in that flat. When I staggered to the bathroom I was tripping. On videos and leads, emptied glasses, cans. A mess. And if you hit the floorboards too hard or suddenly, he had warned me the first time I came to stay, it would set off the burglar alarm on the smart disc drive he kept on the carpet under his desk. His work was in computers. His were sensitive and registered all kinds of tremors.

Then he found he had to switch this failsafe off when I came to stay. We shagged on the bed-settee he'd fetched from his parents. The metal supports jingling, jangling, the computer alarm screaming. When I came it meant he couldn't do his e-mailing.

Tonight I lay, tense and knowing that when I turned over they would hear it downstairs, if they'd been quiet enough for a moment. Surely when we had sex it drowned out all the noise they made? I'd always thought orgasms loud.

Then, deafened, chastened, they would see us the next day when we came out of the door together and walked past their snooker hall windows. Two blokes. Fucking hell.

Poor David could do without that kind of hassle. This was his home. I told him to keep his gob shut the night.

It was the suspense I liked.

Waiting elbow to elbow with a whole crowd, some of them reading novels. It was a city of novels, it seemed, that spring. Looking at the small yellow numbers overhead as they ticked the minutes down. The soft warm fart of the approaching train. Everyone stirring.

Imminence.

That plunging, anticipatory moment.

In my head, watching the stations notch by, watching the diagram directly opposite, orienting myself, the pleasurable threat of a possible mistake. How easy to rectify it – popping back the way I'd come – like running a tape back and forth – maybe to find the exact start of a song.

Here I was safe and braced in suspense.

His style was jaunty. He began: 'Hi there!' and he said he was 'Youngish, professional, financially secure'. He was seeking an 'unselfish, masculine, kind, strong-minded, tolerant, northern guy. Photo?'

He was from the South. South of the river, in fact.

He lived in a windowless flat in a high street of kebab shops and Irish pubs, above a snooker hall.

I took down his PO Box number, holding my breath. I'd do it for a laugh. I mulled this over as I fed the plants, dripping Baby Bio neat from the bottle on to crusty soil like it was soy sauce.

No, I'd do this for real.

He wasn't 'straight-acting' or 'smooth'. At least, he never said that. Those were the ones to avoid, I thought.

We would meet.

His leap in the dark, the odd gallantry of his putting himself on the line like this, would prevent the necessity of *my* having to advertise. I had let him take the initiative.

So. Here we were.

I was coming to London, anyway. To see people about my novel.

It was a busy time for me. My own hectic pace drowned out London's for me, for a while. I would slip him in somewhere, along the way. Just another appointment. See how it would work out.

'Good, very honest letter important and humour too.'

Yeah. Don't expect too much.

I'd built up my hopes in the past.

Fashioned terrible, unsustainable fictions from them.

When he decided, out of all the letters he must have received, that mine was the one for him . . . well. It was like I'd won something.

'You won't have to water the plants,' I said. 'I've done them.'

My house-mate Ian looked up from the living-room carpet, where he lay curled watching *The Time, The Place*, smoking Marlboro Lights in his navy dressing-gown. His hair was still bed-rumpled and he had four empty glasses around him, streaked with sour milk.

'Depends how long you're gone for,' he said. 'They might need doing again.'

'It's a week. They won't.'

He was taking over my shifts that week. We were care-workers together and we shared a house. We tended the differently-abled like we tended my houseplants, almost wordlessly and routinely. As scrupulously as we maintained our distance from each other.

Our best time had been a couple of years ago. Working together in the same place, the same home. The air charged with our attentive care.

Anyway, I took the train.

So we met . . . and we got on fine.

We met in writing. Via those tersely worded invitations to . . . what? Romance? Sex-only? A members-only club where you're given a key and shown to a steamy, ill-lit basement full of plastic plants, muted lift music.

Guarded statements, the width of a thumb; these are what gave us away. No proud, dressed-up in-laws. Tokens of phrase, easy conventions and yet, in their own coded way, gaudy and provocative as birdplumage signalling desire.

Although he wasn't one for writing, my new lover. He e-mailed and sent brittle, clipped phrases around the world. 'Hi there!' just to keep in touch. 'Hailing frequencies open, Cap'n.' Turned out he was a big *Star Trek* fan and when I went back to his flat the first time, south of the river, it was to a dark flat, walled in with videos of every episode ever made. They all looked the fucking same to me.

We were born on the same day, in 1971. Two years after the original *Star Trek* finished. He had a look of always being somehow belated because of this. He'd missed the train.

We had both answered a lot of ads. That was something we established, soon after we met at King's Cross, that first tea-time. I'd had a day swanning around Bloomsbury, meeting people, signing things. In Samuel French I'd sent home a postcard of a woodcut entitled 'Ophelia Distracted' and said that I'd 'see you in days'. Which might – or might not – mean that I'd be back soon.

I met my classified man in a shabby café by the station. We shared coffee in glass mugs. It was a change after all the posh places I'd seen on my trip so far.

Long lonely weekends at our opposite ends of the country we'd been spending writing these letters to people we'd never met. Writing things out with the same dogged hope I did Saturday lottery tickets. Sneaking into photo booths in Woollies . . . flash! Trying to look suitably . . . flash! . . . tolerant and honest . . . flash! . . . looking professional and smooth-bodied . . . flash!

Snipping the strips of photos into four and popping them into envelopes along with chatty, worked-over and mildly salacious letters.

At King's Cross while we talked we found that we both wrote our letters on Sundays. My weekends were always for writing. My novel, the screenplay, these letters. My weeks were full – or had been – of caring. Carrying and lulling and wiping people. He worked in computers, in lists of letters and numbers much terser and more complex than those in the classifieds, for a South London council.

As we talked at the formica breakfast bar at King's Cross

PAUL MAGRS

I was entranced by his floppy-fringe. The brown inner run of his arms and wrists looked smooth and he was, in fact, straight-acting. My heart sinking, I thought: is gayness new to him? A virgin maybe? Someone playing games? When I asked how old he was he said, surprised, twenty-six. And I thought, how nice. Someone old enough to be sensible and yet he was still gangling and dippy, full of sixth-former charm.

In a brief moment over coffee dregs he went serious, said he must go home. Come over London Bridge, he said, with a circumspect, too-casual sniff, come to sleep over the snooker hall, fuck south of the river with me.

On the platform at London Bridge we took bars of Fruit and Nut from the machine and stood about, shoulder to shoulder with the crowd. It was a crowd of single people. How rarely they commute in couples, I thought. He was in his worksuit, looking clumsy. We drew closer without really thinking about it.

Everything was in one room, compact and tight as a cheap sit-com's set. I undressed him by his bed-settee as the answer-machine gave chastened clicks and whines. Only then, under his poise-lamp, did we take a good look at each other, having maintained till then a distance, a not-looking-too-closely, in case we got disappointed. Seeing each other in the flesh, after a life so far only in text, was a rare treat, not to be bolted.

So that our whole selves were eroticised. The whole of what we both looked like, of what we were composed, became as mysteriously alluring and breathlessly anticipated as, usually, in an ordinary pick-up, the unseen bits of body are.

We were for each other entire objects of desire. We couldn't help it. Democratised body parts, freed of the phallus's false tyranny, exploring for all we were worth, tangled up in our jeans, fallen on the bed-settee. Oh yeah . . . right . . . freed of the phallus's false tyranny, sure . . . and yet not happy, not quite blissfully content till we'd taken each other's cocks in our mouths and made them bright and sticky and smarting.

34

And, eventually, pumping oodles of spunk on to the already splodged fabric.

Work in the morning, for him at least.

So we didn't talk much. Slept, playing some London station.

I watched his face. A square nose, it looked moulded. A flinching mouth, his nervousness. Deeply expressive, almost Irish eyes. All his hair was so black it was Prussian blue in the night and his flesh was milk-bottle creamy. While he slept the end of his cock still protruded lazily out of a foreskin slack as a badly put-on sock. I tried to sleep, clasping his thin body. When I poked a thoughtful forefinger into his navel it was wet with come inside.

That morning in South London I woke on the bed-settee and I told David all about the Tube dreams.

There were strikes going on then. You had to listen to the radio each morning to check if you could get to where you wanted to be. The question was: are the Tubes running? Which sounded revolting to me.

David asked this, turned the radio on. He fiddled blindly with tapes. He liked to play Philip Glass. Round and round in fucking circles. Good for fucking. Getting nowhere fast.

All that cosy prevarication. Awful for getting where you need to be.

He listened to my dream. He had a slight frown.

Oh, and he had deepdeepdeep Celticy eyes. And a pale pink hyphen of a mouth. Pale as the scar on his dick where someone had given him an accidental semi-circumcision. Novelists call it a pursed mouth. But it wasn't. It hyphenated the last thing he said and what he wanted to say next. It made me hang on his response. A pink hyphen in a blue half-mask of baby beard. In the morning his hair lay every which way. It was ridiculous, but wonderful, and could have been cut like that.

He was ready in a matter of minutes. Me just lying there. He sat on the Kotex-thin mattress of the bed-settee to sip at spoonfuls of Fruit and Fibre, dribbling milk down his chin.

'I won't be in till seven.'

'It's like we're married.'

'Frightening, isn't it?'

He put his breakfast down and we hugged earnestly, as if it really was frightening.

'I can't go!' he complained. 'I don't want to!' Like it surprised him.

He watched the alarm clock over my shoulder as it counted up to seven. His shirt and tie got all rucked up and I was staring at his taut belly, the fine line of black pubes up to his navel. I had his work trousers unzipped and he was poking erect, a healthy, wet dog's nose through the fabric of his boxers. I sucked him gently through his shorts. And it shocked and delighted me all over again that I should take him for granted now, that I could turn him on so easily. That when I'd squeezed his cock's end with my teeth a shudder ran powerfully through him and he didn't care about getting to work any more. He just wanted his work clothes back off again. He struggled with them like they were on fire and he flung himself on me, so that I laughed, almost spoilt the mood. But he was mad for it.

'You're mine,' I said.

Through his pores his sweat came all garlicky. From dinner in Soho last night. Even his come tasted of garlic, when he came it was with a great cry. I thought he would burst into tears when he exploded on to me. A cry half-apology. All the night's tension gone. He lay face to one side on my chest, smearing his spunk on to me. It slid between his newly shaved chin and my chest. He said his own come tasted of garlic.

When he'd gone, dressed again, and I lay thinking about getting ready, going into town for my meeting, I felt a twinge of *angst*. He was out in the world by himself.

I'm just daft, mind.

I was going into town. Early for me, in with the workers. My two-zone travelcard in my pocket, beat up and sweaty already. I worried it wouldn't slip safely into the machine at the station.

New Cross Gate was leafy and dingy and I saw a fox on the opposite side of the rails. The other commuters standing about had novels out. Jeffrey Archer, Alice Walker, all that shit. Easy to read. They barely had to look up when the train came.

Where was I going?

By now I hardly had to think about travelling round London. I did it by rote, half-noticing landmarks. The bits I really saw were people's offices or bedrooms or pubs at night.

Or from a train I'd be looking in open windows and at signs. Tattooists' studios with lime green interiors, photos all up their walls. Flatblocks with old mattresses wedged on open landings, mattresses stained the colour of just-done toast. A closed boutique by a station that was called 'Fancy Pants'. Tell a lie: 'Fancy Pants' is a closed boutique by the station in Newcastle.

In the White Swan on the Corporation Road.

It was where, they say, Michael Barrymore came out, live on stage, and took the whole pub back to his house for a party.

It was where we met.

Ah. That's the truth. There were no classifieds. We just bumped into each other. Turns out neither of us have ever used the classifieds. The closer he comes to it is e-mailing and I can't bear the idea of paying someone else for my own words. I made an attempt at fiction there but now I've let it slip. One Christmas, last Christmas, we bumped into each other on the dance floor at the White Swan while the drag act was on and within three minutes we were in each other's arms. Bless our hearts. We were near the front and the artiste made loud, scathing remarks at us for not listening and we were not listening to the extent that we had to be told about the loud scathing remarks afterwards.

We went back for a sentimental night out and a dance. A return to where we met, three months on.

Packed. Valentine's.

Two big screens showed fuzzy hard-core porn.

Dancing wasn't his thing. I stood him in the middle of the beer-sticky floor and we danced to a disco version of Charlene's 'I've Never Been to Me'. I was shouting all excitedly into his face that this song had been a house favourite back in L., with me and Ian, when we lived with M. and A. It was a theme tune.

> I've been undressed by kings
> and I've seen some things
> that a woman ain't supposed to see . . .

We ran across the dark field from the river in L., to our house, singing it out loud, pissed out of our heads.

Our half-hearted anthem.

I shouted this all out to David in the White Swan.

He smiled, picking out one word in three, wanting to go home.

The Tube again, through North London, then the overland, where the stations were clean and backed on to streets with old shops. I stood by a set of grimy windows and looked in. The shop was crammed with sandwiches. Mozzarella, basil leaves, fat tomato slices. I ate one, standing in Kilburn, waiting for my friends. They were coming in a new mini and I was staying with them for a few days. We'd spent little time together since graduating all in the same place, in L., four years ago. I quarrelled some change out of the newspaper man and went and bought some fleshy pink tulips.

That weekend we drove around town in the mini. We paused in one dark street so I could look up at St Paul's. Huge.

We drove late at night and the roads were unfamiliar. I was used to trainlines, shunting through London at the height of the roofs' eaves.

I sat in the back of the mini, looked up at St Paul's, and that was when I was coming down with flu.

Saturday morning saw us in a Portuguese café on the Portobello

Road. Before the book came out, quite by coincidence, I had some photos taken there. Me hanging off chains in a kids' playground. Stood louchely outside a pink naughty knickers shop. I'd bought a Carpenters' vinyl LP for a pound off the market. And almost – I wish I had – given a fiver for a pair of brass peacocks.

In the Portuguese café you had to fight for a table. Bea said, watch what cakes you're getting. We came here once for egg custards and they tasted of fish. Something to do with too-raw eggs.

I thought: complicated tastes, or just plain awful?

And isn't it often the way?

We brought ourselves up to date.

Heavy marble tables. Urban, cultured. Weathered faces and clamouring children. Coffee arrived, overly milky in tall glasses.

We sucked up the skin of milk or whisked it out with a spoon. Bea looked at me and asked if I was used to the city. Used to the Tube.

I looked at her; she'd broken my dream.

It sounds so formal, the way that I put it, doesn't it?

The 1971 Tube Journeys. It sounds like a title. The name of a book. And it was only a dream. Something that came to me, very informally, the way that dreams do. Sneaking up and coaxing round and tipping themselves in your ear. Rounding off the night with a little sleep. Shucking themselves into you.

It got the title 1971 Tube Journeys because David called it that. We were crossing the field in L., a gang of us, heading towards the river, to the station, for a day out. I had told him my dream the moment we woke up. I do that. And then, to the others, as we crossed the field, he gave it this title. I thought, how sweet, he's naming my dreams for me. Like they were progeny. He did it wryly, speaking as someone in the know. Shaking his head at me, like he couldn't account for it, but he was keeping tabs.

I always told them – my lovers – what I had dreamed

of, the moment I popped back into the land of the living. They thought I was daft, but I never cared. I'd sit bolt upright, thwarting whatever conclusion I was probably coming to, head spinning, eyes aching, cock throbbing, and me all bursting with the morning story.

Once I woke and told someone:

'*I was just in a field, on a gingham cloth, with Sylvia Plath. Oh, I know – not Sylvia Plath – but that's your fault, bringing her up last night, honest, I don't think about her much usually. But we were having a picnic and talking about nice things, as it happens, and she seemed so carefree I was surprised. In the next field, over the high hedge, the English Civil War was going on and the Cavaliers and Roundheads were on horseback, going at it like hammer and tongs.*'

Someone must have had something new delivered. Something in unwieldy cardboard boxes stuffed with these protective spongy white question marks. The main street was scattered with packing material, drifted up, lodging in every grimy crevice. First twilight they'd shoved all the boxes out, ready for the binmen. David's old bed, the one he'd replaced with the bed-settee – his decrepit, childhood, single bed – propped against the pillar box outside the snooker club. The mattress slumped over it. The binmen weren't supposed to take stuff as big as that. David knew that. His job was controlling and coordinating the binmen via his computers and everything. He went out on site sometimes, with a mobile phone and a laptop. He was a troubleshooter. Maybe he was engineering something tricky with his room's computer. Could he make someone in a van turn up and take his old bed away?

Odd, that his tapping in codes and instructions in the clamminess and the clutter of his room could result in material effects. The endless shunting of what is disposed of.

Anyway, the street first thing in the morning was full of old crap and thousands upon thousands of question marks.

Why was I walking back at this time?

Had I been out all night?

Where was the night in between?

Was he safely asleep on the jingling bed-settee?

What was I doing out without him?

In the night-time I'd been out patrolling the Tubes. Skirting and exploring and plunging into the map. Seeing how the land lay.

While he slept, rumpled and content, once he had managed to slip above the druggy, relentless cover of downstairs' racket.

Was he dreaming of The Next Generation of Star Trek?

At this time in the morning, their lights were still on. They were still going on down there.

I braced myself to take the fire escape, up two flights, one storey, climbing right past their barricaded window, in full view of the people downstairs. Of course they would see where I was going.

I wouldn't ring the doorbell. He needed his sleep. He worked.

Oh God, how I got used to that. Falling, at first, with a self-mockery and a kind of warped glee into the sit-com patter: How was the office, dear? And he would scowl – because of the work, because of the reminder that we were enacting a parody anyway.

I'd let myself in. I still had my key. I was, at that point, exactly three months away from sending him his keys back. That final, irked, desperate gesture. I would send them back on May the 1st. Pop them in a jiffy bag, in a pillar box in Edinburgh, where I had just decided I was going to live. I was on my way with the crowds up to Calton Hill to see the Beltane Fires. Midnight: it was quite a moment. My moment of resolving to go further north. Snapping the cautious elasticity of our few months of relations.

I dealt with two locks and, glancing backwards to make sure no one was following, stepped inside.

What it should have been – the Dali prints in the hallway, the shelf units of the complete *Star Trek: The Next Generation*, the wardrobe of all the clothes he had ever owned, the kitchen with his mountain bike propped against the washer and the blinds that he had never ever opened – well, it all wasn't there. It had fucked off. Like it had had enough of the waiting, or enough of the noise.

A. L. Kennedy

AWAITING AN ADVERSE REACTION

IT'S UNMISTAKABLE, ORGANIC, the flavour of something live.

'Oh, that's dreadful.'

She shifts in her chair while the doctor pads across to his fridge.

'Dreadful?'

'The taste. I don't get a sweetie for after?'

'No.' He turns back with a blur of smile. 'No sugar lump to go with it and no sweetie for afterwards.' Quietly teasing between the slim and softly shining shelves. 'Sugar is bad for you and here we don't ever dispense what is bad for you.'

'A small piece of fruit, then?'

'This is a surgery, not a restaurant.' He coughs out a small laugh and decides to risk, 'And that's a Scottish medicine – if it tastes bad, it must be working,' before glancing to check if she takes him in good part.

She grimaces back, not entirely unhappily, and swims the flavour round her tongue, hoping it will weaken. Under the tickle of spreading salt, the cold initial weight of the vaccine, there is something familiar about the taste. She knows that if she concentrates, identification will come.

Her doctor advances, hands benevolently folded round a stack of suitably chilled inoculations: the start of any truly happy holiday.

'I'll need the use of both your arms.' Laying out his packages and snapping the first needle free, 'Diphtheria and tetanus this side . . .' he grins curatively, 'typhoid and malaria that.'

Something about his casual enumeration of plagues is strangely enjoyable, a comfort to her. She is being made safe; a part of her bloodstream is welcoming something foreign, so that none of her will go wrong when she takes all her body abroad.

She swallows and briefly considers the matter of Gordon. Gordon will not be made safe, because he will not go with her, because he does not like abroad. He does like her, but not abroad. She does like abroad. The thought of abroad is something she likes very much.

'I won't hurt.' The doctor draws a careful epidemic up inside his syringe.

'I know you won't. I will.'

She rolls up her sleeves, hoping that she can offer him flesh high enough on her arms. She would rather not take off her blouse. In the past, her doctor's acts of examination have been both medical and polite; a nurse discreetly attending, should any extensive explorations be required. Even so, undressing is always more awkward than being undressed – stumbling her clothes off while the doctor slips outside and the nurse presses breaths through the disinfected silence and shifts tinily on white crêpe soles, observing. Nothing to enjoy. But that won't happen today.

He nods, 'Good,' then pushes a pinching kind of pain inside her skin; holds it, dabs around it, withdraws and dabs again. 'Terribly bad?'

'Not bad at all.'

'Mm. I am actually quite good at giving injections. I still practise, you see. Others I could mention do not. How's the polio doing?'

'I can still taste it. In fact, I think it's getting worse. It reminds me of, I don't know what.' He slips in another needle, while she thinks. 'That wasn't fair.'

'Some people would rather not know what's going on.'

'It's my arm, I like to keep tabs on it.'

'I quite understand. Other side now and then we're done. We just ask you to wait for a few minutes more, in case there's an adverse reaction.'

As soon as he says this, she feels a rush in her circulation, a burst of strangeness, but nothing she would call adverse. Her flesh is being fortified like wine, science defending her against nature more deeply with every prick.

'You're getting tense – this will be painful if you don't relax.'

'Sorry.'

'Not to worry. You've been a very patient patient. And. Last one. There. Will you be going away for long?'

'A month.' A month away from Gordon, during which time she will try to phone him and will certainly write him postcards and may nevertheless experience increasing bouts of what she might well call relief. She has already suffered from immanent release.

'Terrific. A month.'

One whole month of release.

They probably will fire her when she gets back home. She has calculated the likelihood of summary dismissal. She finds that it doesn't scare her – not in the way that disease might, or a month staying here with Gordon and his list of things they shouldn't talk about.

'Yes, I've saved up my holiday time,' pausing, recalling the polio taste and where she met it once before, knowing it, making a smile, 'And I'm taking four days off sick.'

'Really?' He pauses to look quintessentially medical: phial held high, a glimmer at his needle and obviously chill but steady hands. 'What will be wrong, in your professional opinion?' His voice relaxes into a type of wink – his eyes being unable to do the same, for reasons of professional distance and confidence.

'Wrong? Oh, probably flu. Probably not typhoid, or cholera, or – '

'Or tetanus, or diphtheria, or polio. Yes, I think that flu would probably be best. In my professional opinion.'

Or polio. She licked against her teeth and smiled again. On their second anniversary, last spring, when Gordon had asked her to do it and she'd finally agreed, when he'd got his way – this is how he'd tasted. The gagging nudge in her throat, repeating, and then warmed polio vaccine. It's just like him.

'As you're away so long . . .' The doctor ponders, above her notes. 'I could write out your next prescription for Trinovum.'

'For?'

'Your contraceptive.'

Her passport for Gordon to travel, pregnancy free.

'Oh yes, thank you.'

'No problems, periods normal?'

'No problems at all.' She can say this because it will be true soon and might as well be now.

She waits as he checks the pressure of her altering blood, not minding the hard fit of the cuff, and taking – for the sake of politeness – the prescription for an oral contraceptive she intends never to use.

'Thank you.'

'We aim to please.' He opens the door so she can start to go away. 'Do have a nice holiday.'

'I will.'

She is aware that, when she speaks, her breath is vaguely coloured with the taste of something not unlike seminal fluid. She is aware of something not unlike the cloy and tang of spunk. She is aware that her husband has the flavour of a tentatively sweetened disease.

John Forrester

PSYCHOANALYSIS AND THE STRANGE DESTINY OF ENVY

IN CHAPTER III of the First Book of Kings, two harlots come before King Solomon to ask for his judgement. They lived together and had both given birth to sons a short time before. In the night one of the women had inadvertently crushed her child while sleeping and had secretly exchanged the dead baby for the living one of her friend, who on waking immediately recognised that the dead child was not her own son and tried to take back her baby from the other woman. Both women disputed the other's version of the events. Solomon said: 'Bring me a sword . . . Divide the living child in two, and give half to the one, and half to the other.' The Bible continues:

> Then spake the woman whose the living child was unto the king, for her bowels yearned upon her son, and she said, O my lord, give her the living child, and in no wise slay it. But the other said, Let it be neither mine nor thine, but divide it.
>
> Then the king answered and said, Give her the living child, and in no wise slay it: she is the mother thereof.

When I was young, I thought the point of the judgement of Solomon was to demonstrate the chutzpah of the King. It was a story whose structure was rather like certain detective stories, demonstrating the skill and acumen of the hero-detective. Solomon's strategy is a case-study of how the master dialectician acts, as he ostensibly sets off in precisely the opposite direction to his actual goal, knowing that the other actors will inevitably carry him back to precisely that goal. He, the King and absolute Master, orders the baby to be cut in half precisely so that the baby will not be cut in half. We could call this the Zen master reading of the parable.

My second reading of the parable, when I was a little older and had decided that stories were not usually about the intelligence of men but about the tragedy of life, emphasized the selfless and tragic action of the true mother, who gives up her claim on her beloved child and is prepared never to see it again, in order to preserve its life. Perhaps her child means more to her than her own life – perhaps she would, given the choice, substitute herself for the child and die in its place. So in giving up her claim, she gives up something more valuable than her own life for the child; she certainly gives up her motherhood in the act of saving the baby. Her conscious motive is thus paradoxical in a similar way to Solomon's: she acts in the opposite direction to her ostensible goal. In order to save her child, she abandons it. In this way, the judgement also becomes a parable of the relationship between parent and child – of how the parent gives life to the child, carries it through life and exchanges his or her own life for that of the child.[1]

I was entirely blind to a third possible reading until I read it in a passage in Freud's *Group Psychology and the Analysis of the Ego*, in the chapter where he discusses the existence of a primary herd instinct in human beings:

What appears later on in society in the shape of Gemeingeist, esprit de corps, 'group spirit', *etc., does not belie its derivation from what was originally envy. No one must put himself forward, everyone must be the same and have the same. Social justice means that we deny ourselves many things so that others may have to do without them as well, or, what is the same thing, may not be able to ask for them. This demand for equality*

*is the root of social conscience and the sense of duty.
It reveals itself unexpectedly in the syphilitic's dread of
infecting other people, which psycho-analysis has taught
us to understand. The dread exhibited by these poor
wretches corresponds to their violent struggles against
the unconscious wish to spread their infection on to
other people; for why should they alone be infected
and cut off from so much? why not other people as
well? And the same germ is to be found in the apt
story of the judgement of Solomon. If one woman's
child is dead, the other shall not have a live one either.
The bereaved woman is recognized by this wish.*[2]

Freud's reading of the Judgement of Solomon focuses neither
on Solomon nor on the true mother of the baby, who gives up
her claim on her own child. Instead, he focuses on the woman
who maintains her claim against the other woman. Freud's
simple interpretation is something of a shock. Focusing on
the third party, the woman who maintains her claim, reveals
how it is *we*, and not Solomon or the true mother, who
are led away, by the narrative structure of the parable,
from her. The parable-work, to coin a term along the lines
of the dream-work and more proximately the joke-work,
conceals the fact that it is the second woman, the woman
who maintains her claim on the child, who is the principal
actor. We have been duped by the structure of the parable.

Freud's interpretation has textual support in the Bible.
Uncannily repeating the lofty impartiality of King Solomon,
the envious mother says: 'Let it be neither mine nor thine,
but divide it.' Freud generalises this principle in the following
rather dry way: 'Social justice means that we deny ourselves
many things so that others may have to do without them as
well.' This is the joke-work of political theory. The high ideal
of social justice tendentiously cloaks something altogether
more individually self-interested: the envious woman is not
truly interested in half a baby, as if half a baby were better
than none. Her true aim is to ensure that the other woman
has no baby, just like her. For her, no baby is better than

one. Her idea of justice, then, is not stably redistributive, nor is it entirely impersonal, despite the iron logic of equal shares for equal subjects; its motivations and its manifestations are destructive and personal, aimed not at any general other, but at any specific other who has the thing she does not have.

To highlight the personal and specific aspect here, we can contrast the woman who wishes to see the baby cut in two with the woman who gives up her claim on the baby, rather than see it cut in two. You do not have to be the baby's mother to wish to see its butchery avoided at any cost – it does not take a specifically *maternal* love to withdraw a claim under such circumstances. Any *ordinary* human being would prefer the child to live rather than see it cut in two. Therefore what requires explanation is why any human being would *maintain* her claim under such circumstances. Freud's explanation shows that the parable's structure misleads us into thinking the baby is the centre of the dispute, whereas it is more fundamentally the envy of one mother for what the other woman has that provides its motor. Do not forget that the mother who wishes to see the baby cut in two is in mourning for her own baby. The dispute is primarily an attack on the other woman, not an attempt to win her baby from her.

Freud's discussion of envy and Solomon's judgement formed part of an attack on the plausibility of a herd instinct. Freud wished to show that, in contradiction of Trotter's theory of the herd instinct, human beings are not by nature social animals.

For a long time nothing in the nature of herd instinct or group feeling is to be observed in children. Something like it first grows up, in a nursery containing many children, out of the children's relations to their parents, and it does so as a reaction to the initial envy with which the elder child receives the younger one. The elder child would certainly like to put his successor jealously aside, to keep it away from the parents, and to rob it of all its privileges; but in the face of the fact that this

*younger child (like all that come later) is loved by the
parents as much as he himself is, and in consequence of
the impossibility of his maintaining his hostile attitude
without damaging himself, he is forced into identifying
himself with the other children. So there grows up in
the troop of children a communal or group feeling,
which is then further developed at school. The first
demand made by this reaction-formation is for justice,
for equal treatment for all. We all know how loudly and
implacably this claim is put forward . . . If one cannot
be the favourite oneself, at all events nobody else shall
be the favourite.*[3]

For Freud this argument clinches his case against the assumption of a primary, innate social feeling: 'Thus social feeling is
based upon the reversal of what was first a hostile feeling into
a positively toned tie in the nature of an identification.'[4] At
the core of this argument is the demonstration that the call
for justice and equality is founded upon the transformation
of envy. Without envy, not only would there be no *need* for
a judicial apparatus – there would be no *desire* for justice.

It is this conclusion, this link between an emotion and a
principle for the organisation of society which I want now
to explore further. Before I do so, I want to make a few
digressionary remarks – remarks, which, I hope, will show
the interest of this inquiry. Envy as a fundamental fact of
psychic life is well known in two different psychoanalytic
theories, both of which have had rather mixed fortunes. The
first is Freud's thesis that a little girl becomes a woman via
the transformation of penis envy into the wish for a baby.
Aligning his theory of general social envy with the specific
theory of penis envy reveals immediately their closeness of fit,
if I can put it like that. The primal scene of penis envy is very
similar to the primal scene of envy in general: the girl, like the
sibling, sees the other child with an object that she thinks gives
him complete satisfaction, and she falls prey to envy. What
is missing when Freud discusses envy of the penis compared

with envy in general is the subsequent reaction-formation: the identification with the other child and the clamorous demand for equality.

I don't think I need say more about this theory, since it is very well known, a part of our intellectual mythology. However, I would like to ask the question: in the debates that Freud's notorious account started, which element of the concept of penis envy aroused the most passion: the penis or the envy?

The other psychoanalytic theory is contained in Melanie Klein's short book *Envy and Gratitude*. Klein advances the hypothesis 'that one of the deepest sources of guilt is always linked with the envy of the feeding breast, and with the feeling of having spoilt its goodness by envious attacks'.[5] Beneath the Oedipus complex, which in Klein's view manifests itself principally in the primal scene of the parents making love, enjoying one another endlessly, there is a deeper fantasy: that of the breast endlessly feeding itself on the good things contained in it – including the father's penis. If there is any failure in the relation to the breast, if there is any frustration, then the child's response is envy and the attempt to spoil what is good.

Klein's theory sees envy as a direct derivative of the destructive impulses, the death instinct. The destructive impulse attaches itself immediately to the first object of love, the breast. The breast is the immediate object of destructive impulses precisely because it is loved. Destroying what you love most: this fundamental response to the world is summarised in the emotion of envy.

Klein's theories have received an uneasy response, in large part because the theory looks very like a psychoanalytic version of the doctrine of original sin. This comparison is appropriate, yet gives the biblical account of the Fall an interesting twist: the breast is an Eden spied from far off, a paradise where there is no lack, from which the human subject is excluded. Interestingly enough, St Augustine perceived the relation of the child to the breast in exactly the same way as Klein, and made clear that the envy of the child confronted with the feeding breast supports the doctrine of original sin:

> *Who can recall to me the sins I committed as a baby? For in your sight no man is free from sin, not even a child who has lived only one day on earth ... I have myself seen jealousy in a baby and know what it means. He was not old enough to talk, but whenever he saw his foster-brother at the breast, he would grow pale with envy. This much is common knowledge. Mothers and nurses say that they can work such things out of the system by one means or another, but surely it cannot be called innocence, when the milk flows in such abundance from its source, to object to a rival desperately in need and depending for his life on this one form of nourishment? Such faults are not small or unimportant, but we are tender-hearted and bear with them because we know that the child will grow out of them. It is clear that they are not mere peccadilloes, because the same faults are intolerable in older persons.*[6]

In Lacan's commentary on this passage, he accentuates one feature, only implicit in Klein. Lacan affirms that the object of envy is not something useful to the subject – the child no longer has need of the breast as he watches his brother feeding. The object of envy is not what I desire, but rather what satisfies the other with whom I compare or identify myself. It is the image – and it is important for Lacan that envy is a sin of looking, *invidia*, of looking outwards – of the other's plenitude closed in upon itself, of another gaining satisfaction through enjoyment of an object, that is the scene of envy. The object is given as separate from and outside the subject in the very inception of envy; included in the very idea of envy is a throwing outwards, a projection.[7] It is then the dialectic of inner and outer that characterises envy. The very concept of the subject's interiority depends upon the subject's attention being directed primarily to the other, in the moment of perception of its being satisfied by the object of envy.

At this point, I wish to turn to Nietzsche's genealogy of morals to explore a parallel analysis which, in my view, proves to be very similar to Klein's analysis of the original sin of envy. It is these passages that also form the starting-point for Max Scheler's influential essay on *Ressentiment*. Nietzsche's *Genealogy of Morals* sets out to analyse the development of the concepts of good, bad and evil. He counterposes two fundamentally different principles, associated with two different peoples: the aristocrats and the Jews. The aristocrats' morality consists in a 'triumphant self-affirmation' – though Nietzsche questions whether such a principle of self-affirmation can ever give rise to what *we* call morality. But the morality of the Jews – and by Jews Nietzsche obviously means Christians – develops from their vengeance and hatred, manifested in *ressentiment*, rancour or resentment against the noble aristocrat. Out of their hatred grows that 'deepest and sublimest of loves' as expressed in the 'ghastly paradox of a crucified god'. With the universalisation of this slave morality, the people, the slaves, the herd have triumphed over noble values.

> *Slave ethics ... begins by saying* no *to an 'outside', an 'other', a non-self, and that* no *is its creative act. This reversal of direction of the evaluating look, this invariable looking outward instead of inward, is a fundamental feature of rancour. Slave ethics requires for its inception a sphere different from and hostile to its own ... the 'enemy' as conceived by the rancorous man ... is his true creative achievement: he has conceived the 'evil enemy', the Evil One, as a fundamental idea, and then as a pendant he has conceived a Good One – himself.*[8]

In his commentary on Nietzsche's genealogy of the slave morality, Scheler characterises the envy that so often leads to the attitude of *ressentiment* towards the world as arising from a sense of impotence.[9] The awareness of the object envied and the awareness of one's own failure, one's own emptiness, go hand in hand, they are inseparable. Envy thus turns out to be the most 'sociable' of the passions – it is the one that reveals one's fundamental failure in relation to the world, at the very moment where it reveals the causally linked success of another.

From envy Freud derives the sense of justice: 'If one cannot be the favourite oneself, at all events nobody else shall be the favourite.' In a more indignant tone, Nietzsche called this attitude 'world-destroying':

> *This man fails in something; finally he exclaims in rage: 'Then let the world perish!' This revolting feeling is the summit of envy, which argues: because there is something I cannot have, the whole world shall have nothing! the whole world shall be nothing!*[10]

For Klein, envy's effect is to undermine gratitude towards a good object and lead to indiscriminate spoiling and destroying of the objects in the world. For Nietzsche, the man of *ressentiment* embodies the reactive, negating attitude of the slave, of the common man, of democratic man. As Bertrand Russell put it in an uncharacteristically Nietzschean moment: 'Envy is the basis of democracy.'[11] Thus Nietzsche, Freud and Klein each offer a genealogy of the social and moral world as derived from envy.

It is this project of conjoining an affective state to a configuration of the social world that interests me. Nietzsche characterised the foundation of part of the project as follows: 'moralities are also merely a *sign language of the affects*'.[12] Yet Freud derives considerably more than a moral stance, or a moral universe, from the affect of envy; he also derives a socio-political regime. Why have so many political theorists, sociologists and anthropologists regarded this argument as illegitimate?

To answer this question, we should inquire further into the history of discourses of the passions and the place of psychoanalysis within that history. The *OED* defines passion as 'any kind of feeling by which the mind is powerfully affected or moved' and it gives as its chief examples 'ambition, avarice, desire, hope, fear, love, hatred, joy, grief, anger, revenge'. Psychoanalysis is a modern discourse of the passions, but one that frames the passions within a structure of quantities, of relations of conflict between abstract mental forces, or of the relations of subject, object, signifiers and the symbolic. The traditional passions are thus accepted as elementary units, as phenomenological givens. But they are in many ways deprived of their traditional force – their compulsive quality is taken as their primary characteristic, and a quantity such as the Q of Freud's *Project* is postulated as their underlying substance, or their universal currency. Hence there are two discourses in psychoanalysis which are often in tension: on the one hand, a traditional discourse of the passions, in which greed may be linked to jealousy, love to hate; on the other hand, a discourse of quantity, of the rationality inherent in quantification.

Yet our modern discourses of public life, of the social, political and moral orders, do not offer an easy welcome to the passions. However, political discourse was not always silent about the passions.[13] One of the founding questions of sociology requires that one pay attention to the development of discourse on the passions, since, ever since Max Weber, Ernst Simmel and R. H. Tawney, the political foundations of modernity have been traced to the transformation in the Church's attitude to business, commerce and banking. Put crudely, although not altogether falsely, avarice became transformed from one of the seven deadly sins into the foundation stone and guarantee of stability of the new social order. Alongside the thesis of religion and the rise of capitalism is the thesis of passion and the rise of capitalism.

One long-standing transformation of theology into political philosophy has regarded the passions as effects of external social and political arrangements, rather than as causes of these. To quote one early example, from Winstanley in the 1640s:

> *I speak now in relation between the Oppressor and the oppressed; the inward bondages I meddle not with in this place, though I am assured that if it be rightly searched*

> *into, the inward bondages of minde, as covetousness,*
> *pride, hypocrisie, envy, sorrow, fears, desperation and*
> *madness, are all occasioned by the outward bondage,*
> *that one sort of people lay upon another.*[14]

The contrasting of inner with outer, of the passions with the social relation of oppression, is the radical twist on a millenarian theme. The passions are themselves the products of man's fall from grace, of his expulsion from Eden. The restoration of that Eden, in the form of equitable social relations, will bring a revolution in the inner world – freedom from the bondages of the passions.

It is also clear that these passions – Winstanley's covetousness, pride, hypocrisie, envy, sorrow, fears, desperation and madness – overlap considerably with the Christian table of the seven deadly sins. Elaborated gradually from the fourth century on, given some stability by Gregory the Great, the seven sins provided a way of organising a discourse of the passions which subordinated worldly to eschatological concerns. Christianity always gave the discourse of the sins and thus of the passions an individualistic bent; one can see this in stark evidence in St Augustine's conviction that one should never tell a lie, not even one that might save another person's life, since what did another person's earthly life count when put in the balance against the fate of one's own immortal soul? Yet the revival of classical learning and its routinisation in the universities allowed what came to be known as morals to fuse the Aristotelian study of practical philosophy – ethics, politics and household management – with consideration of the passions in human affairs. More concretely, a less formal consideration of the foundations of politics grew up within the courts of the European states, from Machiavelli onwards. And it was in the courts that the new moralism of the seventeenth century analysed the place of the passions in a secular context. The theory of the State came to depend upon a depiction of man as he really is.

In his stimulating essay on 'The Passions and the Interests', Hirschman has traced the development of the discourse of the passions into the theory of the interests from the late seventeenth century to the end of the eighteenth century. As well as being threats to one's state of grace, the passions were threats to political and moral stability. Hirschman outlines three theories within which the necessary controlling and disciplining of the unruly and dangerous passions were envisaged: firstly their coercion and repression; secondly, their being harnessed, moderated and refined by the action of civilisation, of civil society; thirdly, the principle of the countervailing passion, the principle that one of the passions become the principal ally of the social order in disciplining the others. Gradually, the general framework of benign passions being capable of moulding and containing the malignant passions was developed. The court and salon societies which gave rise to the merciless dissection of human motivation by La Rochefoucauld, Nicole and La Bruyère produced the conviction that self-love is the one founding and unshakeable passion. Passing out into a more mercantile society, self-love could become transformed into self-interest, which could be assayed as the stable element in the taxonomy of motives for human action. And it was avarice, the love of money, the most constant and dogged of all passions, Dr Johnson's 'uniform and tractable vice',[15] that could be granted the position of universal and perpetual passion, in contrast with envy and revenge, which, according to Hume, 'operate only by intervals, and are directed against particular persons'.[16]

Avarice and greed, the 'calm desire of wealth',[17] thereby became officially sanctioned, benevolent and innocuous passions, the master passions with which anger and sloth, envy and pride could be tamed – without recourse to religiously founded precepts. Hirschman dates the decline of the doctrine of the countervailing passion to Adam Smith's *Wealth of Nations*, which established a powerful economic justification for the untrammelled pursuit of individual self-interest, rather than the political and moral account that the story of the passions and the interests previously gave. Yet the search for an underlying master-principle that is universal, that is unifying, that is rationalising, is characteristic of the nineteenth-century sociologies from the utilitarian calculus of pleasure and pain, via Marx to Weber, Durkheim and the Frankfurt School. Tentatively, I would suggest that the key document here is the chapter on money in Marx's *Capital*, which demonstrates the way in which the specific qualities of things are transformed by the inner logic proper to money into quantity; we find its echoes in the internal logic of rationalisation that Weber and Simmel perceive in modern society. What is eliminated – most conspicuously in the eighteenth-century mechanical algebra of utilities, and in the rational decision theoretic calculations of 'interests' with which Elster toys – is the specific colour and force of the passions. The passions become epiphenomena, mere effects of the underlying shifts of interests, mere signs of conflict and clashes of interests, particularly of different self-interests; or else they are privatised, and only retain their own character and flavour in the separate world of the family.

And it is in the family that Freud and Klein find them again. The archetypal scene of envy, remember, is of two children, one at the breast, the other looking on. Or, in the Freudian drama of the sexes, there is a girl who looks, sees and is instantaneously seized by envy. However, psychoanalysis blithely takes no notice of the logic of money, or of self-interest even – although part of that concept's force is recaptured by psychoanalytic theory in the new principle of universal narcissism, albeit in a form which is much less easily assimilable to the arithmetic of financial self-interest. And this is why its social theory so often has an archaic tone to it. Quite clearly, psychoanalysis harks back to the eighteenth-century principle of the countervailing passion. The story of superego, ego and id is a new morality play, in which one sin is pitted against another, one passion is subverted by another. For analysis, it takes the always passionate and vindictive superego to curb the unruly passions of envy and greed. The narcissistic pride of the ego can only be tempered by the fear of loss, itself akin to the *acedia* or withdrawal from connection to the world of the early Christian Fathers. Anomie might be the best modern translation for the sin of *acedia* (or sloth). So, in the psychoanalytic morality play, it might well be the balance of pride and anomie that determines the true sources of moral action.

Some summarising and concluding remarks. I have suggested that psychoanalysis includes a discourse of the passions that has some similarities with the moral and political thought associated with the French moralists of the seventeenth century and with certain strands of 'Establishment' political theory of the Enlightenment, before the legitimation of capitalism and the stability of the social order could be attributed to the invisible hand of the money market. Freud and Nietzsche are on common ground here, seeking in a genealogy of the passions and the principle of the countervailing passion the only possible derivation of so-called higher principles, such as the concept of equal rights, of justice or of a universalised morality such as 'Love thine enemy'. In Freud and Nietzsche we find arguments concerning the origins of morality and society which bypass the structures arising out of the inner rationality of money. In particular, the passion of envy is the source of a society founded on the idea of justice and of individual rights.

And finally we must return to the question of penis envy. Given the more general context I have now supplied for thinking about envy within psychoanalytic theory, it is possible that the criticisms of the theory of penis envy are as much directed at Freud's more general project of locating the cement of the social fabric and its institutions (such as the requirement of social justice) on the vicissitudes of the passions, in particular of envy, as they are against the image of the penis as the dominant symbol of the good, the achieved, the fulfilled. I want to make two final comments about this.

My first comment stems from this image of the full penis, the enviable penis. It is the envying subject who encounters this image of plenitude, who experiences impotence, that impotence that Max Scheler located as the source of envy, in the face of this image. The impotence or lack upon which this image in the other is founded is remarkably similar to the account of desire that we find in Lacan's work: the fundamental lack upon which desire is based, and the axiom that desire is always desire of the other. Isn't this concept of desire remarkably like envy? If this is the case, then penis envy and the general formula of desire are one and the same.

Secondly, we should ask ourselves why the Freudian account of the derivation of the sense of justice from the passion of envy is regarded with such suspicion, why it is thought to be reductionistic? Is the very idea of the countervailing passion, the idea that we are protected from one malignant passion by the force of another an implausible one? I presume we all find plausible the idea that we can be shamed out of acting upon cruel impulses, or restrained by fear from making love to someone we love. Or is it, as Klein suspected, that we still hanker for some higher foundation for what we value in ourselves and our social worlds, something more like love than hate, something more worthy than envy or avarice? La Rochefoucauld noted that we are often proud of even the most criminal of our passions, 'but envy is so shameful a passion that we can never dare to acknowledge it'.

There is one additional factor at work here. We may be more prepared to accept a base genealogy for religion and Christian morality – or at the very least the Freudian and Nietzschean critiques have habituated us to the idea that humility and brotherly love may be based on fear and resentment. But how relaxed are we about seeing our sense of justice based on envy? It seems we are now accustomed to God being dead, but would be reluctant to admit that social justice suffered the same fate.

NOTES

1. This theme could be developed in a different direction by exploring the image of the parent who bears the child, in its uncanny mode (the Erl-King), its religious mode (St Christopher, the Madonna) and its psychoanalytic mode (Winnicott's emphasis on holding and dropping babies).
2. Sigmund Freud, 'Group Psychology and the Analysis of the Ego', in: *The Standard Edition of the Complete Psychological Works of Sigmund Freud*, (24 volumes), edited by James Strachey in collaboration with Anna Freud, assisted by Alix Strachey and Alan Tyson, (London: The Hogarth Press and the Institute of Psychoanalysis), 1953–74, Vol XVIII, pp. 120–1.

3. Ibid., 119–20.

4. Ibid., 121.

5. Klein, 'Envy and Gratitude', in: Melanie Klein, *The Writings of Melanie Klein*, under the general editorship of Roger Money-Kyrle, in collaboration with Betty Joseph, Edna O'Shaughnessy and Hanna Segal, 4 vols, (London: The Hogarth Press and the Institute of Psychoanalysis, 1975), p. 195.

6. St Augustine, *Confessions*, trans. R. S. Pine-Coffin (Harmondsworth: Penguin, 1961), Bk I, Ch. 7, pp. 27–8.

7. Jacques Lacan, *Le Séminaire. Livre XI. Les Quatre Concepts Fondamentaux de la Psychoanalyse*, 1964 (Paris: Seuil, 1973), pp. 105–6; *The Four Fundamental Concepts of Psychoanalysis*, trans. Alan Sheridan (London: Tavistock, 1977, reprinted in paperback by Penguin, 1986), p. 116.

8. Nietzsche, *The Genealogy of Morals*, Essay I, Sections VIII-X, in Friedrich Nietzsche, *The Birth of Tragedy and The Genealogy of Morals*, trans. Francis Golffing (New York: Doubleday Anchor, 1956), pp. 168–73.

9. Max Scheler, *Ressentiment* (1912), trans. William W. Holdheim, ed. Lewis A. Coser (New York: The Free Press, 1961), p. 52.

10. Friedrich Nietzsche, *Daybreak: Thoughts on the Prejudices of Morality*, trans. R. J. Hollingdale, intr. Michael Tanner (Cambridge: Cambridge University Press, 1982), para. 304, pp. 155–6.

11. Bertrand Russell, *The Conquest of Happiness*, (London: George Allen and Unwin, 1930), p. 83.

12. Friedrich Nietzsche, *Beyond Good and Evil*, trans. with commentary by Walter Kaufmann (New York: Vintage, 1966) #187, p. 100.

13. We might propose as a general rule of thumb that any system that takes as the primary object of political philosophy the relative distribution of goods in a society (rather than the absolute good each individual possesses) is more concerned with envy and its consequences than with enjoyment of goods.

14. Gerrard Winstanley, 'The law of freedom in a platform; or, True Magistracy Restored', 1652, in George H. Sabine (ed.), *The Works of Gerrard Winstanley* (New York: Cornell University Press, 1941), quoted as epigraph in Carolyn Steedman, *Landscape for a Good Woman: A Story of Two Lives* (London: Virago, 1986).

15. Samuel Johnson, *Rasselas*, Ch. 39, quoted in A.O. Hirschman, *The Passions and the Interests* (Princeton: Princeton University Press, 1977), p. 55.

16. David Hume, *Treatise*, Book III, Part II, Section II, quoted in Hirschman, op. cit., p. 54.

17. Francis Hutcheson, *A System of Moral Philosophy*, 1755, Vol. V, p. 12, quoted in Hirschman, op. cit., p. 65.

Dannie Abse

EVENTS LEADING TO THE CONCEPTION OF SOLOMON, THE WISE CHILD

AND DAVID COMFORTED *Bathsheba his wife, and went into her, and lay with her; and she bore a son, and he called his name Solomon: and the Lord loved him.*

I

Are the omina favourable?
Scribes know the King's spittle,
even the most honoured
like Seraiah and Sheva,
and there are those, addicted,
who inhale
       the smoke of burning papyrus.

So is the date-wine sour, the lemon sweet?
Who can hear the sun's furnace?

The shadow of some great bird
       drifts indolently
across the ochres and umbers
of the afternoon hills
       that surround Jerusalem.
Their rising contours, their heat-refracting
       undulations.

The lizard is on the ledges,
the snake is in the crevices.

It is where Time lives.

Below, within the thermals of the Royal
            City,
past the cursing camel driver,
past the sweating woman carrying water
            in a goatskin,
past the leper peeping through
            the lateral slats
of his fly-mongering latrine
to the walls of the Palace itself,
the chanting King is at prayer.

            Aha, aha,
attend to my cry, O Lord
who makest beauty
to be consumed away like a moth;
purge me with hyssop and I
            shall be clean.
Wash me and I shall be whiter
            than the blossom.
Blot out my iniquities.

Not yet this prayer, not yet
            that psalm.
It is where a story begins.
Even the bedouin beside their black tents
have heard the desert wind's rumour.
They ask:
            Can papyrus grow
where there is no marsh?
They cry:
            Sopher yodea
to the Scribe with two tongues,

urge him to tend his kingdom
    of impertinence.

II

When the naked lady stooped to bathe
    in the gushings of a spring,
the voyeur on the tower roof
    just happened to be the King.

She was summoned to the Palace
    where the King displayed his charms;
he stroked the harp's glissandos,
    sang her a couple of psalms.

Majestic sweet-talk in the Palace
    – he name-dropped Goliath and Saul –
till only one candle-flame flickered
    and two shadows moved close on the wall.

Of course she hankered for the Palace.
    Royal charisma switched her on.
Her husband snored at the Eastern Front,
    so first a kiss, then scruples gone.

Some say, 'Sweet victim in the Palace,'
    some say, 'Poor lady in his bed.'
But Bathsheba's teeth like milk were white,
    and her mouth like wine was red.

David, at breakfast, bit an apple.
    She, playful, giggling, seized his crown,
then the apple-flesh as usual
    after the bite turned brown.

III

In the kitchen, the gregarious, hovering flies
where the servants breakfast.
A peacock struts
            in its irradiance,
and is ignored.

On the stone floor and on the shelves
the lovely shapes of utensils,
great clay pots, many jugs of wine
            many horns of oil,
the food-vessels and the feast-boards.

On the long table, butter of kine, thin loaves,
bowls of olives and griddle-cakes,
wattled baskets of summer fruit,
flasks of asses' milk and jars of honey.

What a tumult of tongues,
            the maids and the men,
the hewers of wood,
the drawers of water,
            the narrow-skulled
            and the wide-faced.
What a momentary freedom prospers,
            a detour from routine,
a substitute for mild insurrection.

They ask:
    In his arras-hung chamber
    did the King smell of the sheepcote?
    On the ivory bench, did he seat her
            on cushions?
    Did she lie on the braided crimson couch,
    beneath her head pillows of goat hair?

Who saw him undo her raiments?
Who overheard Uriah's wife,
Bathsheba of the small voice,
      cry out?
Was it a woman made love to
or the nocturnal moan
      of the turtle dove?

Will the priest, Nathan, awaken
who, even in his sleep, mutters
      Abomination?

Now she who is beautiful to look upon
leaves furtively by a back door.
She will become a public secret.
She wears fresh garments of blue and purple,
the topaz of Ethiopia beneath her apparel.
But a wind gossips in the palm trees,
the anaphora of the wind
      in the fir-trees of Senir,
      in the cedars of Lebanon,
      in the oaks of Bashan.
It flaps the tents where Uriah, the Hittite,
is encamped with Joab's army
on the Eastern open fields.

Does purity of lust last one night only?
In the breakfasting kitchen, the peacock screams.

IV

The wind blows and the page turns over.
   Soon the King was reading a note.
Oh such excruciating Hebrew:
   'I've one in the bin,' she wrote.

Since scandal's bad for royal business
   the King must not father the child;
so he called Uriah from the front,
   shook his hand like a voter. Smiled.

Uriah had scorned the wind's whisper,
   raised his eyebrows in disbelief.
Still, here was the King praising his valour,
   here was the King granting him leave.

In uniform rough as a cat's tongue
   the soldier artlessly said,
'Hard are the stones on the Eastern Front,
   but, Sire, harder at home is my bed.'

Though flagons and goat-meat were offered,
   the Hittite refused to go home.
He lingered outside the Palace gates,
   big eyes as dark as the tomb.

Silk merchants came and departed,
   they turned from Uriah appalled –
for the soldier sobbed in the stony heat,
   ignored his wife when she called;

sat down with his sacks, sat in the sun,
   sat under stars and would not quit,
scowled at the King accusingly
   till the King got fed up with it.

'Stubborn Uriah, what do you want?
   Land? Gold? Speak and I'll comply.'
Then two vultures creaked overhead
   to brighten the Hittite's eye.

'Death.' That's what he sought in the desert
   near some nameless stony track.
And there two vultures ate the soldier
   with a dagger in his back.

The widow was brought to the Palace,
  a Queen for the King-size bed,
and oh their teeth like milk were white,
  and their mouths like wine were red.

V

Should there be merriment at a funeral?
Stones of Jerusalem, where is your lament?
Should her face not have been leper-ashen?
Should she not have torn at her apparel,
          bayed at the moon?
Is first young love
        always a malady?

When Uriah roared with the Captains of Joab,
        the swearing garrisons,
the dust leaping behind the chariots,
        the wagons, the wheels;
when his sword was unsheathed
amidst the uplifted trumpets
and the cacophony of donkeys;
when he was fierce as a close-up,
        huge with shield and helmet;
when his face was smeared with vermilion,
did she think of him less
        than a scarecrow in a field?

When she was more girl than woman
who built for her
        a house of four pillars?
When his foot was sore
        did she not dip it in oil?
When his fever seemed perilous
        did she not boil the figs?

When the morning stars sang together,
face to face, they sang together.
At night when she shyly stooped
         did he not boldly soar?

When, at midnight, the owl screeched
         who comforted her?
When the unclothed satyr danced
         in moonlight
who raised a handkerchief to her wide eyes?

When the archers practised
         in the green pastures
whose steady arm curled about her waist?

True love is not briefly displayed
like the noon glory of the fig marigold.

Return oh return
pigeons of memory to your homing land.

But the scent was only a guest
         in the orange tree.
The colours faded
         from the ardent flowers
not wishing to outstay their visit.

VI

The wind blows and the page turns over.
    To Bathsheba a babe was born.
Alas, the child would not feed by day,
    by night coughed like a thunderstorm.

'Let there be justice after sunset,'
    cried Nathan, the raging priest.
Once again he cursed the ailing child
    and the women's sobs increased.

So the skeletal baby sickened
   while the King by the cot-side prayed
and the insomniac mother stared
   at a crack in the wall afraid.

Soon a battery of doors in the Palace,
   soon a weird shout, 'The child is dead.'
Then Bathsheba's teeth like milk were white,
   and her eyes like wine were red.

Outside the theatre of the shrine
   David's penitent spirit soared
beyond the lonely stars. He wept. He danced
   the dance of death before the Lord.

That night the King climbed to her bedroom.
   Gently he coaxed the bereaved,
and in their shared and naked suffering
   the wise child, love, was conceived.

CODA

Over the rocky dorsals of the hills
the pilgrim buses of April arrive,
one by one, into Jerusalem.

There was a jackal on the site
        of the Temple
before the Temple was built.

And stones. The stones only.

Are the omina favourable?
Will there be blood on the thorn bush?
Does smoke rising from the rubbish dump
        veer to the West or to the East?
So much daylight! So much dust!

71

This scribe is
           and is not
the Scribe who knew the King's spittle.

After the soldier alighted,
a black-bearded, invalid-faced man,
stern as Nathan, head covered,
followed by a fat woman, a tourist
wearing the same Phoenician purple
           as once Bathsheba did,
her jewelled wrist, for one moment,
a drizzle of electric.

But no bizarre crowned phantom
will sign the Register
           at the King David Hotel.

Like the lethargic darkness
of three thousand years ago,
once captive, cornered
within the narrow-windowed
           Temple of Solomon,
everything has vanished into the light.

Except the stones. The stones only.

There is a bazaar-loud haggling
           in the chiaroscuro
           of the alleyways,
tongue-gossip in the gravel walks,
even in the oven of the Squares;
a discontinuous, secret weeping
of a husband or wife, belittled and betrayed
behind the shut door of an unrecorded house.

There is a kissing of the stones
a kneeling on the stones,
           psalmody and hymnody,

winged prayers swarming in the domed hives
of mosques, synagogues, churches,
ebullitions of harsh religion.

– For thou art my lamp, O Lord . . .
– In the name of God, Lord of the Worlds . . .
– Hear the voice of my supplications . . .
– And forgive us our trespasses . . .
– The Lord is my shepherd I shall not want . . .
– My fortress, my high tower, my deliverer . . .
– The Lord is my shepherd I shall not . . .
          . . . my buckler, my hiding place . . .
– I am poured out like water . . .
– The Lord is my shepherd . . .
          . . . and my bones are vexed . . .
– The Lord is . . .
              – Allah Akbar!
              – Sovereign of the Universe!
              – Our Father in Heaven!
              – Father of Mercies!
              – Shema Yisroael!

There is a tremendous hush in the hills
        above the hills
where the lizard is on the ledges,
where the snake is in the crevices,
after the shadow of an aeroplane
        has hurtled and leapt
below the hills and on to the hills
        that surround Jerusalem.

Isobel Armstrong

NO-ING

I

By no effort can we think space to be away, although we can readily think of space as empty of objects.

Kant

Window, white window, choked with snow,
Pure matter, obdurate, through glass.
Snow's white intransigence
Turns matter to its opposite – nothing,
Makes all rhymes the same word,
All words homonyms.
Glass and glaze,
Frozen sand, frozen water,
Window, snow, converge,
The same crystalline morphology
Fused to a white mirror.
Images die outside, blanched
By an icy light.
Inside, blank surface I importune to release
Some sign, to unseal
A gleam from the window, separate
Its radiance from the ice, to deny
White on white
The negation at the heart of snow
The structure of nothing.

II

*Space is . . . a pure perception. For we can be conscious
only of a single space.*

And yet there's space.
Empty, as the philosopher says, blank,
Never nothing.
As snow melts back to water,
Molten glass resolves to sand,
Liquid, debris,
Rediscover
Singularity.
And still there's pure space
Through pure glass
Fused together.
Pain from flesh
Self from thought
Love from the lover
Sunlight in water –
Words
Tear them apart

Windowscapesky

III

*But it is just in this way that space is thought of, all its
parts being conceived to co-exist* ad infinitum.

white flowers froth
surfing the air
from a narrow glass before
a lace curtain whose
threads reticulate
light
which quivers

at the core of the vase
and along the table, stirred
by wind in
the trees' network
beyond

Robin Robertson

A Decomposition

The horse decoded on the killing floor:
a riddle of hair and bone
unknotted here
by a bad fall,
a buzzard, some
unkindness of ravens.
Then dogs came
for the dismantling:
splayed the legs to cord and cable,
emptied the chest,
snapped the brooches of the back.
The forelock sits
intact on the skull's white crown,
like a wig;
the head's cockpit
fizzing with maggots.
The horse drones.

Three days later,
a bone rebus;
the horse is parsed.
The ribs at sail, the body like a boat
in a surf of horsehair,
hollowed, resonant.
The wind's knife wedged in the keys
of an organ and left; the horse
playing itself, its singular note, its cipher.
A signature, legible and bold.

Lithium

After the arc of ECT
and the blunt concussion of pills,
they gave him lithium to cling to –
the psychiatrist's stone.
A metal that floats on water,
must be kept in kerosene,
can be drawn into wire.
(He who had jumped in the harbour,
burnt his hair off,
been caught hanging from the light.)
He'd heard it was once used
to make hydrogen bombs,
but now was a coolant
for nuclear reactors,
so he broke out of hospital barefoot
and walked ten miles to meet me in the snow.

Anthony Thwaite

OBJECT LESSONS

I

'But there's no index,' I said, turning the pages.
'Ah yes,' he said, 'And you're not the first
To comment on that. But we wanted to give more space
To the stuff itself, which is what most people want.'

The stuff itself flicked under my fingers,
Lots of it, moving at speed, till it seemed
Like those fat little joke-books I had as a child:
A cartoon animated by the turning pages.

Then I got to the end, and no index. Then
I made my comment, and he responded.
It seemed the end of the conversation.
A blur of pages, with no index at the end.

II

Because it was damaged, he said, he would bring down
    the price.
I couldn't see any damage, but I kept quiet,
Not wanting to show I'd not noticed. With a set face
I turned it round in my hand, and thought it all right.

He brought down the price, and I bought it. And now
    and again
I fetch the pot down from the shelf and examine it all

In the palm of my hand, never finding the flaw or the mend
That made me buy it at the price at which he would sell.

III

I found it on a market-stall in Skopje,
Not knowing what it was: bright tapestry,
Orange and red. It was a mystery.
My mother made it into a tea-cosy.

Now, when I'm pouring out a cup of tea
From this transmogrified fragility,
I sometimes face a visitor with a query:
'What do you think this curious thing might be?'

It seems it was, at least originally,
A decoration for a trousered knee
Worn by some Macedonian. But could it really be
A relic of the sole one-legged evzone in Skopje?

Tibor Fischer

BREATHING, EPHESUS

TWO TURKISH JETS rasped overhead as Andy squirmed
out of the taxi; he locked on to them professionally as they
snuggled together in the unchallenged blue, and thought of
the army of armies that had sunk into the hillsides around
there, humming in the humus.

Lucy had sauntered over to the booths that clogged the
entrance, booths buckling under the howling rubbish that
the sightseers were consumed by. Poised to make a perfect
purchase she stood by a stall, the consummate shopper,
Andy mused, grumpily aware that he had no need of a
placard requesting 'Fleece me black and blue and invite
your extended family to have a go' since his face did that
job.

Wanting a guidebook, he had to brave a booth, worried that
the absence of prices meant haggling. As feared, the proprietor
came out with a price that even Andy, with his total uninterest
in Turkish currency and on-the-spot arithmetic, understood
was a numerical expression of 'I think you are really, really
stupid'.

After a mild refusal, Andy gave the proprietor his back.

'Aren't you going to send some postcards?' Lucy asked.

'Can't be bothered. Why don't you get some? Aren't you
going to send one to that attentive dentist you were telling
me about?'

'You know me. I prefer them insolvent, not letting me get
a word in edgeways, and treating me like dirt.'

It was ironic that his work was, however dressed up,

haggling and that he was so bad at it: that here on the street, in the most rudimentary fashion, he had impotented out.

'Discount, discount,' urged the proprietor tagging after Andy, terrified that he might take up one of the dozen other opportunities ahead of him to purchase a guidebook. No wonder that Turkey was so far behind if they wanted to ponce around over the price of a sodding guidebook. Andy ambled on, forming his features into the look of the last man in the world who would want a guidebook.

'Do you want a guide?' they were asked most politely further on by a grey-haired man using the rich English of the fifties, acquired from BBC Radio no doubt, cultural light from a long dead star. He and Lucy hadn't been chatting and Andy was disappointed to think he looked so incurably English. The prospective guide's voice was from an era when learning and polish held sway.

'No,' Andy lied, convinced any hardship was better than being cozened.

'You're so ridiculously English, Andy,' said Lucy, 'I can't understand how you can be any good in bed. You're the one who wanted the trip here. More culture than you've had hot dinners, you said.'

He had been looking forward to it. Rome, Athens, Thebes, Izmir – whatever their illustrious roots, they were mostly deeply buried; your imagination stumbled on the traffic jams, the ghastly high-rises and the television antennae. When he had seen the sign by the road *Efes – 3 Km* he had felt a thrill he had never experienced before; the Ruins were isolated. They were a direct line back to the past, no taint of the present. He had eaten for years in a Turkish restaurant in London called the Efes; when he had discovered yesterday that this was the Turkish name for Ephesus he had instantly re-enjoyed all those meals that had unwittingly been bringing him closer to the ancients.

His excitement had been quickly quelled by the car-park with its mob of tourists, junk-junkies, touts making history dance like a distempered bear.

They made do with an outline map Lucy had picked up in town.

As they entered the site, there was a guided group immediately ahead of them and, reconnoitring, Andy spotted two couples from their hotel. They hadn't talked, but now Andy was forced into an acknowledgement. He and Lucy hadn't mingled much, partly because he always felt uneasy about the question that was never more than third down the list: 'What do you do?' When he said 'Aerospace' sometimes it was those who didn't figure out what that entailed, sometimes it was those who did figure it out, who irritated him.

At one party, sozzled, chatting with a dancer with whom he clearly wasn't going to be visiting Nudesville, he had broadsided the truth: 'Mainly, I go to hot countries to meet short people with unpronounceable names and try to convince them that we're the dog's bollocks in hi-tech death, hoping that while we're conducting our business they're not gassing or bombing their own populace or some moaning minority in a newsworthy way.'

Apart from the extreme unseductiveness of his résumé, it had suddenly struck him that the job description was flawless. Shithole? Oafish military regime? Flimsy dictatorship? Dire night-life? Send Andy.

Not that he was any good at it. He had never been remotely in the vicinity of a worthwhile sale in his entire career; but he wasn't discernibly bad at it either. He had never disgraced himself, never dropped the tray. The trick was to come back and swear blind: 'You know how much the French bribed them?' Then in the internal post-mortems to blame someone extremely unpopular or who had left the company for initiating the project or running it with the wrong pitch.

'Who were the Ephesians anyway?' Lucy asked.

'That's a tough one. The ancient authorities are divided on the origin of Ephesus. Some say the city was founded by the Amazons. Androcles, son of an Athenian king, is a popular choice. And there was an Ephesus who was son of the river Cäyster. The trouble with ancient authorities is that they're . . . well, dodgy.'

The theatre loomed massively ahead of them, a slope of stone. Striding up the steps, Andy was repeatedly reminded of how unfit he was and how hot it was. They hadn't even done the first item and he was knackered. The interior of the theatre was fenced off, which disappointed Lucy, since she wanted to play with the acoustics, but it didn't bother him as it was the most beautiful of excuses for not climbing any more steps.

Its splendour was accessible to the eye though; his gaze swooped up and down over the vast amphitheatre. It was stupendous that this construction had been left sprawling around. The adjacent stadium however had been rubbed out by wrathful Christians when they had got their era, as payback for their brethren who had been offered to the lions. Andy imagined the heat, the reeking felines, grumpy and starved. The dingy martyrs wanting to get on with it. The management fretting about the lions looking too mangy or pegging out, wondering where the next batch of condemned would be coming from, whether the crowds were wearying of feline-felon action anyway. Any job dealing with people was more trouble than it was worth.

'Fantastic, isn't it?' Lucy remarked.

'Eye-catching . . . but, you know, these ruins are a bit . . . *nouveau*. Imperial Roman tat. The really interesting stuff was going on here five, six, seven hundred years before the Romans bulldozed in.'

'You don't think you're being a little hard to please? But of course, you're a hard-core antiquist or whatever the word is.'

Antiquist? Antiquary? Ancient historian? Fan of the Ancient World? Paid-up member of the Society for the Real Past? Long gone freak. Craver of the fully crumbled? Most of what he had studied at university had evaporated over the years, but oddly, plenty remained. Ancient History, the degree that had more usually been referred to as the Gracchi 'n' wacky baccy.

Another group milled past them, which included a beautiful twelve-year-old girl. Andy took a moment to explore what he would do if order evaporated.

'But they were Greeks, were they?' Lucy asked.

'Mostly, but like all these ports Ephesus attracted anyone with an idea, something to sell, or a knife. Every army worth its salt has been up and down this coast. Ionians. Goths. Arabs. Dozens you wouldn't have heard of.' And in their wake, someone who would sidle up to the swordsmen saying 'You don't want to be killing with that. Buy one of these. Have a butcher's at that finish.'

Perhaps he remembered so much, Andy concluded, because the subject had fascinated him. He had had no regrets about doing the BC thing even when he had graduated and splattered on the granite wall of job rejections. He had sweated over reams of application forms, those masterpieces of bunk. Only a fraction of those to whom he had applied bothered to send him a drop dead, but the ultimate humiliation had been the four thank-you-for-your-interests from accountancy firms; he'd seen the offer of his services as a colossal favour, unparalleled in human history. That still burned.

His overdraft had got to the stage where the bank manager had wanted to see him to make sure he existed and to personally extend some unpleasantness. Andy had even taken out an ad in a magazine: *Switched-on graduate in Ancient History seeks employment. Anything considered.* He still had the rhomboid cutting hidden at the bottom of his desk, the loneliest scrap of paper in the world. Hadn't been a single feeler, nothing shameful, nothing criminal, nothing preposterous, no one minded even to con or exploit him.

At the age of twenty-one he had the knowledge that he was not anywhere near insignificant (insignificance was a rank far above his station) blasted through him like a soldier vaporised by a missile on its way to a large armoured object. Although things were far from over he knew he was not going to be a great spy, the billionaire's billionaire, a breeder of sundry brilliances, a name of any sort, a target for adulation, because he couldn't even manage a crap job.

Re-examining that year he could still make himself sweat with the authentic sensation of being totally redundant, having career-repellent caked thick on his skin, so far down the tunnel of debt there was no light.

Then Aunt Carol had died. He hadn't thought much about her. No one in the family had. He had had no contact with her since he had been nine (which he decided, on reflection, had been a boon since otherwise he would easily have found a way of infuriating her); so he was left three oil paintings, so awful he wanted to burn them; but he didn't – he had them auctioned and got a tidy windfall.

He was very grateful to Aunt Carol, not only for the bequest, but for croaking at the most opportune moment. If she had expired a year earlier the lolly would have been entrusted to an élite group of bong masters, record shops, restaurants and travel agents. It would have taken him and his favourite freeloaders a few months' hard spending, but he would have nothinged it. But by the time he got his mitts on it he had been flat-packed for long enough to have constant nightmares about spending eternity in his parents' house.

He had done well at the business school; he had done well because he had viewed it as an act of complete prostitution, and if you're going to prostitute yourself: swallow deeply. The entire course as far as he was concerned was raw charlatanry, ritual bone-waving. His tail had wagged on demand, he didn't squander any vitality thinking. He slapped on the bullshit, and unlike that old inhabitant of Ephesus and idea ace, Heraclitus, who it was said had smeared himself with dung when he was dying in the hope of remission, he flourished, or at least got a job.

'Who cares about the Carians?' he asked.

'Sorry?'

'The Carians. Do you worry much about them?'

'No. Should I? Would you recommend it?'

'You would have if you'd been round here in the seventh century. They were in charge of throat-slitting. What about the Lelegeians? Are you concerned about the Lelegeians?'

'No. Don't think so. And you?'

He paused and browsed his sentiments.

'Not really.'

They sauntered along the Marble Way to where the brothel was marked. They overheard a guide explaining that the outline of a foot carved on a paving-stone was the sign for the brothel. How did they know that?

'It's where you got your kicks,' commented Lucy.

'Bloody archaeologists; they have to rewrite their books every twenty years, replace one heap of speculation with another.' He was taken aback by how much burst there was in his outburst.

'I know this was one of the great cities, but in what exactly did their greatness lie?'

'Everything. The works. Philosophy. Poetry. Science. The Temple of Artemis was one of the Seven Wonders of the World.'

The brothel was eminently unexciting.

'Bricks are pretty much the same everywhere, aren't they?' observed Lucy.

Nevertheless, Andy thought, if he had made detours from the things held admirable in life, he had also side-stepped the ridiculous. He wasn't like Doug, a seller of double-glazing. And Doug's degree should have been more inclined to procure dignified employment since he had done Modern History.

Doug had shifted from castigating civilisations for their gaffs, scolding governments for their short-sightedness, tut-tutting wars and reprimanding revolutions that hadn't tucked their shirts in properly to trying to persuade a retired car-park attendant that he needed to spend a few thou on more glass.

The look on Doug's face had been unforgettable: shock, like coming home to find that your entire family had been murdered and the killer had already sold the rights for a seven-figure sum. He, the tweaker of societies' nipples, the fondler of cultures' bottoms, was selling double-glazing.

Doug was laughing now. Last month when he had stayed at Doug's country retreat he had moodied on Doug's bathroom fittings topping the value of his flat. Laughing Doug: golden children, a view of paradise out of the window; but you could detect at the edge of his eye a mote, a microdot to be unravelled and read: I am spending my life selling people glass they generally don't need.

Andy raised his eyes upwards; the sun was leaning on him.

'I was thinking about Stacia, the other day,' Lucy said. 'I can't remember any more, was she at the graduation do?'

Andy wondered whether it was the heat that had triggered Lucy's thoughts; he remembered the graduation party particularly well because it had been one of the three sunny days he had known in England.

'Of course she was.'

'We should have a reunion.'

He didn't see the necessity. Apart from Stacia their lives had pincered together every so often. He wondered why he remembered graduation day so well. Memory had such bizarre taste.

Him, Doug, Raj, Adam, Stacia, Lucy, Lucy's mum, all gathered around, as if posing for a photo. He had been cheesed off in the midst of the cheese and wine because a beautiful Danish girl in whom he had seen years of future, who did fifty sit-ups every morning, who was some great-grand-something of Kierkegaard (the closest he would ever get to enjoying philosophy) would summarise him as a minor, not unpleasant, incident in her English tour. That misery was ably supported by no money, no job and people he hated effortlessly picking up crushingly remunerated jobs.

'Enjoy yourselves,' Lucy's mother had said. He had known, in gory instalments, of her jugular-busting divorce. 'You think things are bad now. Wait and see, they'll get much worse.' You must be joking had been his response. He had been convinced he had been to the back of the disappointment shop. And he couldn't help thinking that your marriage sinking without any goodwill surviving had to be partly the result of negligence.

Andy stared down at a stone between his shoes; a chip off an old block, a fragment on its way to being a pebble, a petrous infant, separated from its family, wailing stonily.

During one of Doug's baby daughter's elongated, pole-vault

bawls, the question that had occurred to him was when and where she would die and in how much pain, which he doubted was a healthy reaction to the sight of new life.

Naturally, he was now aware that negligence was rarely the villain; keeping your eye on the ball wasn't enough, gluing the ball to your face wasn't enough. Misfortune's first name was versatility, and the world's soundtrack was various strains of straining, woe's beats, the yelp of someone striking a pain main.

This orb was no respecter. At that function, he had yet to discover that everyone gets hosed down with absurdity: the deservers of better get wetter. You're older, less oomph, less grit, less hope, but the same yokes: no money, no lover, no job-u-like. And new nettles, outlandish bodily complaints hidden in ageing's special stash, other specially flown-in impoverishments of your existence: children who hate you, your skills no longer considered skills.

He wasn't bloated with failure. It didn't hang out beer-bellyly; no, part of the thriving from afar. Unmarried, un-cohabiting at thirty-four, however you costumed it, was not good. Divorce was superior, a treading on each other's hearts achieved only at the closest of quarters; the solitary had a spoor no raffish aftershave could ever submerge.

Even a divorce like Lucy's was better, initiated the day she had returned from honeymoon: 'It would have been quicker but the tickets were non-refundable.' Her husband had broken his arm on their first day at the skiing resort, slipping on some ice. 'Careful, it's slippery,' Lucy had said. 'I can see that. Of course it's slippery, it's ice,' he had retorted, launching his legs into the air and snapping his arm cleanly as it was unexpectedly transferred into the role of sole. His wholehearted failure on the dignity front and inability to sherpa the pain 'was like ten years' concentrated marriage'.

Andy had been surprised by the union capsizing. Lucy was so ordered, calm. It was as if she had a delay-switch that gave her ten seconds to prepare. Even in her private life it was as if everything were a business deal, where clarity, courtesy and cool were paramount. But no exemption for poise.

Andy watched Lucy casting around the brothel for something that might produce a memory. There was an aptness in her being there. She wouldn't cause men's heads to revolve wildly, but she had worked through more liaisons than the rest of them put together. Two French skiing instructors in one afternoon. 'I didn't see why not.'

The absence of daunting attributes was her fortune, no hurdles of exceeding beauty to dissuade suitors. Once you made contact however . . . when it came to the carnal, there were two dénouements: those women in whom you had to work to surplus, and those in whom you had to work not to surplus. Lucy was lucky. You had it or you didn't.

'Lucky in fucky,' he said, pleased with his formula. Lucy gave him the despairing look women reserve for occasions when men manifested their innate unreformability.

'You've never heard anything from Stacia?' Lucy asked.

'No. Why would I?' No one had. Which was odd. Stacia had been a natural letter writer, a forwarder of new addresses, a true stayer-in-touch. Like Lucy, in control, a tidier of kitchens, a shopper of bargain goods, a switcher-off of lights, though not so inclined as Lucy to test-drive men, certainly not flash ski instructors. A teacher, whose hobby had been hospital visiting. Andy had wondered at the time how you could go through life to find yourself ill and friendless, unvisited and abed; it had only occurred to him recently that the answer was: very easily.

Swallowed by the globe. No report for years. It would be interesting to know what had happened to Stacia. Whether one of them had made it, got through, reached a four-bedroom contentment, didn't have to beat down despair every night.

'I'm curious to know what's she's up to.'

'Arms-dealing, probably. More Germans than Berlin,' Lucy added. The Marble Way was a pedestrian indicator of who was loaded. Germans. Japs. Americans. A few bewildered Brits you could spot from a hundred yards: maggoty white, poorly dressed, not knowing where they were going, squabbling uncolourfully. Was it true they couldn't get over the end of Empire? Wind up like some Amazonian tribe on the bottle, blotto? The Germans were white, but better cut, as if they all used personal trainers, with swagger and a sure sightseeing manner.

'You know what Doug was telling me?' Lucy continued. 'He said you'd be out of a job in a few years because the Germans and Japanese will own everything and they won't tolerate any wars that would damage their investments.'

'They could collect on the insurance, surely?' There goes the analyst, the sphere-feeler. Doug wouldn't have told him that, even as a joke, because he knew he'd be mocked senseless. It wasn't that simple. Why they were so successful, that was simple. Andy could never believe the number of books he saw about management and systems in Germany, Japan and elsewhere, stacked up on airport shelves. Nothing arcane or clever involved: they worked their guts out, and unlike back in Blighty, people took responsibility, not dodged it like a white hot tank; a belief predominated that things should be done properly. But how long can you keep it up? Affluence softens. Luxury had always been a dirty word in the ancient world.

He watched: the Americans had a hint of uncertainty. The Koreans, not as slick as the Japanese, coarser clobber, not such good teeth, were thuggishly getting into tourism: See? we're part of it, we camcord old stones too.

At the three-arched gate of Mazaeus and Mithridates Andy felt his sweat had sweat. He hobbled through the Latin of the dedicatory inscription, so Lucy understood that Mazaeus and Mithridates, former slaves of the emperor Augustus, made good in Ephesus, had paid for this construction as a very public token of their gratitude, a monumental grovel.

'They must have spent a fortune on this,' Lucy reflected. 'Toadying must be the oldest profession. I can imagine when we clambered down from the trees one ape was yammering to another: "I really admire the way you clobbered that gazelle with that tool-like thing. What genius. What vision. Do you mind if I tear off a haunch?"'

'No. Killing's the oldest profession. But crawling gets a harsh press; it's demanding work. The queue of people who wanted to weasel into Augustus's favour must have gone twice round the world.'

Was he serious enough about his career, Andy pondered. He didn't scrape to his boss at all. Or his boss's boss, or his boss's boss's boss on those rare occasions when he was winched upstairs. Promotion didn't do anything for him, he had his routines pat. Of course, not wanting a promotion was dangerous, he'd have to speculate about getting one otherwise he might get back to find one waiting for him.

Harvesting sweat with his handkerchief, Andy was mown down by the Celsus Library. These were ruins for people who didn't rate ruins. Much as he despised Imperial remains, he couldn't resist unpacking an amazement.

A tidal wave of masonry, columns and statues, it seemed implausible that something so extravagant could sneak past the millennia. Only a façade now, the body of the building and its contents gone. As always when the word façade appeared in Andy's mind, Raj tagged along behind, in tow.

Andy hadn't been shocked by the affair, because Raj's peccadillo wasn't that shocking when you could read about women and children being seasonally slaughtered in any morning paper, and when vicars asphyxiated themselves in ornate bishop-bashing exercises; not shocking, but it had been surprising.

Raj had always acted older, wiser, as if he were doing everything for the second time. You never saw him doing nothing; even if you saw him lolling in a chair gazing at the ceiling, somehow he was still making money, scheming some scheme. Maybe a bit stuffy – Raj wouldn't keep you up late with his aardvark jokes or selections from his love life, he wouldn't rip off his shirt and lead the dancing at a party – but on the other hand he always had the answer: where do I buy a top hat for a tenner, Raj? Dates for Henry II, Raj? Should I dump Julie, Raj? Raj always had the answer, and if he didn't, he behaved as if he did – which, Andy supposed, was the trick. No wobbling.

'I'll never understand how Raj managed it,' he said, letting the end of his thought caravan out.

'Can't you stop going on about that? We all have our odd habits, don't we?'

True. But this was beyond the valley of the odd habit. Anatomically, he still didn't comprehend how Raj had managed it. And Raj should have quietly acquiesced in the charge. Perhaps he had been counting on it being a my-word-against-their-word affair; and that might have been the result if the neighbours hadn't videotaped the activity. The drawback of living in a posh neighbourhood: no tolerance and good evidence-gathering. Discussion had also focused on why Raj had left the bedroom window open. Repeatedly.

Raj was unabashed, showed no dents, but he had stopped talking about standing as a candidate for the Liberals.

Andy had been disappointed because he had regarded Raj as a man whose sock drawers and bank accounts were exemplary, who cha-cha'd over the disruptions and misdeals. It was good to know that it was do-able; nevertheless he had taken heart that Raj was fallible, incomplete. Certainly, shafting your own rear as a coda to the day spoke of a lack: the want of someone to perform that service, or at least to join in.

You didn't need bars to be in solitary confinement. He found himself inspecting single women of his own age for the rampaging derangements or goring idiosyncrasies that would explain their being on their own, and noticed they were undertaking the same vetting. Looniness vs. loneliness. The twenties were rapporting, a pleasanting body in your bed, then a row and a split, or a move and a split, but another companion would come along, until one day the companions vanished mysteriously.

She was the only one of his girl-friends with whom he had succeeded in achieving the legendary good friends status, so when Lucy had suggested they go on a snap holiday he had been glad, and quite flabbergasted when she had said: 'If they only have a double room, that'll do.' He was only too happy to have a chance to refresh his memories of their intimacy, to resurrect for a week their romance which had originally been of that duration.

Andy didn't take much holiday and suspected he wasn't much good at it.

Bulgaria: first morning he had strolled down to the restaurant and surveyed the beach with two distant, toplessing, sun-soiled female figures, beauties he had as much chance of getting to know as he had of flapping his arms and hitting the moon. In an excess of good humour, pleased with himself for being inserted into such a relishable sky-sea sandwich, he accosted a waiter: 'It's so beautiful here.' 'No it's not,' responded the waiter in knockabout English, 'it's shit. I can't wait to get out of here.' Andy never had a chance to delve into the worthlessness of the resort, succumbing within hours to food poisoning and botulisming away the rest of the fortnight.

Rhodes: impulsively, he had booked a last-minute cut-price package, a bargain that was not such a bargain, he discovered at the airport. The other passengers were whisked away by couriers but he had no hotel. The bargain was only the flight and not the full board he had been expecting, a computer blunder, or perhaps the universe-defying stupidity of the travel agent. Everything was either booked or stratospherically expensive, and the small amount of cash he had brought with him was only enough for a room in a dilapidated guest house between two plenteously noisy auto-repair yards.

Spain: buffered with medication, traveller's cheques and credit cards, he had gone for a week in August. It had rained incessantly and so heavily he hardly left his room and he caught a rotten cold.

So the idea of travelling in tandem was appealing. In a pinch there was someone to call an ambulance, identify your body, collude with in grousing about the weather, and if the arrangement didn't contain the extremism of a holiday fling, decent conversation had its merits, and there was the charm of someone who knew you well, but still liked you.

'Sophia.' Andy read out the legend under one of the statues. 'Ephesian letters.'

'What?'

'Ephesian letters. *Litterae Ephesiae*. A.k.a. *Ephesias Grammata*. This was a huge centre of magic. They exported it. One of their most successful products. They were fascinated by the power of the letter, they hadn't had the alphabet that long, I suppose.'

'Doesn't look as if the magic did them much good.'

Indisputably, the countryside was of a voracious, relentless greenery into which miscellaneous blocks of stone had been plonked down. Not even a loose resemblance to a city, to a great port. The river Cäyster wasn't just silted up, it had done a bunk.

'Maybe they used it all up.'

'How did the magic work?'

'Search me. There were six formulae. One contestant was disqualified from the Olympic Games because he was nabbed with one of them down his leggings.'

'It was a good idea to come here,' Lucy said fiddling with a strap, 'my cultural levels are at max. No wonder St John did his writing here.'

'How did you know that?'

'You told me. Twice. Are you all right?'

'It's hot.'

Andy sat on a boulder, feeling as if the sun was treading on him with all its weight. Lucy meandered off to see if the slabs were slabbier on the other side. Drained, he decided to axe the visit to the house of the Virgin Mary up the hill where some anaemic nun had had visions.

A group, thoroughly toured, was being ushered out. There we go. See the sites, do the rites, on your bike. You paid more or less attention according to the quality of your guide or your mood. It was all here. Education. Sport. Entertainment. Graft. Trade. Rituals: obeisance, grovelling, snivelling, importuning, appeasing. Church, temple, shrine, mosque, fetish factory. Bird with big bristols, Cybele, Artemis, Diana, Virgin Mary. Help. The pleading places piled up on top of each other. Myrrh, fatted oxen, weaker people: burn the burnables. Eat, drink as much as you can, or at least more than your neighbour.

Why did so many people regard his business as evil, Andy wondered. He liked to look at it in this light since it made it less mundane. But it was difficult to feel sinister when the work was so poorly paid and most of his energy was devoted to things like getting a parking space and arguing with a jafa about his right to claim a cappuccino at Zurich airport on his expenses. With all the backhanders, sweeteners, loans, costs, he couldn't see how anyone made any money out of it. Like a painting, if you got too close, you wouldn't see a picture, just mangled colour and roughness.

'I do miss Adam,' Lucy said, returning from her stroll.

He nodded. Adam's death, while depressing, hadn't been much of a surprise. Adam's promiscuity had impressed him in a way; an achievement of a sort, although he had learned that it did require doing it with unappetising men. Adam usually played away matches (he had been especially fond of fire-escapes), returning in the morning to exclaim to him and Doug: 'Girls, you don't know what you're missing.' But once he brought back to the flat a scrawny coffee-coloured disc jockey who was a repository of the ugliest features of both races. Adam's jockeying of the jockey had mainly been linked to his immaculate access to illegal substances (of clinical quality and in quantities to scupper an aircraft-carrier), the consumption of which had been made doubly pleasurable by their flat being next door to the police station.

Still death was a harsh sentence on someone who, one way or another, had spread a lot of joy, especially when you considered how many monsters were torturing and murdering and guffawing, making a living out of killing in their seventies or eighties. One person was such an intolerable loss, let alone a whole civilisation.

'You know what the Gnostics said?'

'Remind me.'

'It's all a mistake. We're droplets of the divine, mislaid in flesh, stuck in steak. Clerical error, but as government spokesfolk say after a slip-up, everything will be rectified.'

His reverie then struck the roadblock of her ultramarine bra, assertive under the gauzy white blouse; it was the kind of outfit teenage girls wore to say: 'Tits.' His gaze was celestial, he had been bleached of beast by the sun, but it still caught her attention.

'Hotel,' she stated.

'Hotel.'

Going back was a relief, and although she was looking stunning, he was apprehensive about her intentions. Having a florida was an impossibility since even his bones were floppy but perhaps his tongue, that flaccid but loyal organ, could smooth things over.

The first night at the hotel, in his manhandling of her breasts, he had sensed a bud in the left. He had hesitated, skidding effortlessly from perplexity to anxiety, his mouth open, waiting for his wits to come up with some seemly line.

'I know,' she had said. She was taking physicians. 'If the drugs don't sort it out, they can always chop.' He was resupplied with astonishment. Why had she chosen to go away with him? He'd have been too busy polishing church floors with his tongue, amassing good works, hiring busloads of doctors, gibbering.

They walked exitwards. Having been extensively worked over by the presiding nuke, he was half staggering, his thoughts broken by the heavy light. Lucy was a couple of steps ahead, annoyingly unflustered.

Retracing their steps on the Marble Way, two of their conversations rattled in his head. When he had been having one of his moans about his job, she had inquired:

'So what would you like to be?'

'A man,' he had said, wondering where the answer and his candour had come from.

'A man? You do a passable imitation.'

'That's just it.'

'So what's the true qualification?'

'Being self-standing.'

You enter the world with a confidence that all history has been a warm-up act for you; you settle for not getting squashed and cowering uncoweringly.

Over breakfast, when he had moaned about London, she had inquired:

'So you think civilisation's in a tail-spin?'

'Yes,' he had replied. She had been teasing but he was in earnest as he reached out for another croissant. 'We're finished.' Diagnose and reach for another croissant, what else was there to do? A dab of jam, a dash of rite.

Near the car-park, amid the giant fennel, two boys old enough to have some acquaintance with compassion, were shunning the sophisticated diversions of what was practically the twenty-first century for the lure of some traditional cruelty and were engaged in furiously ramming a stick under a rock, mashing some small creature.

'I want everyone to be happy,' he said as quietly as you could while still saying; the wish didn't catch up with Lucy.

Who wouldn't sacrifice themselves, renounce the worldly for the world? To dispose of disposability. To provide a fitting of sense. To im up all mortals, to put everyone in the vault. Unwound the wounded. Arm of comfort as long as an equator. As much compassion as sky. Pain drain. Fear weir. Grief thief.

That too passed.

Julia Darling

BREAST

THE WHIRLPOOL IS my secret place down by the graveyard, behind a rotting wall held up with vines. It is the only place I know in the city where you can't hear the low drumming of Cripps' Shirt Factory. To get there I must climb down a weavy bank of tree roots, and there is the pool. It is a perfect circle, and the banks are mossy and green. The water curls round in a spiral and disappears into a narrow underwater pipe, which you can't see from the surface. I first swam through the pipe when I was six, and I didn't know where it led. I trusted in my imagination.

When Auntie finds out she has breast cancer, I am twelve and my breasts are two ideas swelling beneath my skin. It is thick summer and I am down at the whirlpool with Char who is a girl too, but thinner and more worried than I am. We walk about with our shirts knotted so that our belly buttons show. Then we strip off at the whirlpool and jump into the green water with only our knickers on. The water tangles us together into a knot, and we struggle apart and swim like eels to the underwater pipe, then we hold our breath and drop down into the weeds and slither into the black opening, and suddenly we are being pushed through the darkness, feeling the hard contours of the narrow pipe, and then splashing, into the light, in a completely other place with buttercups and a bridge, screaming, being born, like babies.

That day, later, I stand in the sitting-room with wet hair and three aunts weeping on the sofa, hanging their heads down in an auburn waterfall.

Auntie shows me her lump. It is hard and nobbly and sticks out of the side of her breast like a tangerine.

I think, Auntie only has one breast anyway; her whole front is a fleshy mountain harnessed up in iron vests and ancient brassières, so it doesn't seem such a big thing.

For once no one is smoking, and Auntie sits with her mouth open as if she has been caught shoplifting.

Char is there too and she whispers in my ear, 'Have you got any cake?' but it doesn't seem right to eat cake now Auntie is going to hospital to have an operation, so I say we haven't and Char goes home, looking anxious, as I doubt if there is much cake at her house.

The night before she has the breast off Auntie enters a wet T-shirt competition and dances at a disco with all the other aunts. There are seven of them, counting the removed cousins. They are all big as wardrobes and between them they have enough hair to stuff a mattress. Together they look alarming. They sing too loud and their skirts ride up their legs. I am the next generation. One of the aunts is my mother, although our family is so huge, I sometimes forget who my real mother is. I will fall asleep on any aunt. They all smell similar; of beer and starch.

She didn't win the competition, although she showed me her breasts in the wet T-shirt when she came in. They looked very dramatic. Then she drank some vodka. Then she danced the polka. Then she cried, ate some chocolate, and finally she fell asleep, still wearing her moist, sweaty T-shirt, her hair tangled amongst the cushions of the settee.

Auntie has to go into hospital straight away. She packs a small tartan suitcase and I am sent to Sid the Indian's Corner Shop to buy a copy of *Hello* and a packet of Kleenex tissues.

Sid says, 'Tell your Aunt we're thinking of her,' and gives me a card, and his wife mutters and nods her head, and the beads shake on her sari.

We go and visit Auntie in the hospital which is high up on a hill. We all go on the bus. A boy throws some chewing gum at me from the back seat and Auntie Madeleine cuffs him with her handbag.

'You're disgusting!' she yells.

'Don't make a scene. Not today,' whispers Elsa.

The old hospital is a long yellow place that smells of cigarettes and rubber sheets. Auntie is right at the end by the window, but we can hear her voice complaining from the moment we step out of the lift, holding carnations that die instantly. We walk past lines of women with no hair and night-dresses fastened with string around their necks. Auntie Melanie says, 'Don't stare,' when I hesitate by a Spanish woman who calls, 'Talk with me. Somebody talk with me,' and I walk towards her, but already a nurse with mottled skin is pulling the curtains around the bed and clicking her tongue.

Auntie is a funny colour too. Her cheeks are bright red and she is plumped up on her pillows. As soon as we get to the bed she starts to undo her buttons.

I back off, but she winks at me and says, 'Don't worry, there's nothing to see,' and I look and it's just a space where once there had been rolls of big bosom. It reminds me of an empty envelope. We sit around the bed patiently and stare at her, and she looks back at us.

She says, 'Somebody speak!'

She doesn't look like an ill person, she looks more like an eiderdown.

Every single female in my family works at Cripps' Shirt Factory. It's a corrugated shed on the edge of the river, and the air is so bleachy inside it starches your face. There are vats of bubbling cotton, and sewing machines with cruel needles, and the floor is blue and covered in broken white buttons.

I think about Cripps' shirts as we sit there dumbly in the old hospital. They are stiff and uncomfortable.

I notice Aunt Elsa secretly pressing her bra under her jacket.

JULIA DARLING

The next day I go swimming with Char in the rain, and we slither through the pipes and are born again, and float in the calmness on the other side.

Char says, 'Is she going to die, your Auntie?' and I say, 'No, I don't think so.'

'Will she get sick pay?' asks Char pragmatically.

I think of Mr Cripps with his tight collar and creased trousers. 'Bloody well should do!' I say in my Auntie's voice. My breasts are just big enough to be two small islands in the water. I rub them.

A man is walking along by the church wall and we have to turn over like otters and stay still in the water until he passes. I wonder what he would think if he saw a woman with only one breast. Would he still whistle?

We live in a part of the city where all the women are big and the men are small and jumpy, like ferrets. When my aunts go out with men they look ridiculous, as if they might squash them by mistake. My own father works on the oil rigs. When he comes home he is a shadow in an armchair. Once my mother sat on him.

When Auntie returns from hospital she has a false breast in her handbag. We throw the breast around the sitting-room. It's made of spongy stuff and is nothing like the breast that has been cut off. Auntie seems uninterested in it and watches the telly. She is like a mother that won't bond with her baby. Later I find it in a waste-paper basket.

That night I go and sit on the lavatory and find blood on my knickers. When I tell the aunts they all hoot and wail and make me lie down. They shout advice at me until I am dizzy. I feel guilty, as if the spotlight is on me, when it should be on Auntie with her empty chest.

By the time they have calmed down it is nearly midnight and we are all suddenly quiet, and all that we can hear is the thumping machinery from the shirt factory from the other side of town. Auntie says she has to have chemotherapy, and we all nod, not really knowing what she means. Then all the aunties start asking questions, and it's obvious that no one knows anything. The cancer was in her lymph nodes,

102

she says. Mentally I see a line of miniature telegraph poles stretching up into her armpit.

'What does it mean?' I ask suddenly. Auntie shrugs.

'What did the doctor say?' chorus the aunts.

'I just told you what the Doctor said,' says Auntie and yawns.

The next day when Char comes round I say I don't want to go swimming because of my condition. Char is jealous because she hasn't started her periods and she is thirteen. She slumps on to my bed and says indignantly, 'What am I supposed to do then?'

'We could go for a walk,' I say hotly. The curtains are still drawn even though it's eleven o'clock in the morning, and all the aunts are at work apart from Auntie who is watching television with her one breast.

Char nods crossly and we get dressed up in tight T-shirts and little skirts and put lipstick on. We go walking down in the town and stand with all the other teenagers at a bus-stop by the bingo hall. People look down at us from the buses as if we are vermin. Starlings shit on us from the ledges. A boy comes up to me and offers me a cigarette. He is very ugly with flapping ears and dirty trousers.

Char smirks and won't look up. I refuse the cigarette even though I quite fancy one. My arms are all goose-pimply.

'Come on, Char,' I sigh, 'let's go home.'

She lopes after me like a dog. The boy starts following us. We walk back along the river and every time I turn round he's there with his big ears flapping. The river is frothy and still and the trees are full of rubbish caught on the wind. Cripps' factory is smoking away and wheezing, and the machines are whirring and manufacturing stiff white shirts. A pebble hits my shin and I realise that the boy is stoning us. He has a friend with him now; a freckly, red-faced boy with red hair and a torn rag of a vest that barely covers his sunburnt shoulders.

A stone hits Char on the cheek and she starts to cry. The red boy yells, 'Show us your tits!' and we start to run. We run right up until the whirlpool, and the boys are out of sight, then I say, 'Quick!' and we strip off our clothes and hide them under a bush and I jump, in blood-stained knickers, into the pool and plunge down to the pipe.

Char is behind me, and before long we're lying face up in our quiet oasis and I feel safe again.

Char says, 'That's the last time I go for a walk with you,' as if it's my fault, for being a thirty-two B size and attracting attention.

After a few weeks Auntie has to go back into the hospital for chemotherapy. She lies vacantly in a bed with a drip going into her vein. At first she tells jokes and shrugs, but then she turns green and won't eat the biscuits we've brought her. All she'll eat is dry bread and pot noodles and she doesn't seem to have any energy. Around her the other patients grow balder and greyer. We stand around her bed just looking, and there doesn't seem to be anything much to say.

While we're sitting there, listening to the bleeps of faulty drips, the wig woman comes round with her trolley of hair. Auntie cheers up for a bit and tries on a Dolly Parton style, but settles for a short black one, which makes her look strangely young and smart. We leave her staring into a mirror with wide eyes.

We pass a doctor in the corridor, and Aunt Elsa looks as if she might pounce on him and start asking questions, but he bends his head away from us, and none of us want to shout.

'I just want to know the odds,' says Elsa, as if it's a horse race.

'What's the point?' says Madeleine.

The Spanish woman's bed is empty and tightly tucked in.

The summer is suddenly over and Auntie is still wearing her wig. She takes it off when she gets hot and wanders around the house looking like a monk. Her sisters keep telling her to put it back on, but she leaves it lying on the settee where it gets mistaken for a sleeping cat.

She is back at work, at the shirt factory, sewing on buttons faster than a machine. I am thirteen. I have had six periods. Char has still not started.

The whirlpool in winter is a terrifying place with silver water and icy weeds. I sometimes go there just to look at it. Char is going out with a boy she dredged up from the youth club. His face is flat and his skin is the colour of stone. I have no one. I lie in bed, listening to my Auntie chewing sweets in the room next door, wishing I was someone else. The sound of the shirt factory makes me feel unhappy.

Then one day the aunts come home with brown envelopes in their hands. The shirt factory is closing down. Auntie's hair is grown back now. It's thick and tufty, and she is her old self, although sometimes she looks at the sky and sighs. I'm not sorry about the shirt factory, although everyone seems to think it's the end of the world. Char comes round with her pondlike face and throws herself on to my bed, messing up the covers with her long thin arms.

'What's the matter?' I ask.

'What are we going to do?' she wails.

I realise that she is doing an imitation of her mother who sews collars.

On April Ist the town is suddenly silent. The machinery dies in one last gasp. Everybody stops what they're doing and listens. They say that Cripps has gone to the Philippines to make night-dresses. That evening people go and stare at the factory, as if it's a wake. There are bales of unwashed cotton piled up in skips, and bags of buttons spilling out on to the ground around the factory. Dogs sniff around the doors then scurry off. The river is full of blue dye and a dead cat floats on the water.

I am glad that the factory is closed, but somehow the silence in the town is deathly, and the vegetables in the grocers look grottier, and the ice-skating rink closes down, and there are fewer buses and the summer takes a long time arriving. In this time the aunts become middle-aged. They cut their hair short and Elsa marries a butcher and Madeleine gets a part-time job emptying sanitary bins. The biscuit tins are empty. I know who my mother is, and she gets on my nerves. She sits in the kitchen clearing her throat and chopping up onions so the tears run down her cheeks.

All through the winter I grow. My breasts feel heavy and hard. My nipples are two raspberries. My stomach is a smooth mountain. Hair grows everywhere, like weed. By spring I am a totally different shape.

Then Auntie gets another cancer, but this time it's deep in her body, in her ovaries, and she says that all the doctors do is smile.

None of us know what to say. I have nightmares about her insides; that they are riddled with woodworm. Suddenly she gets into bed and doesn't get up, and her face becomes milky and heavy. Our house is like the hospital.

The day that my Auntie dies I play truant with Char. The house smells of boiled eggs and daffodils, and everyone is whispering. Auntie has even chosen the colour of her gravestone. They tell me to come straight home after school. The local vicar is hovering at the end of the street.

Char says sentimentally, 'Your Auntie would want you to enjoy yourself,' although the truth is she can't face double chemistry, and Char is going down the drain with her anxious eyes and boring boy-friend.

We walk down to the whirlpool, singing a Take That song. There is a delicious quietness about schooldays. Nothing is quite normal. When we get to the whirlpool it is deserted, and it feels as if it belongs to us and to nobody else.

'Let's go naked,' I whisper, and Char's eyes shine, and it occurs to me that this is the most precious thing that will ever happen to Char, and that if there was still a shirt factory Char would work in it, but as it is she will become a woman with no biscuits in her tins.

We strip off and jump in and the water wraps itself around us like an enchantment. I am suddenly light and strong. I hold my breath and disappear down into the silver depths. Then we lower ourselves down to where the pipes are, and

Char disappears into the dark hole, to that other place, where the buttercups grow. I wriggle my shoulders into the opening.

And I push.

Philip Hensher

DEAD LANGUAGES

I DID NOT know when I was a boy that most people in the world went away to school. I only knew that no one from my family had ever left the stilted house in the forest river, to travel fifteen miles in two days to arrive, with the mud dry on my bare feet, at the big white school where they laughed at the way my family had always spoken.

They kitted me out with clothes which scratched and made you sweat; clothes which either gripped you like ropes and made you want to pluck and itch, or hung loosely over your hands and feet and got in the way of running. And a pair of brown shoes which, eight months later, my father would take from around my neck, where they had been hanging during the journey back home, and sit with them for an entire week, looking at them and thinking his thoughts no one ever asked about.

The mister of the school was a Christian and had a wife. They lived in the school, in a separate wing, which the boys called the House. It was the way of the school, and the mister, for one of the younger boys, or one of those less accustomed to shoes and stuffed square beds, to be taken into the House to learn its clean domestic ways, the ways of what I learnt to call civilisation. I was the youngest boy, at least at first, and unused to the life of the school, and of schools like it. So, like boys before me, I was taken into the House to work.

When I first went to see the mister to be told of this, I shook in my shoes. I stood at the end of the long dark wood room and waited to be shouted at. But the mister did not shout;

he said good morning and, with his way of pausing before speaking, asked me to come closer. He asked about the place I came from, and he asked how old I was, and my family, how was it. And then he stopped asking, and in the room there was silence for so long that I raised my head, and I looked at what he looked like. He was just looking at me, in silence, without talking. And his big black eyes were sad in the way the eyes of animals are sad. Or look sad, when you know that in fact they are really nothing of the kind.

There were few duties for me, and they did not interfere with what I had to learn. I learnt that I lived on an island, too big to walk around. I learnt not only what I knew, that you could add things and take things away, but that things could be multiplied and, more often, because it was harder, divided. I learnt that there were languages which were dead, and civilisations which were gone, and I chanted the words which humans once spoke freely and in feeling, to say *I love* and *you love*, and I felt nothing except what I happened to be feeling at the time. And I learnt other things, in the mister's House.

Every day, at four, I would walk around the trim square of grass to the House. For two hours, I was supposed to do the housework. At first I dreaded going round there, because the boys of my age told me stories about the mister and the mister's wife. They said they would fight in front of you. They said he would punish you. They said the mister was afraid of his wife, and he took it out on you. I was afraid that these things would come to pass, and then quickly I saw that they would not. It did not occur to me to tell the boys who said these things about my meeting with the mister; it seemed to me then that nothing happened, when he said nothing and gazed at me.

I was intended to dust, to tidy, and to iron clothes; to make certain preparations for food. But in fact, I did not do these things. After some time, each afternoon, perhaps no more than half an hour, the mister's wife would call to me. 'Come and sit,' she said. And I went and sat, and drank *totosa* with her in the heat of the late afternoon, and we talked. I liked to listen to her.

The mister was immensely tall and his limbs were immensely long. They were insect-like, or lizardy, his limbs, in the way they gave the sense that through sheer length they would easily break, or easily turn themselves backwards. When I think of him, I think first of his loping vaguely across the thin lawn of the school; but then I think of his wife. Because the mister's wife was round and sweet and idle like a sweet yellow bun, and reminded you of the mister because she was so unlike him.

'Come here, Bobo,' she would say. A silly name she had for me. Her voice comes to me, it still comes to me; her husk and hint of a rattle which made your own throat ache with the urge to cough, and clear it. And her conversation, the silliness we let ourselves jabber about. She would ask me things which I was certain, once I knew enough, I would be able to answer. 'Why is the sea sometimes blue, and sometimes not at all?' Or she would ask me about my family, and I would tell her about my tiny mother, no taller than I, and my little brothers, and my new sister or brother who now must be born, whom I knew nothing about, and the long stilted house no more than fifteen miles, and no less than half a world away, which my father and his father together built. I did not talk too much about my family; I had a constant fear that one of them might have died, and I would know nothing about it. It would be bad to sit and talk fondly about my father and laugh about what now seemed to me the funny way he had of putting a little yaw in the middle of words. A bad thing, if he was dead and I did not know it.

We talked once about death, the mister's wife and me, and it was like another fancy of hers. 'If there was a day,' she said once, 'when nobody in the world died, nobody anywhere died, who would notice?' I sat and thought about that world without death, for one day; how it would be happy and untouched by suffering, and yet no one would know until long afterwards, when suffering and death and pain had returned. Enchanting, these conversations, and a secret they were, from the mister.

I came to understand that he slept upstairs after he had

finished teaching, while his wife talked to me in the dark cool rooms with their resiny smell of teak. The creak and lollop of his coming downstairs was, for me, a sign to rise and be busy with the furniture and a rag; and, for her, a sign to sigh and stretch and smile for her husband.

'Who built the school?' I said once.

'Long long ago,' she said. 'It belongs to me now.'

I digested this.

'It was the mister's,' she said. 'But he thought he would lose it, so he gave it to me.'

'How could he lose it?' I said.

'It could be taken away from him,' she said. 'He was afraid it would be, so he gave it to me.'

I thought about it. It made no sense, to give something away because somebody would otherwise take it from you.

'And now he'd like to be off, to be rid of his old baggage, but he can't,' she said. 'He's stuck with me, and I'm stuck with him, because the school is mine.'

I thought.

'If you gave it back to him,' I began.

'They would take it away from him,' she said.

It made no sense. In the dark corner of the sitting-room, I heard the quick creak of the ceiling which meant he was getting up, and I reached for the duster.

The boys in the long room where I slept laughed at me at first, and soon I learnt to speak as they spoke, and to wear my shoes always, and not to scratch myself, under their laughter. And soon I joined in with their fanciful night talk about the mister and his wife. The tales of shouting, tales of hurled insults, the names of vegetables and beasts they yelled at each other, the throwing of objects in their epic rows; I listened, and soon I too found I could tell of arguments I had not heard. I joined in when the boys said that they knew of a machine for punishment the mister kept in his upper rooms, and they knew of a boy who, five years before, had died of fright when he had merely seen the terrible machine. I thought that there was probably no such machine, but in my duties I did not go upstairs. I did not know what punishment and secrets and humiliations lay in the bedroom of the mister, and the bedroom of the mister's wife, and I kept quiet.

'Does the mister ever speak to you?' she said to me once, one afternoon, as we sat with our cooling *totosa*.

Her conversation was like that, simple questions you could not understand.

'Yes he does,' I said.

'Does he speak to you when you're on your own?' she said.

'I don't know,' I said, after a while.

'If he asks you to come to the House when I'm not here,' she said.

There seemed to be nothing more. She was looking at something, with sudden fierceness. She was looking at a big fly, making a noise like thick paper tearing at the far wall. I sat and waited for the next thing she would say. But she said nothing more. And in six months, I was no longer the youngest boy when I came back from my six weeks with my family in the quiet stilted house in the mud by the river. Before long, the fat progress of the creamy yellow flesh of the mister's wife through the shady cloisters was as comic to me as to every other boy. For years behind and years to come.

That was the way to talk about her, in a funny story. Because I told the stories to the dormitory, the stories of how she talked to me. But it was no story, and the boys in the long room after dark laughed at me for thinking it was something to be told. And yet it was.

Years passed; they always do. And the time came to go; and I was exactly the same. Except that I knew more, and I talked differently, louder, I suppose. And I knew my father, when I jumped out of the boat back from school, would, as he had every year, seem smaller. I knew his way of talking would have suddenly developed a funny, unexpected yaw I would want to correct. The dead languages we learnt at school, we guessed at their pronunciation, I knew, and guessed wrongly; and I knew that if a speaker of those dead languages was to leap out of a boat and talk to us, his way of saying even *I love* and *you love* would seem strange to us. But it would be a way of speaking we had once known, and had forgotten; a way newly unfamiliar to us, because we have so changed.

The time came to go, and not to return, and I did not know where I was supposed to go. The mister asked me to go to his room, once more, and I went. He was sitting behind his desk, as he had before. This time I looked at him, but his eyes were dark and sad as they always had been; and we looked at each other.

'Here,' he said eventually to me. 'You've been good. We ought to be proud of you.'

'Thank you, sir,' I said.

'I'd like to give you a leaving present,' he said. 'Something you will always keep.'

'No need, sir,' I said.

'No need to call me sir now,' he said.

'I would like to say goodbye to your wife,' I said after a time.

'My wife is out for the afternoon,' he said. I did not understand the mister and his wife. I did not know what contracts passed between them in the dark. And, in fact, I still do not. He reached for his wrist, and unhitched his watch. He glanced at it, as if checking it still told him what Now it was, and offered it to me, across the broad expanse of his desk. I shook my hands at him. His smile insisted, and I carried on shaking my hands at him. And I did not know whether my refusals were the sort of polite refusals which always intend to finish in acceptance, or if I did not want the watch. I did not know, and on either side of the desk, I shook my hands at him, and he smiled at me, and proffered.

The mister's tiny wrist-machine was what I once called *tiktik*. Knowing no better. And with every *tik* another second gone, and another moment, and a chance lost, and, perhaps, no new chances to take their place. Once I wanted to learn and learn, until I knew enough. But now I know that I will never know enough; that the exams in that unmastered subject, Enough, have never yet been set; that they have never been passed, and never will be.

Duncan McLaren

SOAP CIRCLE

TO THE RICHARD Long exhibition at d'Offay's.

Three stone circles made from blocks of slate have been installed. One can be stood inside; I step into it but don't linger. Another has a perimeter which is several blocks thick and would require a leap to be entered, a leap that would disturb the calm ambience here so I don't make it. The third is entirely infilled, jagged edges pointing upwards, and must be viewed from without. I walk round it, considering the red slate – some edges sliced straight by quarrymen or the artist – before turning to the gallery walls.

Stone circles also appear in most of the half-dozen large, framed photos. I stand in front of a wide, flat New Mexican landscape; a lightly clouded sky over miles of featureless, scrubby desert. The circle of wayside stones in the foreground hardly dominates the scene. Does the presence of stone circles over the gallery floor encourage me to engage more with those the artist has assembled and photographed in New Mexico, Iceland, Australia (a bark circle this one, actually) and Dartmoor? Oh, I think it does.

How would I have gone about making this New Mexican stone circle? I'd have reassured myself about the water/sun/ temperature situation before getting involved . . . I'd have established that there were enough loose stones of a suitable size lying around . . . I'd have marked the centrepoint of the circle-to-be, and collected a few stones together . . . I'd have paced out maybe eight radials and placed a stone at the end of each one . . . I'd have completed the circle by making as few short trips for stones as possible ... And then I'd have made the most of my handiwork in whatever way came to mind at the time. Before contemplating the wider view, taking the photo and being on my way ...

As well as photos there are a number of large, framed texts on the walls. Including this:

DUSTLINES

KICKING UP A LINE OF DUST EACH DAY ALONG THE WALKING LINE

A 7 DAY WALK ON THE EAST BANK OF THE RIO GRANDE

EL CAMINO REAL   NEW MEXICO 1995

The text doesn't tell me whether the trek was to the north or south, unless 'EL CAMINO REAL' somehow gives that information. In this year's other walks, the artist specifies which way he was going: from the south to the north of Ireland; east from the mouth of the Loire. In New Mexico, perhaps he walked in one direction for a few days then retraced his steps ... but this takes me nowhere.

I'd also like to know in which season the walk took place. I suppose the landscape picture gives clues but I don't know enough about the annual cycle of desert plants to make use of them ... Presumably the walk came after the All Ireland winter walk, but did it come before or after the French walk?

Another thing – mileage. France: 121 miles in 3½ days; Ireland: 382 miles in 12 days. Very good going – more than 30 miles a day. But last year's progress across the middle of Iceland was slower – 220 miles in 14 days is only an average of 15 per day. How fast did he get through New Mexico? – the exhibition doesn't say.

I ask the young woman at the desk about this walk. But she knows no more about it. I ask her about the personality of the artist. All she can say is that at the private view he came across as quiet and self-contained. She asks why I want to know. I shrug and say something about writing.

We talk about the other artists I've written about so far,

the stances I've taken and the slim prospects of the material being published. She discloses that she once wrote a romantic novel, but, although she felt she'd followed all the rules of the genre, the book wasn't accepted by Mills and Boon – the only feasible outlet for it, and so that was that. She goes on to say that she still writes, that she's been offered a job by *Sight and Sound* to write film reviews and other articles, and that she's really excited by the prospect. We smile at each other.

I walk once more round the stone circles on the varnished wooden floor of the gallery and, smiling again, go on my way.

On to Saatchi's where Young British Artists are showing.

Soaps and washroom fittings dominate the list of Hadrian Pigott's exhibits. As I cross the huge, white space towards rounded, white shapes, perfume pervades the air.

I veer towards what appears to be an open travelling case. Closer and from a different angle it seems to be the case for a bulky wind instrument. But as I look down into the velvet-lined interior I see a hand-basin complete with taps, plug-hole and plug. Also set in the velvet is a bar of soap and plumbing components which could, I presume, enable the wash-basin to be plumbed in. Did Richard Long saddle himself with such luggage on his New Mexican trek? Certainly it would explain embarrassingly slow progress across the desert.

My eye is drawn to a group of three round, white boulders. One of them has two taps at the top of it, and is, I now smell, a huge soap. I suppose the boulder shape reflects – materialises – the interior of a sink. Anyway, there is also a plug on a chain resting on the soap boulder, and a plug-hole between the taps. If the taps were turned on, some of the water from them would go down the plug-hole into the soap, but most of it would spill down the sides of the boulder. Of course, you no more get water from taps set in a soap boulder than you get blood from a stone. Unless your name is Long, you're in the middle of the New Mexican desert, and you're hallucinating.

I look towards what turns out to be a row of pristine, white bars of soap, equally spaced, each resting on a white, plaster soap-dish set into the wall at about waist height. Each soap has a word stamped into it, but not a manufacturer's name. I walk along the row, reading: FEET, LEGS, ARMS, SHOULDERS, NECK, EARS, CHIN, CHEEKS, NOSE, FOREHEAD, HANDS . . . I stop at HANDS.

I'm aware again of what I'd forgotten about on entering the building. After eating a bag of chips for lunch, my hands reek of vinegar and could do with a wash. I walk away from the soaps 'n' sinks display towards a washroom proper where I give my hands a good seeing to with an almost new cake of white soap.

Back in the gallery, a second glance at the list of exhibits tells me that the eighteen soaps refer to the artist's order of washing himself in London on 23 March 1994. I'm now doubting if I went along the row in the right direction. Sure enough, the reverse order makes more sense given the effect of gravity on soapy water. So: ARMPITS, CHEST, BELLY, PRICK, BALLS, ARSE, BACK, HANDS . . . I stop at hands as before, puzzled.

I can still smell vinegar. I raise my left hand to my nose and confirm the scent of acetic acid. How come? . . . I suppose the handle of my bag and the pocket of my jacket were contaminated by the vinegar before I washed my hands, and that contact with handle and pocket subsequent to the wash has . . . oh, it's obvious enough. So what I have to do now is return to the loo and soap my hands again, as well as washing the tainted parts of jacket and bag. Wrong. After all I haven't been kicking up dust for a week along the Rio Grande; I am relatively clean and the best thing would be simply to move on to a different part of the building and another artist altogether.

Kerry Stewart's 'Sleeping Nun' has a room to herself. I try not to feel like an intruder as I approach the figure. She is made of plaster, I think, which has been painted – flesh colour for face and hands, white for the head-dress, but mostly black. She is lying on her right side and her front, with her habited head resting on her right wrist, and her left forearm stretched out with its palm flat against the floor. Her eyes are shut, her expression . . . difficult to read.

I back away from the sleeper and sit in a corner of the room. But from here the figure is entirely black so I slide along the floor until I have sight of pink and white as well. The still predominantly black figure seems to hover above the grey floor. I lean my back against the wall, close my eyes in sympathy with my room-mate . . . and visualise each stage of my journey home.

Home, I step on to a cold bath and under a hot shower. It's not hot yet though.

I imagine a wide, flat landscape with a stone circle in the foreground. Iceland. Inside the circle lies a sleeping nun. The circle is made out of little soaps with words such as . . . No, the circle is formed by blocks of ice, the nearest of which has 'SLIP IT TO ME' written on it . . . No, the ice-blocks are wordless, but are moulded into bathroom forms: a sink, a cistern, a lavatory pan . . . Nonsense, the ice-blocks are rocks, smoothed-down limestone perhaps, white and slippery to step on, but warm now.

Hot water pours on to the nape of my neck. Another wide-open landscape, a New Mexican stone circle. In the circle is the girl from d'Offay's. She is sitting at her desk . . . no, she is sitting at the piano I recognise from my first visit to the gallery, years ago. Joseph Beuys installed the piano and lined the walls of the space with felt. Indeed, I now see that the circle is made out of rolls of felt, standing tall, roll to roll, blocking out my view of the woman . . .

My hand passes through steam and picks up the nearly-new bar of orange soap. I turn it around in my hands. I keep turning it and see that by moving my thumbs I can rotate the soap on its long axis, at speed. The soap spins round in my hands, lathering up. What do I do with all this liquid soap? I put the bar back on its dish, stick my right hand in my left oxter and my left hand in my right oxter, and rub away. Soap overflows from my armpits and I smooth it over my chest and belly. Am I going to wash in Pigott order, then? Certainly I have started that way and will finish with my feet for practical reasons – the slipperiness of this bath. I carry on with my ablutions.

I could have said much more to the woman at d'Offay's. She told me that *Sight and Sound* intends to give space in their review section to avant-garde films and videos. And I did recommend *Humiliate* by Bob and Roberta Smith which she took a note of. But I didn't give her an idea of what that work was really like even though I could very easily have done so. My prick is clean.

Also, I mentioned to her that I'd been to the Richard Long show held at d'Offay's a couple of years back. But I didn't go on to say that I'd been stimulated by it into making a walk of my own. I remember the event well, and how I commemorated it:

THE RIDGEWAY
ROADS PATHS AND ANCIENT TRACKWAYS FROM GORING
TO PRINCES RISBOROUGH
A 25 MILE NIGHT WALK WITH JOANNA
FULL MOON 4–5 JULY 1993

My balls are . . .

WALK OF THREE STOPS
A STOP UNDER A RAILWAY BRIDGE FOR A MIDNIGHT FEAST
A STOP AT CART GAP THROUGH GRIMS DITCH FOR REST AT 2 A.M.
(THE EARTH MIGHT BE UNINHABITED)
A STOP AT NUFFIELD CHURCH FOR WATER AT DAWN
CHILTERNS SUMMER 1993

My balls are clean. My arse and hands too. The soap is spinning round in my hands again. I use the tips of fingers of both hands to rub soap into my forehead. I slowly pull my hands down over my face – two fingers sliding down each side of my nose, the heel of my thumb slipping over my cheeks. I use the tip of my right index finger alone to rub soap into my chin but change to the middle fingers of both hands to clean my ears.

Soap circle; neck. I place my left hand on the back of my

neck above where the right hand lies. I make little circling movements of both hands, then alter the action and hands are encircling back and sides of the cylinder. Letting go, I clasp myself around the throat, right-handed, and slide my hand up and down until all the soap has gone. I place the tips of my fingers at the base of my skull and draw them down over the back of my neck to the tops of my shoulders, flesh squeaking. My neck has never felt cleaner.

I suddenly realise that the whole tenor of today has been set by a couple of things that happened yesterday. Seeing Gilbert and George's 'Naked Shit' pictures at the South London Gallery. And, more important, meeting Joanna in the evening and parting from her by mutual consent until the second week in December – a trial separation. I wash on . . .

Both my feet have been lathered and rinsed. I help the last soapsuds down the plug-hole. Am I disposing of all traces of my lover? I don't see it that way. Rather, I am cleaning up my act for when we get together again.

I hope I'm doing the right thing. I hope I'm doing the right thing but fear I may be overdoing it:

Two nuns in a bath.

First Nun: 'Where's the soap?'

Second Nun: 'It certainly does.'

SOAP CIRCLE

ARMPITS

CHEST

BELLY

PRICK

BALLS

ARSE

BACK

HANDS

FOREHEAD

NOSE

CHEEKS

CHIN

EARS

NECK

SHOULDERS

ARMS

LEGS

FEET

A HALF-HOUR SHOWER TOWARDS THE END OF THE AFTERNOON
FOREST HILL   SEPTEMBER 28 1995

JOANNA

Edwin Brock

FUCKADUCK!

The season began in early summer:
thirteen of them whistled behind their white mother
as we ran to the baker for dry bread
saying How will she rear so many?
and These will be fed by faith hope and charity!

On the following day we thought we had miscounted:
six could not be missing presumed so quickly dead.
And are mother ducks so mathematically stupid
they cannot calculate the sum of minus half a brood?

By the third day we were waking pale into nightmare
saying with our first breath Good morning!
How many are there left? Still she marched on
looking resolutely ahead and keeping tight
to a route which traversed minefields
of cats and moorhens, killer fish and motor cars
leaving behind a debris of dying expectations.

Now it is this humid July afternoon.
Curtained by willows and willow herb
and lulled by the background music
of an idyllic mill race, I hear
the last yellow duckling's tiny whistle
choke in the throat of our legendary pike.

No flower stops growing,
the mother duck is unperturbed
and I do not know whether my curse is calling
to fish or water, duck, Darwin or God.

Simon Armitage

THE FOX

Standing its ground on the hill, as if it could hide
in its own stars, low down in the west of the sky.
I could hit it from here with a stone, put the torch
in the far back of its eyes. It's that close.

The next night, the dustbin sacked, the bin-bag
quartered for dog meat, biscuit and bone.
The night after that, six magpies lifting
from fox fur, smeared up ahead on the road.

AQUARIUS

We take exception to that chain of hotels
that asks us to think of the dying planet
by skimping on towels and not flushing the toilet.
This is about metered water and laundry bills, isn't it?

Nevertheless, we write in the mist on the bathroom mirror
how we drank from the vapour that hangs in our breath,
    washed
in the shower of blood that rains from a slashed wrist,
dried off on the mops and rags of our own flesh, in
    assistance.

Nick Drake

THE DISAPPEARING CITY

(i.m. Anna Vondraček-Drake, born Prague 1904,
died London 1992)

The disappearing city in her head
has street names blanked; façades fall to the wind
and cobblestones in waves shine under rain.

One street still stands, and at the top she lives
by a window, closed, unshattered, the last one
of a city of windows waiting for the sun.

Zigzags where stairs once led. A golden grove
by a black river. Snow falls in the night.
She is a gargoyle stone hunched in the eaves

in company with dragons and angels carved
leaping the walls and arches, their moss eyes
pecked out by all the winter birds she loved.

But they have flown away, and the dark doors
stand open to the cold, old enemy
who loots eggs, children, music, cakes and flowers.

At dawn the stormtroops execute the clocks;
birthdays, deathdays, anniversaries
are secrets which her dreaming heart unlocks

once in a while or once upon a time
now she is blind, and spring, shot in the back,
has fallen down into a pit of lime.

The door is bolted. Liars shout at her
from the next room. The lift whirrs up and down
inexplicably, each stop an error.

Phone off the hook; the new directories
of a foreign city; a stranger has no name;
the numbers are all wrong; no one is home.

Upon the pillow her dandelion head
which time has breathed upon, is gently laid
awake and listening to the radio's crack and hiss;

voices, languages, somewhere a lost tune
for chandelier and dancer, long ago;
a midnight waltz, round and around, alone.

CEAUSESCU'S DAUGHTER'S BEDROOM

(Bucharest, 1991)

Impossible but true;
I am insomniac
in the land of Nosferatu's
spooky dark,

in the shrivelling bed
of an attic boudoir,
awaiting the Undead
kiss of Romania's bad daughter;

her parents were booed
to their rooftop helicopter
by the chanting crowd
in Revolution Square,

then shot by firing squad
on Christmas Day,
their absolute, iconic heads
shown on TV.

Abandoned here,
was she the teenage sacrifice
slaughtered by soldiers
for her father's sins,

her only defence
the innocent chocoholic
in the haunted palace
of *realpolitik*?

No one seems to know
the truth of her fate,
and much less care; snow
falls, and I speculate

in her dark chamber which contains
no personal possessions,
but stray bullet-hole burns
in the yellow curtains,

dusty official tomes,
a Sixties sunken circle
of seats in collapsed foam,
a swirly carpet from hell;

no water runs
in these taps at night,
petty tyranny's
B-movie set.

My head on her pillow,
I could almost
pity her,
spoiled adolescent ghost

night-stalking the city
in Undead rage,
this winter curfew's
vampire of revenge

who will not acquiesce
to the stake of light
driven for peace
through her ordinary heart.

Something creaks: the snow, a door;
I switch on the lamp's
small pale against fear
of the dark and sleep;

but no one is there.

Ron Butlin

THE KING AND QUEEN OF WINTER

When the king and queen walk side by side their breaths
come
web-cracked, their footsteps trample silence.
A waterfall has hardened into pipes and swollen stops
jammed
with massed sound – next year's Spring.
The king points a royal finger at the moon,
'We wish: true harmonies of reflected light.'
He pauses, listens, smiles, approves.

Around them, so many old men who have nothing
more to say. Too weighed down:
days, weeks, months are piled on them. 'They need,'
observes the queen, 'that touch of sun they'll never get
this side of the mountain.' The living attend,
merely; the dead, cut and stacked, suggest
the perfect feasting-place.

Chocolates, cognac – all the pleasures of a lawless reign.
The royal calendar's rewritten, and once again
the bridge they should return by thaws too soon . . .

When the king and queen lie side by side they cling
together: the ending of their kingship seems
a maddened dance to a maddened tune.
The sun, in exile, burns into their dreams.

David Malouf

SNAPSHOTS AND AN ALPHABET

SOME TIME IN the 1880s my grandmother, Alice Razi, left her widowed mother and younger brother and sister and set out from the small town of Zahle in Lebanon for Australia, in the company of neighbours who were emigrating. My grandmother was not. Aged just twelve, her instructions, or so the story goes, were to get off the ship in Melbourne, dig up the biggest nugget she could see, and go right back home again.

In fact she never got home, and none of the seven little Australians she bore, the second of whom was my father, ever saw the place of her birth. She became what in those days was called a Syrian pedlar, travelling from town to town and homestead to homestead in western New South Wales selling ribbons, buttons, trimmings and baby clothes and bringing news of the great world and local gossip. Somehow she saved enough to send for her mother and the other children, and at sixteen married my grandfather. He too came from Zahle, but was older, already thirty, having misspent the better part of his youth in Rome. They settled in Brisbane and their children, my uncles and aunts, like those of the dozen or so other families that made up their small community, were by the time I was born in the middle thirties almost completely assimilated.

Christian, of course, as one had to be then to enter Australia from Arab lands, they had originally belonged to different sects, Maronite, Greek Catholic like my father's people, Greek or Syrian Orthodox; but with no church of their own in the new place, and finding the old controversies that for so many

129

centuries had divided them, such as whether Christ had one nature or two, increasingly difficult to maintain in a place that had its own great schism – the simpler one between Catholics and Protestants – they soon fell into the local pattern. One lot became Roman Catholics, the other Anglican, and that was that. My father and his sisters and brothers went to mass at St Mary's South Brisbane, were schooled by nuns, and for all the difference it made might have been called O'Reilly or Mahon. My sister and I, growing up at a time when the word ethnic was still confined to the more arcane reaches of the dictionary, were plain Australian – a condition compromised only by the fact that our mother remained irremediably English.

When I lived in England in the sixties I planned a trip to the east that would have included Lebanon, but the Arab-Israeli war intervened. I tried again in the seventies, but by then Lebanon was involved in its own bloody conflict. I made it at last a year ago, in company with my friend Carmen Callil, whose family on her father's side was also Lebanese, but real Lebanese, from the white mountain itself that gives the country its name.

The road south towards Sidon hugs a flat, dispiriting coastline. The traffic is headlong; every driver has his palm on the horn. But after three or four kilometres the great stream of cars, trucks, taxis, slows and coagulates. A double line of red-and-white-striped tyres, a vertical one set in one laid flat and weighted with a broken-backed sandbag, leads to a pillar-box emblazoned with a cedar of Lebanon. Our driver gives us a half-hearted glance of apology. Roadblock.

Armed guards approach and take our passports. But almost immediately a plainclothes figure in dark glasses emerges from the box. The armed men hand over our papers and stand deferentially aside. Bored but suspicious, the plainclothes man lowers his head to the window and peers at us over the top of his shades, then turns away, returning our passports to the army men as he goes.

'Syrian,' the driver tells us.

All along the median strip as we push on are banners with

representations in garish colours of the political figures to whom the locals pay allegiance: President Assad and his son Basil; the Ayatollah; various mullahs in white turbans, either ancient and saintly or mad dogs. Uniforms are everywhere. Impossible for the outsider to tell from the berets of different colours, pine green, mauve, royal blue, whether it is a soldier of the Lebanese or Syrian army he is dealing with, or a military policeman or militiaman, and what power he holds beyond the fire-power in his hand.

At a turning of the highway we come upon a tank that takes up half the road. It is backed in among poppies and yellow marguerites and carries a gun that could blast a house away. On a bit of road in the middle of nowhere a soldier sits on a camp-stool, half-dozing with an automatic across his knees. A little further on we pass an encampment of bell-tents set out along a ridge. The men on guard are uniformed but others, who move among them, are wearing bathing trunks and pegging out washing on an improvised line. On the other side of the highway still more are splashing about in the lank sea while others again, like institutionalised children, kick a football up and down the sands in a walled enclosure.

In the open stretches between villages are road-stalls offering plastic baskets full of strawberries the size of tomatoes and piles of the velvety, pale-green almonds that at this time of the year are eaten whole, soft shell and all. They are in the charge of small boys who recline in genoa-velvet lounge-chairs or sit tilted back in detached car-seats – a bizarre effect against a stand of reeds or rows of broad-beans in full flower. At an open fish-stall a young man sits with his head in a book that lies open on the marble slab before him. On the concrete below live fish flop round his bare feet.

This is one of those societies where only private spaces are respected and cared for; public spaces are no man's land. Which would explain the ruthless exploitation of the coast by developers, who need fear nothing, it seems, from government interference, and the tides of litter that choke the one-storeyed villages.

A triumph of improvisation involving breeze-blocks, timber, chicken-wire and sheets of corrugated plastic, they consist of open cafés where men sit at rickety tables drinking coffee or arak and smoking water pipes, butcher shops with a couple of freshly decapitated goats' heads at the door, crowned with parsley but still dripping, and brightly lit shops selling chandeliers, gilt-framed mirrors, chickens in tiered coops, nets bulging with cerulean blue and yellow soccer-balls, hub-caps new and second-hand arranged fanwise like shields or family crests, and something I have not come across before, great bunches of grey-black feather dusters of an extraordinary opulence like Prince of Wales ostrich plumes.

Only next day do I discover what these magnificent objects are for. Going round to the boot of the car to collect my bag, I am startled when I raise the hatch by a grey-black bird the size of a scrub turkey that comes flying at me.

Every Lebanese car has one of these creatures locked away in the boot. Under the murderous bombardment of five years ago Beirut collapsed in a cloud of dust. Beiruti drivers, armed with dusters, wage a continuous war to keep it out of their engines.

I never get used to the demented bundle of feathers that roosts in the darkness of the boot; like some household demon, maddened beyond endurance, that under the unnatural conditions of war has amazingly transmogrified, broken free of the domestic and found a new life on the streets.

Just beyond Deir in the Shouf mountains, a pretty well-kept town all golden stone, we visit a mock castle above a terraced ravine.

The castle too is of golden stone. Heavily rusticated, it is stuck all over with emblems and carved inscriptions: a sun face, a bird of prey, a relief showing 'les Phéniciens portant l'alphabet au monde', another proclaiming 'rien n'est impossible' – advertisements for a national energy and achievement that still appeals. The forecourt is crowded with newly-weds and exuberant but orderly schoolchildren.

Passing over a moat and under a leather curtain we are

confronted with a diorama that runs the whole length of the building: scenes from Lebanese village life in what I take to be the middle twenties.

Very boldly modelled and wittily observed, the figures are mostly still but enough of them are in motion to suggest lively activity. A woman turns an old-fashioned spinning-wheel, another rocks a cradle with one hand and with the other turns flat-bread on a little metal stove. In an animated café scene, men in costumes denoting different classes and religious groups are in friendly argument. They include a comic priest in high hat and robes and a waiter in baggy pants who pours coffee from a long-spouted pot into little decorated cups. Downstairs, in wire cages, are scenes of a more specialised sort. In one, three boys sit cross-legged studying the Koran with a mild-looking teacher; in another, small children in Western dress line up in front of a travelling peepshow.

The attempt, one sees, is to present small-town life as rich and inclusive, but not without its comic side. The overall impression is of vigour and industry, of energy in the control of a disciplined purpose.

In the largest and most impressive of these tableaux a whole schoolroom is presented. Twenty or more boys of thirteen or so, no girls, are lounging at their desks, each one individually created right down to his dusty footwear. At the front, the master is boxing the ears of one of their fellows, who yowls and cringes. In the corner by the blackboard another delinquent is being punished by kneeling bare-legged in a box of stones. The message is clear – one recalls those Phoenicians bearing the gift of the alphabet. Education is all-important. It is what sets you apart from your neighbours, takes you out into the world – meaning westward. It is civilisation. Most of all, it is wealth.

I hear more of this next day from my neighbour at a Saturday luncheon party.

Mrs C., an elegant woman in her fifties, is the wife of a former Attorney-General. She is from Zahle, was born Malouf, and wants to know where my grandfather belonged in the family tree; we may be related. I cannot tell her. Her husband, a Maronite from Bcharri where Carmen's people come from, has the same name as her grandmother. They too may be related.

We are in a fashionable restaurant on the road towards Byblos. In contrast to the miles of shattered apartment blocks we have driven through to reach it, with one-armed or one-legged *mutilés de guerre* at every intersection selling cartons of Marlboros or Kleenex tissues, the restaurant is gleamingly intact, a monument to Beirut resilience and style. I divide my attention between Mrs C., who speaks excellent English but whose preferred language is French, and the waiters, for whom the occasion is clearly a kind of theatre of which they are privileged spectators. They seem unaware of the extent to which they themselves are a source of almost continuous comedy.

There is a strict hierarchy among them.

The smallest in number are those at the top. Very sleek and self-important in their brushed dinner-jackets and immaculate cuffs, they smile, make recommendations, shift a fork or two, take orders with a large-handed flourish of the pen, use their eyebrows with eloquent emphasis to instruct the second and larger group who do the serving.

These too wear dinner-jackets but move faster, are less complacent, do not speak. Their hands, I notice, as they bring dish after dish of *mezze*, are the broad hands of peasants, a little roughened from digging and tying vines in some plot in the suburbs or the nearby hills, though they all wear rings of heavy gold with a coloured stone.

The third group consists of boys of sixteen or seventeen, smooth-cheeked and pliant or stocky with a two-day growth of beard, whose job it is to fetch dishes from the kitchen and carry away the trays of used plates. They wear long-sleeved silk shirts of a pale buff-colour, and when they are not working, hang about the delivery table in the centre of the room, laughing, gaping, or just looking dreamily vacant and bored. When a new group of customers arrives, the whole body of waiters springs alert and presses forward to peer through the plate-glass windows as the newcomers step out of their cars; then, under the mobile eyebrows of the head waiter, shuffle themselves into two lines at the door.

I notice this especially when a limousine pulls up and an overdressed, bejewelled woman of forty emerges with her husband and a little lord of maybe ten in long trousers and an embroidered waistcoat.

A ripple of excitement runs through the waiters, which may be inspired by the woman's heavy glamour but may also be a response to the sexual glow that is given off by money. They surge and jostle, stand on tiptoe for a better view, at last make for the entrance and form their line.

Now the real show begins. The members of the couple's party, some of whom are already seated, begin on the extended business of greeting. The waiters, grouped in a circle on the sidelines, practically fall over one another to catch every detail of the kissing and clasping, as if this were a performance to which they had taken tickets. Their interest is candid and unashamed. They crane their necks, they stare. It is as if there were some mystery here, a psychology of affection and duplicity and affectation and desire whose secret, once grasped, would show them how to manage these people to their own advantage. The spell is broken only when the last guest is seated, the head dinner-jacket has dropped the last napkin into a capacious lap, and the ritual of ordering begins.

Meanwhile Mrs C. has been relating her experience of the war.

I am surprised by her coolness. Like almost everyone else who comes here, I am obsessed by the war. The ruins are so new that I feel it has barely ceased, I still have my ears tuned to the echo of bombardment. But for Mrs C., civil conflict has been replaced by the sort of normality our luncheon represents, the easy conversation, the spanking whiteness of the tablecloths and napkins, the professionalism with which the waiters produce dish after dish. She answers my questions with great politeness but soon brings the conversation round to her son, who is at this very moment en route between Paris and the United States, and then to the house she grew up in in Zahle, which she seldom visits, she tells me, but often dreams of, and which she opened recently so that an *émigrée* cousin who knew it as a girl could revive her memory of its lovely old rooms. She tells me, with a nostalgic affection of her own, how they unhooked the shutters and looked out together into the overgrown garden with its laurels and pomegranates.

'Here,' she says, 'you must taste these chickpeas. I'm sure you've never had them done like this. Now, aren't they *good*?' She is settling us firmly in the present. Not denying the war but denying that it is the only reality here, or even the most important one.

Though they are Christians, she Greek Catholic, he Maronite, they spent the larger part of the war in West Beirut, the Muslim sector, cared for by their Shiite neighbours and Mr C.'s Muslim employees. The apartment in the East where we had drinks this morning, served by a Filipino maid, stood empty and undamaged except that the glass fell out of the floor-length windows.

What strikes Mrs C. now is the mistake that was made in her education. Growing up in a Greek Catholic town, speaking French and looking always to Paris and the West, she learned nothing of her Muslim compatriots, of their long and glorious history, of their culture, or the injustice they feel at being forced into a secondary place in the world. 'I had to learn all that for myself. When I was grown up. By study, and by listening to my Muslim friends. And even now I can't *think* the way they do.'

Mrs C., like most Lebanese I spoke to, is resentful of the Syrian occupation. She sees it as an attempt to deprive Lebanon of its independence and restore the Greater Syria that existed before 1919. But when I ask her what she feels when she looks out of the long windows of her apartment and sees, as we did this morning, a Syrian tank squatting toadlike at the gates of her garden square, she replies without hesitation, 'Safe.'

The Byzantine church of St John the Baptist, Byblos: Palm Sunday.

The crowd in the sunken courtyard is waiting for eleven o'clock mass. Little girls in flounced dresses, their brothers in slacks and long-sleeved shirts, carry candles, as long almost as themselves in some cases, tied round with a frill of pink or pale blue or silvery nylon and trailing satin ribbons. Along the road above, and in the unweeded side-streets among the parked cars, are soldiers in battle fatigues carrying automatics, about the same length as the candles but without ribbons.

This is a Maronite stronghold and such feast days in the past have provided the perfect opportunity for a massacre, most often by rival branches of the same sect.

The soldiers are young and for all their fierce-looking moustaches look more like play soldiers than real – children armed with toys and wearing another sort of holiday dress. Hard to believe, in the warm spring sunshine and the heady scent of pittosporum, that they might suddenly turn murderous.

Last night in Beirut we joined the Saturday evening throng on the Corniche: family groups in their best clothes, strolling and pausing to greet friends, power-walkers in expensive tracksuits and joggers, the usual lounging youths with ghetto-blasters. A young man moved back and forth along the line of parked cars at the kerb clinking a pile of coffee-cups in one hand and in the other swinging a long-spouted pot. The light dimmed from gold to indigo.

Pausing a moment to look back from the darkening sea towards the piled-up city, we were confronted, on the other side of the road, with a multi-storeyed building whose entire façade had fallen away – gone perhaps in the same blast that made a shell of the American Embassy on the next corner and killed two hundred marines. It was like looking into a giant doll's house. In every room, on every floor, was a soldier, some sitting on cots, others combing their hair at mirrors, others again playing cards. One, in full uniform, feet apart, stood at the very edge of the drop, surveying the scene below – the strollers, *us* – through a pair of field-glasses.

A ladder led up from the ground to the first floor. We watched a boy in an emerald-green windcheater with a purple rucksack over his shoulder shin up the ladder and disappear into a stairwell, then emerge again at a door five storeys up. A soldier on a cot sprang forward to greet him. Like figures in a computer game they leapt vividly together, then apart.

The whole image as it presented itself was both very lively and utterly unreal. What was disturbing was to find oneself caught for a moment in the space here that armed men create and keep open between play and real.

Lebanon's national symbol is the cedar. The last of the local cedars (there are hundreds, of course, in European gardens) stand in a fenced enclosure above Bcharri. We are driving to see them via the Qadicha valley, climbing swiftly from the sluggish warmth of Tripoli towards the great white bulk of the Mountain. This is the Lebanese heartland, a place of saints and fanatics, and of a mountain people, pious, tough, intransigent, who for more than fifteen hundred years have defended themselves against all comers.

'Farouche' is the word Carmen's guidebook uses for the landscape. Carmen immediately appropriates it for the people themselves and, with a great loose laugh, for her family, of whom, as we swing round curve after curve, she has extravagant stories to tell. Tidy villages cling to the slopes, some only a few hundred yards from others, equally precariously nested, across a drop so sudden and blue that your mind dizzies at it. Scrub oak and juniper choke the rocky outcrops, every inch of cleared land is set with vines, and high above hangs the Mountain, nine thousand feet above the sea we left less than an hour ago and which would still be visible, if the haze lifted, ten miles off in the world below.

The cedars, though bedraggled and much doctored, are of almost mystical significance. Legendary even four thousand years ago, when they went out from the port of Byblos to timber the building projects of the Pharaohs and Solomon's temple at Jerusalem, they are the last shaggy survivors of one of the earth's great forests, a sorry huddle in their snowfield enclosure, resembling nothing so much as a remnant herd, wolves perhaps, or buffalo, mangy and cringing, packed together against extinction but too weak any longer to defend themselves or breed.

Just across the Mountain, but the pass at this time of the year is closed, lies Baalbek, a place that plays an antithetical and demonic role in the life of Bcharri. In the old days, we are told, Baalbek men used to creep over the Mountain and steal sheep. Carmen asks her Beiruti cousin about people in Melbourne of the same name who she thinks may be relatives. 'They are,' he confesses, 'but we never mention them. They come from Baalbek.' But when we reach the place at last, and its ostentatious ruins – everything at Baalbek is on a colossal scale, the biggest or tallest in existence – we get the other side of the story.

'No doubt,' our guide tells us, 'you have seen the famous cedars. They are our national symbol. Well, we have our own national symbol right here,' and he points to the six surviving columns, familiar from many posters, of the temple of Jupiter, the tallest ever raised, which, in that excess of monumental effort that is one of the wonders of the ancient world, made a voyage in the opposite direction from the cedars, being quarried in Upper Egypt, floated down the Nile, shipped to Byblos, and then hauled, by countless slaves, all the way up here. They are, I suppose, a kind of reserve symbol in case the other lot, which belong to the more precarious realm of Nature, should die out. But why, one wonders, does the genius of this nation embody itself only in objects that barely survive against the odds?

Later, in Damascus, but from a source that can only be thought of as malicious, we hear of yet another reserve, a separate and rival stand of cedars, equally authentic, also at risk. They are in the Shouf, in Druze territory; Walid Jumblatt, the Druze leader, has made them his special concern. Jumblatt, our Damascus friend tells us, is the nearest thing in Lebanese politics to a green, but he is a green *à la libanaise*. He has surrounded his precious relics with a barbed-wire fence, and the approaches in all directions are mined.

In the village below the walls of Krak des Chevaliers we

get our first real sight of Syria. The unmade pavements are streaming with boys and girls coming back from school, handsome young people, healthily exuberant and many of them blond, and all in military khaki. Some of the boys wear flashes and loops of scarlet across their chest like little generals.

Hama. A dark rose grows over the wall of a public building, in front of which stands a sentry-box. A soldier, overweight and capless, in an ill-fitting uniform, emerges from the box, reaches up, and with some difficulty plucks one of the blooms. He stands on the pavement for a moment, taking in the scent, then, holding the rose awkwardly before him, steps back into his box.

A week later, emerging from our hotel in Damascus, I find a truckload of military policemen in the square, all very young and many with the regulation three-days growth of beard that is part of the Basil cult, a version perhaps of the cult of Antinŏus, the much-loved youth cut off in the flower of his beauty and raised to the status of a god. They sit laughing together and spooning chickpeas out of plastic trays. What disturbs my view of their youthful high spirits is the foot-long truncheons in their belts.

Friday morning, the Muslim sabbath. The streets are full of family groups or fathers with small children. We sit in a brightly lit shop, all chrome and glass, where sheets of yellow pastry are hung to dry over round, three-legged stools, which makes the stools look like golden lampshades. Three older men are making a fuss over a little girl of maybe eighteen months in the arms of her youngish father. He is delighted at first. But one of the old men, chanting a litany of Arabic nonsense, gets carried away. He pinches the child's cheek so hard that the father protests and has to push him off. Carmen has a flash of memory: of 'the Uncles' as she calls them, whose voracious affection when she was tiny was a source of continuous terror to her, and I of Uncle Harry from New Zealand who on his yearly visits used to alarm me by taking my cheeks between thumb and finger and saying, 'I think I'll take these sweet little apples back home with me.'

*

Carmen is a woman who is used to being noticed, to having people take account of her commanding energy. Here she is engaged in a never-ending battle against invisibility – and not only her own. The sight of women veiled in black, which is the regular thing in this fundamentalist town, drives her to fury, and she has no patience with my wishy-washy view that some of these women may wear the veil because it means something to them.

Under the cloud of her anger and frustration I keep to myself an even more shameful observation: the attraction these figures exert.

The veil is just fine enough to offer a phantom vision of mouth and eyes that is both tantalising and confusing, since the face is hidden but other, more intimate parts of the body, the calves and ankles for instance, are not. Standing in ordinary sunlight at traffic-lights, they have the air of visitants from another reality, from myth or dream. To see one moving towards you carrying a bag that says *Shop till you drop*, or with a child in tow licking an iced lolly, makes you wonder for a moment what life or century you are in. They seem utterly present but at the same time remote – and that surely is just what is intended. It allows strangers, a salesman for example, to deal face to face with a woman while pretending she is not there. As for the woman, she must somehow preserve a sense of her own presence without the comforting reassurance, a thing incomprehensible in our culture, of being seen.

We are in the *souk* at Hama and stop at a stall to buy spices which come in little sachets of clear plastic. Carmen does not recognise them by sight, and has no sense of smell, so to the salesman's amusement we go through a little routine in which she chooses a packet, passes it to me, and I sniff and provide the name: cinnamon, nutmeg, cumin, etc.

An audience gathers, two veiled housewives, a couple of small boys, a pair of schoolgirls wearing ponytails. As I produce the name, which they more or less recognise, they nod their approval, and the salesman, a dignified old fellow, gives a gap-toothed grin. It is an impromptu comedy. Two foreigners are making themselves pleasantly ridiculous. We are all enjoying ourselves. Carmen makes her choice, the salesman tots up the bill and hands it to *me*. Explosion! Carmen grabs the bill from my hand and begins beating herself on the chest. 'Me,' she shouts, 'you are dealing with *me*. You give the bill to *me*. Not him!' – and she gives me a rough shove.

The onlookers are astonished. The veiled women turn and flee, the children gape. The salesman looks as if a tornado had hit him.

What Carmen wants him to see is a woman who is standing up for her right to be treated independently and as herself, a woman naked-faced and with a will and money of her own. She is teaching him and all his kind a lesson.

What he sees is a lady tourist, already admittedly a little queer, who has suddenly gone off her rocker. And even more disconcerting, a man who possesses a woman (this too is infuriating to Carmen but we have no way of making the difficult thing clear) over whom he has no control. In this I am very much the more serious offender. Carmen, though she has given him a fright, he can make invisible. She is very nearly that already. But me he cannot ignore. He accepts the money Carmen counts out for him, but coldly and with his face averted. He clearly wishes he had never laid eyes on either one of us.

This matter of seeing and not seeing, and more specifically of being there but remaining unseen, intrigues me.

It is one of the rules of begging, for example, that the beggar should never meet the eye of those from whom he is seeking charity. He sets on the pavement before him a cap with a few coins in it, or he holds out a cupped hand, but as if the hand, like the cap, were not part of him, and in every case he lowers his head, hides his gaze. And this cannot be simply to show submissiveness or false shame because the giver in his own way does the same. He too supresses himself. In this way the beggar is relieved of indignity and the giver of the temptation to hubris. The coin moves as of its own accord, in a space where the clear injustice of one man's being rich and another poor is for the moment suspended. Two little violations of this convention make it plain to me.

The first takes place in the ruins at Palmyra.

Carmen has wandered off to take photographs. I am sitting on a fallen column hugging the bottle of mineral water I have just acquired at an inflated price from a couple of school-aged entrepreneurs, when I am approached by the dirtiest child I have ever seen. Runny-nosed and filthy-handed, in an out-at-elbows woolly, he is maybe nine years old and comes, I guess, from the bedouin encampment at the edge of the ruins. Setting himself squarely before me, he points in a very forthright, little-mannish way at my water-bottle, puts a dirty thumb to his lips, tilts his head back and waits. I pass him the bottle and he takes a long drink, then cleans the rim with a twist of his palm, recaps the bottle, and with just the slightest inclination of his head, hands it back.

Two of his friends appear. Since he is the one who has made this interesting contact, they defer to him and he obligingly indicates their presence. Once more I hand over the bottle. When the younger has drunk I give him leave to pass it on to the other who very nearly finishes it off, but at the last moment saves himself from that breach of courtesy. Then all three thank me brusquely and go off.

Asking for water is not begging, even when it is the rare and expensive and maybe magical stuff that tourists pay so much for. It is a transaction between equals.

When a little girl comes running over the stones towards me – she is perhaps five years old, young enough anyway to have all her pretty milk teeth, and is even dirtier, if that were possible, than the boys – I have only the dregs of the water to offer her. But what she wants is something simpler. She wants me to shake the grimy little hand she holds out to me. That achieved, she grins and skips joyfully away.

To be visible, to be recognised.

Two days later I am drinking coffee on the terrace of a café in Damascus when a small boy, very ragged, maybe ten, steps out between the angle-parked cars and begins to prowl the rails. He has his eye on a group of substantial-looking Germans at the next table to me. He cocks his head, grins, nods, and when they continue to ignore him turns his attention to me. I shake my head. A moment later I see him dancing round the skirts of a young woman in a head-dress so snowy white that it seems luminous. She too waves him off and when I look again he is back, settled now against the fender of a car, but crestfallen. I have the change from my coffee. As I step down from the terrace I hand it to him. Utterly surprised, he lights up like a figure coming into focus on a screen, three-dimensional, dazzling, and I am taken back nearly thirty years to when I was first hitchhiking in Europe; to the extraordinary joy that struck me, the affirmation of being and well-being, when the first car of the day slowed and halted, the sense, like a sudden access of sunlight, of being acknowledged, chosen – not by some as yet unknown motorist but by the *world*, as the sky, the fields, the whole morning opened to let me in. The child's pleasure is that. It is delight at being admitted to the realm of the visible, at having the world turn for a moment in his direction and acknowledge that he is there – and he is still young enough to break all the conventions by showing it.

A Little Alphabet

(Pour les Phéniciens)

A: for Asphodel, the miles and miles of their sparky pink towers in the plains above Aleppo.

B: for Birds. There are no birds in Lebanon. They have all been slaughtered or scared off by hunters. When I see what I take to be crows sailing over a field of new spring wheat they turn out to be black plastic bags.

C: for Car horns. Lebanese drivers lean on them almost without stop. Between six in the evening and dawn the Corniche in Beirut is a twelve-hour-long Mahler symphony.

F: for Fawzi Malouf, whose bust is in the corner of a little garden in Zahle; one of four brothers, all poets, of whom he is the most renowned. At a lunch in Damascus Dr Georges Jabbour tells us how a young woman in their company once dropped her coffee-cup and all four poets produced extempore lyrics on why the cup had failed to reach her lip.

G: for Khalil GIBRAN (or Kellogs Allbran as he is rather irreverently known in Australia), the author of *The Prophet*. When we try to visit his museum in Bcharri along with a busload of students, the curator, who does not want these noisy young people in his museum, tells us we cannot go in because the lights have failed, the great poet's works are lost 'dans l'obscurité'. 'But I have come all the way from Australia,' Carmen insists, 'the *obscurité* does not worry me. I love the *obscurité*!' When he can't be budged she loses her temper and calls him a national disgrace. As we stomp off, one of the students comes leaping down the rocky path behind us. We are to be let in. But the curator, the boy warns, is deeply offended and Carmen must say nothing more. So we see the museum in the *obscurité*, every room, every painting; followed throughout by the student, who is more impressed by Carmen, even under the imposition of silence, than by the great man's half-erotic, half-mystical, half-visible works of art.

J: for JOSEPH, my third name, and the reason why, departing from Damascus airport just before dawn, I am detained for an anxious twenty minutes while the Syrian police decide I am not the Joseph Malouf whose delinquencies, great or small, have got him into their machine.

N: for NOISE (see CAR HORNS). One of the things Carmen suffers even less easily than fools, German tour groups and salesmen (see TALK) who will not keep their mouths shut while she examines their wares.

P: for PEPSI BOTTLES. Ubiquitous. Most remarkably in the form of ten-foot high replicas, sometimes single, mostly in threes, in the snowfields round Bcharri.

S: for STYLITES. We visit the ruins of the church of St Simeon Stylites near Aleppo. He spent forty years on top of his column there, setting off a local fashion that included one infant ascetic so young that he still had his milk teeth. If what we saw in the ruins is any indication the craze is not yet dead. Young Syrian soldiers had climbed to the top of several columns and were dangling their boots and eating almonds or swaying about and waving to their friends.

T: for TALK, and Carmen's insistence whenever she enters a shop in the markets that the salesman should not. 'I'll only look,' she tells him, 'if you do not talk at me. If you say a single word I'll go right out again.' Also for the TORMENTS suffered by these keepers of carpet-shops and vendors of curios, torn between the need to tout their wares (and on this occasion losing a sale) and keeping silent and losing it anyway.

V: for VISA and Carmen's attempts to convince the local traders that if they want to make sales they must take cards. 'You put the price up,' she explains when they insist they would lose on the transaction. 'Look! For cash, six hundred Syrian pounds, for cards six fifty.' And for her VINDICATION at last in the market at Palmyra when a carpet salesman says just that: this much for cash, this much *more* for a card. 'I can't believe it,' she cries. 'At last! Someone with a *brain*! Now show me your carpets. But don't talk. If you say a single word, I'll walk right out of your shop.'

Shena Mackay

THE LAST SAND DANCE

AFTER THE TAXI dropped him off, Alfred rode on beside her in a dark shape of Eau Sauvage and cigar smoke. Zinnia was driven south, with her eyes shut to retain his presence and her fingers closed on the note he had folded into her gloved palm to pay the cab, unsettled by his scent, once familiar and now exotic, and the impression of his heavy coat that she still held in her arms. The nylon spiracles of Zinnia's wide fur collar, electrified by the long-ago lovers' brief parting embrace, made an aureole round her small head like that of a red squirrel's tail against the light and stirred her own hair into the tiny scarlet-tipped feathers of an African Grey parrot.

It was late March. Passover and Easter just round the corner, and the clear moonlit night was cold enough to encourage a thin frost. She was on her way home from the theatre. When Alfred had telephoned her to ask her to go with him to a play he had agreed to review for a literary journal, although his subject was really Byzantine art, Zinnia had accepted, thinking it might be a lark, especially as they had not seen each other since the funeral of a reprobate dramatist six months ago.

Zinnia was an actor, with an unreconstructedly actressy West End glamour about her even though she had not appeared on a stage north of Wimbledon for several years; Zinnia Herbert, one of those stalwarts who never quite become a star, whose kindness to their fellow thespians and the humblest ASM are legendary in the profession, whose obituaries will make even those readers who had assumed

147

they had died long ago sigh at their youthful beauty and long to go backstage to express their belated appreciation. Zinnia had been born into show business, to a variety act called 'The Two Herberts', which while not entirely responsible for the death of music hall, was certainly in at its demise. Zinnia herself had made her début at the age of three, at the Hackney Empire, singing 'I've Never Seen A Straight Banana'. In fact, as it was wartime, she had never seen a banana at all.

She might have guessed, she thought in the taxi, that any production staged at a venue with such an unpleasant name recalling ancient cruelties would be dire. The Pillory Theatre was the converted billiard room of an old gin palace, and specialised in previously unperformed and often never seen again works by young playwrights. Zinnia and Alfred had perched uncomfortably on the fringe of the avant-garde, on an itchy banquette which was a superannuated bus seat blobbed with polished strings of chewing gum, and scarred by cigarette burns that sighed puffs of dust at every shift of haunch and hip.

A fellow critic acknowledged Zinnia and Alfred with a languid wave, another rolled his eyes towards the kippered ceiling, and one or two people stared as if they thought they ought to recognise them, for Alfred, with his speckled red beard, yellow silk scarf, fedora and unlit cigar, cut as theatrical a figure as Zinnia in her russet fur, sniffing a scented handkerchief as if it were an orange stuffed with cloves or a nosegay wafted by a disdainful spectator at a historical scene of public humiliation. The air was rancid with the smell of unwashed hair and the heaped coats and jackets, and loud with the ripping of ringpulls and the crackle of discarded plastic cups that had held wine. Zinnia consulted her programme and groaned.

'You didn't warn me that there are only two characters, I can't stand two-handers. I'm always hoping for a knock on the door or for somebody to come jaunting in through the french windows.'

No scenery and not a french window in sight, not even a telephone to relieve the tedium; it was quite obviously not going to be her sort of play, and then red wine was splashed over her ankles as latecomers barged past with a surly demand of ''Scuse me.'

'I'm afraid I can't. You are inexcusable,' Zinnia told them, adding to Alfred, 'Do you remember the days when people said, "Excuse me, *please*?"'

'You are at your most *grande dame* tonight. I love it. Marry me,' he whispered into her hair.

'Well, they might at least do the perpetrators of this sorry entertainment the courtesy of arriving on time, particularly as it started twenty-two minutes late. Besides, I'm married.'

Afterwards, outside on the pavement, wrinkling her nose at her coat sleeve, Zinnia said, 'I feel as if I've spent the evening in an old chip pan, or in the dustbag of a hoover that hasn't been emptied for years. And I'm sure several vertebrae have fused.'

'You might have woken me,' Alfred complained. 'You know I always sleep through the first act, and as there was no interval . . . which was a wise directorial move, pre-empting a mass escape at half time . . . did you manage to get your head down at all?'

'Only forty winks right at the end. Why can't young people speak any more? That dreary sub-dialect they all use – I mean *yewss*. They're all at it, actors, weather girls, broadcasters. And have shampoos and dry cleaners gone out of fashion?'

'Yoo hoo, Dolly!' A middle-aged woman was waving at them across the street, calling the name of a character Zinnia had played in a recent television sitcom, one of the dotty next-door-neighbour parts which casting directors had made rather her forte.

'Yoo hoo yourself!' Zinnia responded, waggling a zany little wave, with a daffy smile, through a gap in the traffic.

'Let's get out of here,' she said. 'Where would you like to eat? *I'm* taking *you*, as you treated me to that delightful show. Such a glamorous life you lead, my dear.'

'Don't be silly, *I* invited *you*. What do you feel like eating? I don't know about you, but I'd just like a bowl of noodles.'

Zinnia slipped her arm through his, remembering with affection how this big, powerful, rich man had always sought comfort from food served in round, simple peasanty or nursery shapes; a plate of pasta, a bowl of soup, a pot of tea, a dish of lentils, and how he was not above tucking a napkin under his chin on occasion, and how his chopsticks would glean the last grains of rice from a succession of ceramic lotus leaves; and a whiff of his *eau de toilette* brought a pang of regret.

'Let's find you some noodles, then. How about the Golden Dragon over there?'

'Or you could just come home with me, and I'll bring you something delicious on a tray.'

It was as much the impossibility of superimposing her present-day self on Alfred's memory of her as the thought of her husband Norman at home that made her pull Alfred briskly to the restaurant. They both had children older than most of the Pillory audience, she a daughter by her first marriage and two granddaughters, Alfred two sons and three grandchildren, and Norman's son's girl-friend was expecting a baby. Zinnia was more excited than Norman by the good news; she adored babies and shopping for them. Norman was grumpy about becoming a grandfather, although he was well of an age for such an event.

Zinnia felt a frisson of desire, a flattered flutter at Alfred's suggestion. But at her age. And she had spent so many years atoning for her own successes and polishing Norman's fallen star that she had lost all sense of herself as desirable. Norman Bannerman had been a big name in television drama in the seventies, and now, when there was such a dearth of new plays on the small screen, he was all but forgotten.

'I wonder if old Norm's plays have stood the test of time?' mused Alfred, painting a little pancake with plum jam. 'Do you think they'd hold water now?'

'Of course they would! They're plays, not sponges or colanders! If you take that away from Norman, you leave him with nothing. As a matter of fact, he's working on a stage play now, and I'm sure it's going to be wonderful. You have a noodle in your beard.' Zinnia took a searing sip of jasmine tea from a tiny cup of scalding porcelain emblazoned with a dragon.

'I don't know – I'm afraid they might have dated badly. Poor Norman,' Alfred persisted.

'Noodle. Remove it, please.' Zinnia was starting to feel a remembered irritation.

'You'll have to fill me in on tonight's débâcle,' Alfred went on. 'I don't suppose you thought to make any notes, did you?'

Habit made her apologise.

'Come home with me. You can fax Norm to say you won't be back.' He flipped the last pancake on to her plate.

'Just along there on the right, please,' Zinnia told the taxi-driver. 'Past the big tree.'

Ingram Road was a curve of white stuccoed terrace houses, like a thousand London streets, with nothing taller than a slender eucalypt, a magnolia or an occasional misshapen pollarded lime in its walled front gardens, but there was one Olympian plane tree growing out of the pavement, whose shadows dappled the house on either side and across the road with light and shade like the patches on its great trunk.

The plane's bare branches, hung with shrivelled fruits, splashed moonlight over Zinnia as she stepped out and the taxi's running motor set off a scolding car alarm. She hurried into the house before an irate neighbour could identify her as the culprit, without asking for the receipt which Norman would demand in the morning. A paper lantern shone in the front room of the new young couple next door. It was not Joel and Maxine's fault that they knew nothing of the history of Ingram Road, or that to the older residents number 18, where they had moved so cheerfully and noisily with a hired van and a gang of friends helping, would always be the house where widowed Jim Bacon had been barbecued on his late wife's electric blanket. Joel and Maxine had a little silver cat called Mignonette who wore a pearlised flea collar that was reflective in the dark.

*

Upstairs, Norman switched off his bedside lamp and lay resenting the discreet clatter of Zinnia washing up his supper things. At last he heard the stairs creak, and the sound of the bathroom shower and the whine of the hair dryer. She came soundlessly into the bedroom on velvet mules, bathed the dressing-table in a kindly apricot glow, and sat down to brush her hair.

He thought she looked like a B-movie actress playing a film star. There ought to be light bulbs round the mirror reflecting that slithery kimono slipping off one shoulder, he decided, the sleeve falling back up her arm as her hair leaped to the bristles of her silver brush. A ritual hundred strokes for the head that had long ago lost its golden lustre. Norman blacked out several of his imaginary light bulbs, swept aside the pots of theatrical unguents and goo to make room for a bottle of gin, and tacked a broken star to her dressing-room door, to show even the least cinematically literate voyeur that here was a dame on the skids. Box office poison. Then, in embittered inspiration, he had her peel off her eyelashes and pull off her wig to reveal the bald, clichéd head of a drag queen.

'Well, well, well, if it isn't Mrs Norman Maine! Tell me, my dear, how went the show tonight?'

Zinnia's gasp at his voice, and the clashing of glass bottles on the glass-topped dressing-table as she dropped her brush gave Norman a visceral wriggle of pleasure.

'Darling! I hope I didn't wake you. I was trying to be so quiet.'

'I heard you taking a no doubt much needed shower.'

'You're not kidding! I felt absolutely soiled – contaminated.' Embarrassment as fine as a cloud of powder from a powder-puff drifted across the room as Zinnia, realising the implications of this exchange, unscrewed a jar of face cream. Norman was at his most dangerous in his *A Star is Born* mode.

'So, apart from that, how did you enjoy the play, Mrs Lincoln?'

'It was filthy. The theatre was filthy. That's what I meant about needing a shower, as if I don't always have one, and the play was filthy. Self-indulgent, illiterate, pathetically boorish. So depressing, it's as if Shakespeare, Chekhov, Ibsen, you of course, Beckett, Noel, Frank Marcus, Rodney Ackland, etc. had never been . . .'

Zinnia worried that she should have placed Norman higher in the pantheon, perhaps between Shakespeare and Chekhov, but all he needed to know was that the play had been rubbish, and relieved, he said, 'Sorry you had a rotten evening, but I did warn you, didn't I?'

'You did,' she said ruefully and gratefully. 'I should have listened. I thought it might be a lark, but it turned out to be' – she thought of the Chinese restaurant – 'a dead duck.'

The smell of the cream which Zinnia was smoothing into her arched throat brought a memory to Norman of lying in his mother's bed, a sick child propped up on her pillows, watching her rubbing in Pond's Vanishing Cream. It had never worked though, he reflected. Mother was with them still. He decided to visit her the following afternoon. It would beat another long day in the garden chewing the lonely cud of nonentity, while Zinnia was off recording voice-overs for washing-up liquid commercials, and then watching television with his unfinished play dozing fretfully like an untended baby on his desk, and the classic serial he was adapting for radio clogging up his word processor.

Zinnia got into bed and reached for his hand beneath the covers. Deliberately mistaking her intention, for neither could remember the last time anything more than a homely hug had passed between them, Norman, a dog with the bone of jealousy clamped in his teeth, said,

'Do you mind awfully, old girl? Sorry to let you down, but I'm feeling somewhat queasy. That casserole you left me must have been a bit off. Been in the freezer too long, I guess. Nothing to worry about, I'm sure – I hardly touched it. Chucked it in the bin as soon as I realised. Blimey, Zin, you've been on the garlic, haven't you? Hope your chum was too, for his sake. Or should I say saké? I've seen that gin bottle in your dressing-room. You'd better get a grip on yourself, people are starting to talk.'

Bewildered and hurt, flushing in her smooth night-dress that suddenly irritated her skin, Zinnia asked, 'What on earth do you mean?' but Norman had rolled over into contented sleep. She wished with all her heart, with her clenched fists and tears leaking into her lavender-scented pillow, that she was in Alfred's kelim-covered bed in his richly dark and frankincense and myrrh fragrant mansion flat. Alfred's antecedents had sailed from Smyrna, and his grandfather had opened the family carpet business in the Burlington Arcade, and his uncles and brothers were importers of dried fruits and nuts, and dealers in works of art and sweet heavy wines, otto of roses, attars, orris root and amber.

Zinnia pictured heaps of dates and figs, salted almonds, cashews, pistachios, halva, Turkish delight sleeted with soft sugar, frosted glacé bonbons, glowing embroideries and sheer bolts of silken colour. While Alfred lay in damask sheets beneath exiled textiles, the personification of the romantic Levant, Norman the Nebbish snored softly beside her in striped pyjamas buttoned to the neck with his breath giving little snickers as if he were making jokes at somebody's expense in his dreams.

If only she had married Alfred when they had first met, but she hadn't, and they had both married, and divorced, other people. Then when she was single again, and her beloved daughter Nerissa away at university, she had fallen for Norman's lanky English charm. Zinnia had forgiven and forgiven Norman for his cruelty, because she knew it stemmed from his own pain, but she felt unable to bear much more of his malice. Yet, even now, if bitter, going-to-seed Norman were to turn to her, she would take him in her arms.

In the morning, Norman found himself alone in bed, vaguely aware of a breakfast tray on his bedside table, of gilded strands in the marmalade and rainbows playing about the facets of the crystal jar, and lay half-dozing. His thoughts were tender vulnerable things, green walnuts, soft-shell crabs on a damp seashore, a violet snail reflected in a pavement after rain, unfledged birds in pink and mauve, the fuzzy green almond buds of the magnolia, little boys.

Norman wrestled languorously with his conscience, hardly breaking sweat, knowing he could lick it with one hand tied behind his back, overpowered it and flung it into a pathetic whimpering heap beside the bed. He reached for the forbidden bookshelf in his memory and took down a faded volume with a picture of schoolboys on its torn cover, riffling through the speckled pages until he found his place. What Norman liked best was the beating of boys, preferably in some raffish educational establishment on the South Coast, but what he could never determine, which made him go back to the book again and again, was whether he wanted to be Old Seedy the gowned and mortar-boarded avenger, or one of Seedy's devil-may-care but ultimately chastised and chastened young tormenters. The swells and eddies of desire, the sucking surf, the quivering rod, the crashing waves outside the mullioned windows, the breakfast tray flying, caught by a guilty elbow as his wife, with misplaced levity, popped her turbaned head round the door to enquire brightly, 'Can I do you now, sir?'

In a second she was on her knees, scrabbling among the spilled breakfast things, apologising.

'I'm so sorry, I thought you'd have finished by now. I'll get you some fresh tea and toast as soon as I've mopped this lot up. Entirely my fault.'

'For God's sake, woman. You're not in *ITMA* now. You always have to be on, don't you?'

'What do you mean, *on*? And you know I'm not old enough to have been in *ITMA*.'

She sat back on her heels to face him.

'*On*. You of all people should know what *on* means. On stage. On camera. Performing. Playing to the gallery. You can't even do a bit of housework without getting yourself up like Mrs Miniver in a pinny or Lucille Ball prancing around with a feather duster, can you?'

Zinnia's hand flew to her scarf-wrapped head, she glanced down at her striped matelot top, toreador pants and ballet slippers, and a blush crept up her neck and burned her face.

'I just bunged on the first things that came to hand, to do a few chores.'

'Forget the breakfast, I don't feel up to it anyway. Just get me some Pepto-Bismol and a glass of water. You'll be pleased to know that by barging in like that, you've completely broken my train of thought and probably destroyed my play. I hope you're satisfied.'

Zinnia stared at him in horror, a person from Porlock who had pranced roughshod in ballet shoes through her husband's dreams, opening her mouth to beg forgiveness for something that could never be put right.

But before she could speak Norman went on, 'Isn't it time you were off to do your washing-up commercial? Don't let me keep you. Your public awaits, and you're dressed for the part. "These are the dreams of an everyday housewife . . ."' he sang.

At the sneer in his voice, Zinnia, her lip quivering, said, 'Funnily enough, when I was putting out the rubbish I didn't see any sign of that casserole you said you threw away. You used to do that once, remember? Put the garbage out on dustbin day.'

'Perhaps it wasn't food poisoning after all. Could be a recurrence of my old complaint, chronic Zinniaphobia. Anyhow, don't bother about leaving me lunch, I'm going out, as I expect you've forgotten, but I can't expect a star of stage, screen and the kitchen sink to remember the mechanics of my dull life, can I?'

'I hadn't forgotten, as you didn't tell me. Look, Norman, I had hoped that we could make a fresh start this morning, but I see I was wrong. I'm sorry I went to the theatre with Alfred last night. It was a mistake. But it was all perfectly innocent, I assure you. Don't humiliate me by pretending to think otherwise. That's what all this is about, isn't it? You're jealous because I saw Alfred.'

'You flatter yourself, duckie.'

*

When Norman stumped off to the bathroom, Zinnia caught sight of herself in the mirror and saw that she looked very silly indeed. She wanted to telephone Nerissa, but it had never been her way to whinge. She blew her nose and was wiping her eyes when Norman came back into the bedroom with his bare chest looking its age in the morning sunshine.

The ache of affection she felt then was obliterated when he said, 'Chin up, Mrs Miniver. Smile though your heart is breaking, laugh, clown, laugh, and all that crap. Even when the darkest cloud is in the sky, you mustn't sigh and you mustn't – Attagirl, big blow now, troupe away, my brave little trouper, the show must go on.'

Zinnia screamed at him, 'You're not Norman Maine! At least Norman Maine had the decency to walk out to sea and look like James Mason! You know who you are? Norma Desmond! That's who you are, Norma Desmond!'

'That makes you a dead monkey then.'

Ingram Road was where the boys of St Joseph's School came to smoke and eat takeaways in their breaks, and the residents often slipped on the greasy bones of birds. As he left the house, Norman came upon old Father Coyle, a shrunken praying mantis who occupied a grace-and-favour apartment in the attic of the Palladian school building, prodding with his stick a vinegary chip paper that had adhered to the trunk of the plane tree. Father Coyle, in his little black suit and biretta that was too large for his head, often took his constitutional along Ingram Road, hoping to catch out truanting pupils, even though he was too frail now to do more than shake his stick at them.

'Not long till Easter now, Father,' Norman remarked pleasantly, perhaps in a wish to console.

'Is that so, so?' replied Father Coyle.

Norman went on his way, in real life, in a blue morning pouring through the spreading, arching, gracefully trailing twigs of the tree, where Old Seedy's gown was a grubby black rag stuffed away somewhere and forgotten, and a pair of passing schoolboys in their untucked shirts and black blazers attracted neither a thought nor a glance. The daytime Norman who would sicken at the notion of striking a child set off on his journey to visit his mother.

Maria Bannerman lived in sheltered accommodation in West Kensington. She had had to sell Norman's birthright, the family home, to afford her self-contained flatlet in Glebe Park, a purpose-built block with a resident warden on the premises in case of emergencies. Norman's father, who had died at ninety in full possession of his faculties, had owned a small engineering works which had specialised in making tin openers. The recession had almost put him out of business and the ringpull revolution, particularly in the petfood industry, would have bankrupted him, had he not had the vision to diversify into shackles, leg irons and handcuffs for home use and export to select regimes abroad, and electric prods that were licensed to teach cattle a lesson but destined to burn softer flesh as well.

The company, Bannerman Aluminium & Steel (GB), had been sold at a loss on Norman's father's death so, as Zinnia had remarked, Norman was spared making any Shavian or Ibsonian decisions about his inheritance by its perpetual trickling into the coffers of Glebe Park, and he was glad to be shot of the firm and his father's disappointment that it was never Bannerman & Son. He had hated working there in the holidays, fearing the sharp, ribald apprentices and the cynical, laconic foreman, but what a success his television play *Pigs and Spigots* had been, set on the shop-floor, with cradles and ladles of molten steel and dialogue that had jammed the switchboard with protests.

His mother was ninety-two and fit as a flea, although, with her bright eyes magnified by the spectacles clamped to her beak and her fuzz of white hair, she looked, to Norman, like a hawk chick in a flowered overall. He found her pegging washing on to the communal lines in the garden behind the flats. Her next-door neighbour Jack Bedwell, whose television could be heard shouting a racing commentary through his closed window, was holding a basket of wet clothes which contained, to Norman's distaste, several items of his mother's underwear.

'Norman! What a lovely surprise! I hope this doesn't mean you won't be coming at Easter?' she added anxiously.

'No, mother. I just felt like coming to see you. We'll be there at Easter, three-line whip, eh?' He knew how vital it was to the residents' prestige to have family visits on the prescribed occasions.

'Zinnia's not with you today then, son?' Maria looked hopefully down the path, through borders of forsythia at its yellow apotheosis with the green about to take over.

'Sorry. I did ask, but you know how it is with these famous actresses . . .'

'We was just talking about you,' put in Jack, passing a pair of bloomers, 'I was only saying to your mum, when's your Norman going to get the old BBC to put on some of his plays again? With all the old rubbish and repeats they have on nowadays, they can't be any worse than them, can they? You want to have a word. It's all cops and crime and hospitals. Where's the entertainment in that? Get enough of that as it is, thank you very much. Old Elsie had 'er pension snatched last week, only a young kid, he was. I'd chop off their hands if it was up to me. I'd do it myself.'

'Shall we go in, Mother, if you've finished?' Norman took the plastic basket from the old man.

'Used to be a really pleasant area round here in the old days,' Jack went on. 'Now it's liquorice allsorts. Remember, Marie, when we had the old muffin man come round, and the milkman with his horse and cart, the cats' meat man . . .'

'The cats' meat man!' exclaimed Maria, and the two old people stared mistily into the distance, as if the cats' meat man would descend from the clouds to save them all.

In his mother's flat Norman drank tea from a cup that tasted of bleach. The muffin man, he thought, that's pushing it a bit, and pictured a nursery rhyme figure in striped stockings, with a bell and a tray round his neck, but he had to sympathise a little with the old people who felt like aliens in their childhood landscape changed out of all recognition.

'When you live on your own,' his mother explained, not for the first time, of the bone china scoured with bleach, 'you can't afford to let things slide, you've got to keep everything up to scratch. Of course Shirley, my home help, comes in as you know, but she's from the criminal classes, bless her. One of those big families of the criminal aristocracy. I suppose, being brought up to prison and hospitals from an early age, it was natural that she should be drawn to disinfectant. She doesn't need to work, you know, her husband's got a shop off the market, specialises in reproduction antiques and chandeliers, all the genuine article. Shirley was a nursing auxiliary for a while and then she cleaned the police canteen, but that didn't suit her either. Her home's a little palace from what she tells me, a regular Aladdin's cave. More tea, son? A piece of cream cake, it's only just past its sell-by, Shirley got it for me.'

As Norman sipped and nodded, his *alter ego*, in exaggerated blackface – Larry Parnes in *The Jolson Story* – detached itself from his body and fell to its knees, clasping Maria round the waist in its white-gloved hands and burying its face in her flowered lap. Don't you know me, Mammy? I'm your little baby!

Norman departed uncomforted, leaving his mother in her few square feet of life, scouring the stainless steel sink, keeping things up to scratch. Exhausted and irritable after the long journey home by tube and bus in the rush hour, he breathed the air of Ingram Road with relief, noting the song of a blackbird on a satellite dish and daffodils in the gardens. Maxine from next door was coaxing the little cat Mignonette down from the lowest branch of the plane tree.

'Beautiful evening,' said Norman, 'there's a real hint of spring in the air at last.'

'Yea, I know. Everything coming into bud, and the blossom out.' Maxine patted the tree trunk, with the cat over her shoulder, its collar silvered with the glimmering early evening light.

'Dear old tree,' she said. 'I'm going to miss it.'

'What do you mean, miss it? You're not moving again already, are you?' She was a pretty girl, her arms poignant in the sleeves of her boy-friend's pink polo-shirt.

'Oh no. It's just our insurance company. They say it's got to come down. I'm really really sad, because I'm very much a tree person, very into trees, but they won't insure us unless it comes down, because of the roots. In case they cause problems in the future. Ouch, Mignonette, you're scratching me. I'd better go in.' She backed away, clutching the struggling cat.

'No, wait! You can't just land a bombshell like that and walk away!' Norman grabbed her arm, the cat leaped away, and Joel appeared, with a can of cola in his hand, saying,

'Everything all right, Maxie? Take your hand off her arm. What do you think you're doing? I'll have you for assault if you don't watch out.'

'Is it true, what she just said, about the tree?'

''Fraid so, mate. Shame, but there you go.'

'But you can't just do that! You can't just move in like vandals and chop down mature trees to suit yourselves. There are laws about that sort of thing. It's ridiculous. We'll see what the Council has to say about it. I'll get a preservation order if necessary.'

'Too late, mate. The Council has given its consent. It can't afford to take on the insurance company in the courts, so it's caved in under the threat of litigation. What's called market forces, old chap.'

'No it isn't, it's called hooliganism!' said Norman. 'I don't believe I'm hearing this. Tell me I'm dreaming, somebody. Are you two aware that the paid thugs of cable television have destroyed the roots of thousands of trees all over London so that their pornography can be piped into the homes of people like you? Are you?'

'Let's go in, Joel,' said Maxine.

'Hang on,' Joel shrugged her off. 'Nobody talks to me like that. I've a good mind to kick his head in.'

'Just try it, punk.' Norman thrust a clenched fist under Joel's chin. 'Come on, I dare you.'

'Oh, leave him, Joel, he's not worth it. He's just a twisted old looney.'

'Old looney, am I?' Norman swung a punch, which Joel side-stepped.

'Zinnia!' Norman yelled, with tears of rage in his eyes, 'Zinnia! Where are you, you stupid cow? Come and give me a bit of support for once in your life, damn you!'

He turned back to Maxine and Joel.

'I thought you young people were all about saving the planet? What about the environment you're all so keen on? What about the Newbury Bypass protesters, then? Young people, and old, risking life and limb to try to save those trees, yes, and the opponents of the export of live veal calves have lain down their very lives for their principles and you stand there calmly telling me that you have arranged the murder of the oldest, noblest, most majestic tree in this street. Old Jim and Edith Bacon must be turning in their graves! You ought to be ashamed of yourselves. Is this the sort of world you want for your children? Don't you walk away from me! Come back here!'

Norman kicked their gate, hurting his foot on wrought iron.

'Goths and Visigoths! Barbarians! Veal-eating, Diet-coke-swilling pigs! I hope you die of mad cow disease!' he shouted at their slammed front door.

Where the hell was Zinnia when he needed her? There was no note, no sign of any supper. Not knowing what to do with himself, Norman poured a glass of whisky and went into his study. He saw at once that the pages of his play had been disturbed, but he was in such turbulence himself, agitating his drink into a whirlpool that spiralled out of the glass and splashed everything in its radius, that the violation of his work scarcely registered. As the hideous confrontation replayed in his mind, he became aware of faces watching it from neighbouring windows. He put down his glass and went out again, to ring the doorbell of the Patels who lived opposite.

*

After Norman had left the house that morning, Zinnia had not known what to do with herself either. She had worked hard all her life, she had paid her dues. Surely she was entitled to enjoy what success she had without Norman spoiling everything and making a nonsense of her life?

Yes, she was a trouper. Was that something to be mocked and sneered at? Why could he not just let her *be*, without judging her every action like some sarcastic schoolmaster or a vicious director humiliating her in front of the rest of the cast and making her forget her lines? She had a recurrent nightmare now, of being late for the theatre and running and running along endless backstage corridors, through doors which opened into surreal dressing-rooms, until at last she stood on the stage in tears, trying to force her voice through locked lips above the babel of the audience but no sound would come, and when she looked down at herself she was naked or dressed in a clown's costume.

She remembered how Norman, on his way out, had asked, 'Anything in the post?'

'Nothing to write home about,' she had replied, concealing the letter inviting her to open the fête at their local hospice.

At a loss, in the kitchen, she stared at the vermicelli of a hydroponic hyacinth on the window-sill, and saw that overnight two strawberries left on a plate had bloated and their seeds turned black like the bristles in a drunk's bruised red face. She drifted into Norman's study with the feather duster still in her hand. The Heart of the Evil Empire, she thought.

She was forbidden to touch Norman's desk, but this morning, with the sun casting a tracery of plane tree twigs and bobbles over the word processor, the papers, books and writer's paraphernalia and toys, and glinting on the gold pen Norman's dad had filled with the blood of unknown prisoners in remote countries, the pen that Norman had to use for all his 'real', his creative, work, Zinnia picked up the manuscript of Norman's unfinished play, *The Last Sand Dance*.

Act 1, scene 1. A seedy theatre somewhere in the provinces. The stage is lightly sprinkled with sand. Enter stage left, shuffling, two sad old vaudevillians, male and female, in striped blazers and flannels, bent stiffly at the waist and waving straw boaters and clutching canes. Turning to the sparse audience of comatose pensioners, HE *sings in a cracked cockney voice,*

> *'When you wore a turnip,*
> *A big yellow turnip,*
> *And I wore a big red nose . . .'*

while SHE *executes a grim little dance. Onstage costume change . . .*

Zinnia sank back into Norman's chair. Her legs were weak and tingling, the little hairs on the back of her neck and arms standing on end. 'You bastard! How could you do this to us?' He had dug up her dead parents and was killing them again with his pen. She read on, clammy in her matelot top, the horripilant pages trembling in her hand.

. . . Onstage costume change. The straw boaters are sent whizzing into the wings, and Egyptian robes and red fezzes with black tassels thrown unceremoniously on, at the aged pair who catch them clumsily and struggle into them over their blazers etc. They break into a grotesque sand dance, à la Wilson, Keppel (kepple?) and Betty. TOT *runs on, stage left, tripping cutely over her too-long Egyptian robe, holding on her fez with one hand and staggering under the weight of a giant papier-mâché banana. Sings, 'I've Never Seen A Straight Banana' . . .*
'Wakey, Wa-key!! Hey, you down there with the banana!'
At the disembodied voice of Billy Cotton, the trio cower and crouch like victims of an air raid as an enormous balloon with the spectacled features of the great bandleader floats down from the gods, and his

signature tune blares out, 'Dah, dada dah dah dah, Somebody Stole My Gal' . . .

Zinnia was shaking, and nauseous at the knowledge of her own innocent collaboration in this parading of her family to public scorn. It was she who had told Norman how the Two Herberts had been turned away from their audition for the Billy Cotton Band Show on the wireless and how it had broken the Two Herberts' hearts. 'Boater? What boater?' she heard her father's voice in memory, 'I thought you said put on your bloater!' He had a large fish on his head.

Her eye caught the glitter of Norman's fountain pen. The murder weapon. Although she could hardly bear to touch it, she picked it up, feeling the weight of its machine-turned gold in her hand.

So that is what they mean by the banality of evil, she thought. Its agents are the jovial grandpa finding a sixpence behind a grandchild's ear, the benevolent boss with a pen clipped to his clean overall pocket as he jokes with his employees on the shop-floor, the Rotarian adding an afterthought to his speech at the charity dinner.

'Your play stinks, Norman,' she said aloud. 'It stinks to high heaven. The only place bad enough to stage it is the Pillory Theatre.'

Zinnia threw the pen to the floor and stamped on it, but it would not break. It rolled from her ballet pump, hard and inviolate. She tried to grind it into the carpet. The cap came off but still the pen was unharmed. She tried once more and failed, and then she picked up the shiny barrel. It was bleeding a little blue ink from the nib and had caught a piece of fluff, like a feather in a crossed bill. Zinnia opened the window and flung the pen and its cap as hard as she could, and heard them fall somewhere in the vicinity of next-door-but-one's dustbins.

Then she telephoned her daughter.

'Nerissa, I have nourished a viper in my bosom.'

Much later that night the telephone rang again in Nerissa's house. Nerissa's husband picked it up.

'Stephen?' said Norman's voice, 'I don't suppose you have any idea of where my wife might be? She seems to have disappeared, and I'm getting a bit worried. It isn't like her.'

'She's here, if it's any of your concern,' said Norman's stepson-in-law, and put down the phone.

A fortnight or so after Easter, Zinnia's taxi-driver stopped his cab at the corner of Ingram Road.

'I can't get through. Seems to be some sort of disturbance going on down there, or an accident. Looks like they've got the emergency services out.'

'Oh, I do hope it isn't anything dreadful! Can you wait for me here then? I'll be as quick as I can, I've just got to pick up a few things. Oh dear, there seem to be lots of people, and the police!'

It flashed through her mind that Norman had killed himself, but reassuring herself that he was no Norman Maine, she hurried on.

She could see spinning blue lights, flashing amber, yellow machinery, a heavy digger slewed across the road, a television camera crew, a banner strung across the street, a crowd holding hands around the trunk of the plane tree, spilling over the pavement and into the road, shouting and singing, 'We Shall Not Be Moved'.

Zinnia stopped, and looked up into the branches of the tree, and saw huge black and white birds, vultures, huddled there, and realised that they were boys from St Joseph's. At the top of the plane tree, as high as he could climb, stood Norman, arms outstretched, straddling two boughs.

His face, patterned by sun and shadows, was radiant, as if he had found his element, the air, at last, or was an ancient tree deity returned to redeem the world of men. Below him, his people waved broken branches and twigs and sang hosannas. Tears were streaming down Zinnia's face. Everybody was there, all the neighbours, the Patels, the Smiths, the Peacocks, the Patterson-Dixes who spoke only Esperanto, Joel scuffling with somebody, that family of Exclusive Brethren who never spoke to anybody, and now, unbelievably, the boys were hauling old Father Coyle up in a hoist, with his skinny black silk ankles poking out like sticks and everybody cheering him.

A television reporter had made it almost up to Norman, who shouted down into the furry boom they called a dead rat, 'We are the people of Ingram Road, and we have not spoken yet! But now we have found our voice, and we are saying, for all the world to hear, "Save Our Tree!" This is the will of the people and the people will be heard!'

The wind ruffled his hair and billowed his white shirt, cleansing him of old diffuse familial shame and failure and recent guilts. He could hear, lower down, the buzzing of a saw, a policeman shouting, and he was aware of the boys scrambling and swinging from the branches like monkeys in their black blazers, and as he heard the quavering benediction of Father Coyle through the swaying bunches of twigs, withered fruits and new baby growth, it came to him that all he had needed, all along, was an audience to make him whole again.

Far beneath his triumphant feet, Old Seedy was cut to pieces by the teeth of the saw and sent flying in fragments of dry dead wood, haloed like an icon in golden sawdust.

The crowd was swelling with the red-blazered girls of the comprehensive and latter-day punks and hippies with their dogs. Norman heard faint chimes of an ice-cream van over the din, and he almost lost his grip and his footing as he thought he saw Zinnia's distinctive head, tiny and scarlet-tipped above her foreshortened daffodil-yellow jacket, ducking into a black cab parked at the corner. It happened so quickly, and she was lost to sight so fast, in the blink of an eye, in the whisk of the tail of a rat leaping aboard a ship bound for the Gulf of Izmir before the tide turned.

Robert Irwin

UNREADABLE BOOKS: FICTIONAL LANDMARKS IN TWENTIETH-CENTURY BRITISH WRITING

BRITISH FICTION IN the twentieth century resembles a large Victorian house – as it appears in a recurring nightmare. It has corridors which seem endless and which do indeed go nowhere. Its windows look out on nothing. There is a bad smell from the drains. Some of the inhabitants of this house are busily engaged in trying to strip the lead from the roof, others are bemusedly trying to find a way out. There are also dark things stirring in the basement. It is the job of the critic to bring some order to this turbulent ménage.

By common consent Sebastian Knight, Herbert Quain, X. Trapnel, Gwynn Barry and, perhaps, Jude Mason have been the dominant figures in British novel-writing in this century and the discussion which follows will concentrate on these writers. However, it is desirable first to set these novelists within a broader cultural context. It has been well said by one of our academic critics that 'modern British writers all come out from under the shadow of Soames's *Fungoids*'. Although Enoch Soames was little appreciated in his own time, his reputation has grown vastly over the last hundred years, as is evidenced by the forthcoming colloquium, jointly sponsored by the British Library and the British Museum, to be held on 3 June 1997 in the British Museum Reading Room.

Soames's *Negations* and *Fungoids* are landmarks in the British modernist movement. In *Negations*, Soames advanced the bold thesis that good and evil are not found in Life,

168

but only in Art. This was of course a position which was later to be endorsed by some of the leading novelists and poets of the Diabolic Movement. In Soames's vision, Life, though it always aspires to the condition of Art, usually fails lamentably. *Negations* was a ground-breaking anthology of short stories and essays, none of which yield up their meaning easily, though the effort spent on trying to read them invariably proves worthwhile. In *Fungoids*, his second and, as it turned out, final book, he collected and commented on his poems. As the *Preston Telegraph* presciently noted at the time of the volume's publication, the poems 'strike a note of modernity throughout'. Some later and less discerning critics have hailed Soames as the 'English Baudelaire'. However, the truth is that Soames ventures far beyond what he would have characterised as Baudelaire's bourgeois mind-set. (Incidentally, 'Max Beerbohm', a separately published and little-known short story about an imaginary wit and essayist obsessed with his own prospects of literary immortality, is a great imaginative creation and one of Soames's rare ventures into comedy.) Enoch Soames died tragically early, a victim of his beloved *sorcière glauque*, absinthe.

After Soames, British fiction in the twentieth century is one long disappointment. It is, I think, the job of the critic to point this out and to stand looking over the shoulder of the reader, muttering 'This is awful, isn't it?' So it is that canon-formation, which is after all the highest aspect of the critic's art, turns out to be as much a matter of exclusion as inclusion. It is peculiarly the task of the critic to rule out utterly ghastly specimens of genre-writing, such as sci-fi, fantasy, the historical novel and the whodunnit. Foreign influences should also be deplored and sniffed out. The central tradition of twentieth-century British fiction deals in a realistic manner with shared common perceptions. This great tradition is at one and the same time both robust and elegiac. It is true that not many books have been written in this tradition of elegiac robustness and none of them are really satisfactory, but that is what the critic has to work with. If fiction writing in modern Britain has languished, higher criticism is staking a claim to be the leading art form and many novelists who are too clever by half have been taken down a peg or two by the discerning critic. Successful criticism will necessarily depend on a kind of woodenness, or critical density, in which enthusiasm is kept tightly reined in.

Soames was a John the Baptist crying out in a literary wilderness. Contemporary and subsequent British novelists have failed to match his robust seediness and the world of fiction is, I think, still waiting for its Messiah. Be that as it may, the influence of Soames is detectable in the works of Soames's younger contemporary, St John Clarke. Those works include *Fields of Amaranth*, *The Heart is Highland*, *Dust Thou Art*, *Match Me Such a Marvel* and *Never to the Philistines*. Of these the most considerable are surely *Fields of Amaranth*, with its melancholy elegiac quality, and *Match Me Such a Marvel*. However, the latter's reputation has suffered from the film version in which the book's homosexual decadence and rather fascinating gynophobia were comprehensively ignored. Clarke's fame was at its highest in the Edwardian era. It is perhaps now due for re-evaluation.

Clarke's literary rival, the grand old man of letters, Gilbert Strong, has recently been the subject of a lively biography by Mark Lamming. According to Mark Lamming, all Strong's novels and in particular *Once in Summertime* are intensely autobiographical. Many now find Strong's tub-thumping, lapel-grabbing manner offensive. Moreover, Strong, who held that novel-writing was 'just like cookery', spread himself rather thinly, also producing plays (including *Queen Mab's Other Island*, biographies (including *Disraeli*) and travel books (including *The Road to Anatolia*). Those who have been enchanted by Julie Andrews's impersonation of Queen Mab in the film of the play may be rather surprised when they turn to what Strong actually wrote. His fustian stuff has not worn well.

Although Sebastian Knight's father was Russian and Sebastian himself was born in St Petersburg, his mother was English and in 1919 he settled in England where he became thoroughly assimilated and wrote novels in English. Indeed Knight's use of his adopted language, which is delicate and subtle, has exercised an enormous influence on those British writers clever enough to be influenced by him. Viewed as a whole, his novels reveal a strange mixture of controlled fantasy and painfully thinly-disguised autobiography. Knight plays (chess-like) games with his readers, but they are serious games, life-and-death games. His novels include *The Prismatic Bezel* (1924), *Success* (1925–7), *Lost Property* (1929) and *The Doubtful Asphodel* (1935). *The Funny Mountain* is a collection of accomplished short stories.

The intellectual whodunnit, *The Prismatic Bezel*, is thought by some to be his *tour de force*. Although the novel opens conventionally enough, very soon a 'new plot, a new drama utterly unconnected with the opening of the story . . . seems to struggle for existence and break into light'. Twelve people find themselves staying at a boarding house, but twelve soon become eleven as one of their number is murdered. Suspicion falls on a passing collector of snuffboxes, Old Nosebag. However, while the detective sent for from London is making his way by train to the scene of the crime, not only has Old Nosebag been cleared, but it has been established that the boarding house is not a boarding house at all, but a country house, and that the eleven 'lodgers' are in fact the family who live there. By the time the detective turns up, it is reality itself which is under suspicion. Old Nosebag, formerly the chief murder suspect, turns out to be in truth the murder victim – at least he would be, if only he had remained content with that somewhat passive role. Enough has been said, I think, to indicate the extent of Knight's ambition. But perhaps the multiple perspectives suggested by the prism of the title point not only to ambition but also to a lack of confidence about its achievement. Be that as it may, alleged inconsistencies in its plotting prevented *The Prismatic Bezel* from receiving the Golden Dagger, the premier award for British crime writing. (Knight's and, for that matter, the reading public's fondness for crime novels is to be regretted; crime novels are a diversion from the great Soamsean tradition. The current popularity of trashy female crime novelists like Harriet Vane and Emma Sands is deplorable.)

Knight's next novel, *Success*, in part the detailing of a romance between a commercial traveller and a female conjuror, has been criticised for its excessive length and self-indulgence. The romantic story serves as a pretext for a lengthy examination of the nature of coincidence. Knight's subject-matter here (though not his style) seems to have influenced certain British Surrealists. *Lost Property*, the most autobiographical of his works, tackles the theme of exile. Its protagonist is an exile not just in space, but also in time. It also provided Knight with an opportunity to take stock of his life. *The Doubtful Asphodel* deals with the perceptions and memories of a dying man, right up to the terminal darkness. When the man dies, so does the book and it is Knight's doubtful privilege to have given a new meaning to 'the death of the novel'. Certainly, one senses some fatigue in the writing here. Does one really want to sit for so long at someone's deathbed? Nevertheless, despite these reservations, Knight, who died in 1936, is the flawed genius of post-modernism. Goodman's *The Tragedy of Sebastian Knight*, which points up the novelist's failure to withstand 'the anguish of the epoch', is fundamental to understanding the man and his work.

Although some critics would probably wish at this point to discuss the similarly experimental Dublin writer, Dermot Trellis, it does not seem to me that there is any real comparison, for Trellis lacks Knight's mastery. Indeed, Trellis does not seem to like his characters and he never seems very securely in control of them. Moreover, Trellis's account of gunfights between cowpokes in the streets of Dublin shows signs of genre contamination – unusually in this case from the Western. So I pass on to the hardly more successful experimental novelist, Darley. A whiff of the *Fungoids* is detectable in the work of this expatriate writer with his (surely largely autobiographical) novels about cosmopolitan layabouts in Egypt before and after the Second World War. The influence of Jacob Arnauti's *Moeurs* on Darley's first novel, *Justine*, is also hard to miss. Trellis and Darley are difficult writers and you probably would not understand their books even if I took the trouble to explain their plots to you.

Darley's somewhat pretentious reflections on time and his related experiments with a fractured time sequence in his novels probably result from a rather dim understanding of the investigations of philosophers into the nature of temporality. Here one thinks not only of Bergotte with his elastic concept of time but also of the more sceptical philosopher Van Veen, whose *The Texture of Time* was gleefully plundered by many novelists looking for a stick with which to beat reality. De Selby, Britain's foremost thinker, has also queried conventional beliefs about the nature of time – in the same way as he has queried so much else. De Selby characterised the commonly experienced sensation of progress through time as a series of hallucinations and he went on to define human existence as 'a succession of static experiences each infinitely brief'. De Selby apparently reached this conclusion after examining some old spools of film. The philosophic legacy of De Selby perhaps accounts for the cinematic quality of many modern novels.

Although Herbert Quain is Roscommon's most famous son, it will become immediately evident that Roscommon does not have much to boast about. In his first novel, *The God of the Labyrinth* (1933), Quain, like Knight, allowed himself to be seduced by the lure of genre writing, for this book is an intellectual sort of whodunnit. Despite being superficially conventional in its plotting and materials, the book, in seeming to come to one solution of the crime, actually points to another, for Quain's carefully chosen closing words undermine the obvious solution. The famous last sentence has often been quoted by genre aficionados: 'Everyone thought that the encounter of the two chess players was accidental.' Having read and understood this conclusion, the fuming reader then has to read the whole damn book all over again. *April March* (1936) is a better novel. It begins (or ends?) with a group of people standing on a railway platform. In the following three chapters the reader is presented with three alternative scenarios, any one of which might have led to the meeting on the platform. In the next nine chapters, Quain sketches out the various and divergent incidents which might have led to the three scenarios in the previous chapters. Quain's story-line is a regressive one in which, as it were, Time's Arrow has been made to travel backwards. Although I prefer it to *The God of the Labyrinth*, I still do not like it very much, as its ramificatory structure smacks of foreign influence. (The obvious comparison would be with the Chinese novelist Ts'ui Pen's *The Garden of the Forking Paths*.)

Quain's last novel, *The Secret Mirror*, begins in a country house belonging to a certain General Thrale and features his daughter Ulrica Thrale and her admirer, the playwright Wilfred Quarles, as its leading characters. However, as the novel progresses, there is a lot of slippage and characters begin to change their names and locations redefine themselves. Quarles turns out to be a commision agent in Liverpool. He has never met Ulrica Thrale and the country estate turns out to be something more like an Irish-Jewish boarding house. Surely Quain's indebtedness here to Knight's *The Prismatic Bezel* is too obvious to require elaboration.

Finally, *Statements* (1939) is a literary manifesto masquerading as a series of short stories. Each story starts off promisingly, but in each case the reader's expectation of seeing the plot successfully developed is frustrated. It is rather as if on a winter's night a traveller should start off, heading for a designated destination, but then after a short while, change his destination and then change it again and again. In his suspect European experimentalism, Quain reminds us of Osberg, whom Van Veen has rightly summed up as a 'Spanish writer of pretentious fairy-tales and mystico-allegoric anecdotes'. Quain and Osberg are all a bit too clever for me and I am sure that if I cannot understand them, no one else can. The poet and aphorist *maudit*, Pursewarden, spoke for this class of pseudo-intellectual writers with unusual plainness when he declared that 'I have always believed in letting my readers sink or swim.'

*

I take it as axiomatic that it is the novelist's job to hold a mirror to reality. Anything that encourages the writer to turn away from the reflection in the mirror should be eschewed. I have no hesitation in condemning science fiction for seeking to tackle matters which are outside the given world of commonly shared experience. American pulp science-fiction writers have certainly had a deleterious influence on British fiction, by encouraging our best writers to stray from the robust yet elegiac tradition.

The American writer, Van Veen, who (under the pseudonym Voltemand) published *Letters from Terra* in 1891, has claims to be regarded as the father of science fiction. His first and only novel presents a satirical account of an alternate world, Terra, and its imaginary history peopled by fantastical Nazis, Soviet Communists and so on. Van Veen's lead in creating an alternative universe has been followed by many later sci-fi writers, of whom the most notable is probably the reclusive Hawthorne Abendsen. Abendsen's *The Grasshopper Lies Heavy* presents a playful alternative history of the world in which Germany and Japan are imagined as having lost the Second World War. Abendsen seems to enjoy playing literary games (always a bad sign in my view) and his novel features a wholly imaginary novel entitled *Man in a High Castle*, attributed to the no less imaginary and rather tiresome-sounding Philip K. Dick.

Novelists have a tedious tendency to write novels about novelists on the mistaken assumption, I suppose, that such folk are the lords of creation. Even so some notable, often comic, inventions have been the result. The names of Anthony Powell, Lawrence Durrell, Vladimir Nabokov, Jorge Luis Borges, Iris Murdoch, Muriel Spark, John Updike, Flann O'Brien, Kurt Vonnegut, Simon Raven, Peter Ackroyd, Philip Roth, Arthur Machen, Stella Gibbons, Bernard Malamud, Thomas Pynchon, David Lodge, H. P. Lovecraft, M. R. James, A. S. Byatt, Martin Amis and P. D. James come to mind.

Finally, on the distasteful subject of science fiction, the prolific pulp writer Kilgore Trout cannot be ignored, much though I wish he could be. His *The Gutless Wonder* (1932) concerns the social acceptability or not of a robot with bad breath. *Oh Say Can You Smell* is thematically similar and features a dictator who succeeds in getting rid of bad smells by cutting off people's noses. As for *Venus on the Half Shell*, one only has to read the novel's opening sentences to get a clear notion of Trout's unwholesome preoccupations: 'Queen Margaret of the planet Shaltoon let her gown fall to the floor. She was wearing nothing underneath. Her high, firm, uncowled bosom was proud and rosy.' In *A Plague on Wheels* the diminutive alien hero, Kago, while attempting to warn earthlings about the perils of the motor car, is mistaken by an automobile worker for a matchstick and is killed by being repeatedly struck against the bar. Where did the man get his ghastly plots from? But all science fiction resembles the Trout *oeuvre* in that it is so busily determined to invent specifically detailed future worlds or alternative worlds, that it takes no trouble to give its protagonists emotional roots in those worlds. (There is, I think, something very unBritish about Kago.)

English literature is like a large family – half of which is not talking to the other half. It is with some relief that we return to the literary mainstream. The novelist X. Trapnel first attracted public attention in 1945 with the publication of *Camel Ride to the Tomb*. His other works include *Bin Ends*, *Profiles in String*, *The Heresy of Naturalism* and *Dogs Have No Uncles*. All these books can be seen as chapters in a sustained paradoxical literary campaign designed to demonstrate that naturalism is merely a convention and an unnatural one at that. An adroit promoter of his personal legend (rather in the manner of T. E. Lawrence), Trapnel let it be understood that *Camel Ride to the Tomb* was autobiographical. The book remains enduringly popular among adolescents, and its Levantine setting seems to have been subsequently annexed by Darley.

Fungoids casts a long shadow indeed and there is an unmistakably damp feel about his last book, *Profiles in String*. Trapnel was really better at talking about literature than at actually producing it. He was a flamboyant poseur and, for example, he seems to have copied the habit of ostentatiously parading about with a swordstick from the Surrealist painter, Caspar. Yet, though Caspar and Trapnel inhabited the same louche Fitzrovian world, they do not seem ever to have crossed paths or sticks and the novelist does not feature in the painter's memoir, *Exquisite Corpse*. Trapnel's swordstick, of course, furnished Russell Gwinnet's thoughtful biography of the man, *Death's Head Swordsman* (1968), with its central image. Some readers have fallen into the error of enjoying Trapnel's novels, but more correctly read, those books furnish us with an example of the inevitable disjunctions of the post-*Fungoid* writer.

Trapnel, who always drank heavily, died after collapsing in a gutter. Although Fielding Gray is widely perceived as having picked Trapnel's mantle from that gutter and as having inherited his status as our flamboyantly louche writer *par excellence*, Gray handles his somewhat disreputable subject-matter in a more middle-brow fashion (and was therefore much more to the taste of the jury of the Joseph Conrad Prize for Fiction). His *Love's Jest Book*, which chronicles the downfall of a gilded youth and his successive expulsion from school and university, strikes a note of elegiac seediness of which Soames would have been proud. In subsequent novels, Gray has returned again and again to the themes of opportunities squandered and sexual betrayal (by members of both sexes). In *Operation Apocalypse*, for example, Gray tells essentially the same story but he sets the story in the officers' mess of a smart regiment. Gray's novels chart a raffish rake's progress. It is hard not to see the *oeuvre* as on the whole a *roman à clef*, in which the reality comments on the fiction. The man who undertakes the task of presenting a critical account of British fiction in the twentieth century is like a judge at a knobbly knees competition; he is in the business of assessing and comparing flaws and deformities. Gray's knees are knobblier than most.

The Approach to al-Mu'tasim, by Mir Bahadur Ali, though much vaunted by Philip Guedalla, is really nothing more than a pretentious mixture of Islamic allegory and a would-be traditional British mystery story (that tell-tale genre contamination again!). Mir Bahadur Ali would like to be British, but no matter how hard he tries, he is not going to succeed. He lacks that quintessentially British elegiac robustness, and I take it as axiomatic that English literature must be rooted in the English landscape. Unfortunately, however, twentieth-century English literature is not something that has been cultivated in a sealed bell-jar. Novelists are often tempted to go whoring after strange gods. I therefore now turn with considerable reluctance to consider the question of contamination by foreign influences.

The French writer Pierre Ménard's fragmentary experimental novel, *Don Quixote*, with its affected mock baroque style and fusion of antiquarian subject-matter with showy, post-modernist tricksiness, has exercised a baleful influence on some pseudo-intellectual writers in Britain. Ménard's famous declaration of faith, 'Every man should be capable of all ideas, and I believe that in the future he will be', is nothing more than continental swank. The British novel has suffered from contamination not just from foreign novels, but also from pretentious alien philosophies. One thinks here of the Abbé Fausse-Maigre and his alleged intellectual masterpiece, *The Higher Common Sense*. I should have thought it was impossible to read the Abbé's famous chapter on 'Preparing the Mind for the Twin Invasion by Prudence and Daring in Dealing with Substances not Included in the Outline' without feeling that one is being confronted by continental flim-flam masquerading as daring speculation. Nevertheless the book has its fans and surely *The Transfiguration of the Common-place* by 'Sister Helena' (a.k.a. Sandy Stranger) owes a debt to the Abbé's ill-conceived attempt to wed strategies for dealing with day-to-day problems with high Catholic theology.

Transatlantic writing provides British literature with dubious models of a different kind. Henry Bech's first novel, *Travel Light* (1955), was acclaimed for its lyrical celebration of American space and life on the road — a young man's dreamworld of speeding motorbikes, Zen mechanics and beautiful young girls. Although it remains a cult book among latter-day hippy students, it has dated badly and, besides, the Americans cannot manage the elegiac. (It is salutary, incidentally, to meet the real Henry Bech in the flesh. I assure you that he bears no resemblance to the portrait of a *dharma* bum on a motorbike that he so lovingly painted in the novel.) Bech's second book, the surrealist-existentialist-anarchist novel *Brother Pig* (1958), proved less popular, perhaps because it was intellectually more challenging. Finally, his third novel, *The Chosen* (1963), is universally reckoned to be a failure. After Bech, Nathan Zuckerman, a specialist in the painful detailing of the sexual problems of Jewish American intellectuals, is perhaps the most admired of American writers. But enough of all this! For what in all truth have the sexual problems of Jewish American intellectuals got to do with English fiction and its celebration of a land of leafy oak-trees, cricket matches and shared readings of *The Pickwick Papers*? It is not some hand-me-down, second-rate English version of Henry Bech or Kilgore Trout that we should be looking for. Instead we should be asking where are the Percy Graingers of the modern British novel.

It is inevitable that men dominate my discussion of seriously important British novels. However, it is possible that some women writers deserve to be taken more seriously than they have. Ada Leintwardine is typical of the writers I am trying to ignore in this survey of important fiction. Her *I Stopped at the Chemist* was published in 1947 and later filmed as *Sally Goes Shopping*. Other novels include *Bedsores* and *The Bitch Pack Meets on Wednesdays*. Published in the fifties, these were feminist novels *avant le mouvement*. Then the clever, brittle novels of Fleur Talbot, among them *Warrender Chase*, *All Souls Day* and *The English Rose*, hardly seem more satisfactory. Of them *Warrender Chase* is the most profound. This book, which deals with the literary legacy, the *damnosa haereditas*, of the eponymous great man bears some resemblance, surely, to *The Aspern Papers*. Although, the predilection of novelists for writing about other writers is certainly tiresome, Talbot's speculations about Life's imitation of Art and indeed her belief in the power of fiction to generate reality can be seen as a heartening revival of great themes first raised by Enoch Soames.

However, as I have intimated at the beginning of this chapter, Soames's true heirs are to be found in the Diabolic School. The Diabolic tendency in British fiction has its roots in developments in academic research into mythology and occultism. British fiction was in trouble when Casaubon's fine *Key to All Mythologies* was replaced as a standard reference work by *Unaussprechlichen Kulten*. The literary researches of figures like Russell Gwinnet may have also contributed something to the Diabolic revival. Gwinnet's scholarly *The Gothic Symbolism of Mortality in the Texture of Jacobean Stagecraft* has led to a reappraisal not just of that strange, dramatic (and proto-philatelic) masterpiece, *The Courier's Tragedy*, but has also encouraged a more general re-evaluation of the dark tradition in English literature. (The recent reprinting of the sinisterly beautiful baroque prose of the seventeenth-century essayist, Nicholas Dyer, is a straw in the wind.) It has been under the impetus of these and similar academic works that the Diabolic Movement in British fiction got under way. Writers of the Diabolic School, having taken the medieval *grimoire* as their model, have produced fictions in the maledictory mode. Diabolic works are often anonymous or pseudonymous. Among the most important titles in the 'black library' are *The Yellow Book*, *The King in Yellow*, *The Three Impostors*, *The Tractate Middoth* and the *Necromicon* of Alhazred the Damned. Only the bravest of bibliophiles dares keep these works on his shelves. Dangerously fashionable though such books may now be, Soames was there first with his diabolically written story in *Negations* about the murder of a mannequin by a *midinette*.

Some critics are inclined to place Jude Mason in the Diabolic movement. The latter's *Babbletower: A Tale for the Children of Our Time* (1966) was, as its title suggests, directed at the youth of the 1960s and it has indeed become a cult book among the drug-dulled, disaffected, anomic young.

However, Mason's parable is an ambiguous one and it is doubtful that many of his long-haired, unwashed readers understand the text that they so fervently worship. The novel, set in the period of the French Revolution, deals with an attempt to set up a sort of anarchist sexual utopia in which no impulse, no matter how vicious or perverted, will be suppressed. The book's apparent delight in the infliction of pain and its fierce misogyny have attracted criticism. In addition, while it is probably true that *Babbletower* should be read as a warning about the dangerous tendencies of Utopian libertarianism, the prose in which that warning is couched has a strangely seductive quality. Even so, the novelist Anthony Burgess has praised the book for its deeply moral content. According to Burgess, 'Jude Mason is both didactic and pornographic: it is to be supposed that he believes his own stance to be that of his creation, Samson Origen, who professes a Nietzschean eschewal of the libido and all its works. But he has chosen to construct his fable, his *machine*, his clockwork, in parody of the devices and drives it criticises, the sado-masochistic panoply of straps and knives, the pornographic relish of human surfaces and orgiastic contortions.' Burgess's verdict notwithstanding, the strong influence of such foreign thinkers as De Sade and Fourier means that Mason's novel lacks the essential virtue of thoroughgoing Britishness.

It is a cardinal rule of literary as well as of dramatic criticism not to judge things on the basis of the first night. I like to think of myself as a second-nighter – that is as someone whose responses have been tempered and refined by the critical consensus. It is with some anxiety then that I turn to novelists of the 1990s. Richard Tull can probably be dismissed fairly briefly. Although he is the author of a cycle of novels entitled successively *Untitled, Unpublished, Unfinished, Unwritten, Unattempted* and, finally, *Unconceived*, only *Untitled* merits a critical reading. The book has a fine description of an escort-agency advertisement done as a chapter-long parody of the *Romance of the Rose*. Later on in the same book, Tull offers us a miraculously sustained *tour de force* chapter in which five unreliable narrators converse on crossed mobile-phone lines while stuck in the same revolving door.

I actually prefer this book of Tull's to anything produced by his hip and knowing rival, Gwyn Barry, but it is to Gwyn Barry I now turn, for there is no doubt that Gwyn Barry is setting the literary pace today. His first novel *Summertown*, a novel about Oxford, did not attract much attention at first (despite its containing a hilarious and thinly disguised portrait of Richard Tull). Success (and money) only arrived with Barry's second novel, *Amelior*. It is possible to argue (and I have argued the case elsewhere) that Barry intended this novel as a riposte to Mason's *Babbletower*. In Barry's book twelve fair-minded young people come together to set up a kind of rural Utopia in an unnamed community. The composition of the Utopian community is somewhat curious, as not only is each racial group represented, but each of the participants in the Utopia sports a non-disfiguring affliction. Thus Piotr has haemophilia, while Conchita has endometriosis. 'Of these twelve, naturally six were men and six were women; but the sexual characteristics were deliberately hazed. The women were broad-shouldered and thin-hipped. The men tended to be comfortably plump. In the place called Amelior, where they all had to dwell, there was no beauty, no humour and no incident; there was no hate and no love.' This strangely deformed community do not do much, except sit around and talk about such matters as astrology and roof mainte-nance. Like *Babbletower*, it has become a cult book: unlike *Babbletower*, it presents a portrait of a Utopia which works, in its own terms at least. Since the jury is still out on the sequel, *Amelior Regained*, I refrain for the time being from delivering a critical verdict.

Is it possible that my fellow critics and authors of liter-ary biographers bear some responsibility for the deplorable state of British fiction today? I think so. It is a matter for considerable regret that novelists have not been as well served as poets by their biographers. *All Fouled Up*, Jake Balukowski's exemplary life of the poet Philip Larkin, should serve as a model for all subsequent literary biographies, as with unerring insight Balukowski shows how the poet's public work was shaped by private anguish. Similarly, the reputation of the American poet, John Shade, has benefited enormously from the unfailingly informative commentaries provided by his learned associate Kinbote. It is not the least of Kinbote's merits to have drawn attention to a hidden subtext in *Pale Fire* which might otherwise have eluded us. (Sadly, Britain's answer to John Shade, the workmanlike F. X. Enderby, still awaits his biographer.) The lack of worthwhile biographies of our leading novelists is surely all the stranger, in that biography is nothing other than the deformed sister of the novel. After all, as our leading biographer, the prolific William B. Dubin, has observed, 'there is no life which can be recaptured wholly as it was. Which is to say that all biography is ultimately fiction.' Yet only Dubin, Lamming, Goodman and Gwinnet have produced literary biographies worthy of mention (and only of mention).

When it comes to literary criticism, I am sure my fellow practitioners in the craft will not mind some frank speaking. The old-fashioned man-of-letters approach of the likes of Professor Lord Pinkrose is now happily behind us. But the more academic approach of university-based literary theorists is not much of an improvement. Philip Swallow, best known for his *Hazlitt and the Common Reader*, seems excessively timid in his approach. Persse McGarrigle and Morris Zap, on the other hand, are the wild men of academic criticism and their critical judgements often seem overbold, even euphoric. Arthur Kingfisher's enormous reputation as arbiter of the critical profession is as yet unsupported by any correspondingly large body of work. Looking around me, I sense a widespread loss of critical confidence. The burden of the future weighs heavily on post-modernity. Perhaps this obvious critical unease looks forward to a world in which there will be no books. Such a future has been predicted by the Neo-Marxist political philosopher, David Crimond. Working in the tradition of the Frankfurt School, Crimond austerely looks forward to the death of the bourgeois individual (and with it of bourgeois literary culture). If he is right, 'the world in the next century is going to look a lot more like Africa than Europe'. But Crimond is not necessarily right in his predictions and, in the meantime, it is one of the additional tasks of the critic to seek out hints of Africanness in the English novel and condemn them.

In summing up, it is hard, I think, to see the wood for the trees. However, some general tendencies can be discerned. From Enoch Soames to Gwyn Barry, British fiction is the story of the long journey of the British nation – a fairly aimless tramp from the British Museum Reading Room towards some, as yet unrealised, rural Utopia. Plainly the achievements discussed above are somewhat insubstantial. There is a feeling, is there not, of what can be termed 'unearned literature' and a sense also of a recurring literary *mise-en-abîme*? For all the wealth of experimentation, there has been a discouraging lack of realism in the problems our best novelists have chosen to tackle. If one were to judge from their chosen topics, the major problems facing English society today are those posed by country-house murders, *doppelgängers*, mirrors, alternative worlds, recurring nightmares and suchlike. Are these really the central concerns of a condition-of-England novel?

Canon formation is, in a sense, a form of self-definition in which one defines oneself in terms of one's response to the works of others. After years of reading and disliking other people's novels, I have at last realised that I can do the job better myself. Almost a hundred years ago today Enoch Soames flung out a mighty challenge to those engaged in the production of serious fiction. Now it is time for a response. In my own forthcoming novel, *Spirits from the Vasty Deep*, I shall show how to do the job properly. I am going to write a self-consciously naturalistic novel which will foreground the critical enterprise and celebrate adventures in agonistic reading. At the plangent sound of the Critical Last Trump, novelists shall be summoned up from their graves. The English landscape will heave and the earth crack. Novelists will stand bewildered amongst the clods of soil, and there will be much weeping and gnashing of teeth as they come up for judgement. Those found wanting by the Hero-as-Critic shall be cast out of the critical canon. But the saved shall gather round while the Hero-as-Critic reads from his triumphantly successful novel, *Spirits from the Vasty Deep*. The notion of having an imaginary novel set within a real novel and of giving that imaginary novel the same title as the real novel is rather a neat trick and it has not, I fancy, been tried before. Well, there it is. It only remains for me, in my self-appointed task as critical policeman of novel-writing, to acknowledge the help and advice of the poet, Adam Dalgliesh.

Keith Ridgway

The Problem With German

ANGER IS A place to put things, for a while. It is like a refuge, temporary, constructed from what is at hand, filled with huddled fears, and confusion, and the failure to understand. It serves a purpose. The contents rattle and knock against the edges, contained only by the hardness of the anger, its width and its depth. It is a weak structure. And when what it holds is strong, anger is brittle and thin. It splinters and its contents spill.

There is a strange bench at the corner. It is a circular heap of concrete with a flat hollow top where flowers should be, but which is filled instead with dead mud and litter. A ledge in the concrete, lined with wooden slats, serves as a seat. The bench is ugly and the wood is scratched and written on, and cold. Robert sits there, angry.

His legs are stretched out before him and crossed at the ankle, the upper foot twitching furiously. He folds and unfolds his arms, puts his hands in his pockets and takes them out again. Every few moments his head jerks tightly to his right and stays still, and then slowly turns back again in an arc, looking up at the sky and down at the hard ground where the grass is losing its colour.

When he looks to his right it is a distant corner that interests him. And every time a figure appears from around that corner Robert squints at it for a moment without moving, except for a kind of craning, a barely perceptible stretching. And then he looks away again, moving his head through the same arc, resuming his twitching, rearranging his arms once more.

186

It is dusk now, and quite cold. Robert smokes a cigarette and decides what to do. He jumps from one notion to the next, fixing on one thing and then another, his insides raging, deciding to go here and there and elsewhere, but in the end staying exactly where he finds himself – sitting in anger on the ugly bench. He will do nothing. He will stay where he is and do nothing. It is not up to him to do anything. He will sit here and wait.

Across the street is a bar, its window filling with a watery grey light, a couple of shadows moving about in its gloom. He thinks of going in for a drink, of sitting at the window and watching the distant corner from there. But he does not want a drink. And anyway, Karl would not see him in there. He wants Karl to see him. Karl will stop when he sees him, and then approach him and sit down. And Robert, after a long pause, will say something angry. Something memorable, something so fucking precise and to the point and perfect, that it will cover everything, and that will be that. There will be no need for anything else to be said. Then Karl will realise what has been going on, and he will feel in his heart what Robert feels, and he will apologise, and they will sort it out.

Robert considers what he might say. He decides to leave it until the moment. Maybe Karl will speak first. Maybe he will have spent this time on his own considering everything that has happened and not happened, and he will realise what he needs to realise, and he will apologise, and speak about the future and will not need to be told. It should be like that. He should apologise. After all, if he thought for a moment, for even a moment, about why it is he is on his own in the launderette, then he could not possibly fail to realise what the situation is. What the problem is. If he even spent half a minute thinking about what had gone on in the last ten days, about how he had treated Robert, about how he had behaved, about how he had left everything unsaid after all this time, then surely he would realise. Robert had, after all, come all this way. Across Europe. For silence? No. It would not take a lot of figuring out.

If he did not apologise straight away then there would be

something seriously wrong with him. With them. With the whole situation.

Robert will say nothing.

It is not up to him to say anything.

Cars move slowly around the corner where Robert sits. Some drivers look out at him and Robert stares right back. What the hell are you looking at? It pleases him that his aspect, his appearance, his demeanour attracts attention. Damn right. He holds the gaze of those who stare at him.

There are passers-by. Some couples, some in threes and fours, some alone. He does not like the couples who walk in silence. He does not understand them. He does not understand the ones who talk either. Robert knows no German. Except for the few phrases and curses that Karl has taught him. Karl teaches the German first, getting Robert to repeat the words over and over until he has it right, without telling him what it means. Then he reveals it with a laugh – that what Robert has learned to say is in fact 'Fuck yourself in the knee' or 'My penis is a little flower'. You would teach a parrot to say stupid things that way.

Robert does not like the sound of German. You cannot whisper in German. You can only argue and be adamant and stubborn and precise. He does not believe that a German speaker ever has to search for the right word. Karl wants him to learn the language. He will not.

He looks up the street to the distant corner, and keeps looking. He has to turn his head to do it, and he can feel an ache begin in his neck. He thinks of moving around the bench so that he can face Karl directly. But he stays where he is, so that Karl will be unsure whether or not he has been seen. Every figure looks like Karl now. But Karl will be carrying a bag, so he rules out those who carry nothing. Once or twice he is sure that he sees Karl. But it is not Karl. From a distance, strangers can look like Karl. They have his shape and his stride. Robert looks at them and thinks about being with them. Sleeping with them. Arguing with them. Being angry. He looks at them and wishes they could just go back to the apartment and go to bed and hold each other. Then he realises that the person he looks at is not the person he thinks of. It is some German man who does not know anything about him. What does that mean? To be so easily mistaken.

He glances at his watch occasionally. He tries to work out times and distances. He tries to remember how long it had taken the two of them to walk from the apartment to the launderette. It could not have been more than twenty minutes. He calculates in his mind. He takes into account the time they left the apartment and the distance to the launderette and the distance from there to where he now sits and waits and the length of time they had spent together in the launderette before he had walked out, and the length of time that had passed since then and the length of time it might take to wash clothes and bedclothes and tablecloths and the time it would take for them to dry, taking into account what had been completed while he had been there, and he looks at the sky and sniffs the air and decides that it will be as much as another hour before Karl appears.

Robert stands up and sighs and feels the muscles stretch in his legs and walks towards the distant corner. He looks again at his watch and stops. Maybe he is wrong. He feels wrong. Maybe they left the apartment earlier than that. Up the street a woman pulls down shutters on a shop. He turns around and walks back to the bench.

Robert lights a cigarette and stretches out again and turns his head to gaze up the street. The light is fading. Shadowy Germans move around against the background of grey walls and buildings like figures in old film. The only colour is in the sky. He does not like this place. Not the bench on the corner, not the street, not the city. It goes on and on and on as if nothing can stop it or split it or shame it. Or kill it. It spreads like a stain with no centre and no heart. It is all shadows and old films. Here is where this happened, and here is where that happened, and here is where this voice said that and that voice said this and now there has been so much laid down here that it is impossible to take a step without stepping on a shadow. On the long shadows.

*

The night before, they had gone to a bar in Kreuzberg, a bar curiously inconspicuous on a quiet street. Karl had sat there watching Robert, waiting for him to be impressed. Robert had not been impressed. He had noticed that all the gay bars which they had visited in the city had about them a kind of grim, bored utilitarian aspect. He did not know if that was the way of things in the city, or whether these kinds of places were to Karl's taste. One was for leather, another for younger gays, another for older, another for young gays who liked older gays. Most had cruising in mind, with dark rooms and videos. Others concentrated on music or drugs or drinking.

This one, it seemed to Robert, though now virtually empty, might, when full, be dedicated entirely to bitching. It was a gaudy, depressing place, without atmosphere or imagination. Silver glittered stars and moons and baubles hung from the matt black ceiling, reflecting endlessly in the mirrors that cluttered up the walls. Between and above and below the mirrors hung black and white photos of movie stars and body-builders. The bar counter itself was veiled in a bead curtain and lit from below by a dull red neon, giving the barmen the look of embarrassed corpses. A circular bed with bright pillows and cushions occupied a raised platform by the window. It seemed that nobody was allowed near the bed, surrounded as it was by the kind of red rope which is found holding back the public in museums and galleries. The furniture was wooden and old and painted black. The centrepiece was, of course, a fountain. A rather dazed-looking cherub stood holding a large drooping leaf in his outstretched arm, from which the water trickled down into a dirty pool lit pink and blue and studded with coins and bottletops.

'What do you think?' asked Karl, adding, after the shortest of pauses, 'It's great, isn't it?'

'It is, yeah.'

'It is.'

'Great,' said Robert, as enthusiastically as he could and overdoing it.

Karl frowned at him and drank from his bottle. Robert lit a cigarette.

At a table in the corner two men sat talking animatedly, loudly, laughing with shoulders that went up and down as if they were only pretending to laugh. Robert looked at them and tried to work out what they were talking about, even roughly. But he could not. The words blurred into each other and every barked-out sentence sounded like an order to shoot. This way to the showers. *Achtung*.

A barman leaned on the counter, his head hooded by beads, writing on a postcard. At a small table by the fountain a black man with blond hair and torn jeans stared into the water. Three men and a woman watched him and whispered to each other. A man coming out of the toilets caught Robert's eye and smiled. Robert smiled back.

'I must ring Elsa,' Karl said.

'What, now?'

'Yeah. Can you see a phone?'

'Why now?'

'I said we'd meet up with her later.'

'Oh.'

He wanted to ask why. He wanted to ask Karl why he had said that they'd meet up later. Why did they have to meet up later? Why Elsa? Why again? Why couldn't they spend just one night together, without meeting anyone? But all he said was 'Oh.'

Karl went to the bar and spoke to the barman with the postcard, who pointed towards the front door. Robert thought that he was directing Karl to a telephone on the street, but then he saw Karl stand into an alcove at the end of the bar near the door and scrunch his shoulder to his neck to grip the receiver and reach into his pocket.

Elsa spoke very little English. She and Karl spoke in German. Then they would turn to Robert and speak in English. Then they spoke in German.

A man came into the bar from the street and the black man by the fountain stood up and they said something to each other and embraced and kissed. The man who had come in went to the bar and bought two bottles of beer and came back and sat down next to the black man. They started talking. Robert thought it strange to hear a black man speak German. It worried him, as earlier that day he had been worried by a playground full of blond kids ordering each other out of the sand-pit and into the swings. *Himmel. Gott in Himmel.*

The man who had come in suddenly got up and walked over. He stood by the table and looked at Robert and smiled. He opened his mouth and spoke.

'*Pllggtgfur?*' he seemed to say.

Robert stared at him. He widened his eyes and his head jerked a little.

'*Tlugerggtfur?*' It was like a spit. An operatic spit.

The man looked at Robert and shrugged and looked around as if for assistance. He was embarrassed. He leaned down, precisely, as if giving a small bow, and in a very loud voice, with his eyes on Robert's eyes, he fired out a string of clipped metallic words as if he thought that Robert was perhaps deaf, or retarded. Or foreign. Robert raised his hands and displayed them, palms outward, and shook his head.

'I don't speak German.'

Then Karl appeared at the man's shoulder, sighing. He leaned over the table and stuck his hand into Robert's shirt pocket and took out his lighter and handed it to the man and said something that sounded apologetic. The man laughed and went back to his table where he lit a cigarette for the black man and for himself. Then he handed the lighter back to Robert and said something else and laughed again.

Karl sat down and drank from his bottle and shook his head slowly.

'What?' said Robert.

'What what?'

'What are you looking at me like that for?'

'He asked you for a light.'

'Well, I know that now.'

'But I told you that one. You have that one learned.'

'I have not. I hadn't a clue what he was on about. I thought he wanted to see my papers.'

192

Karl frowned.

'Is that your only joke?'

'What?'

'Whenever anyone says anything you go on about the fucking war. It's really pathetic. Why don't you try and learn something?'

'You have to understand the way I am, *mein Herr*.'

'That's your other joke. Cabaret is your other joke.'

'I do what I can – inch by inch – step by step – mile by mile – man by man.'

Robert hummed quietly and lit another cigarette and glanced at the couple by the fountain. The black man spoke and moved his hands and his eyes and the muscles of his face, and the other man nodded and made small noises, '*Ja, ja, ja*', engrossed.

'What did Elsa say?'

'We're meeting her at eleven.'

'Where?'

'Outside the theatre.'

Robert could think of nothing else to ask.

At the airport, they had smiled and fumbled an embrace and spoken at the same time. They had travelled across the city in a bus. In the first silence Karl had asked how long Robert was going to stay. Two weeks he said. Then the second silence fell. A week or more had passed since then, and the silences had grown and grown.

Robert drank and looked at Karl, at the dark hair that fell over his forehead and which he brushed back with a new gesture, learned in the time he had spent in the city. His city. He had slept with men here. Robert knew that. They had spoken about it, in a way, and Robert had claimed to have slept with men at home, when he had not. He looked now at Karl's hands and felt inside his chest a strange feeling, like a flood of something.

'Diddley de de dee – two ladies', he hummed.

Karl smiled at him and shook his head again.

'Another beer?'

'Yeah, okay.'

Karl stepped across the floor of the bar with their two empty bottles. He leaned on the counter and spoke to the barman, who smiled as he opened two new bottles, and then put them on the counter and held the bases of the bottles while Karl clutched the necks. They stood like that for a moment, the barman talking, and Robert looked at them and felt the flood inside him rise and felt himself breathless as he saw the back of Karl's body. It was as if he saw it from a great distance, but clearly. It was as if he was not meant to see it. As if it had nothing to do with him. But he had made love to that body only hours before. He had lain down beside it and had matched its length with the shape of his own body, and they had dozed in the sunlight that streamed through the yellow sheet that served as a curtain and was better than any curtain could be. But here, in the bar, the body was different, like a version of Karl that he could not understand because it was not directed towards him, or because he did not know its language. And it was that which was closed to him that caused the flood.

He turned away and swallowed and waited to be told what things meant.

'The barman says that it doesn't really get lively here until ten or so.'

'Oh.'

'And we'll be off to meet Elsa by then.'

'We will, yes.'

'What's wrong with you?'

There was no concern in the question, just impatience.

'Nothing's wrong with me.'

'You're sullen.'

Robert drank.

'Talk to me,' said Karl.

'What?'

'Talk to me.'

'About what?'

'Talk to me. Talk to me.'

'Stop it. I am talking to you.'

194

'No you're not. Entertain me. Charm me. Make me like you. Talk to me.'

'What do you mean? You don't like me?'

'Not at this very moment, no. You're being very boring.'

Robert frowned as severely as he could and in his head he prepared a sentence about how it should not be necessary for him to entertain Karl. That was not what a relationship like theirs should be about.

'I . . .'

'Talk to me,' interrupted Karl.

'I . . .'

'Talk to me. Talk to me. Talk to me. Talk to me. Talk to me.'

'I'm your guest,' said Robert quietly. 'I'm the one on holiday. You have to talk to me.'

Karl shook his head.

'I'm fed up talking to you. I do all the talking. Ever since you've arrived I don't think you've started a single conversation. So I'm tired and I'm not going to say a thing.'

Robert sipped his beer.

'How's Elsa?' he asked.

'She's fine.'

Robert nodded and drank.

'Talk to me.'

Robert put down the bottle.

'Talk to me.'

He looked around and saw the black man glance at them.

'How far is it from here to the theatre?' he asked.

'I don't know. Talk to me properly.'

'What's properly?'

'Talk to me.'

'About what?'

'Talk to me. Talk to me. Talk to me.' His voice was like a clock. There was a look on his face that might have been amusement or might have been hate. Robert could not tell.

'I think you must . . .' he began.

'Talk . . .'

'You must have been a real little fucker of a kid,' Robert

said, and Karl smiled. 'Horrible. Nasty. I think you must have caused your parents all kind of grief. Were you very obnoxious?'

'I was,' laughed Karl.

'A real little brat I'd say. A noisy little monster. Answered back all the time. Annoyed all the adults. Hung out of sleeves moaning about everything.'

'I did.'

'I knew it. You learn some manners, young man. Did they ever say that to you – learn some manners? They called you "young man" all the time, didn't they? Called you "young man" and told you that if you didn't behave you'd be sent to your room. That shut you up. Being sent to your room was hell. There was no one there to annoy.'

Karl smiled. He leaned across the table and spoke softly.

'You see,' he said, and touched Robert's hand. 'That didn't hurt, did it? You can do it when you want to, you know.'

Waiting on the bench at the corner, Robert tries to cling to his anger as if it is a balloon whose string runs through his fingers. He feels it slipping. It is quite dark now, all the cars have their headlights on, lighting his face briefly from different angles. He peers into the distance and peers at his watch, not at all sure now of his calculations, or of the assumptions he has made. He feels a rising unease. Surrounded by the unfamiliar. Robert on his bench. The cars and their lights seem to threaten him, their engines become louder, their beams fix on his face.

A sudden shouting starts behind him, a rough voice barks out cluttered German, tumbling over itself with aggression and hostility. Robert stiffens. He feels his back like a bow. The voice comes closer and is joined now by another, just as loud, a laugh contained in it like a cough. He thinks of standing up and walking off, but before he can move he is aware of two figures stepping up on to the bench behind him, boots hitting the wood with a thud that he feels in his thighs. They come around the seat in a circle on either side of him, like two arms. Pincer movement, they call it. He is frozen, not knowing what to do, thinking that perhaps it would be best not to look. But he is aware of the boots, like Doc Marten boots, and he is aware of the pause, and of the moment of quiet that comes when they see him, and of the closeness of them, and of their physical shape, distinct as a cut. He feels them near him like a charge in the air. Then they jump down and walk ahead where he can see them.

They are skinheads. They walk backwards, looking at him, curious. Their jeans are tight against their skinny bodies. They wear short jackets with zips. One has a tattoo of a hammer over an ear. They speak to each other and Robert knows that they are talking about him. One of them nudges the other and turns away. But his friend continues to walk backwards, staring. Robert knows he should look away. But he cannot. They are standing now at the roadside waiting to cross, one facing one way, one the other. Robert does not move. They wait for a gap in the traffic. The one who looks at him is the one with the tattoo. He has a dog collar around his neck and his nose is pierced. He shouts something. The other one turns his head. Robert looks at them blankly. The one facing him takes a step forward and shouts the same thing again. He jerks his head. His friend turns back towards the road, sees that it is clear and begins to cross, shouting something impatiently.

Robert looks at the man in front of him. He is young. He moves closer to Robert. He is a tall thin creature with eyebrows cut darkly across the surface of his skull. His hands are stuck half way into his pockets and Robert notices some kind of symbol on the back of one of them. The right. Robert sits stock still, believing that the slightest movement will provoke an attack. He plays dumb. Dead. He does not move or speak because he believes that if he is given away as a foreigner or as a queer he will be beaten. Better to appear stupid, mad. If he keeps his mouth shut and does not move then the skinhead will be uncertain. He might even think that Robert holds some kind of threat. They stare at each other. After a moment there is an impatient shout from across the road. The skinhead mutters something and spits, and then says to Robert the same thing that he has said before. It sounds like contempt, like a dismissal. Robert takes it in and does not move. The skinhead spits again, mutters, and then turns suddenly and runs after his friend, shouting and laughing, disappearing behind the flashing cars.

Robert breathes. He breathes deeply, closing his eyes and shuddering slightly, relief sweating from his body. It is cold on his bench.

With his head back he smiles a little, trying to remember the sound of what the skinhead had shouted at him. He will repeat it to Karl, find out what it means. He says it to himself a few times, then says it out loud. It sounds close. He looks towards the corner. There is no sign. He looks in the direction the skinheads have gone, wondering what they had thought of him, sitting there in the dark. It was lucky that one of them had seemed in a hurry, that they had been on their way somewhere. If they had been bored, nothing to do, well . . .

Karl.

Suddenly he sees Karl and is confused.

Karl is walking past on the other side of the street, directly opposite Robert. He has come the wrong way. He is not looking at Robert. He is walking by slowly, one hand in his jacket pocket, the other holding the bag, his head down. The bag is heavy. He has not seen Robert.

Robert watches him for a moment, considering. He will have to go after him. Fuck. He stands up and walks slowly away from his bench, watching Karl. He quickens his pace suddenly, thinking that perhaps he can overtake Karl and wait again somewhere further on. But it is too short a distance to the apartment and Karl will see him. Fuck. He slows down again.

It annoys him. It does more than annoy him. All his preparation has been for nothing. Now he feels humiliated and slightly panicked, as if it is he who is in the wrong, he who will have to apologise, uncertain of the response.

What will he do now? He will have to call out to Karl, stop him in the street, approach him. Or else follow behind him all the way back to the apartment. But he will have to attract his attention before he disappears inside. Robert has no key.

He cannot think.

He watches Karl on the other side of the street, slightly ahead of him. Karl looks at his watch and runs his hand through his hair. He swings around suddenly and Robert stops. But Karl still does not see him. He is checking the traffic. He crosses the road at an angle and arrives on Robert's side, some fifty yards ahead, his back to him. Again, his back.

Robert whistles, surprising himself. He cannot whistle. This is stupid. Shit. He whistles again, feebly. Karl does not hear, does not turn around. Robert walks a little faster, comes closer and whistles again. Karl swings around, nothing on his face. He looks at Robert for a moment, and Robert, to his disgust, feels a smile crawl to the surface. He tries to stop it, twisting it into a grimace. He thinks he sees Karl roll his eyes upwards as he turns around again, but he isn't sure. Karl walks on towards the apartment, his head down, and Robert follows, no anger left, just the biting of the bottom lip, and the panic that he has done wrong and cannot make it right.

By the time they turn on to the street where Karl lives, Robert is at his shoulder. He can say nothing. Karl opens the street door and goes in. He holds it open for Robert without looking back. They walk through the front building and into the courtyard, lit only by the light from the windows which face on to it. A woman comes out of the back house and smiles at Karl. He stops to talk to her. Robert feels stupid, standing at Karl's shoulder with his silly grin, not understanding a word. The woman looks at him and smiles. She asks him a question. Before Robert can react, Karl says something to her and they both laugh. She turns towards the front house and walks away, still laughing.

'What did she say to me?' asks Robert as they go up the stairs.

Karl stops and turns, two steps above Robert. He looks down.

'She asked where the fuck you've been.'

He does not wait for a response. He turns and continues up the stairs.

Inside the flat Karl moves about, putting away clothes,

lighting the stove, tidying the kitchen, saying nothing. Robert follows him, talking, making no sense. Karl's silence frightens him. He does not know the edges of it.

'Say something, for Christ's sake!'

'I've nothing to say.'

Karl lights a cigarette and sits at the kitchen table. Robert does the same.

'I'm sorry I walked out like that. I needed to. You were treating me very badly, you know, like you didn't want me there.'

Karl stubs out the cigarette with a single swift movement and an angry look, and gets up from the table. He goes towards the bathroom.

'I don't know what you expect from me,' says Robert, going after him.

'Oh, don't be ridiculous,' says Karl from behind the door. 'I expected you to stay and help me dry the fucking clothes.'

'That's not what I mean.'

'You don't mean anything. You mean nothing.'

'What's that supposed to mean?'

'Mean, mean, mean. Everything's meant to mean something with you.'

'I think we should talk.'

'We are talking. I don't want to talk.'

Robert smokes his cigarette, walking back to the kitchen.

'I'm the one who's meant to be angry, you know.'

'What?'

He looks around the kitchen, at the cartoons in German stuck up on the wall which he does not understand, at the German magazines which he does not understand. He does not understand the words on the milk carton, or on his packet of cigarettes. He does not understand the titles of the books on the window-sill.

He puts out his cigarette and wanders around Karl's apartment. In the bedroom the bedclothes are lying on the floor, not quite dry. He thinks about putting them back on the bed anyway, but you need two people to do it, to slip the elasticated corners over the mattress, to smooth it out, to get the cover on the duvet. He puts the pillowcases back on the pillows and sits on the edge of the bed, tired and unsure. He wants to lie down and sleep, wake up somewhere else. He feels that he should make some kind of decision, think things through. He doesn't know how to start. Everything seems vastly complicated, obscure. He thinks suddenly that he can leave, that he will leave. In the morning.

He stands up and walks to the bathroom door.

'I'm going home in the morning,' he shouts. There is no reply.

He goes back to the bedroom and finds his suitcase and begins to pack. He has everything in before he realises that he needs clothes for the morning. He opens the case again and takes out things that are close to hand.

Karl appears in the doorway and watches for a moment.

'You can't go in the morning. You haven't a flight booked.'

'I don't even know why I'm here. Do you?'

Karl is silent for a moment. Then he comes into the room and sits on the bed.

'I asked you.'

'Why?'

'I missed you.'

'You regret it now, though, don't you?'

'No.'

Robert looks at Karl and does not believe him.

'I'll get a ticket at the airport.'

'It'll cost a fortune.'

'I have credit cards.'

Karl sighs.

'Sleep on it, will you?'

Robert looks up at him, wondering.

'I mean, you're overreacting a little,' Karl continues, smiling now. 'You're being a bit dramatic. We've had a fight. It doesn't mean you have to go running to the airport.'

'I'm not running.'

'Well, just forget about it. We'll talk tomorrow. I'm tired. We'll fix up the bed and get some sleep, okay?'

Robert is still for a moment and then he nods slowly. He

remembers that he has been angry, but he cannot remember why. It is gone from him and he cannot follow it. Karl stands, and as he walks out of the room he trails his hand across Robert's shoulders. There is forgetfulness in the touch. And a small request. That is always the way. They will sleep. Tomorrow they will go on. In a few days they will have nothing left of each other.

They tidy up the bedroom, put away clothes, fix the bed. Karl makes tea and they drink a mug each and smoke, saying very little. What they do say is gentle, inconsequential. Eventually they climb into bed and lie together in the dark. Robert stares at the ceiling, trying to stop himself from thinking, from going over the evening again and again. He can hear Karl's breathing slowing down, relaxing. He does not want to disturb him, but he cannot help turning on his side and laying his head on Karl's chest. Karls cups him in his arm and breathes.

'I waited for you on the bench at the corner. You didn't see me.'

'No,' replies Karl, sleepily.

'There were these two skinheads . . .'

He tries to remember what they had said.

'What does "*Get ess eenen gut*" mean?'

'*Geht es ihnen Gut?*'

'Yeah, that's it.'

'It means "Are you all right?"'

'Oh.'

Robert closes his eyes. In the darkness as they drift out of the world he holds on to Karl and he does not let him go.

Charles Tomlinson

MORNING

When we open the curtains,
will it be white or wet?
Will it (remembered) blaze back at us,
or shall we then forget

the grey irresolution
of rain against frost,
the distances melted away
and the far view lost

to a closed-in glance
across sweating flagstones,
catching what little light there is,
what wine-dark tones?

The choice is not ours to make,
so we await the chance
of weather's looming, loosening
in its long advance

up the valley reaches
and straight at our panes,
not to be predicted, contradicted:
let us draw back the curtains.

THE SISTERS

(Recalling the Westminster Piano Trio:
Shostakovich Op. 67)

This is not music for the wedding.
The Hasidim are dancing on their graves.
Muted in its highest register,
The cello mourns, and the passacaglia
Paces through one burial the more,
Notes sounding up out of the darkness as
The bare arms circle their instruments
Hacking the downbows, stroke on stroke. How young
They seemed, wielding the weapons of the music,
Burdened by a time they had not lived through,
Yet recognising the lineaments of its sorrow
And the severe exactness art had called them to.

John Hartley Williams

ON VAUXHALL STATION, I THINK OF SHIRTS

A slow train comes. Doors stand open
to the light. Beneath a poster
                    of a man in mirror sunglasses,
(bare to his waist), the platform
is an ironing board.

The train is an iron.
Life is a shirt.
            What follows
are my weird rules
for pressing:

1. If you're not the signal, you're
                        reading it.
2. Do not stand too close to the edge.
3. Do not stand too far away.
4. Continue reading.

The man in blue jeans
assaults me with his
            homo-erotic leer.
He's beginning to lose face.
Pollution is scrubbing him out.

In the stopped train
are men in suits, England's virtues,
                    with crooked elbows
to hang umbrellas in. They do
the crossword with a straight pen.

At fifty, they've learned
to enjoy the silent maracas
          of their bones,
how to dance
the hush-hush skeleton tango.

If this train started,
& scandal jolted her leg
          against them,
over points, & she
brushed closer, whispering

in the entrance
to a tunnel, that moment when,
          the lights gone out,
a shock pitches her to them,
soft as a thought, they'd get the clue.

But they wouldn't show it.
The train hums quietly to itself,
          not leaving.
I do a step from side to side
in the patient shuffle of waiting.

I think
of a woman in a shirt-shop
          fingering someone's neck
as if it were marble, smiling
blindly into the face of a customer.

The unworn shirts
of the dead rustle
          under cellophane,
& a kaleidoscope of stripes
that shiver and seethe.

Then loudspeakers rip open
the still packet of the quietness,

           names pulled out like electric pins
in a rich cascade
of incomprehensible destination –

& far off down the track, another train
comes silent up the line. I don't know
                    where it's going,
but when it stops I stretch my arms out wide
& slip into the armholes of the afternoon.

Penelope Shuttle

GOD

Green sea and blue heaven.
Hot sun and cool tree.

The complete silence of Me
reflecting on my faults.

My faults?
I sit beside them, no more, no less.

They coil and doze and bask,
half-shadow, half-snake.

While the blue heaven
and the green sea

continue to provide Me
with the ideal weather of antiquity.

C. K. Stead

BRIGHTNESS FALLS FROM THE AIR

THE SNOW HAS come back. Henry knew it this morning before getting up and looking out – 'sensed' it; which means, he supposes, that his waking eyes registered the different light, its whiteness.

And Albie has gone again. That too Henry knew while he lay there, because the silence that comes with the other-worldly light of the fallen snow was undisturbed by the poet's frantic work at the typewriter in the next room.

Now, looking out through a window, Henry is watching a cat making its way through the snow, which comes up to its shoulders. It tries a high-stepping walk; then an intermittent leaping. Henry isn't sure what it's looking for, but he supposes food. It stops to shake itself, disliking the sense that its fur is becoming wet, uncertain now whether to go forward or back.

He wonders why the sight of animals going about their daily business gives such pleasure, and decides it's because what they do exactly matches, in scale, what they need to do, whereas our doings are always an excess. He imagines them taking over when we, the human race, become extinct. They must be kin, he thinks, or there would be no pleasure in that thought.

During the past couple of days, while Albie bashed away at his typewriter and raced in and out to the kitchen and to the bench press on the cold front porch, Henry has observed the squirrels. There was no sign of snow then, and they darted about the campus lawns digging for buried nuts. Though the cold out there was intense even in the sun, it was as if spring must be just around the corner. But yesterday, while the sky was blue and the sun continued to shine, the squirrels' demeanour changed. They knew something Henry didn't know. They were anxious, and not for food. They hung upside-down on the boughs and trunks of trees, stripping bark and running up to repair their nests. This morning they're gone, hiding away in those newly patched interiors, and all down the Jersey Shore the snow is falling.

There is no sky, just a low grey blankness out of which the flakes sail like an invasion of paratroopers; and the brightness seems to come, not down from above, but up from below. Light has taken on substantial form. It has broken up and is tumbling out of the heavens. Still shining, it covers lawns and paths; heaps up on hedges, statues, fences, gates; on outdoor chairs and tables. It piles up along branches, and falls from them in sudden, splintering showers. Soon the ploughs will be out to clear the road, and the shovels will attack paths and sidewalks. But for now it comes thick and fast and lies undisturbed.

Henry – Professor Henry Bulov – turns on Woodlake's 'Memory Station' which plays 'the greatest music of all time', by which is meant the popular songs of the 1940s, '50s and '60s. He begins to make breakfast and then, feeling the need of company, changes his mind, puts on overcoat, scarf, gloves, hat, and walks to the campus dining-room where the nuns will smile and urge him to eat more, to keep warm, to look after himself.

That over, he will wait for the ploughs and shovels to do their work before walking the mile or so to the supermarket. There's nothing he needs there, but it's somewhere to go. Meanwhile, there is the latest batch of poems Albie has given him to read – more of the same he has read and reread this past fortnight. By now Henry knows what to expect. They will be sharp, pictorial, 'Japanesy', occasionally witty, now and then gritty. But where has the grand sweep gone, the larger scale? Where are the Modernist ambulations, the parodic dislocations of the post-Modern? What has become of the great Canadian epic-maker and courage-teacher, delineator of northern wastes, servant of the mythical White Queen, poet-father of the Snow Maiden? Where among all these miniaturist nail-parings is the majesty that was Alban Ashtree?

Crunching through the dry snow, up to his ankles in it, Henry says over to himself lines from a seventeenth-century poet whose name eludes him, and wonders whether they have sprung to mind because of the snow or because of the decline of a once major poet:

> *Brightness falls from the air,*
> *Queens have died young and fair,*
> *Lord, have mercy upon us.*

But this is a story, and we must go back two weeks to take up the thread.

Henry Bulov, recently appointed full professor by his university in New Zealand, arrived at JFK with his modest and battered baggage and was met at the foot of the escalator below the American Airlines desk by a Gofar Limo driver holding up a sign with a version of his name he hadn't encountered before:

PROF BELOVE

He shook hands with the driver and they joked about the mistake. Henry told him about the fax from Woodlake College saying he would be met by a representative of the Gofar Limp Company.

There was a sixty-mile drive south to Woodlake. Henry sat in the back and pretended to read papers, pretended to sleep, did sleep – but not before he had had his views of the Manhattan skyline across water in the fading light, and seen the Staten Island 'hills' that were really New York's garbage mountains. When he woke it was dark and they were somewhere in the State of New Jersey, pulling in at the doors of a restaurant built out over a river or tidal inlet.

Ashtree, known now as Albie Strong, met him at the door. It was their first encounter, and the greetings were loud and enthusiastic, the smiles broad, the handshakes strong.

'We're dining alone,' Albie explained. 'There are things I have to get straight with you.'

There were indeed. The circumstances of Henry's invitation had been mysterious – not surprisingly since it was generally understood that the poet Alban Ashtree was dead, killed (though the body had never been recovered) in an avalanche in the Austrian Alps. It was a death which had always given Henry anxiety. It lacked the sense of perfect closure that ought to accompany a genuine demise. There was an air of fiction, even of contrivance, about it. It had been too good to be true – iconologically apt (Ashtree was poet and theorist of the Snow White Goddess), and lexically perfect, the author's name piling up in alliteration with place and event. 'Alban Ashtree,' Henry's book on him began, 'died in an avalanche in the Austrian Alps.' It had been the easiest sentence to write and the hardest to believe. Even the Canada Council, afflicted by doubts, had frozen the funds set aside for the posthumous editing of Ashtree's work.

But this uncertainty had only added to the aura surrounding Ashtree's name and his poetry. The man for so long known only in his own country was soon being talked about in New York and in London. Two years after his 'death' the work, previously published only in Canada, was available everywhere in English, and translations into several European languages were appearing or planned. And Henry Bulov, the first non-Canadian to write seriously about Ashtree, and the only person (no one knew how this had come about) to have read his private notebooks, had found the academic escalator, for so long stalled beneath his feet, all at once lurching on up to full professorial status.

Bulov had helped to make Ashtree famous; Ashtree's fame had helped to make Bulov respectable. These two, it seemed, needed one another; and now, improbably ('It's like a story,'

Henry said, as they gave up the handshaking and embraced one another), here they were meeting for dinner in a New Jersey restaurant that looked out over moonlit waters.

Albie (as he asked to be called) was a tall, well-constructed fifty-two-year-old with a good head of grey hair tied back in a pony-tail. He wore jeans, boots, a shirt of red corduroy, and a leather jacket. He talked fast, ate fast, seemed impatient, but also excited to be meeting the critic who had done so much to promote his work and his reputation.

The Austrian avalanche, he told Henry, had been real. He had been taken up by it, swept down the mountain slope, and then, by some miracle, or quirk of the rolling snow, had been ejected – cast out on to a ridge from which he had been able to make his way down to a village on the lower slopes. He was bewildered, slightly concussed, and it was some hours before he recovered his sense of who and where he was. By that time the news was everywhere. Seven were missing, four already confirmed dead.

With the least possible fuss he returned to his ski lodge, where he had gone unaccompanied, removed a few essentials, and departed, leaving gear by which he could be identified. Next day, from a village further down the mountain he rang two newspapers, one in Toronto, the other in Vancouver, to report the death of the poet Alban Ashtree. It was meant only to bring him a little attention, but the story ran all across Canada, from east to west, from west to east, its authenticity never seeming to be checked. Though for a time he travelled on his own passport, and drew on his own bank account, no one appeared to notice. As far as the Canadian literary and academic community were concerned the fact was established: Alban Ashtree the poet had died in that avalanche.

During what remained of his sabbatical year Ashtree's fame spread, promoted especially by an article Henry Bulov wrote for the *Times Literary Supplement*. Unused to his work receiving the kind of attention he always believed it deserved, Albie now found the condition of being dead difficult to give up. Casually at first, and then, as time passed, purposefully, he contrived a new life for himself, one which allowed him to keep his death alive. This involved difficulties and sacrifices. Posing as a former anti-Vietnam defector-to-Canada whose previous identity had to remain undisclosed, he had been able to get a teaching post in a minor, though well-endowed, Catholic college. But he was not able to profit by, or to enjoy (except as an observer), Alban Ashtree's increasing fame. Part of him wanted to reclaim it as his own; a more cautious self recognised that to 'come back' might be to lose it.

'I'm like the lover on the Grecian urn,' he told Henry. 'He lives for ever because he's a work of art. But because he's a work of art he's not flesh and blood – he can't kiss the girl.'

But was he intending to stay dead for ever? – that was what Henry needed to know. He put the question in a way which sounded odd even as he said it: 'Will you ever come back to life?'

Ashtree smiled. 'It's a hard one, Henry. If I do, there's going to be hell to pay. A massive critical backlash, wouldn't you say? That's why there have to be new poems first, and they have to be good.'

What he impressed on Henry during that first meeting was that in the meantime his real identity must remain secret. It was not known to anyone – not to Woodlake College which employed him; not even to the woman in his life, Joy Gates, also a teacher at the college. During the past few years Albie Strong had acquired a modest reputation as a poet of the Jersey Shore. Woodlake College had issued two small collections of his new work. He gave readings, poetry workshops, was interviewed on local radio and written about in the local papers.

'No one connects my work with Ashtree's,' he explained. 'The new stuff is different. Smaller in scale.' There was a look of uncertainty as he said this. 'Tighter. Closer to the knuckle.'

After a short silence, which Henry couldn't think how to plug, Albie murmured, 'Hopefully.'

Henry was to share Albie's house on the edge of the campus. He was to read the new work, comment on it, prepare for a time when it might seem right to reveal that the two poets,

Alban Ashtree and Albie Strong, were one; but he was to say
nothing until Albie gave the word, which might be soon or
might be years away. It was possible even that it might have
to wait until he died – in which case Henry would be named as
his literary executor. This was something they would discuss.
Together they would arrive at a strategy.

'I need someone to tell me how I'm going with my work,'
Albie said when the meal was eaten and they were sitting over
their decafs. 'You're the critic I can trust, Henry. The only
one.' Again there was that uncertain look, but also a glimmer
of courage. 'You have to give it to me straight, man.'

In the days since that first meeting Henry has begun to
understand why Albie's confidence is less than perfect. With
his real name and nation has gone, it seems, his real strength
as a poet. Away from Canada and the northern wastes that
were his inspiration, Alban Ashtree's talent has shrivelled. As
poet of the Jersey Shore, he is Samson after the haircut. What
remains of his former strength is a sort of sad afterglow.

So the visit, embarked on with such enthusiasm, has turned
into a trial of character for Henry. Should he be truthful, and
if so when? When a poet says, 'You have to give it to me
straight, man,' is he to be taken at his word? Even if he means
it, that's not to say he won't react badly when he gets it. And
wouldn't the truth be like a death sentence? It would be saying
in effect, 'Don't come back to life if you want Alban Ashtree's
reputation to continue.'

But there are more immediate problems for Henry. Albie
is not easy to share a house with. More precisely, Albie is
extremely difficult to share anything with. All day, when he's
not teaching, he sits at a desk in his room, hammering away
at an old-fashioned typewriter in furious bursts interspersed
with long silences and occasional eruptions of swearing, or
singing, or muttering, or laughing – the last a kind of dark
laughter, more sinister than the swearing and muttering.
Albie, Henry writes in the journal he is keeping, is a sort
of Glenn Gould of the lexical keyboard.

At intervals of about half an hour the poet jumps from his

chair and rushes either to the front porch or to the kitchen. On the porch he has set up his bench press and weights. The lifting is accompanied by huge orgasmic groans and sighs. When the rush is to the kitchen he fills a bowl with fat-free granola and a fat-free fruit yoghurt drink, downs it at speed, and returns to his room and his desk. There are no regular meals, but if Henry wants them he can take them at the university dining-room.

'This is better than my old regimen,' Albie explains, leaning against the door-jamb of Henry's room while he spoons out the last of a bowlful. 'Before Joy I only used to eat every second day. The starvation days were hell. You wouldn't have liked living with me then.'

Albie works till late, then unfolds an ironing board and stands at it while he watches a replay of the old *Star Trek* series. He irons not only shirts and handkerchiefs, but underclothes, sheets, pillowcases, towels – everything. When there's nothing left, he re-irons clothes already done. The ironing, Henry has come to realise, is only because Albie needs something to do, can't sit still while watching.

Then he takes sleeping pills, puts a rolled towel across his bedroom door, and turns on what he calls 'radio static', a sort of white noise, to drown out all external sound. When Henry gets up in the night to go to the bathroom he hears that strange loud continuous hissing coming from Albie's bedroom.

Fortunately Albie is not there all the time. There are days and nights when, as now, he is at Joy Gates's house, twenty miles away in a town called Brick. Then Henry has only to cope with the loneliness of the little suburban house at the edge of the campus, a house in which the furnishings and pictures provided by the nuns, sober, dull, proper, self-abnegating (and including by way of uplift only a golden Christ on a midnight-blue cross over the living-room door), fight a Cold War with the items Albie has introduced – a Tiffany lampshade over an art deco dining-table in black glass on a red central column; a shiny red plastic wall-hanging representing an English telephone box; an Algonquian shield and spear; several big-faced 1940s electric clocks advertising dairy products, motor oil, piston rings; a white sofa with red cushions; a telephone in transparent plastic which lights up in blue when it rings; a print from the Utamaro brothel series. Slowly the sensibility of Albie is winning its interior décor war against the pale restraining hands of the Sisters of Mercy, but there are battles yet to be fought and in the meantime no truce is in prospect. The Joseph House, as it is called, is not a house of peace.

Henry leaves it to walk to the supermarket. By now the ploughs have done their work on the roads, and the pavements are partly cleared, but patches of ice make the going on foot slow and dangerous. Up and down the street men are out with shovels. Without exception they are dressed in black with broad-brimmed hats, some with a long lock of hair trailing somewhere over face or neck. These are Hasidic Jews, and the suburb is full of them. Their wives wear wigs so their hair will not be seen by strangers, their children are innumerable, their cars are large old station-wagons with many dents, and their lawns are covered with plastic toys in bright colours sticking up like wreckage through the whiteness of the snow. The Hasidim are devoted to prayer and propagation, but also (Albie's *Random House Dictionary* informs Henry) to joy. Their responses to his morning greetings, however, are mostly grim and formal.

It is almost two miles to the shops – far enough for Henry's ears to feel the cold painfully. He buys fruit and cheese and chocolate and wine. At the liquor store he checks his ticket in the New Jersey lottery. He has not won a prize; but the storekeeper tells him there is a huge jackpot coming.

By now the ears have thawed and he is ready for the long march back.

Joy Gates, the woman in Albie's life, is a glamorous, energetic divorcée, a woman in her forties who wins Henry's approval not by cleverness (though she may well be clever, and probably is) nor by charm (though he's quite sure she could charm if she chose), but simply by smiling. Joy's smile is warm, wry, and self-sufficient. It seems to come from good

217

health, acceptance, and an inner electrical charge. No doubt, Henry reflects, it could be defeated, but the circumstances would have to be dire – flood, famine or slaughter.

Joy seems, in her egocentric way, to love her poet and to do all she can to promote his work. She doesn't live with him, however, except overnight, or sometimes for two nights on end, and Henry understands why. No one, not even Joy Gates, could live for long with Albie and keep smiling.

Today, a Saturday, is Joy's mother's seventy-fifth birthday, and they are to take her to New York to see a matinee performance of a play by Edward Albee, *Three Tall Women*. Joy has ordered a white stretch limo as part of the birthday treat, and it arrives at the Joseph House a few minutes early. Joy's mother, Gay, is already in the car. They will drive next to the town of Brick to pick up Joy and Albie, and then on up to New York. The driver is wearing a suit and bow-tie. 'Do you have boots, sir?' he asks at the door.

Henry says he doesn't need them.

The driver frowns, looking at the path deep in snow. 'I'll try to clear some of this while you're getting ready, sir.'

Henry tells him not to be silly. 'Wait in the car and keep warm.' But when he emerges the driver is waiting on the porch with a golf umbrella. His eagerness, and the size and whiteness of the stretch, which seems at one moment to vanish into the snow, at another to be materialising out of it, signal generous expense. This is something grander than the Gofar Limo Company. Joy is turning it on for her aged parent.

Inside the limo there are two pairs of leather chairs, facing one another. There is a drinks cabinet, and ice. Gay, in furs and a fur hat, has a face that must once have been pure Hollywood and is still glamorous. She introduces herself, they shake hands and he wishes her a happy birthday.

'Happy birthday?' she repeats, puzzled. And then, 'Oh yes. Sure.' She laughs, revealing a perfect bow of upper teeth, all her own.

It is Saturday and the Jews are walking to the synagogue in family clusters, not along the sidewalks, but in the middle of the suburban street where the snow ploughs have made the deepest impression. The men have shed their broad-brims and are wearing immense fur hats out of Russia or central Europe. The limo crawls behind them. When it tries to go around them there are angry shouts and gestures of protest.

When they get out of the Hasidic suburb and on to the highway Gay begins to tell stories about Joy's infancy. 'She didn't creep like other children. At eight months she just got up and walked. Her first words were, "I do it."'

'"I *do* it"?'

'"*I* do it,"' Gay says, putting the emphasis in the right place. 'She was always very independent.'

Yes. Henry can imagine that.

'From the time she was seven,' Gay goes on, 'I never had to manage money. Joy looked after it. When we went shopping, she had the purse. If I bought something, she paid. If I wanted something too expensive she told me I couldn't have it – there wasn't enough in the purse.'

'From the age of seven,' Henry repeats, not disbelieving, but by way of showing that, though his eyes are on the woods and the river and the white, transformed landscape, he is listening.

He is aware that Gay must be a widow. He asks about her husband. 'He was a Sioux,' she tells him. 'A beautiful man with a fine body. He was a pilot.'

'So Joy's father was an Indian . . .' He corrects himself. 'A Native American . . .'

But Gay is shaking her head. 'Joy's father was Samuel. Walter was the Sioux.'

'He was your second husband?'

'My third,' she replies, and then appears uncertain. In any case Henry is not sure whether they are now talking about Samuel or Walter.

'What did he – Joy's father – *do*, so to speak?'

Gay's eyes have gone dreamy with reminiscence. 'He was a beautiful man, a pilot, and I lost him . . .'

But wasn't it the Sioux who was the pilot? He gives it up. 'I've heard good things about this play,' he says.

She sighs, still sad at the thought of Walter. 'Is there an

orange juice in there?' She is pointing to the drinks cabinet. He opens it and finds what she wants, a bottle, up to its neck in ice. 'I won't have it now,' she says. 'Later.'

He pushes it back into the ice. 'Drinks can make you think you need to eat,' Gay says. 'I eat only once a day, in the morning, and it's all I need. It's how I kept slim. Of course,' she acknowledges, 'I'm not so slim now . . .'

She is not slim, it's true, and he lets this invitation to contradict her pass. There is a long thoughtful silence. Snow has begun to drift down again, and now she is telling him what she cooks for that one meal. There are many items, and she explains in what special way each of them is nutritious.

He stops listening. And then, 'Yes,' he hears her say. 'A play. He's a talented boy, isn't he?'

Henry wonders how to deal with this. 'I'm sorry,' he says. 'I drifted off for a moment. Who is talented?'

'Albie.'

'Albie, of course. His poetry . . .'

'His poetry. And now his play.'

His play? Has she confused Albie and Edward Albee? To get it clear which of them is confused, Henry asks, 'What did you say Joy's father did for a living?'

'Samuel,' she says, in a tone both firm and dismissive, 'worked for my father. He was an instructor.'

They are driving now into the town of Brick, and she makes him promise he will not let Joy know that she has told him things about her daughter's infancy. Albie and Joy are waiting at the door of Joy's townhouse.

Before they leave Brick Albie gets the driver to stop at a shop that sells tickets in the lottery. There's a jackpot draw coming that's to be worth at least $35 million. They each put in five dollars. That will give them twenty shots at the pick-six. Albie comes back waving the tickets. 'Thirty-five million among four,' he says. 'I make that eight and a half each, with a million over for a party.'

He stuffs them into his bill-fold.

'I might go on a world cruise,' Gay says. 'I've never been to foreign places.' She stares out at the snow. 'Or maybe Miami.'

'Los Angeles for you, Mom,' Joy says. 'Hollywood. They'll put you straight into a movie. You'll be a star.'

Gay says, 'When I was young that's what everyone told me. "Go to Hollywood," they said. "You've got the looks. You'll be a star."'

'With eight and a half,' Albie says, 'you could be a star without doing the movie. You could just buy yourself a big house in Brentwood . . .'

Gay purrs. 'I'd like that.'

Albie is restless as they drive on. He keeps checking their speed, the distance covered, the time the play is due to start, the state of roads and weather. He takes ice from the drinks cabinet and sucks or chews it, presses it to his wrists and along the back of his neck. As they get nearer to New York Gay becomes excited. It's a long time since she has seen the city, which was once her home. She recognises landmarks – fuel depots, derelict warehouses, refineries, generators, ash heaps, wreckers' yards – greeting them as if they were things of great beauty. When they come out of the tunnel into Manhattan she lowers her window. 'Halloo, New York!' she shouts up at the skyscrapers. 'Hi there, New York! Halloo!'

She turns her face to them, at once smiling and tearful. 'Ah, New York,' she says. 'Isn't it great? And Gene Kelly had to go and die on me. That was a man I would have married.'

The Edward Albee play turns out to be about an unpleasant old woman, attended in the first half by a sadistic nurse and an angry lawyer. These are the three women of the title, and they are named in the programme as A, B and C. There is a lot about A's imperfect control of her bodily functions, and at the end of the act she suffers a stroke. In the second half A, B and C represent A's three selves, old, middle-aged, and young. Her sex-life is recounted – a beautiful teenage experience, unappetising marital sex, and a brief violent affair with a groom in her husband's stables. Throughout this half of the play A, the terminal stroke-victim whose earlier selves these three now represent, lies unconscious in a big bed wearing an oxygen mask.

It is hardly a play to celebrate a woman's seventy-fifth

birthday and Henry feels such embarrassment at what seems like a bad mistake he finds it difficult to concentrate. During the second half he's relieved to see that Gay has fallen asleep. Joy rolls her eyes at him across her mother seated between them, as if to signify that she too is embarrassed. But as they come out of the theatre Gay seems refreshed and cheerful. 'Did you write that about me?' she asks Albie.

'Write what?' he asks; and then darts forward in the crowd, looking for the white stretch.

'Of course he won't ever admit it,' Gay says in an undertone to Henry.

They get the driver to take them to a famous deli on Broadway where they order a soup of barley and beans, and then pastrami and gherkin sandwiches which are so large they must contain, each of them, a pound of meat. Gay appears to have forgotten that she eats only once a day. Albie jokes with the waitress, who comes from Costa Rica.

'I like your horse-tail,' she tells him, flipping his tied-back hair with her pencil. 'What else you got like a horse?'

'Hey,' he says. 'Will you marry me?'

'I don' marry no one,' she says. 'I was married once and you know what I say? I say marriage sucks.'

'I see a poem here, guys,' Albie tells them. When she returns with their orders he asks her what was the worst thing about her marriage.

'Getting married was the worst,' she says. 'I was fourteen. And best was when I leave him.'

It is already dark as they drive away from Manhattan with their brown-bags of unfinished pastrami which give the heated interior of the limo a strange salty aroma.

That night Albie comes back with Henry to the Joseph House. He doesn't work at his typewriter, is restless, seems constantly on the brink of saying something which doesn't get said. He suggests a walk around the campus and Henry, wanting to be agreeable, goes with him, slipping and skating in the dark along the icy paths.

'I used to love this place,' Albie says as they walk under trees and down towards the lake. 'I'd done that thing in Austria – killed myself off. I didn't belong anywhere. Didn't know what I was going to do. The nuns gave me work, didn't ask too many questions, made me feel at home.' The tone in which all this is said seems to put it firmly in the past.

'Joy . . .' Henry offers.

'A wonderful woman.' Albie says that, too, with a kind of retrospective finality.

They stand staring at floodlit statuary above the lake. It belongs to the time when the grounds and buildings were the mansion estate of a rich railroad-owner. There are classical columns and a naked Grecian youth. On the far side of the water the nuns have added a statue of the Virgin. The Virgin and the boy stare at one another across the ice. 'For ever wilt thou love and she be fair,' Albie quotes.

As they head back towards the Joseph House he says, 'It's truth time, Henry.'

Henry feels a nervous tremor. 'Truth time?'

'My new poems.'

'They're good.' He says it too fast, too brightly, conscious that if he meant it sincerely it would have sounded different. Also that Albie will have registered a lack of conviction.

'How good?'

'I think I need time . . .'

'No, you've had time.'

'To assess . . .'

'You're leaving . . . When?'

'Next week.'

'And before that there's . . .'

'Yes, my visit to Princeton.'

'So let's have it, man. How do they compare?'

'Compare?'

'Compare, Henry, for God's sake. With the earlier stuff. With Ashtree.'

'You wrote them, Albie. They're good. What else could they be?'

Albie doesn't press it any further. There's no need. He knows the thumb has gone down on his new work. They walk on in silence. Back at the Joseph House Albie says, 'You were supposed to give it to me straight.'

Henry has gathered himself now. He has been brought all this way, it seems at Albie's expense, or at least at his behest, and he owes it to the poet to give him what he asks for.

'OK,' he says. 'They're nice publishable poems. Well-turned, sharp observation, some brilliant images. But no, they're not as good. The range is lost, or the punch, or the guts, or something, I don't know what. The life. Something's missing, Albie.'

Albie smiles at him. 'Attaboy,' he says. 'It wasn't so bad, was it?'

Henry doesn't know how to respond. There seems no bitterness. For just a moment, and it's the only time it has happened since they first greeted one another, Albie looks at ease, as if a weight – of doubt maybe, or responsibility – has been lifted. He pats Henry's arm. 'Thanks for that, friend.'

He goes to his room and shuts the door. Henry waits for the sound of the typewriter. Or will it be a gunshot? After a time he hears the hissing of Albie's white noise machine.

Henry is away for most of a week. He spends three days at the Princeton university library studying books and manuscripts. There are a couple of days in New York, looking at libraries, visiting museums and art galleries. When he gets back to Woodlake he notices changes in the Joseph House. Albie's room, looked at from the passageway, has become more orderly. The clutter of books and papers seems reduced. The old Olivetti is down on the floor, replaced on the desk by a laptop. There is a cardboard box piled high with discarded files.

The bench press and weights are gone from the front porch. In the living-room the Algonquian shield and spear are missing from the walls; so are the Utamaro print and the wall-hanging representing a phone box.

'I was getting tired of those things,' Albie says. 'Time for some changes.'

He does no work at his desk, apart from more tidying and

clearing of old papers. That night he borrows two video movies and they watch them together. Both are about life in prison. In one the hero is found guilty of a double murder he didn't commit, and locked up for life. Most of the movie takes place in the prison where he spends more than twenty years. It's a bleak story, but at last he escapes, gets right away to start a new life for himself in some idyllic place with a long white beach, blue water and palm trees.

The other, based on a true story from the old San Quentin days, is much darker. A prisoner, guilty only of stealing five dollars from a post office, tries to escape and as a consequence spends three years in solitary confinement, only taken out at intervals to be beaten and tortured by a sadistic prison superintendent. Driven mad by this treatment, he murders the inmate who gave away the escape plan. His defence lawyer reveals the nature of the torture he has undergone and the prisoner is found not guilty. He is returned to San Quentin to serve out his other sentence and three weeks later is found murdered in his cell.

After four remorseless hours of prison life the interior of the Joseph House looks strange to Henry. To Albie too, it seems, because he says, 'Prisons aren't like that any more'; and then he adds, 'They're more like this place, I guess.'

He opens a bottle of whisky and insists on a nightcap. It's not something Henry likes or wants, but he accepts one drink, then a second, to be sociable. He sleeps soundly but wakes some time after 3 a.m. and heads for the bathroom. There is a light on in Albie's room and the door is open. The bed is unmade and the room wildly untidy, as if stirred by a gigantic spoon. The rolled up towel has been pushed back by the opening of the door. The white-noise machine is issuing its loud hissing static.

Henry tries to think of a rational explanation – that Albie has gone out for a walk, that he has gone to his office, that he has driven over to Joy's house. But the word that springs into his half-asleep brain is 'Escape'. He looks out to the street and sees that Albie's car is still parked there.

Next morning nothing has changed. Henry calls Joy but

Albie is not at her house. He is due to give classes but he doesn't turn up for them.

Two days later Henry is ready to leave Woodlake, and there is still no sign of Albie. He has vanished. Everyone is worried. The nuns are saying prayers for his safety. The police have been notified. There is talk of dragging the lake.

Joy comes to say goodbye. It is early March and a Jewish festival is taking place. All the children in the neighbourhood are in fancy dress. The men wear their usual black suits and hats, but some have put on red noses, funny face-masks, Batman cloaks. The women bustle about carrying cakes in boxes and string bags. The big old bent and broken station-wagons go up and down, filled with shouting children. An ambulance decorated with balloons and streamers is driven around the streets broadcasting music.

Henry's bag is packed and he's ready to go. He stands with Joy looking out into the street, waiting for the Gofar Limo car that will take him to JFK. Another snowstorm is coming through and he is worried that he will miss his flight.

'But these storms delay the flights too,' Joy tells him. 'They have to plough the runways and de-ice the wings. If you're late, they will be too.' She gives his hand a reassuring squeeze.

'I'm sorry to be leaving you right now,' he says. 'I wish I could be of use.'

She shakes her head. 'He's gone.'

'You don't mean . . .'

'Not dead. Gone. We won't see him again.'

'Did he say . . .'

'No. Nothing. Not a thing. There was no warning. Maybe that's why I feel so sure.'

'He must be mad.'

She looks up and, recognising what he means, smiles and shakes her head. 'If you mean to flatter . . .'

'I mean to praise.'

She pats his arm. 'Well, thank you. But I'm not what he needs.'

226

Henry resists an urge to tell her that Albie Strong is Alban Ashtree. A few minutes later the car draws up in the street. Snow is falling fast now.

He hugs her and they say goodbye. He has his suitcase half way across the porch and is handing it to the driver when she asks, from the door, whether Albie checked their lottery tickets. Henry tells her he doesn't know, hasn't given it a thought. 'He didn't tell you?'

'I forgot to ask.'

'Well, I guess we didn't . . .'

She says, 'Mom tells me there were three tickets shared the prize. One was sold in Trenton, one in Newark, and one in Brick.'

'One in Brick.' Henry thinks about that. 'Thirty-five million?'

'Thirty-six.'

'That's twelve million for each ticket.'

They stare at one another, not speaking. Anything is possible is what they don't say.

All the way to New York the snow goes on falling, the ploughs along the highways and on the turnpike working to clear it and scatter salt. For a time it freezes as it falls and the driver can't go faster than twenty. The vehicles keep a respectful distance from one another. Now and then a car up ahead goes into a graceful slow-motion skid, sliding and circling away out of the traffic into trees or bank or ditches.

Then, quite suddenly, the surface seems to thaw. The snow falls and melts. They pick up speed. 'We'll make it,' the driver says, as Henry takes his last look across the water at Manhattan's alphabet on a pale page of sky.

When they reach the terminal Henry pushes twenty dollars into the driver's hand. The driver thanks him. 'And I'm to give you this, Professor Bulov.'

It is a sheet of paper with a typewritten message, in capitals and with no signature:

HENRY: ASHTREE IS DEAD, AND STAYS [REPEAT: STAYS] DEAD. HE KEEPS HIS FAME AND YOU KEEP THE FLAME

– BEST FOR US BOTH, NO? REPUTATION IS AN INVEN-
TION. WE, YOU AND I, HAVE THE PATENT ON THIS
ONE. LET'S KEEP IT THAT WAY.

ME, I GO AWAY, A LONG WAY, FOR A LITTLE R & R
AND A LOT OF QUIET COMFORT.

And then, in lower case, are the lines from Keats Albie has
quoted or referred to more than once:

> *Bold Lover, never never canst thou kiss*
> *Though winning near the goal, yet do not grieve,*
> *She cannot fade, though thou hast not thy bliss.*
> *For ever wilt thou love, and she be fair!*

Who is the 'she'? Henry asks himself. He would like to
think it refers to Joy, but he knows it doesn't. The 'she' for
Albie is, must always have been, Fame.

The driver is already at the door of the limo, opening it to
get in. 'When did he give you this?' Henry asks.

'I'm sorry, sir. I'm not supposed to say.'

'It was Albie. Albie Strong.'

The driver stares at him, embarrassed at not being free
to reply.

'You drove him up here in the night.'

'I'm sorry,' he says, and slides down into his seat.

Henry walks around the car and knocks on the window.
The driver lowers it. 'I'm sorry, sir,' he says again, shaking
his head in refusal.

'Just tell me this,' Henry says. 'I'm not asking who, or when.
But the person who gave you this message for me – did he give
you an unusually large tip?'

Silence.

Henry is holding another twenty-dollar bill close to his
nose. 'Very large, wasn't it?'

The driver looks away, embarrassed. 'I'm sorry. Please
excuse . . .' He presses a button and the window slides up
between them. He puts the car into drive and slides gently
away from Henry, forward, and then out into the traffic.

*

Henry – Professor Bulov – international expert on the poetry of Alban Ashtree, a scholar of modest means who always travels economy, or as American Airlines call it, coach, is not surprised on this occasion to be told at the check-in that he has been upgraded.

'To business?'

'To first,' the attendant says, smiling.

'Ah,' he says. 'My fairy godmother.' And he guesses it will be the same all the way back to New Zealand.

Pauline Melville

THE PRESIDENT'S EXILE

THE PRESIDENT WALKED up the steps to the entrance of the London School of Economics where he had studied as a young man. He wore a calf-length, navy-blue alpaca coat and a fawn cashmere scarf tied neatly, like a cravat, around his neck. Recently he had undergone an operation on his throat and he worried about protecting the vulnerable area from the cold winds of a London winter.

He passed through the swing doors and stood for a moment on the marbled floor of the large entrance hall. It was not term-time and there were few people about. Nobody recognised him. He remained there for a minute or two. The balding man at the porter's desk was looking down at some list or other and paid him no attention. He hesitated for a moment wondering what he should say if asked what he was doing there. He would simply say that he was President Hercules and that he had studied law here some thirty – or, goodness, was it forty – years previously and that he had now returned to take an affectionate walk around the place.

In fact, he had not been happy there. Nobody would recognise him, he knew that. It was too long ago. Nor would they know that he was in exile.

His hand gripped the bottom of the briefcase under his arm more tightly at the recollection of his new and unaccustomed lack of status. It was still unclear to him how it had happened. However hard he tried to remember, the precise sequence of events escaped him. The transition from real president to exiled president remained a blur. The more he sat in his hotel room and tried to remember, the more it slipped from his grasp. He wondered whether he might not be in the throes of a nervous breakdown.

He remembered entering the hospital for minor throat surgery. The limousine had delivered him to the front doors where a team of Cuban doctors waited to greet him. The sun was blazing down. He remembered the warm wind on his cheeks. Photographers took pictures of him shaking hands with the surgeons before going inside. After that, he remembered nothing.

The president was standing staring at the floor when he realised that by remaining motionless he would attract attention. He walked over to the lift. Inside he randomly pressed a button. He could not recall which floor housed the law faculty and anyway it had probably all changed. But stepping out of the lift on the third floor, he felt a familiar sense of unease as he recognised the shabby corridors and the warm smell of dull, wooden doors and cheap furniture polish. Notices on various offices indicated that this was now the social anthropology department. But it was certainly the same floor that had once housed the department of legal studies.

He looked through the small window in the door of one of the rooms, cupping his hand to shade his eyes from the reflection. The long, solid desks were the same ones he remembered but now each desk supported a row of grey computers. He tried the door. It was locked. He stared through the window.

Why had he felt drawn to visit this place again? There had, after all, been enough successes in his life. Why, he wondered, should he feel compelled to return to where he had suffered an unforgettable, if minor, humiliation? He recalled the episode.

His tutor had waved his essay in front of the rest of the seminar group and then handed it back to him with the words: 'This is remarkably like an essay from one of the current third-year students that I marked last year. I shall give you the benefit of the doubt this time but I warn you that if anything similar occurs again, I shall report it to the Dean.'

Naturally, he had feigned surprise and looked mystified, although he had, in fact, copied the essay from the student whose effort had been marked with an alpha plus. His own work was of a reasonably high standard but it was the certainty of obtaining the best grade that he had been unable to resist.

That same evening, a group of colonial students at the Mecklenburgh Square hostel listened and sympathised as he insisted with righteous indignation, over the evening meal of chops and gravy, that the similarity between the essays had been an extraordinary and unfortunate coincidence. He talked scathingly of his tutor who, he said, undoubtedly shared the racial bias common to all colonial masters and just wanted to see him degraded.

Several of the students from that batch at Mecklenburgh Square had gone on to do well in later life. Two were currently prime ministers of African states. One had gone on to Sandhurst military academy and was now a general in Ghana. He himself had become the first black president in South America.

He prided himself on the fact that he was one of the few presidents on that continent who could mix and feel at ease with the crowd in the market-place. Sometimes he would order his driver to stop the car at one of the street markets so that he could walk amongst the pungent smells of vegetables, herbs, washing powders and cocoa beans or stroll between the stiff carcasses of dried fish, to talk and joke with the stall-holders and ask them about business. In his speeches he often referred to the importance of 'the small man'.

It was the same on open days at his official residence. He enjoyed the *bonhomie*, mingling with people in the grounds, chatting, gesticulating and jostling his way through the guests as those around him closed in and clapped him on the back.

But when he was out of the country, officiating as head of state at some international conference and he bumped into his former fellow students, he fretted over whether any of them remembered the time when he was accused of cheating and the public smile froze on his face.

The odd thing was that even after he had been president for many years, he felt unsure of his position. He felt like a charlatan. And this was nothing to do with the rigged elections that had kept him in power for nearly two decades. He would have felt like a charlatan even if he had been fairly elected.

His father, a civil servant, had once told him he would never amount to anything because he lacked moral fibre. The office of president felt like a carapace he had assumed to cover his failings. The only question he ever really wanted to ask his fellow presidents and prime ministers at those conferences was whether they felt the same: 'Do you feel too that we're all a bunch of frauds?' he wanted to ask, but never did.

He turned away from the seminar room and walked down the corridor back towards the lift. He inspected his Cartier watch. Quarter past eleven. He had nowhere particular to go and for some reason felt reluctant to leave the building straight away.

He abandoned the lift on the ground floor and made his way to the Old Theatre. This was where important visiting lecturers delivered their addresses. Nobody paid heed to him and he walked over to the door on the right and slipped quietly inside.

Here things had changed. The auditorium was at the same raked angle as he remembered but, instead of the parquet flooring and banks of gloomy, high-backed, oak seats, the entire place had been carpeted and the wooden benches replaced by comfortable plush seats like a real theatre.

There was no one there. A microphone stand, an empty glass and dusty jug of water stood on a table on the stage awaiting some phantom speaker. The president sank into one of the upholstered chairs with relief and put his briefcase down on the seat next to him. He loosened the scarf round his neck gingerly. The operation wound on his throat had not healed properly. Sometimes it oozed a colourless fluid. He touched the ridged scar gently with his fingertips. They came away a little wet. He searched for a handkerchief in his coat pocket and held it against the places where the seeping plasma escaped.

Anxious to put out of his mind the unpleasant memories occasioned by his visit upstairs, he tried to console himself by reliving the time when he had won the Best Speaker's Prize for oratory at the Inns of Court. But all he could remember was how he had felt at the time – a sense of incredulity that the judges should reward him for something that was so easy – telling lies in a powerful and persuasive manner. He could barely see the credit in that because even as a child he had recognised the distinction between public lies and private truths. He thought it was second nature to everyone. What was oratory if not the art of public lies? For him, all discourse was to some extent a matter of lying.

Lying had never been a problem. It is easy for those with a good grasp of reality. The same sound grasp of reality made him a pragmatic politician.

'It is simple,' he had said in the early days of his political life. 'I am the African leader. My rival is the East Indian leader.' He would say this quite openly when most of the progressive forces in the fifties supported his rival whom they understood to be leader of the masses. His rival campaigned up and down the country on the basis of racial unity. Meanwhile, he negotiated with the Americans and British and took power knowing he would be able to rely on people to vote on the basis of racial division.

'I deal with realities,' he said.

And it was this that made his present position so disturbing. He was not sure exactly what the reality was. If he knew the events that had led him here, he would know what to do about his current situation. But he seemed to have difficulty in concentrating. He leaned forward in his seat and clenched his fists together, head between his hands. The important matters were vague, yet other irritating and inconsequential memories such as the tutor accusing him of cheating all those years ago remained vividly in his mind.

Feeling a little hot, he opened the top buttons of his coat. For some reason his thoughts travelled back to the occasion when his father had compared him unfavourably to one of his schoolfriends, a certain Michael Yates. He was eleven. He had arrived home from school to find his father standing on the polished floor in front of the open verandah doors, scowling over a letter from his headmaster. It concerned some minor misdemeanour. It was not the misdemeanour that the head-master complained of, however, but the disproportionate and elaborate web of lies and deception that had been fabricated to cover it up.

'You shame me,' his father had roared while his sister looked on with satisfaction from beside the dresser. 'Why you can't be like Michael Yates? Michael Yates is open and honest. Michael Yates is a straightforward boy. You sneaky. Why do I have to have a lampey-pampey sneak for a son?'

Years later, as prime minister, when he was about to make a speech at the Critchlow Labour College, he spotted a familiar figure as he made his way down the aisle to the rostrum. These were the days when he had begun to wear an item of purple every day and to sign his name in purple ink like an emperor. He stopped to shake the hand of his old friend from schooldays, whose hair was now thinning on either side of a peak at the front and who beamed at him from the sidelines.

'Michael Yates. What are you up to these days?'

'I'm teaching in the secondary school at West Ruimveldt.'

The president slapped him on the back. 'Pleased to hear it,' he said, before continuing down to the platform.

At lunchtime, the president arrived back at his office and told his secretary to ensure forthwith that a Mr Michael Yates was sacked from his post at Ruimveldt secondary school and refused a post anywhere else. For the rest of the afternoon he basked in the satisfaction of an ancient score settled. President Hercules had a phenomenal memory for slights. He could remember any politician who had offended or opposed him and the precise details of the occasion.

A cleaner bumped the doors of the theatre open with her behind and entered backwards dragging a hoover.

The president gathered up his belongings and edged between the rows of seats towards the exit.

He found himself in Kingsway. He looked briefly for a

restaurant he used to frequent but it was no longer there. It had been replaced by a print and graphics store.

The traffic streamed past him down towards Bush House. In a gap between two buildings opposite stood a beech tree, its delicate branches traced like a frozen neurone against the blank January sky. Missing the heat and humidity of his own country, he turned and walked in the other direction, away from Kingsway, down the Strand.

There was no doubt that this exile was a temporary state of affairs. He would return eventually. When, was the question. He turned into Northumberland Avenue.

The heavy, revolving doors of the building that housed the Royal Commonwealth Society decanted him slowly and he was relieved to feel the burst of warmth as he entered. A uniformed security official trod silently across a sea of red carpet, presumably to ask him his business. President Hercules took the man by the elbow across to where a photographic portrait of the Queen and the Commonwealth heads of state hung on the wall. He pointed out his own picture in the line-up and laughed off the man's embarrassment, tapping him lightly on the back to show that no offence was taken.

The security man looked confused and apologetic as he returned to his position. The president took the lift to the first floor. He seemed bound by a compulsion to return to the scenes of episodes in his life which had shamed or demeaned him in some way. He could not stay away. It was as if, by returning and concentrating with all his energy on these episodes, he might be able to expunge them from history. And yet they were all minor setbacks compared to his achievements. Why did his achievements mean nothing?

In the lift he began to sweat as he remembered in detail what had happened there.

The incident had taken place when he had already been prime minister for several years and had just appointed himself president for life. He had stopped off in London on his return journey from the Commonwealth Conference in Lagos. The meeting he had chosen to address was not a public one but one held by private invitation only. He must have had something of a premonition because he had left specific instructions that his sister was not to be invited. On his accession to the presidency, he had cancelled her diplomatic post in an act of private spite after she refused him a small piece of sculpture that their father had left her in his will. She had remained in London and he knew that his action still rankled with her. He did not want to see her in public lest she caused a fuss about it.

His sister, however, had persuaded a friend to bring her along as a guest. The president was relaxed and in good form. He wore an immaculate khaki shirt-jack that sloped gently out from his chest to accommodate the foothills of what was later to become a mountainous waist.

As his speech finished to a round of applause, he stepped forward to shake hands, first with the High Commissioner, then with other selected dignitaries and party supporters. At that precise moment, his sister stepped out of the lift into the foyer on the first floor where the small but distinguished audience milled about holding glasses of wine and chatting.

'I will probably get into trouble for this, but I should like you all to know certain things about my brother, Baldwin Hercules.' She spoke in an uncertain voice, but her feet were planted firmly apart and she held her handbag in both trembling hands.

The gathering grew uneasily silent as she stood nervously in front of the lift doors, her head thrown back a little. She continued determinedly, looking straight into the eyes of her audience.

'Nobody knows a man better than his own sister. Baldwin is a liar, a cheat and a bully. As a child, he always lied his way out of trouble. Lied. Lied. Lied. He always had to blame somebody else. He wanted to win everything. Yes, he is clever, but he has a cruel streak. And I am warning you. You have let him have too much power. You all will suffer for it and so will the country. There is nothing he will not do and nobody he will not use to get what he wants.'

A couple of people moved forward to try and persuade her gently to leave. One of them pressed the button to open the lift doors behind her. Nothing happened. The lift had stuck. She continued, speaking more quickly now because she sensed that his security guards might bundle her out.

'Somebody has to speak the truth before it is too late. We all know that elections are rigged. We must be the only country where the government is elected by the dead. Half the names on the lists are taken from tombstones. Eventually, he will kill to stay where he is. Socialist republic?' She sneered. 'Ask him why his daughter had to take up residence in Switzerland. I will tell you why – to caretake his secret bank accounts.'

She turned her troubled eyes to the friend who had brought her there as a guest.

'I'm sorry,' she said. 'I shouldn't have done this. But I couldn't help it.' And she turned away from the lift and walked in silence down the carpeted stairs.

That night she took a flight to Canada.

During most of her outburst the president stood silent, an embarrassed smile on his face, his cheeks crawling with horror. When she mentioned the Swiss bank accounts, he turned away and began to speak with an air of amused resignation to one of his entourage.

'A pity you can't sack your family in the same way you can sack your ministers,' he said ruefully, attempting to laugh the whole thing off. Sweat glistened in the creases of his neck. The man he addressed responded with a bray of palpably false laughter.

Now the exiled president walked softly to the place where he had stood all those years ago. He stood in exactly the same spot on the carpet as if he were once again facing his sister, surrounded by phantom dignitaries. Prickles ran up his neck and along his jaw. He rubbed the thumb of his right hand against the middle finger nervously. He could hear once again every word she said and he shuddered as though his soul were being branded.

He had never taken retaliatory action against his sister for the simple reason that he never thought he could get away with it. She lived in Canada. If she had returned to her own country it would have been different. She would have been within his orbit.

Standing there in those gracious surroundings, he recalled the successful assassination of one of his political opponents. The man was a popular radical who posed him a considerable threat. He recollected the man's death with perfect equanimity and with a sense of satisfaction. He had no reservations about the use of power. Power must be used ruthlessly to be effective. He had never suffered a moment's regret about the murder. In fact, he considered it to be one of his most subtle triumphs.

The assassination had pleased him because there had been no need for him to do more than express a desire that the man did not exist. He had flung a newspaper down on the table at a ministerial meeting, groaned with mock theatricality and wished out loud that the radical could be stopped from holding these mass meetings at which he made inflammatory statements. Although it was not the meetings that had infuriated him. It was the fact that the young man had referred to him in public as King Kong. He then scribbled down a list of eleven names of those he considered to be potentially dangerous. The revolutionary's name headed the list.

'Here is a cricket team that is not batting on our side.' He had looked around the circle of watchful eyes and shrugged with exaggerated regret. 'The captain is one I could do without.'

A few weeks later, the man was blown apart in his own car and he, the president, had been able to say, with his hand on his heart, that he knew nothing about it. Although it irritated him to learn that in a fit of over-zealousness, one of his ministers had issued a statement to the press disclaiming all responsibility for the death before it had actually occurred.

By that time, of course, his henchmen knew how to fulfil his slightest whim. His diet, for instance. He began the day by drinking half a beer-mug of orange juice with two raw eggs cracked in it, whisked around with port wine to form a greyish-purple liquid. It was a longevity diet. Occasionally, he swallowed a turtle's heart while it was still beating so that he could absorb the power of life.

Remembering his opponent's violent demise raised his spirits a little. The knowledge that he had got away with it afforded him some relief from the burning and shameful memory of his sister's denunciation. He pulled up his coat collar, making sure his throat was well protected from the icy weather, then walked slowly down the stairs and nodded politely to the attendant before shouldering his way through the revolving doors and out into the cold once more.

This time he took a bus to the High Commission. He wanted to find out whether his portrait was still hanging there. He screwed up his face a little. Something about those airbrushed official portraits always made him look a little prissy – the too plump cheeks, the thin moustache resting on his full top lip and short, greying beard on the point of his chin gave him the somewhat pampered look of a man both smug and guarded, possibly a little shy. But it would reassure him to see the picture still hanging there on the wall. He would take one more look before returning to his hotel.

He walked past the red-brick, bay-windowed building several times. The portrait was gone. It was no longer there. His stomach muscles tightened with anxiety. As he watched they were replacing it with his successor. The solemn face of his deputy prime minister, bumbling Edwin Jefferson, was being hoisted into position.

He stood in a daze in the street. A small, cockney boy, his face marbled with cold, ran past the railings twanging them with a stick. The noise brought him to his senses. There was nothing to do but return immediately to his hotel. He still suffered fits of dizziness. Clearly, he was not fully recovered from the operation. He should go and lie down and try to work out how to return as quickly as possible before his position became irreversible.

The functional anonymity of the hotel room helped settle his jangled nerves. He lay down stiffly on the bed without removing his overcoat.

The trouble was, these patches of fog in his mind. He

wondered if they were some unforeseen side-effect of the operation. He could remember more or less everything up until then.

For a moment he wondered whether Castro had sent a team of doctors to incapacitate him as part of some take-over bid. Unlikely. And if that were the case, why was the portrait of his deputy prime minister, Edwin Jeffson, hanging in the High Commission? Jeffson was a born subordinate. He could not imagine Jeffson being behind any plot to oust him. That was why he had appointed him as his deputy.

Rack his brains as he might, he had no idea how he had arrived in London. Could he have been drugged?

Perhaps he had done something terrible when he was still under the influence of the anaesthetic – made a fool of himself in some way and been discreetly removed for a while. A military take-over was unlikely. The generals and brigadiers were in his pocket. Although, of course, you could never be certain. What kept troubling him was the idea that he might have suffered some kind of mental breakdown.

He frowned. Suddenly he had remembered his horse. He hoped Jason the groom would care for it properly in his absence. He loved to ride his great white steed arrayed in the splendid leather saddle and harness presented to him by President Lyndon Johnson of America. Villagers became used to the sight of him walking the horse between Belfield and Golden Grove. His favourite official portrait showed him mounted in the saddle.

One thing he did know for sure. He would return. It would not be wise to wait for too long. He did not want Edwin Jeffson to become accustomed to the trappings of office.

Some stains on the scarf that lay beside him on the bed caught his attention. He put his hand to his neck. When he inspected his fingers, he saw that the fluid was a pale pink colour as if there were traces of blood in it. He went into the bathroom, but dazzled by the white tiles and brilliant lights he became suddenly fearful of looking at the wound in the mirror. He stepped hastily back into his room.

Before he slept, he worried briefly about running out of money. But there was always his watch and the gold signet ring. Back home he had encouraged people to kneel and kiss this ring, pretending always that it was a huge joke, but not liking it when people demurred. He could always ask for money to be telegraphed through to him from his Swiss account.

The next morning, he decided to brave the icy drizzle and do something that his official position had never allowed him to do before. He decided to visit Madame Tussaud's. The idea of a hall of notoriety for both the famous and the infamous had always fascinated him. On arrival, he had no choice but to queue in the freezing sleet along with the other visitors in the Marylebone Road.

When he came out two hours later, in contrast to the eminent waxworks, secure and complacent in their history, he was overcome by anxiety and paced up and down the Inner Circle of Regent's Park, going nowhere. It was then he decided that he would return to his own country the next day, secretly, via Surinam.

In his homeland, the president's official residence had remained empty since his departure, but the lights were still left on there at night to allay the fears of the populace. The attractive, rambling building stood in its own grounds, surrounded by royal palms, and clearly visible from the road.

The house was uninhabited. Maids and cleaners attended to their duties as infrequently as possible. Nobody wanted to go there. Even relatives had gone in only briefly to collect their belongings and scurry away.

There were reports that his white horse had been heard moving slowly about in the spacious galleries upstairs. Nobody was sure he was gone for good. The story also gained ground that a black cayman had been seen slithering down the front steps of the residence. On reaching the ground, the creature had stood up in the shape of a man. To cap it all, one of the ex-maids had apparently started to speak with the president's voice.

A storekeeper from the village of Vigilance recounted his dream to anyone who would listen.

'One day I was walking out on to the street. Gradually, I notice many people standing on either side of the road in small groups and knots, kind of muttering and whispering amongst themselves. As I proceeded, the groups became silent and everybody stood looking backwards down the road towards Belfield. A hearse was coming down the road. President Hercules was sitting in it. He shouted out to a man on the roadside in his usual, loud-mouth way: "That business with the house – it fix?" The man said no. "Stop by my house tomorrow. I see to it." And suddenly the hearse jerked and veered to the left.'

The storekeeper leaned over the counter to his customers. 'A burial place should be near a fork in the road, you know, so that the funeral party can make a sudden turn and confuse the spirits. So the African legend goes.'

The dream had so impressed him that he continued telling it to each new customer. 'Then I dreamed I found myself near a small church. A priest stood with a baby in his arms as if for a christening. The baby had the face of an old man – sinister. Gradually, I see who the face belong to. It belong to Hercules. I asked my uncle what music was playing. "The Dead March," replied my uncle. And then, you know how it is with dreams, I was at home once more in Vigilance looking out of the window. The whole area was flooded for as far as I could see. The water reached right up to the top windows. Then it began to ebb and recede like mist until it was gone.'

The whole country abounded with rumours and hearsay. There were rumours that President Hercules had been seen in Moscow, in the United States and now it was even being said that he had been seen standing amongst the waxworks at Madame Tussaud's.

It was just at this time, when such rumours were at their height, that the president contrived to return incognito. The whole operation was clandestine. He wanted to get back into his own country secretly and assess the situation. It was best to stay out of the capital where his face was too well known.

He would spend time in the interior where there would be less chance of his being recognised.

It was a warm, voluptuous night when the president once again felt the soil of his own land under his feet.

The first night of his return he stayed in a disused hut on an abandoned trail outside Orealla. For most of the night he sat in the pitch dark, on a rough, wooden plank, planning what to do. Every so often he fingered his neck gingerly. All night long his ring finger itched and he worried that he had developed a nervous allergy.

It would have been more sensible to travel at night when there was less chance of recognition, but he was not accustomed to the bush and feared losing himself. Transportation was clearly going to pose a problem. Regretfully, he decided he must risk going into the capital to fetch his horse.

Early the next morning, he set off. A storm helped him. He took a lift in a donkey cart. The tropical deluge turned the air grey and allowed him to pull the hood of his green military cape down so that it nearly covered his face.

Worst of all was the fear that he had begun to smell. He had not been able to wash properly since leaving England and in this climate, he feared that the wound in his neck was becoming putrid.

By nightfall of the next evening he had reached the outskirts of the city.

It was a clear night. The presidential mansion was open, unguarded and with the lights blazing as usual from the deserted rooms. He walked down the path, through the door and up the steps directly facing him. It was just as he had last seen it except that all signs of his occupancy, his personal belongings and effects had been removed. He walked through every room, his footsteps making a hollow echo on the shiny, wooden floors, polished to translucence. He breathed deeply. Then he went out and stood for a while on the verandah, looking out towards the statue of a slave leader who had led a rebellion in the eighteenth century.

He could just make out the figure of the statue. Even in the dark there was something bleak about the empty, treeless space surrounding it. In the daytime, traffic swirled round the plinth at a distance. Few people went close up to it. Some said that it possessed a force that pushed people away. Others said that the statue had an intimate connection with the president through magical and arcane writings on the back of its head and that they would never be sure that the president had gone for good until the statue fell.

For a while, he looked out over the city and brooded over what to do next.

As he stepped back inside, a violent snuffling, snorting noise from the next room startled him. He tiptoed along the verandah back to the main reception room.

Standing there, head lowered, eyes looking at him was his white horse. He rushed over to greet it, grasping it by the mane and burying his head in the animal's neck. He ran his hand down the horse's flanks. They felt hot and sweaty as though it had recently been ridden. He cursed the groom for not attending properly to the animal which was steaming with heat. It had not even been unsaddled. On its back sat the magnificent, tooled leather saddle donated by the United States of America and normally used only on state occasions. The president hurried into the next room to see if there was any sign of his purple riding boots. No trace of them. He came thoughtfully back to where the horse waited.

And then, President Hercules mounted his horse. His head reached nearly to the crystal chandelier. The tops of the landscapes and portraits hanging on the walls came level with his shoulders. He moved the horse slowly through the room and after a little persuasion, the white charger edged itself sideways and awkwardly, with clattering hoofs, descended the main stairway.

Horse and rider walked through the main doors of the house, down the path, past the unoccupied guard-hut on the left, past the ghostly trunks of the giant royal palms and out into the sleeping city.

He could not resist it. It was three o'clock in the morning. He took a tour. The city was deserted. He rode past the parliament building. There was a slight drizzle and a chill bite to the air.

'Cold. Cold,' he said to himself. 'Ice-cart coming.'

He cantered on through the empty streets, the horse's hoofs throwing up spray from the waterlogged ground. For nostalgia's sake, he took the road past one particular house. It was one of the enormous, old, white wooden colonial houses. The Demerara shutters opened on to the night. Once his father had taken him to this house, explaining that it represented the soul of the country and all that was good in it. He dallied there for a while, almost wistfully, while the horse cropped the grass at the roadside. Then he moved on.

Dawn came with long streaks in the sky of indigo, grey and pink. Needing to remain unseen, the president spurred his horse into action and galloped between the sleeping villages along the highway out of the city.

In the half-light, he looked down and noticed that the horse's white mane had become dark in places. He put his hand out and touched one of the patches. It was damp. He put his finger to his mouth. Blood. The blood tasted like iron on his lips. He lifted his hand to feel the bandages on his neck. They were sodden. Despite the continuous loss of blood, there was no pain and he did not feel dizzy or faint.

He decided to stick to his original plan and galvanised the horse into a gallop once more. Soon there should be a turning that led to the Arawak village of Hicuri in the bush. It was not signposted but he thought he could recognise it. If he hid somewhere near there, he could seek help should it become necessary.

He turned down the small track that branched off the main highway. The horse picked its way through the puddles and lakes of the flooded savannah. Feeling too visible in the open country now that it was nearly daylight, the president left the wide trail with its sandy, rutted tracks and guided his horse across a patch of scrub towards the forest stretching away to his left.

Once under cover of the trees, he relaxed. There was a faint trail and he let the horse pick its own way through the stinging insects and slashing grasses. Not much light penetrated. The morning was humid. Sometimes he ducked to avoid tangled vines and lianas slapping him in the face. The horse stopped every now and then to chomp noisily on wild vegetation. After a while, they came to a place where the trees thinned out and the horse could wander more freely. Exhausted, the president fell into a profound sleep in the saddle.

The captain of Hicuri village was drunk as usual. Even so, he had managed to go into town and persuade the only man he knew who could mend televisions to accompany him back out to the village. The contraption he drove was a cross between Stevenson's Rocket engine, a tractor and a guillotine cart. The video technician, a scrawny East Indian with a straggly moustache, stood in the back. His leg was encased in plaster from ankle to thigh. Every time the vehicle jolted on the pitted, red road that led to Hicuri, the man screeched with pain.

'Ooouw.'

The only other passenger returning to his village was a young Lokono Arawak called Calvin. Calvin had been working on the dredgers up on the Potaro river when he contracted malaria and had to be sent home. Now he shivered in the back, racked with fits of icy fever and nausea.

It was Calvin who pointed out the trail of blood leading to the forest. The captain did not stop.

'You seein' ning-ning,' he shouted over his shoulder, thinking that Calvin was suffering the delusions that sometimes come with malaria. He himself, these days, often saw crystal balls and beetles.

In the village, the technician worked for an hour. When the villagers heard the generator start up, they began to gather under the open-sided palm thatch shelter which housed the television and video machine. Old and young, everybody came walking across the grey sand, even Calvin, a towel wrapped round his waist and so weak that he had to lean against the shed post for support. They sat in rows on benches. Overhead, a parrot chattered non-stop in the scolding voice of an old woman.

The screen flickered and applause broke out. The technician inserted the video which he had brought with him to test the machine. He was proud of the video.

The whole country had been taken by surprise at the death of President Hercules the week before. He had gone into hospital for minor surgery and died under the anaesthetic. The Cuban doctors struggled to save his life, but to no avail. The technician had opportunistically jumped at the chance of videoing the funeral and hoped to sell the film. It was while he was running home to view it that the man broke his leg.

The state funeral of President Baldwin Hercules had taken place a week after his death and the day before the technician's visit to Hicuri.

It opened with a blurry and confused shot of the funeral cortège. The gun carriage with the body, drawn by the president's own sweating white horse, was hurtling down Camp Street in the middle of a thunderstorm with people running alongside to keep up. Curious onlookers stood in the street, ducking the rain, some with newspapers covering their heads, others with umbrellas. Some just stood and stared as if something unpleasant was passing.

By all accounts, the body had suffered from the frequent power cuts while it was in the mortuary freezer. At one point, the mortuary assistants had taken it out and hung it upside-down in the local abattoir. Nor was the preservation of the corpse helped by the fact that one of the employees had been found drunk on the embalming fluid. Haste was necessary if those attending the funeral were not to be overcome by the stench. The coffin was jolted so violently that both the purple boots, emblem of the fallen warrior, had been tossed off the top into the street.

Then there was a sort of blizzard on the screen. The villagers waited patiently while the technician explained that there was a gap in the video because he had had to make his way to the sepulchre for the rest of the ceremony.

Watching intently, the villagers saw the coffin being placed on the catafalque.

It was only when the solemn face of Edwin Jeffson appeared

on the screen in close-up, giving the funeral oration with tears streaming down his face that the Arawak villagers exploded spontaneously into howls of laughter. The more he wept, the more they laughed. They screeched and clutched each other, helpless with mirth as each politician was shown dabbing his or her eyes with handkerchiefs and throwing flowers reverently on to the coffin. The whole village was swept with wild hilarity.

The laughter carried right out of Hicuri village, across the creek and into the forest on the other side where the white horse continued to put his head down and forage for grass. His ears twitched at the distant laughter. He ambled to the other side of the clearing, the revenant still asleep on his back. There, beneath the trees, the horse continued to graze patiently, until such time as his sleeping burden should choose to wake.

Jane Rogers

CHIPMUNK

THERE WERE ONLY two other cars in the car-park. The kiosk where you had to pay for parking was closed up. Gary turned off the engine but stayed in his seat, fingers clasped around the steering-wheel, staring through the windscreen at the low grey sky. Lisa opened her door and got out, steadying herself with one hand on the back of her seat. She made for the trees at the edge of the car-park; he watched in his mirror as she disappeared into them, reappearing a few minutes later.

'Better?'

'Yeah.' She stopped short of getting in, ducking her head into the car to speak to him. 'Fancy a walk?'

'A walk? Here?'

'Well, it's a park isn't it? Must be pretty popular at the right time of year.' She indicated with a tilt of the head, the size of the empty car-park around them.

'All right.'

He got out and started rummaging in the back for their jackets. 'I can only find one of your gloves. D'you want to leave this handbag here – don't you think it'd be safer in the boot?'

'Yeah. Fine. I don't need gloves.'

'It's cold,' he said, leaning in over his seat to wind up her window before locking the door.

'Not very. It's nice to be out in the air.'

He glanced into the car, checking, remembered the camera and unlocked the door again.

'For God's sake.' Lisa moved impatiently towards the board where a map of trails in the park was displayed.

'What d'you say?' he called.

'Nothing. I'll look at the map.'

It was a rustic wooden board with complacent yellow lettering. Rattlesnake Point, the place was called. Three colour-coded trails snaked across the map; they all started from the Information Centre and Café. She crossed the car-park, heading Gary off.

'Found anything interesting?'

'No. The trails begin the other side of the café. Not much to choose between them.'

'We could have a coffee,' he said.

'If it's open.' Lisa plunged on towards the trails.

Probably a mistake to stop here. Another cold grey crappy walk. Rubbing their noses in it. That single-handedly they had managed to choose the worst time of the year to visit Canada. That the much-heralded holiday (honeymoon, they were calling it: didn't eighteen months of living together and not snatching more than a week in Wales, and that with the girls in tow, and the coming of the baby which would probably mean no more abroad for years, entitle this escape to a grander and more romantic name than 'holiday'? Not to mention the visit to Niagara Falls. It *had* to be called honeymoon, so that people would laugh in the right way); that the much-heralded honeymoon was taken *not in the spring*, as they had imagined, but in the bleak and barren late Canadian winter. They had left England swelling into warm green life; parks full of pink blossom and daffodils; pussy willows turned from silver to dusty polleny gold. Spring certain and arrived. They had caught a plane away from that, to Canada. Where filthy snow still lay compacted at the bottom of the Niagara Gorge, despite the rain; where the wind was freezing and the sky leaden and the grass and trees bleached and leeched by the cold to no-colour, not green not grey not beige not brown – nothing, absence of colour, sodden and colourless as a thing washed up on a freezing beach. A month earlier and there would have been thrilling snow and ice. A week or two later, they were assured, and it would be hot sudden

251

spring. But now – first week of April – now was the very worst time.

'Good idea,' said Gary, catching her up. 'To get a breath of air.'

A mistake.

'How're you feeling?' he said. 'Not queasy any more?'

'No. Thanks.'

'We're pretty close to Toronto now. Another hour or two is all, I reckon.'

The silence felt churlish. 'Right.'

'We could see a film tonight. Go to the theatre.'

We could do that at home. 'We could ring up Matty's brother, visit some real Canadians.'

'Matty's brother?'

'Yes. You know she gave me his number – he lives in Toronto.'

'Why d'you want to see Matty's brother?'

'I don't especially. She just said to say hello if we were in Toronto. He could tell us what to visit.'

'We've got a guidebook to tell us what to visit.'

'Yes, but sometimes people who live in a place have a better idea of what's what.'

'You think it's a good idea to lumber ourselves with some guy we've never met?'

'Oh forget it.'

The path, which had been twisting between trees, came out at the edge of a black silent lake, with a boardwalk around its marshy perimeter. Gary drew alongside her.

'I'm not being funny. We can call him if you want. I just can't help thinking what a treat it would seem at home to have the girls somewhere else and no work and a whole clear evening to go out or stay home in, and the last thing you'd want would be to get landed with an unknown Canadian.'

'Yes,' said Lisa. 'You're right. I'm sorry.'

'What d'you mean?'

'You're right. We came to be together. It would be silly to phone the Canadian.'

'But you wanted to. You're not interested in us having time together.'

'Yes I am.'

'Lisa, listen to the evidence. *What shall we do tonight?* I say, and you want to ring up a Canadian.'

'I don't want to spend the fucking night with him.'

'Really?'

'You're being pathetic.'

'OK. If I'm being pathetic. What *did* you want?'

'Can't it be something we do *together*? You and I together – go and meet a new person and find out about their city *together*; is that so awful?'

'I don't want to spend the evening exchanging banalities with a bloody Mountie, if I wanted that I could have stayed at home and watched *Due South*.'

'You are beyond belief ridiculous, and I'm not going to talk about it any more.'

'Look, we've got eight days left – '

'Eight,' Lisa said. 'Jesus. Eight more days of having to choose where to go and what to do and how to be together. How can we stand it?'

They walked in silence to the viewing platform at the head of the lake, leaned against the rail and stared across. It was peat-black with dead leaves floating, and bare branches reflected in its mirror-still surface. There were no birds, and nothing moved.

'You could almost imagine a bark canoe – ' Lisa began softly, appeasingly, but he turned and walked quickly away ahead of her. She followed, nerves taut with familiar anger.

The trees they were going through now were birch – young, close-growing birch with beautiful silver-white trunks, and strips of bark hanging loose. She pulled one strip gently and it came away; on the inside it was a warm sun-tanned browny pink. The dead leaves on the ground had not rotted but remained as a thick dry brown carpet, where the wind lifted the occasional leaf and sent it scuttling and rattling over the others. She looked ahead through the pale trunks but he wasn't in sight. Oh wonderful. Now he would get lost in some national park the size of Wales that nobody else would even come into till the summer.

She went at her own speed. Her last suggestion had been that they should dump the car. Take it back to a rental place and get the train, cross some of these vast spaces in company and comfort.

'But the car is our freedom,' he'd argued. 'It's the whole point – it's the only way to see a country like this.' He had not bargained on the Lakes being quite so unprepossessing, this time of year; or on Lisa being sick.

'Did you have early morning sickness with the girls?'

'No. It's not early morning.' It wasn't. It was irregularly throughout the day. 'I think it's the combination of twelve weeks and driving. I used to get horribly car-sick as a kid. I guess pregnancy just makes you more queasy generally.'

'You can take pills for car-sickness.'

'Not while I'm pregnant for God's sake!'

He'd been very apologetic after that. 'We could go on the train. I'm sorry, I didn't realise. We *should* go on the train. It's absolute madness driving round and you feeling sick – what could be worse?'

But then he started thinking; what was the point in toiling across a landscape that was as brown and dead as this one? Why not cut their losses and visit the cities? Why not visit Toronto and Quebec and get a feel for them? Toronto, the guidebook said, was a wonderful city with the greatest racial mix and range of cuisines in the world. It had a skyline to rival New York.

'You don't want to go to the cities,' she said. 'That wasn't why you wanted to come to Canada.'

'I've changed my mind. I don't care what we do as long as we have a good time. We've slogged round Niagara in the rain; now let's do what other people do on holiday. Pamper ourselves. Swim up and down heated swimming pools, feast in exotic restaurants, shop.'

'You'd hate it.'

'Why d'you assume that?'

There was no point in pressing it any further. She hadn't wanted to be pregnant again: he wanted them to have a baby together. She had let it happen. And now she must endure his return display of selflessness. (Gratitude, she reminded herself. Affection. Concern. Bitch to call it a display.) She had a vision of standing in a shop with him, holding up T-shirts with wolves or moose on them, urging him to help her choose for the girls. His impatient smile and glance out of the window. 'Yeah, they're fine. They're all nice – get those.' Pointing at the two closest. 'What next?'

Half an hour in a shop would be too long for him. But he would be outraged if she wasn't having a good time. Driving and being sick was a picnic, in comparison. Her own discomfort seemed to her to be manageable and contained, to leave him free to enjoy himself – while his would infect the week and kill the whole thing dead.

Something moved in the periphery of her vision and she stopped, tilting her face up to the sky. Something huge and black up there. A sudden near-terror.

'Gary!'

'Ye – es?' His call came from not very far away.

'Look up!' At first she had thought a bat – or even, a cloaked figure. Now she could tell it was a bird. The kind that soars; hawk, eagle, bird of prey. The biggest she had ever seen. Gary came crunching through the leaves towards her.

'Isn't it incredible?'

'What is it?'

'A vulture. There's a notice up here – I've just been reading about them –'

She followed him up across a bumpy rise in the ground to the top of a ridge. The view was unexpected; a deep tree-lined canyon, and woods and fields stretching away on the other side. They were on the highest point for miles around. 'Look.'

She read the board. Turkey vultures arrive back from the

south in early spring. Have nested at Rattlesnake Point for years. There was a drawing – a hideous bird with a bald vulture's head and evil beak. She looked up again.

'There's two. Three. One down there.'

Two came gliding down like they were on a ski slope – soaring right past Lisa and Gary's amazed faces; big birds, wings six to eight feet across, she could see the individual feathers shifting and tilting in the fan of the nearer wing, as the bird adjusted its position in the air.

'It's like the flaps on a plane's wing.'

'It is,' Gary agreed. 'Exactly.'

A way down the birds began to rise and turn, with one or two languid wing flaps, and then to climb higher up the sky.

'They look so hideous here,' she pointed to the picture, '– and they're so beautiful.'

'More – two more.' Two more came in from the south, dropped, circling, and made their run down the canyon.

'They're enjoying it,' she said.

'Anthropomorphism. They're looking for nesting sites.'

'Yeah. And enjoying it – as much as we enjoy the onerous biological duty of procreation.' She laughed, glancing at him, and watched his still-piqued face break into a smile.

At last they turned away from the canyon. 'It must be spring then,' Lisa said. 'It says they come home at the beginning of spring.'

'Yeah. We know. The birds know. They just forgot to tell the weather.'

'I think we can go back this way.'

They walked in silence, the memory of their argument and the coming oppression of Toronto moving in insidiously to flatten the exaltation of the vultures. All around the ground was carpeted with dead and rattling brown leaves, like old dusty cornflakes.

'What's that?'

'Nothing.'

They walked on and then Lisa stopped again. 'It's *running*. That leaf's *running*. Look.'

One crisp brown leaf was bowling and skittering over the surface of the others, with an impossibly sustained movement, as if the wind was behind it and it alone.

'It's *alive*.'

It stopped, a few yards ahead of them. And they could see that it wasn't a leaf but an animal. A leaf-sized, leaf-coloured animal, with the face and shape of a mouse, and a feathery curl of a tail, like a miniature squirrel. It was brown and black, striped, perfect, with brilliant eyes. It was still for long enough to stare at them, then it skittered off again and vanished.

'How *beautiful*. Is it a chipmunk?'

'Now you see it . . .'

'I never knew they were so quick.'

They waited a bit longer then walked on slowly, passing other rolling and skittering leaves, none of which stopped long enough for them to be quite sure if it was or wasn't.

'I don't want to go to Toronto.'

'I know.'

'How d'you know? I thought you thought you were doing me a favour,' she said.

'Male intuition.'

She laughed. 'Well?'

'Well what?'

'Where shall we go?'

'What you want is for me to choose, and me to be completely responsible when it's not exactly what you hoped for, although you don't care in advance to say what it is you were hoping for.' His voice was light and when she looked at him he was smiling. Maybe it was all right.

'Got it in one.'

'OK. My shoulders are broad – '

'Oooh.' She put on a joke voice. 'I do like a man who's masterful.'

'All right. Let's get the train *north*. We've got time, we can go by train all the way up to Nova Scotia – through Montreal, Maine, New Brunswick – through the northern forests – all the way to the sea. The Gulf of St Lawrence in the last throes of winter – the islands the Highlanders came to after the clearances – there'll be snow and ice and real wilderness, and we can put on all the clothes we own and say fuck to the weather.'

'Oh *yes*.'

'You can stand another week of my company, doing that?'

'I think so.'

'Well thank you for your vote of confidence, ma'am.' He made a sweeping bow and gave her a slightly strained smile.

'It's OK.' For that moment, it was. She tucked her arm into his. 'It'll be good.'

John Harvey

EUROPA

Extract from a novel in progress

FROM THE TRAIN window he saw rain in the distance, strands and skeins reaching from brown clouds to the ground. They made shapes like vague fingers, a shadow hand. But he was pleased with the day. His dealer, Sedgeworth, was optimistic for the prints.

He half-opened the light portfolio, and fingered the giant many-coloured etchings. The Rubens suite. Rubens in England. The figures chunky, part cartoonish, but with sensitive, careful detailed faces: against colours, patterns, of a lusciousness, an opulence . . . Here's 'Rubens asks to have it in Writing': the portly balding man holding a big hat is Rubens, the seated fastidious man is King Charles. It pleased him, this print, he liked the idea of it: the cheek of the painter, asking royalty, politely, to commit itself on paper.

Then Sedgeworth put a finger to Charles's head, 'That's Alec Guinness.' It's true, it's true. He'd laughed at the time, now all he can see is the head of Alec Guinness. I must have borrowed him from a film. What to do? Burnish it out? I can't start all over again.

He sighed, looked out. Ahead of the train the sky was darkening into deep-sea depths, black-purple, unbelievable.

Here's the other print, the gross one, which Sedgeworth, against the odds, had liked: 'Olivarez kisses the Pisspot of the Future King of Spain'. Really he did it – Rubens's boss, the great Count-Duke. The fleshy lips protrude, from beneath

259

the broad down-flattened nose, to wet the raised gorgeous vessel. The young prince turns observing, surprised – he is even amazed, but he is shyly pleased too. Flattery is sugar, it always has sweetness. A gross picture, gross. And Rubens was a flatterer, with his liking always to be kissing hands.

He shut the portfolio. In the distance ahead of them he saw a lightning flash: for seconds afterwards still he saw it, like a bent piece of pink wire, connecting the ground to the pale, lit-up clouds. He thought, it's years since I saw a lightning flash. He's always indoors, head-down to his pictures, yet all the time the colossal energies accumulate for the discharge. Maybe he'll make a lightning-print for Rubens: the war-storm of cloud slowly wheeling above Europe, while Rubens works to cajole plump Peace.

His eyes were on the window, awaiting the next flash. Outside like a wave a hill was building, blocking the dim low sky. Any moment the hill would turn into a tunnel.

There was a shape on the crest. A tree? A person? Then the clouds behind it flared, lit up within, flabby puff-bags of lightning: and he snapped it clear, it was a scarecrow. It was an old-style scarecrow, clothes on crossed poles, its arms stretched wide, slanted forward against the gale which blew its tatters back.

Only for a second he saw it, for there followed another flash, and this time he saw the lightning arrive. Perhaps he only put the sight together later: but he saw the zigzag root-shape of lightning strike towards him out of the sky, then take a jagged turn and reach the scarecrow, which at once burst, all of it, into fire, not as if set light to, but as if with the arrival of such too-big power, every particle and atom, of wood, cloth, whatever, at the same time exploded in incandescence, so the whole figure flashed up as a man of blinding light.

He blinked, dazzled. But the scarecrow now was a burning man, with flames like normal flames, a human cross; but the arms were gone and rags, it was just a burning stick; but they were in the tunnel, it had all gone out at once.

He sat back feeling scarred. His eyes wandered the closed

carriage, but no one else showed signs of seeing anything. Not that he could properly tell, for all he saw wherever he looked, with open eyes or shut, was the figure at its moment of bursting in fire.

He expected rain when they emerged from the tunnel: but it stayed bone dry. He could only sit back, his head damaged by the lightning-strike. It was when they neared home, when the thunder had slackened and a low yellow strip of evening light showed a factory and hospital in clear silhouette, that the lightning did its work. It jogged him. Abruptly he saw the unfinished painting. The picture he had not mentioned to Sedgeworth today. It waits in my studio, under wraps, under cloths. The painting I do not go back to. The portrait of Hetty. Even in his head, he hadn't looked at it in a long time.

Why did I leave it? All I do is evasion. The Rubens prints, they are evasion. Another age, other people, a diplomat with kings. I am running away from Hetty, my Rubens-woman. I've run for years.

With a shifting like the sliding of a too-heavy weight off his shoulders, he let it all come clear. I know what I'm running from, I've known all the time. How much one can hide, if one wants not to know.

The picture in front of his eyes has changed: to a woman together with that other, not like a couple but like one creature, he and she joined and fused in one. But his hand has become iron, harder stuff than they are: he could reach through their chests and pull out the double heart.

Yet what do I know? It's all a guess. But the painting of Hetty – I'll never go back to it.

But there he's caught, too. That painting is the centre-piece. The Rubens prints lead from it and to it. It will be, the huge nude, the centre of his show: a fair woman, and Europe, the soft body of the continent. The nations, like dwarf children, squabbling for their share of her. At the side of the canvas, Rubens the peacemaker, done in broad strokes, seated to paint her, and the picture he is in. But the palette he holds resembles a lute: he could be playing sweet music to her. And the colours – deep greens and crimsons, deep ultramarine, around the glowing gold of the body in the centre.

He'd seen it so clear, it should be so big. And Sedgeworth, before, said he wanted it: he had plans, a big tapestry, the mural for Brussels. If it worked, it would make his name.

And it can't be done.

Hetty, Hetty.

As the train drove forward his case got worse. He arrived at the station a shapeless agitation.

He'd walk home, he couldn't arrive like this.

But up on the railway bridge he looked back. There'd been a shower here, slates caught the light. The wet rails shone, snaking to the west, while a train pulled softly to a halt at the station. Lovely, at peace the evening city. Beside him traffic pulsed, stalled on the bridge. Cyclists nudged him, edging up on the inside.

Tired, I'm tired. At his gate, he stops. I see this picture of an ordered house, warm red brick in a stasis of health. Do I want to knock my house down?

He's opened the door.

'Stephen, is it you?' she calls, muffled, from the kitchen. At her friendly call his structure shakes.

'How did it go?'

He's not answered.

'Stephen?' she's called again.

The murderer stands in the hall of the home. You will see him in the dimness if you look in that corner. Only wait, he won't move before you do.

'Stephen?' she says again, her voice now quite uncertain.

A door's opened.

'There you are. How are you, Stephen? How did it go? Was it all right?'

They stand in the dim hall.

He'll only know what he'll say when he hears himself say it.

'No, no, it was good.'

'Good.' She's puzzled.

'Hetty.'

'Yes?'

He's on the brink now. Will he spill all?

The walls are sliding, his foundations will gape. He feels like a jigsaw held up by the ears: you can see the spaces between the pieces.

Hoarsely, he's speaking. 'Hetty – can we go back – to the painting we were doing? The big one. The one we started. I'm sorry we stopped.'

She looks at him seriously, puzzled, not displeased.

'Yes.'

He nods, they're both solemn. And he – he didn't expect to say this. Has he chickened out, taken the soft option, putting his art before all? Or is he doing what's needed: he'll rebuild his house.

She says, concerned, 'It's been a tiring day?'

'Yes, a tiring day,' he says, and enters his home.

Man and woman will enter the cluttered room, shy, conspiratorial, two on a verge. Around them a trestle-bench; a cast-iron machine; a chaise-longue. The man lugs the couch into the centre of the room, while the woman tries the pile of a length of crimson velvet and strews it on the couch.

While the man potters the woman will undress, shaking her head so her yellow hair swings loose, and settles on her plump pink-white shoulders. Her blouse, abruptly, she chucks in the man's face.

'Music!'

He's tuned to a pop channel.

Swaying she'll withdraw her bra, and shuttle to either side of it held still in mid-air – then flick it away past her head in a sling-shot. Other clothes she'll cast to different ends of the room, while he will have tuned to a slower music, night-clubby, saxophonous, to which she will weave and coil sultrily, her eyes in a tantalising fix on his.

She will stand undressed and white and plump, like a soft glowing statue with yellow hair, before the dressed man who studies her keenly. Her full breasts breathe, in their carriages of muscle which hang from her collar-bones. Her powerful handsome glowing face, blue-eyed and straight-nosed, gazes back at him directly: scrutinising, playful-mocking, turning the tables so he feels abashed, placed before her embarrassed by clothes. Then, with a bounce, she meets the old chaise, and extends her limbs to make a star: while he drags into the space before her a high skeletal wooden construction, and lodges within its wooden clamps a crisp, drum-taut stretcher of canvas, new-sized, white, empty.

While he dibbles colours she plays different poses: Odalisques, Mata Haris, the Venuses of Titian.

So it was, when Hetty first posed, or so now it seems in the drowsings of Bloodsmith, as he surfaces contentedly on the crest of the morning. But how will it go today, is the question. That dancing Hetty is long gone.

He has only more trepidation, as he fully comes awake. It's long, so long, since he stopped work on that painting.

And Hetty, though she said she would come readily, still delays, postponing the moment, fixing the washing-machine to wash.

'Let's go,' he's said several times, weakly hanging there.

'Right away,' she's answered, but still been busy.

The day itself is cold and blowy: the wind flaps and blusters, and snaps at the wrapped striding couple, the stocky man and the tall woman. The burdened cloud-cover thickens to bruise-black: it is dark for morning, and getting darker.

She pauses at his doorway. 'It's a very long time since I've been here, Stephen.'

'Let's get to it then,' he says.

From the roof-window a grey light falls in the room: dim as though the room were a tank of water. Sized canvases show whitely, the large press hulks at an edge of shadow. At least the radiator is on.

They look to each other, but not with roguishness. They've both grown grave, uncertain, a little lost: as if they've paused at the edge of trespass, on the rim of a zone where it's dangerous to go.

'Here's Hetty,' he says, pulling out the big canvas.

They gaze at the unfinished painting, from which the

neglected woman looks back, brightly but fadedly. With a cloth he raises a faint mist of dust: and gazes at the real Hetty, with her classical profile, gazing at Hetty in paint.

She doesn't speak.

'Hetty?'

He studies this concentrated adult inspection, with a crease at the eye-corner: she is looking hard. The face in the painting seems prettily nervous, and falling by the moment into ambiguity.

Finally she turns: 'I don't know.'

'No?'

'I don't know that this is me.'

'Oh.' His mouth and eyes hang open, gone serious.

She doesn't offer more.

He won't show he's hurt. 'I'll make sure it is you now.'

She turns to him a tired eye.

With a gravity, solemnity, with no hint of dance, Hetty undresses, resting her clothes in a half-folded pile. It seems, in the room, to be growing colder and dimmer, as if outside the day is still darkening. He aims the bars of his electric fire at the couch where she will sit.

It's a grave and solemn-faced naked Hetty who stands before him in shivery whiteness, with a don't-see-me tilt away of her body. And he is tongue-tied and limb-tied: as if it were the first time he saw her naked, or painted her, as if they had forgotten they were married.

But, 'Come,' he says, with an odd large gesture not usual to him, almost courtly, conducting her to a couch of state.

She gives an oddly aged smile. 'You need your Muse.'

'I do.'

With a movement of her hand to brush the velvet, she sits a little warily, perhaps even shyly. She eases her limbs while he only watches, stationed by his canvas like a proprietor at a gate.

'It's remarkable, Hetty. You've gone back – exactly to the pose you were in.'

She seems pleased and smiles, and perhaps it is an omen. So he won't need to do all his dodging and measuring, squinting at a brush-stem held at arm's length. When he first began the painting, he hung little weights on threads from above, so as to make a grid by which he could measure her: a fine mesh or cage that boxed her in squares. He doesn't need to do that again: but still he's got his fine adjustments.

'Can you put your foot there?'

'Where, there?'

'No, there.' He squints. 'Thanks.'

A moment he pauses: his head goes down, his eyes go unseeing. He always enters a vacancy like prayer, before he starts his paintings. But his head stays down, the moment extends, as it comes home to him: this is the turning point. If this comes right, I can bring everything right. My marriage – I can bring it right in my art. And it will meet his ambition too, for the Euro-competition, for the big wall in Brussels. His Hetty his marriage his life his art, all come right like a masterpiece in one.

Perhaps she knows from his breathing out that he is ready to begin. He is peering at her with his hard dry artist-eyes, eyes that should look through you but which study especially surface.

'Stephen – '

'Right. Yes. Music.'

He's over among his tumbled CDs. It's not a pop or jazz day, rather William Lawes: sweet notes of viols, with a melancholy, a strangeness.

She relaxes. 'Nice.'

On the wall Rubens seems bland and pleased. And it is such music as might have beguiled the famous Flemish painter, of an evening in his English trip, sitting in the Gerbier house as the consort was composed. The company sits quietly, replete but with a lassitude, and as the haunting notes extend, odd pieces of the past return. Rubens recovers evenings with Isabella, the boys hovering restlessly, as some of his apprentices play, and the young Van Dyck plies his bow, with limpid pale eyes that grow hot and return to Isabella.

'Don't you want the lights on, Stephen? Can you see like this?'

'No, I like it. It's interesting.' Though the room is dim, there is a diffused pearly whiteness. The figure of Hetty is snow-white before him, except where he catches, in her shins, her stomach, the faint reflected gleam of the electric bars. He examines his wife, this fair woman in middle life, her body a little slack with posing (a slackness he may later hide). A mature woman, the belly that has had a child, with a certain bloom and glow still to her. He notes the blue veins round the eyes of her breasts. Her breasts will be the lightest place in the picture. The next lightest is, what, her forehead?

Her head, he notices only now, is up with an obstinate jut. He registers something set and stubborn in her face, tautly closed to him: as if after all she is here only on sufferance, as though she is enduring something he is doing to her, as though, who knows, she is making a sacrifice being here at all.

'Hetty, what did you mean, the painting isn't you? It is you. I painted you.'

From wherever her thoughts have been they return. 'I don't know. You can see her now, I can't. But she looks nice, the woman. She doesn't look stupid. She doesn't look weak.'

'So she's not just my dream of a pretty wife.'

Now she's said it, he sees the woman in his painting gaze back at him with character. Why, then, isn't it Hetty?

'So? What is it that isn't there?'

'I'm not sure. I suppose . . . It's too light and bright.'

'You mean she hasn't got a dark side.'

'Yes. Yes, exactly.' Hetty gives him a steady look, not evasive, he's free to ask more. Both of the women look at him now, one in front of him, one further off, but in identical poses: the painted Hetty and Hetty – the woman without, and the woman *with* the dark side. He's not sure quite how that difference shows – except that the real Hetty's look is more intent, as if searching to see if *he* has a dark side.

'What do you mean?'

She looks at him with a gleam. 'Ah, the dark side is made of secrets.'

She watches as if waiting to see if he'll ask more. Till he

thinks, is it that she wants to say more? Perhaps all it needs is for him to ask.

They gleam to each other.

The question, the question.

The question stands in the studio with them. But how does it look, a question of this order? Well, its body and head are fused together, but it has a big ear like an elephant's ear, and a single bulging big dish-eye. A mouth of fangs runs from side to side of its gut – this question is hungry, it will eat man and woman. Also it is proboscid, its snout extends, quivering, tentacular, a moist snuffing trunk.

But does he want to ask the question? And he asked it, or part of it, the other day. He said, 'What is happening? Is something going on?'

She, sharply, 'What do you mean?'

'I don't know. Are you seeing someone?'

'What, like a lover?'

'Well . . .'

'No. Of course not.' It came so curt and clear, he was left shamefaced for asking.

They got nowhere then. But perhaps today is different. She sits naked, unprotected, studying him directly. Perhaps today she wants to tell. Or wants to be asked. If he persists, insists, she will tell.

But he, today, does he want to know?

Into his head a memory strikes, sudden, as happens, from an age ago: when she posed before, and something was said that caused Hetty, naked and posing, to blush. She flushed in her neck, in her cheeks, in her chest, and then down her body he saw the red fire spread. Irregularly, in patches, but growing and joining, as if an irritation, or fever, or real fire advanced, as if a radioactivity were heating inside her and rising up to the surface of the skin.

It grew, unevenly, till he had her lying all crimson on the crimson-strewn couch, a burning person. Then he, to see it, started to blush, till both were burning. He doesn't want that. Secrets are secrets. Does he want her secrets?

Looking round he sees the question, peering at him from

behind an easel. It has many eyes now, roving apprehensively. The music dips and swerves, pursuing a weird unpredictable curve.

Ask, don't ask. He can neither ask, nor not.

'What secrets do you mean?' he hears himself say.

She frowns, looks down. 'You can't explain these things.' She looks up, meets his eyes again.

What is she telling him? That he knows, or that he'll never know? That he should say more, that he should keep quiet?

He can ask more, she may say more. Obstinacy and fear debate in the air. Neither speaks.

The moment passes.

The question retreats behind the easel.

At a light pattering he looks up, and sees on the roof-lights grey-black splatterings: the rain has started. Light not heavy, but set to continue. The low drumming adds an undernote to the plaiting skeins of music.

He to himself, not without edge, 'Perhaps I'll paint her darker now.' Though he's also thinking, I painted her wrong. I was painting with doting eyes. He's come to an odd mood, cross, frustrated, maybe peevish. I can't paint at all, feeling like this.

Then she, sadly, 'It has to do with wanting death.'

'What does?' He knows she means the dark side. Its meaning is changing as the moments pass.

She doesn't answer.

'Say, Hetty.' She doesn't say.

He looks at her, and paints.

With a sudden gust rain slaps the panes, there is a clash as a bin goes over outside. The downpour has started, drumming to drill you. The sound calls his eyes up, to where thin rivulets of water run down the glass like crooked twigs. For moments, held, he watches the dance of the liquid threads, as all the time they shift their course, branching, bending, joining.

Looking back, he sees on Hetty's white skin, diffused and blurred, the faintest shadow of the coursing water. She is under the roof-light, so streams of faint shadow curve down her bare body: as though she sat behind a thin waterfall; or as though one could see time and life wash gently over her; or as if the plasma of her blood showed through transparent skin so you saw the slow streaming, which most of all is like a flowing sadness, as though in this cold wind-gusted room an unstoppable grieving were under way: as though the room is on the floor of an invisible river, and a torrent of grief on the edge of perception forever washes between its atoms.

Even so he paints, he has at last made a start: it will be a grieving painting, placing dim hue next to hue, with a tenderness, a sadness, as the sweet-sad notes come in rhythm with the rain. Outside the Gerbier house it is raining, the faces of the family are pensive and sombre, even little Sophy gazing at the dancing fire. The pattering on the latticed panes is like light pluckings on the lute, it puts Rubens in mind of raining days in Flanders, the rain forever falling on the Scheldt and on the marshes, falling on the new-drained lands and making his cloak heavy as he rides along the soggy dyke. Yet another afternoon of riding out ending up well washed. On the roof-light still the rain-tracks ripple, throwing their veinings on the floor and on Hetty, the changing profile of a succession of rivers. Bloodsmith is abstracted, gone out into eye, watching the moving marblings of light, while his brush dips of itself in cobalt and in crimson, a note of white, which it stirs to a purple and touches to the canvas, as though it moved voluntarily with him for its spectator. And still the sadness thickens, like a mineral in his head, like precipitating lead.

He returns to asking, 'How on earth do you paint the dark side? How do you paint it in a face?' But the answer's ready: you can paint a knowledge, you can paint it in the eyes. He stops to study the painting's eyes: and its true he's not sure now what they show. Almond-shapes with wheels inside them, what knowledge is in that?

From those eyes he returns to Hetty's. He focuses there and comes to a stop: her set face, blank, gazing at things that he can't see. She does not look obstinate, though still in her face there is something sullen, as happens to the face of a 'sitting' subject: they do not realise, but the expression slumps. And her face, inert, is gazing out but looking in with a mood of, what – deep hopelessness? She is lost and far from him, in her own way dogged, deep in a situation he doesn't know. They are very far from each other. And down her face the shadows course like a weeping far inside her: it is a weeping in him too, in both, for the sadness, the sadness, of where they are now.

His painting's stopped, the music's stopped, there is only the drumming rain and the sudden lifting threshing of wind. At the base of the roof-light, he sees the top fronds of a thrashing tree, tossing like a blinded bear.

Looking back, he sees: she's looking at him – with a serious, sad, divided look, with a look that questions, blue-eyed, intense. It is a look that undoes his art. It is a look that withdraws, that veils its edge, when she sees him looking back.

Both slightly smile, the smile of the withdrawing eye.

He retreats behind his canvas: but he can't go back to painting. He's so still and quiet that presently she asks, 'Have we finished, Stephen?'

From behind the canvas his voice says, 'We've finished for today'. A choked voice, he can hardly speak.

'Stephen?'

She has got up, and come where she can see him. He looks back, red-faced, caught. The tears from the window are on his face now, and wet.

'Hetty – '

'Stephen. My love.'

She has come to him, the naked woman: her white hand takes his paint-greased hand. He has half-leaned against a trestle, his red face turned away, a boy-face shamed by tears.

'Stephen. Stephen.' She shakes her head slowly. 'I'm sorry, my love.'

His face returns, abashed, askance, bewildered: to face her face that is all concern.

'I don't know why, Hetty. Just all of a sudden.'

She takes both his hands and holds them: his eyes with red whites, red rims, gaze.

'Come to me. Come to me, my love.'

She takes the draperies from the couch and spreads them on the floor.

271

Naked, kneeling, she begins to undress him. Garment on garment come off in a pile, till he's standing there naked to her.

'Come to me, my love.'

His hatred and rage, where are they? He had wanted to kill. Perplexed, he kneels and starts to caress her. As he does so, she embraces him: she kisses his shoulders, neck, chest, face. She pauses and looks at him, a sad straight serious loving look.

'My love.'

'Love.'

He can only kiss and embrace her more, only love and caress and hold. All of his rage seems melted to loving.

They have made love on the studio floor, their bare skin warmed by the electric fire.

The pattering of the rain has stopped, a white light grows in the room.

'You've greased me,' she says, sitting up.

He looks at his hands, smeared with cobalt and crimson: and at fainter smears lining her shoulders, breasts, thighs. Her white belly is marked where he stroked her belly.

'Reflected lights,' he murmurs: making now, consciously, more marks on her, emphases. A visible caressing, instant bruisings of love.

Using fingers as brushes, they make light decorations. He makes coloured zigzags, a tree up her middle. She makes birds on him and flowers, in capricious curves, dispersed.

The glass overhead is still growing brighter, a changed light rides in wheels through the studio. The crimson cloth seems deeper red, Hetty's skin, where not painted, more richly white: he sees traces of blue vein he didn't see before. She seems somehow larger, he feels larger, all the colours of the room are growing richer, as if the sun outside has emerged from clouds, so all the world will have more light; also as if, in a further dimension, a greater sun has emerged from its veils. When he blinks his eyes, the room seems different, as if it has more wood in it, there is hanging cloth, richly embroidered, the wall is hung with leather, painted red and stamped in gilt: as if two painters are in the room.

Till the moment when she sits up, quite quickly. 'What's the time?'

He looks round startled, not sure where he left his watch.

She stands, and standing steps into the sun, into a direct beam from overhead, so she, all decorated, flashes up golden. He can only watch this numbly: even with a pang, he quickly blinks.

'I have to go. I'm meeting Hazel.'

They look down at their painted bodies.

'OK, OK. I'll bring the turps.'

It's a joke, he brings the washing-up liquid, and, using it neat, makes coloured lathers of the paint on their skin, and wipes it off with kitchen-towel. A mountain of papers grows beside them.

Finally they rinse, splashing from the sink.

She's dressed.

She says brightly, 'I'll see you at home, love.'

She kisses him warmly, quickly, and goes.

And where's she gone?

But surely not.

Not to him.

He won't think bad thoughts, this is one of the good days.

He settles to sit on one of his kitchen chairs. He's tired, relaxed, he leans his head back on the wall.

And what happened today? Has everything changed? Or was it an episode, a strange interruption? For after all, no deal has been made.

A further knowledge is growing clearer: in spite of what happened, she won't soon come back to the studio.

He gazes at the painting of her. It is still unfinished, and somehow is rougher, and more unfinished than it was before today. And he knows now it won't be finished, they won't, he won't, return to that painting.

Yet, even in this room, the after-storm light is sparkling and bright. He pulls a cord so a roof-light opens. At last, a breath of new air in the room.

What happened was anomalous, did it fit? The pattern was bigger than he thought.

If we return, later, it is to see him sitting still before the big canvas. Can we get closer? He seems so absorbed, he won't hear our approach, so spectral as our footfalls are. All we see now is the strong check of his shirt, and the untidy scruff of back-hair on his head. Or, perhaps he just catches the soft fall of these words, leading us closer to him. For he turns towards us, but though we see him, he does not see us. His glistening eyes cloud. His face is red-streaked, a face confounded. And all we can tell from his misting eyes, as he gazes through us, is that he cannot see clear the person he seeks.

Ian Duhig

NOMINIES*

'. . . *to children the days of the year change at midday
rather than midnight.*'

It is noon. We groan, full of cheer
Well, it's the children's time of year!
and dressing up we never hear
the children changing gear.

It is midnight. The streets are snarls.
Good Englishmen walk their mad dogs.
Drowned by the choirs of car alarms
cogs are biting on clogs:

twelve ghosts turn back into children
with pence for the Red King's shilling –
turning the meter of my song
they'd make me a killing

but their taste for justice runs wild,
turning the mind that cast and kind
round to who could murder a child,
to a curse that would bind.

First of our butcher's eleven
shadows two chapters of our clock;
for two sons come down from heaven
their father's in the dock.

* The title of this poem is a Yorkshire word for children's occasional
chants. Its use is recorded in *The Lore and Language of Schoolchildren*
by Iona and Peter Opie, which also supplies the epigraph.

He killed them both, Walter Calverley,
called 'The Yorkshire Infanticide' –
when his wife held back some money
their eldest children died.

A gentleman of many bloods
who'd see no angels anymore
he swore their eldest were devils;
his wife he named a whore.

They tested him in Wakefield Gaol,
to enter a plea they pressed him
with great stone weights on iron plates.
He died. No priest blessed him.

He said nothing, was somehow brave
when his soft breast leaked out its life –
to save his land, his livestock and
to keep them from his wife.

Yorkshire children mock his grave now
raising a sympathetic noise:
Lig 'em on, lig 'em on Calverley,
killer of little boys.

This song maddens some mums and dads:
What's one black cloud? they shout at me.
When times get bad most mums and dads
can darken days till three.

Three then for children as makeweights
in the parental suicide,
and thrown from flats or drowned or gassed
with carbon monoxide –

of course there's the parents' story,
how pressure got on top of them –
like it did with Walter Calverley.
I think of them. Amen.

Light frames the fourth ghost to enter,
the slight youth who enters our ring;
his is a tale to remember,
and it is his turn to sing:

Father took me from the workhouse
down to a bright-sailed ship;
as Captain Arthur's cabin boy
I felt the Captain's whip.

From Greenland to the Bengal Bay
he had us chasing whale
and there three friends, not just shipmates,
I sewed into one sail.

At losing three good whalermen
he cried as if heartsore,
but when he heard the whale escaped
he cried out three times more –

he posted me to watch for squalls
because I also cried,
but in the gale my soft hands failed.
I lost my grip. I died.

He heard no moan; he slept like stone
till four bells echoed in his head –
he slept no more, threw back the door
and saw me, and me dead.

I held well then with iron hands,
I pressed him to my iron chest –
he'll never roam from his new home
North or, South, East or West.

The Angel of the Red Flower
stands guardian to number five
and weeps for sleeping boys and girls
bad housing burns alive.

The number swells as more hotels
sell bed and rather less than board
in the starving hearts of cities,
cold holiday resorts.

But six is the cannibal hour:
the Devil's name is six three times –
a combination to unlock
civil war crimes.

Six little boys late home from school
but two run off when three ask one,
Won't you play us at penny-up
or paper, knife and stone,
or paper, knife and stone?

I won't play paper, knife or stone,
I've no money for penny-up
but if you'll come one at a time
I'll fight until I drop,
I'll fight until I drop.

Six was the hour of broad daylight
that on this boy began to pound
and six the fists and six the feet –
he fell to stand his ground,
he fell to stand his ground.

Now ask the colour of his skin
and why was wrong with nowhere right;
was that all why such boys must die –
it's just that black and white,
sometimes
it's just that black and white.

Seven put question and answer
in a voice that boomed like a mine:
Why should even six fear seven?
Because seven eight nine!

The Red King burst from the shadows
in seven shades of majesty;
Harp and carp, John Rhymer, he said
O harp and carp said he:

study your sun; study your moon;
study books till your eyes grow blind –
a half-truth about human youth's
a half-truth you'll not find.

But things are very different
in Kynderland, where I am King
and a kinder land to children
no human hand can bring!

Laughter fills our days like swallows
and with laughter our clouds are torn
and happiest of our children
are those who don't get born!

And suddenly the moon blazed out
red as the sun will ever be;
and as suddenly he was gone
in shades of majesty.

And suddenly I rode a horse
and the world was a forest road
through some undiscovered country
where only dead cocks crowed.

And suddenly I heard the harp
tied to the saddle by my knee,
Don't turn your head this gold harp said
Or you'll be history!

Behind our backs the forest cracked –
sang the harp *It's you they're after!*
I heard the snorts of six cohorts
and the Red King's laughter.

Then I knew the harp sang true,
the number up was mine;
that these seven, thrown from heaven,
meant to have ate at nine.

Say your name in Latin backwards!
I did: this was the harp's advice
and horse and harp and I became
three blind mice!

I lost the head, I cursed and said
Golden Harp is this your magic?
If such quests are what you do best
that's just bloody tragic!

Full of pluck was that little harp
it snapped *Lest our tales drown in gore,*
live up to your image Rhymer,
work out a metaphor!

I prayed to the ghost of Carrie,
of the telekinetic powers,
of high school proms that go like bombs
and those traumatic showers.

I raised the shade of Janet Leigh
from a plug in the Bates Motel
and I conjured Norman's Mother
just for the Hell as well.

Silence reigned, then broke like thunder:
light gathered in a wheel:
the temple veil of night was rent
with showers of stainless steel.

A fiery crown came crashing down,
the golden harp and I both cheered,
or rather squeaked. But when we peeked,
the King had disappeared:

he turned to drought, made me a lake –
I mumbled underneath my brim
that water's not what should be bought
but still sucked up to him;

I clouded him, I crowded him,
I gave him vapours till four bells;
the interim I hunted him
from England's holy wells.

I worked him under Yorkshire sky
where the Red King popped his clogs,
who gave no thought to a Yorkshire drought
which rains cats and dogs.

Cheers! the harp said, *The King is Dead!*
But the horse looks disapproving;
you're due back west so, all the best,
but get yourself moving –

now is the house of your nine queens
and my Nine Gabriel Rangers;
beyond your ken, beyond your ten
we'll meet, not as strangers!

Harp and horse sank back into coins
that rolled like stones across my eyes,
for the hour was the eleventh
though ten made no goodbyes.

Where around me once was forest
and the great wheels of clocks,
now the pine-smell surrounded me
and six walls of a box.

But Carrie was still my angel:
she broke me free without a word
and from that hole my captain soul
soared upwards like a bird.

The Republic of Kynderland
lay under and it glowed like bone
and no children were playing there
but broken parents groaned.

Tears like tombstones fell from my eyes
and in their lenses I could see
Walter Calverley's, the Red King's
faces. They looked like me.

The sun hung like a temple gong
and the sky was clear as its bell;
the day boomed and, struck dumb and doomed,
from his glass face I fell.

The moon hung like a temple gong:
sand flowed up and down the timer;
which way is left and right and wrong
and who is John Rhymer?

It was midnight and it was noon:
the light of noon and moonlight swapped;
music of the spheres filled my ears
until the penny dropped.

Michael Foley

MARCEL ET JIM

THESE THINGS CAN happen. Joyce even met Proust. Yes, the drunken Irish immigrant and the fastidious darling of the salons. Of course there was the literary connection but a meeting was scarcely predestined, given Proust's reclusive nature and previous experience of Irish writers. After dining with M. and Mme Proust, Oscar Wilde entertained *le tout Paris* with scathing remarks about the bourgeois vulgarity of their furniture. No doubt he would have been more sympathetic if he had known that Marcel would subsequently use it to furnish a male brothel.

Yet Marcel and Jim had also much in common. Behind a pose of familial piety both killed the slave mothers who created them and, in the final versions of their books, eliminated the younger brothers who rivalled them. Behind apparent indifference to marketing (masterpieces published privately in their middle years) both were indefatigable self-promoters. Generally considered élitist and difficult, both attempted to service the entertainment sector (Joyce failing with a cinema, Proust succeeding with his male brothel). Sophisticates steeped in culture, both lived with uneducated women who never read their books (Nora Barnacle, Céleste Albaret). Reared in Catholic culture, both were attracted to SM (Proust S, being French, and Joyce M, being Irish). Incorrigibly epic, both were the joy of waiters (wildly extravagant tipping) and the scourge of printers (manuscripts swelling by a third in proof). Megalomaniac obsessives, both would go to any lengths to verify facts (Proust writing to a horticulturist for details of verbena

283

and heliotrope, Joyce writing to an entomological laboratory for scientific papers on *forficula*, the earwig) and both imposed their imaginative worlds on reality (Dublin erecting a plaque on the birthplace of the fictional character Bloom and the real village of Illiers adding its fictional name Combray to become Illiers-Combray). Wildly different in visual literacy, both were yet taken by Vermeer's *View of Delft* (Proust had a character die for a glimpse and it was the only work Joyce would allow to share his walls with the family portraits). Finally, their lives, so different on the surface, followed parallel arcs. Prigs in youth, they discovered the comic vision in maturity, at the same time renouncing those aspects of the world and the flesh that so engaged them (Proust retiring from social intercourse and Joyce from intercourse with Nora).

Both were also devious and secretive so that accounts of their meeting must be interpreted with care. According to legend they had the following exchange at Sidney Schiff's party for the first night of Stravinsky's *Renard*.

Joyce: I've headaches every day. My eyes are terrible.
Proust: My poor stomach. It's killing me. I must leave at once.
Joyce: I'm in the same situation. Goodbye.
Proust: *Charmé*. Oh my stomach, my stomach.

Surely this is *too* perfect, *too* banal and anti-heroic and mean — too exquisitely *modern* in fact? Ellmann, a rare sceptic in the credulous world of biography, suspects 'later embroidery'. Another explanation is that the legend was created not by admirers but by *the great men themselves*.

Consider what happened after the party. Joyce left *in Proust's cab* but the Schiffs were also present so that when they arrived at 44 Rue Hamelin Proust had to say to the driver: 'Please ask M. Joyce to let my cab drive him home.' Obviously it was necessary to shake off the Schiffs before bringing Joyce back alone for an intimate meeting away from the vulgar curiosity of the public.

*

Old army greatcoat, stained blue serge suit, black felt hat and dirty worn tennis shoes – a motley outfit Joyce attempts to redeem by jauntily twirling a cane. At length the door is opened by a young man whose pallid features express both apprehension and disdain.

'Are you from the abattoir?'

'*What?*' gasps Joyce.

'Do you have the rats?'

They stare at each other in wild incomprehension. Then Joyce bursts into laughter.

'Not yet, says you. *But Ah will in the mornin.*' Holding a hand to his brow, he feigns drunkenness, not a difficult task in view of his consumption at the Schiffs'. 'Jaysus, it's desperate. Ahm in *bits*, look see.' Laughing again, he reaches out a hand to lean on the young man who starts back in revulsion. At once Joyce assumes a formal, even haughty, pose. 'James Joyce. M. Proust is expecting me.'

Allowing his gaze to travel down over the greatcoat to the tennis shoes, the young man releases a bark of incredulity. Nevertheless he steps aside and allows Joyce to precede him to the lift.

At the door of the fifth-floor apartment Marcel more than compensates for his secretary's bad manners.

'M. Joyce!' he cries. 'Sovereign of the Transitory.' Joyce inclines slightly in acknowledgement. 'And hence of the Eternal.' Joyce bows deeply.

They exchange a fond gaze and then suddenly and simultaneously burst into *fou rire*.

'My eyes!' Joyce shrieks, shading them with an exaggerated gesture.

'My poor stomach,' Proust groans, rubbing it in mock agony.

When the laughter subsides Joyce assumes a grave look. 'But how are you . . . seriously, like?'

At once Proust turns away to hide the strength of his emotion. 'Every day I descend more rapidly a rigid iron staircase that leads to the abyss.'

'But you're lookin rightly,' Joyce suggests.

Proust turns in pique. 'I have been at the point of death on three occasions today. I have coughed more than three thousand times. My back and stomach are done for. *Everything* is done for. It's madness . . . *madness*. And as if this were not enough I am being systematically poisoned by carbon monoxide fumes from a crack in the chimney. I who crave heat deprived of fires!' He staggers slightly and reaches out for support. '*Tout l'hiver va rentrer dans mon être.*' Leaning on Joyce, he squeezes his arm. 'And your poor eyes?'

Joyce looks away. 'Nothing can mend the broken windows of my soul.'

'Have you tried the Coué system?'

'?'

'Keep telling yourself how great you feel.'

'You have tried this, I take it?'

'Oh yes.'

'And . . . ?'

'I was laid up in bed for four months.'

There is a long forlorn silence.

'But sure haven't you a brother a doctor?' Joyce says at last.

'And the author of a classic medical text. Alas, of no use to me.' He sighs deeply. '*The Surgery of the Female Genital Organs.*'

Joyce scrutinises him. 'Like Ahve had a few jars – but *Ahm not that far gone.*'

'Everyone knows I make nothing up.' Turning, a little coolly, Proust motions his secretary to take the guest's things.

Joyce shrugs himself out of the greatcoat in a slow abstracted way. The secretary accepts coat, hat and cane with undisguised repugnance.

'Listen,' Joyce says, 'would you have that about the place?'

'?'

'That textbook, ye know.'

Proust exchanges a startled look with his secretary. 'Not on the premises.' There is an awkward silence. 'But perhaps we can offer you something less potent.' He turns to the young man. 'Have we any of that port from Voisin's, the stuff the

Comte de Polignac said was like milk?' Before the youth can reply he turns to Joyce. 'A little port?'

Joyce grimaces. 'Beefsteak . . . *ugh!*'

Proust turns again to his secretary, a little impatiently this time. 'And champagne for M. Joyce.'

Drinks are served by a tall young woman with severely tied-back hair, black boots, a long plain grey dress buttoned to the neck and a white bib with her single extravagance – a border of Breton lace. Joyce regards her with an undisguised admiration that has no effect on her calm demeanour or the smile as fixed and benevolent as that of an angel in Rouen Cathedral.

'My Céleste,' Proust explains when she has gone. 'Beacon to errant sadness, protectress of the sick, haven of the noble banished into a vile world, obedient daughter of God, delicious flute of the wind that guides the lost skiff home.'

'She's a fair-lookin heifer right enough,' Joyce agrees.

'A child of many extraordinary gifts. *To think what her soft little hands will soon do.*'

Joyce's casual manner fails to conceal a keen interest. '*What's that?*'

Removing the protective wire, Marcel grips the champagne cork and averts his clenched face. At the violent report he cries out and staggers back, shaken.

'Close my poor eyes for ever,' he sighs, directing the foaming liquid into a glass. Only now, presenting the drink, does he appreciate the emotion of his guest. 'But of course she's just an ignorant country girl,' he adds hastily. 'Only today I had to explain that Napoleon and Bonaparte were the same man.'

Far from being disillusioned, Joyce turns towards the kitchen with naked yearning. 'I hate a woman that knows anything.'

Proust scrutinises him with interest. And by and by his own cavernous eyes, hollowed and ringed with black by the vampires of solitude, reveal in turn a spark of speculation and hope. '*Perhaps* . . . no . . .' He appears to reconsider, taking a swift drink of port. Then he sets down the glass and begins to rummage in his pockets.

His features softened by wonder and surmise, Joyce sips his champagne and murmurs, almost to himself: 'A strange beautiful wild flower in a tangled rain-drenched ditch.'

At last Proust succeeds in extracting a packet which he hefts with a solemn pondering look, casting swift doubtful glances at the Irishman.

'These are photographs of women,' he begins carefully. Joyce does not respond – but his features regain their customary shrewdness and reserve. 'Women who have meant *a great deal to me* . . . women I respect and admire . . .' Lowering his countenance furrowed by knowledge and wisdom, Joyce applies himself with scrupulous attention to the pouring of champagne. 'Women I *love*,' Proust concludes at last.

Raising his glass to the light, Joyce turns it about and studies it with grave concentration. 'I understand,' he murmurs softly.

With trembling fingers Proust withdraws the first photograph.

'Comtesse Jean de Castellane, half-sister of Boson de Talleyrand-Périgord, Prince de Sagan.'

Joyce accepts the picture solemnly and bursts into violent incredulous laughter.

'Jaysus . . . *Rosalie the Coal Quay Whore*.'

'You think it's *like* her?' Proust stares wildly at the photograph.

'*Like* her? This *is* her.' Joyce regards the portrait with fond amusement. 'God, we had some nights of it too. Talk about involuntary memory – *Jaysus*.' He shakes his head in wonder. 'They used to have a line about her – *she was only a coal quay girl because the skin on her fanny was slack*. But, like, that was only a joke. She was a great favourite really. Very popular at weddings.' About to produce another photograph, Proust halts in sudden dark mistrust. 'They used to get her to sit in a corner . . . with her legs apart, like.' Proust's frown does not relax. Calmly Joyce returns his gaze. 'To keep the flies off the cake, like . . . *ye know*?'

For a long moment they regard each other in silence. Then, shivering slightly, Marcel withdraws another photograph.

'Comtesse Adhéaume de Chevigné, née Laure de Sade.'

'Jemima from Monto, ye mean.' Joyce sings softly:

> '*Oh Italy's maids are fair to see*
> *And France's maids are willing*
> *But less expensive 'tis to me*
> *Jemima's for a shilling.*'

'Jemima was a right sort – heart o' the corn, ye know, one of Bella Cohen's girls – but Bella had to let her go in the end.'

Proust can scarcely breathe the syllable: '*Why?*'

'Ach, ye don't like to spread these things.' Joyce's face is clouded by responsibility and scruple. Marcel reaches out to give his knee an imploring squeeze. 'Jemima would give ye *anything* – but like she couldn't help getting excited and then she always wet herself.' He sighs heavily. 'I quite liked it meself – but I think a lot of the English officers complained.'

Proust falls back in his chair with a whimper of delight. By and by he withdraws the last photograph, throwing it a quick glance before pressing it face down against his heart. Huge and nameless emotions contend on his ravaged features. Lustrous tears shine in the caverns of his eyes. Slowly, and with the utmost reluctance, he proffers the photograph.

'*Maman,*' he whispers brokenly.

Joyce reaches out for the photograph – only to draw back in shock and revulsion. 'Aw . . . Jaysus . . . Jaysus, this is the *pits*. Ah mean . . . *Half-Gate* . . . Jaysus. Ye'd want to be *really desperate*.' He seizes his champagne glass. 'Ah mean, only *winos* . . .' Shuddering with disgust, he takes a long bracing gulp.

Whimpering in ecstasy, Marcel once again attempts to give him the picture. Joyce pulls back at once.

'Jaysus, ye'd even get a dose from just touchin her snap.'

Issuing from those profound depths where pain and ecstasy fuse, a strange equivocal cry escapes Marcel's lips. He curls up in the foetal position, the photograph once again clasped to his heart.

'Ah mean, ye know what they said about Half-Gate.' Joyce leans to administer the final thrust. *'Even the dogs wouldn't eat the green meat that hung from the fork of her drawers.'*

Like a young girl after her first orgasm, Marcel bursts into tears of inchoate fulfilment and wonder. Sitting back with an air of achievement, Joyce rewards himself with a leisurely glass of champagne.

Bit by bit Proust recovers, still snuffling a little.

'No one has ever done it better . . . *no one.*' With an impulsive movement he seizes the bottle and fills Joyce's glass to the brim. Then he pulls out a wallet and extracts several notes. 'It's just . . . here's a little . . .'

'What do you take me for?' Joyce cries. 'A *Proustitute?*'

'Forgive me the insult. Of course it's not near enough.'

Marcel extracts more notes. Joyce declines – but less vehemently than before. Again the process is repeated, with Joyce's resistance visibly weakening. In the end he accepts twenty thousand francs and a season ticket for the Ballets Russes.

Carefully edging through the door with a bottle of champagne on a silver salver, Henri stops dead at the sight of Proust and Joyce in a tender embrace, swaying slightly, occasionally patting each other on the back. Banging down the tray with a haughty cry, he storms out of the room, violently slamming the door. At once Proust rushes after him and, yanking the door open, draws himself erect with blazing eyes and shrieks into the corridor:

'Henri, you little *salope*, this isn't *Feydeau!*'

When there is no reply Proust disappears into the corridor with a violent exclamation.

Stretched out on the *chaise longue*, tennis-shoed feet on a plant holder, Joyce takes from his pocket a wad of notes which he counts carefully, smoothing out each in turn. At the sound of footsteps he hastily stuffs the money in a pocket but Proust, agitated and tearful, is in no state to notice.

'Sentimental madness!' he cries. 'No possibility of joy or relief. Only exhaustion, anguish, outrageous expense.' He laughs bitterly. 'A secretary who can't spell . . . a companion who can't talk . . . can't even play draughts. And it's not as if even . . .'

He throws himself into a chair and stares wearily at Joyce. 'I have to let him win at draughts.'

There comes a soft knock. At once Proust assumes an expression of implacable sternness and hauteur.

'*Yes?*'

'I have something for you.'

'Don't waste my time.'

'But the man from the abattoir came. He's a *beauty*, Marcel. Magnificent. *Aren't you, my sweet?*' A curious scuffling sound. 'Aren't you . . . *hm? . . . hhhmmmmmm . . . ?*'

The endearments visibly undermine Proust who sinks back in his chair with a stricken look. A sudden flurry of scuffling sounds makes him catch his breath. Joyce turns away.

'Well, perhaps a quick look,' Marcel calls out, adding at once in a warning tone. 'But just a look.'

Henri bears in a cage containing an enormous grey rat, its tail thick as an electric cable hanging out between the bars. Joyce shrieks. Instantly captivated, Proust rushes forward to kneel in rapturous veneration, his hand extended to the cage in an impulsive gesture of homage. Standing up on its hind legs, the creature viciously snaps at his fingers.

'A true prince of the sewers,' marvels Proust, gently lifting the tail and voluptuously passing it through his hands like the hair of a *jeune fille en fleur*. 'A glorious sultan of death and foul decay.'

'Ah Jaysus,' Joyce protests. 'Now hold on a minute.'

'Fetch the instruments,' whispers Proust.

'All is prepared.'

Assuming a grave and purposeful demeanour, Henri opens the door and wheels in a silver hostess trolley, from which he offers his master a pair of immaculate white gloves. Proust reaches out impatiently – but as soon as the gloves are placed in his hand jumps to his feet with a violent cry of repugnance.

'These have been *cleaned*. They smell of *benzine*.' He flings them wildly across the room. 'This is the kind of initiative *I do not appreciate*.'

As Henri rushes off, Proust turns to Joyce who has retreated to the far side of the room. 'Henri is *impossible*. Behind the mists and storms of his nerves the light of an intellect can only *occasionally* be discerned.'

When a fresh pair of gloves arrive Proust tries them on with a wary mistrustful air, flexing his fingers like a surgeon preparing for theatre. Henri selects a hatpin from the trolley and places it reverently in his master's right hand. Once again Proust kneels before the cage, gasping a little from the exertion and turning his flushed face to Henri who pats it with a steaming towel taken from a bowl on the trolley.

'*Again*.' Henri repeats the exercise, only to incur afresh his master's wrath. 'No no no no no *no*,' cries Proust, jerking his head away with an angry movement. 'You *know* it chaps my skin to use the same towel twice.'

Henri discards the towel and gently applies a fresh one. They hunch together over the cage.

'Hold him,' Proust says with surprisingly businesslike calm. And then, in a soft cooing tone. 'Ah my beauty, why resist? Who would want eyes to gaze on such a vile world?' He leans towards the cage with the hatpin.

Utterly rejecting Proust's argument, the animal lunges wildly and utters a hideous shriek of fear and pain.

'And now the other . . .' Again he leans forward, only to be disturbed by a sudden loud noise.

Joyce has collapsed on to the floor in a dead faint.

'Oh for *God's sake*!' Proust cries in annoyance. '*Céleste!*'

Joyce starts at Céleste peering into his face with a solicitous expression. He glances wildly about the kitchen and remembers suddenly with a cry of fear.

'It's all right,' Céleste soothes. 'We have taken you away.'

'It's *not* all right. Seeing a rat is bad luck. Yet another evil omen. Last year was . . . *1921*.'

'What of it?'

'Add the digits yourself.'

Céleste commences to count slowly and solemnly on her fingers.

'I feel so *helpless*,' Joyce suddenly sobs. 'Helpless, helpless, *helpless*.'

Céleste lays a compassionate hand on his shoulder. He springs to his feet and throws himself into her arms.

'O Céleste, my little mother, I am like a child tonight. I could nestle in your womb like a child born of your flesh. I could sleep in peace for ever in the warm secret gloom of your body.' Céleste utters an exclamation. He places his fingers on her lips. 'I am a poor weak impulsive sinful dissatisfied selfish poet – but *I am not a bad man*. I am not a bad deceitful person. Believe me when I say that something in you spoke to my soul this evening. Something frank and noble in your bearing. Something tender and gentle in your dark Jewish eyes.' She seizes his arm and attempts to free her mouth. 'Wait, Céleste! We have so much in common, the Jews and the Irish. Dispossessed, passive, impulsive, irrational . . .'

She breaks free with an angry cry. 'I'm *not Jewish*.'

'It's no shame, Céleste. Christ himself was born from the womb of a Jewess.'

'I am NOT JEWISH!' she shouts. 'I'm from Auxillac in Auvergne and I go to the altar every week . . . or I did until Monsieur asked me not to leave him any more. And my brother married a niece of Monseigneur Nègre, the *Archbishop of Tours*.'

Joyce retreats in wonder before her fury but just as he reaches the door a terrible shriek of animal torment drives him back into her arms.

'*Monster!*' he cries down the corridor. Then, tremulously, to Céleste. 'How can you serve such a *sadist* . . . a *tyrant*? You with such nobility . . . such compassion. You who can look on a wretch like me with pity . . . perhaps even with tenderness. Oh if I am ridiculous to you, *say it*.' Céleste sighs and shakes her head. He rests his brow on her shoulder. She stares into space with an expression of mystical vacancy. 'You know what I imagined when I saw you, Céleste? I imagined a misty evening. I was waiting and you came to me dressed in black, young, strange, gentle and pale.

You looked into my eyes which told you many things – that I am a poor seeker in this world, that I understand nothing of my destiny nor of the destinies of others, that I have suffered and inflicted suffering for the sake of worthless books and that soon, very soon now, I shall leave, having understood nothing in the darkness which gave us birth.'

'No no no,' Céleste murmurs, stroking his hair.

'Well . . .' Joyce sighs. 'I suppose some of the books weren't bad.'

'I meant you won't be leaving. You're still a young man.'

'I'm *old*, Céleste. And feel even older than I am. Also I'm not at all well. But I would let my soul be dispersed in the wind if God let me blow softly for ever on a dark-blue rain-drenched flower in Auxillac in Auvergne.'

Céleste, overcome: '*Monsieur!*'

'Take me into your soul of souls, Céleste. You could be to my manhood what the Blessed Virgin was to my youth.'

'An ignorant country girl like me?'

'At the threshold of death all is different, Céleste. We understand what is important. The power of a simple honourable soul.'

'But I have no education of any sort.'

'I could surround you with everything fine and beautiful and noble in art.'

'*Books*, you mean,' cries Céleste in distaste.

'Not just books but fine gowns and scent and magnificent furs. I would dress you like a duchess from the Faubourg Saint-Germain.'

Céleste glances down over the worn suit and tennis shoes.

'*Is there one who understands me?*' Joyce cries brokenly to the ceiling. Then, to Céleste. 'Can you not see the simplicity that is at the back of all my disguises?' He takes a wad of notes from his pocket and throws it contemptuously on the table.

Céleste stares in amazement. 'But you carry almost as much as Monsieur Proust.'

Joyce thrusts a handful of notes at her. 'Buy a fine evening gown. Buy magnificent furs lined with violet satin. Buy stockings and garters and drawers with frills and crimson bows.' He proffers money with furious abandon. She allows her hand to close over it and he whimpers in gratitude. 'Buy whorish drawers, Céleste . . . and be sure to sprinkle the legs with some nice scent.' He pauses but is unable to restrain his enthusiasm. 'And also discolour them just a little behind.'

With a cry of disgust Céleste releases the money and shoves him away. 'You're all the same in the end.'

Joyce flings himself on her. 'Restraint in this matter would be spiritual death.'

They wrestle, scattering notes on the floor. Céleste soon has the upper hand and thrusts him into a chair.

Joyce buries his face in his hands. 'I have killed your love. I have filled you with disgust and scorn. I have utterly degraded myself in your sight.' He raises a disconsolate face. 'You must be severe with me, Céleste, my little mother. Punish me as much as you like.' As he rises she lifts a threatening arm. 'Yes! I want to feel my flesh tingling under your hand. Smack me as hard as you wish. Flog me, even. *I would love to be flogged by you, Céleste.*'

'You'll be flogged by my husband if you come any closer. Then we'll see who discolours their drawers!' As he approaches she cries out a warning. '*Don't touch me!*'

'I don't want to touch you, Céleste.'

Sighing humbly, he goes about collecting the notes and smoothing them out on the table. She follows him with a wary gaze that increasingly lingers on the table.

'Then what *do* you want?'

Taking care not to make contact, Joyce approaches and whispers in her ear.

'Only to *watch*,' she gasps. '*Just when I'm . . .*'

He flings himself at her feet. 'I could kneel there as the Three Kings from the East knelt and prayed before the manger in which Jesus lay.'

A sudden terrifying high-pitched scream – the final protest of an animal dying in agony.

'Monsieur will want me now,' Céleste says. 'But later . . . you know where the . . . ?'

'*O Rosa mystica ora pro nobis.*' He buries his face in her dress. 'O my sweet little brown-arsed fuck bird.'

'We are drowning in an ocean of *merde*!' cries Proust. 'Not to blush at breathing is the act of a *cad*.'

'Ah it's desperate,' Joyce agrees. 'Desperate altogether.'

'And thus we become voluptuaries of laceration and disappointment. The only true pleasure is picking our scabs.'

Joyce nods solemnly. 'This is it. This is the thing. This is what you're up against.'

'Blackguards, cheats and thieves! Mountebanks with smiling masks!' Proust's breast heaves with emotion. 'It is less absurd to simulate life than to live it.'

'Ah yes,' sighs Joyce, 'where would we be without our books? Put it all in a couple of books.'

'No need for a couple. *One* book.'

Joyce: 'Render luminous the insipid present.'

Proust: 'Set the dross of history ablaze.'

Joyce: 'The here and now.'

Proust: 'Time Past.'

Joyce: 'Mimesis.'

Proust: 'Exegesis.'

Joyce: 'Recreate.'

Proust: 'Analyse.'

Joyce: 'No abstractions, theories, judgements.'

Proust: 'Abstract, theorise, judge.'

Joyce (angrily): 'Essayist!'

Proust (furious): 'Puzzle maker!'

Joyce (thrusting forward his face): 'Just watch your step now. I've taken Brits to court for less.'

Proust (defiant): 'And I have fought a duel with pistols.'

At once Joyce withdraws in fright.

Proust pursues him. 'Or perhaps you would prefer swords.'

'Ah Jaysus now. Wait a minute.' Joyce falls back into a seat. 'You know there's no call for that. *I hate violence.*'

Proust stands above him, eyes ablaze.

Proust: 'Mastery!'

Joyce: 'Submission.'

Proust raises his arm in triumph – then totters, gasping for breath and beating at his chest. He staggers backwards and falls into a chair.

At once Joyce rushes to his side. '*Maître illustre!*'

Proust squeezes frantically at his electric bell and almost immediately Céleste rushes into the room with a saucer of Legras powder already burning and giving off fumes.

She ministers to her master, quietly and efficiently, and eventually his breathing grows more even. Stirring anxiously, he murmurs something and Céleste signals to Joyce to draw near. Proust seizes the Irishman's hand and squeezes with all his remaining strength.

'Heroic capitalist of the quotidian,' he croaks.

Joyce, considerably moved, returns the pressure. 'Epicurean of ordinariness.'

Céleste composes her features into a warning frown. 'Do not over-excite him. He must doze a little now.'

She continues to regard Joyce in silence. The breathing of her master is deep and regular. Reaching into his pocket for a wad of notes, Joyce jerks his head towards the corridor.

'From one disillusion to another.' Joyce dully regards the flat champagne in his glass.

Proust laughs bitterly. 'Desire makes all things flourish; possession withers them. And of all the disappointments caused by expectation none is more bitter than that produced by love.' He darts the Irishman a sudden mistrustful look. 'But they say you have lived with a woman for many years. *Do you believe in love?*'

'I do.'

Proust sits up in sudden fierce anger and points unequivocally to the door.

'I believe in two kinds,' Joyce continues, 'the love of a woman for her child . . . *and the love of a man for lies.*'

Proust's gesture of dismissal becomes a solemn salute. 'Many subtle and quivering chords are struck only by you.'

'When I hear the word love I want to puke. What is it but a temptation of nature in youth?' Joyce comes forward on his chair in sudden animation. 'Every mature man knows the solution.'

Proust nods. 'Set up your own establishment. I have recondite specialists in all the singular pleasures. Disabled young war veterans are *especially chic* this year. But the constant research it takes to maintain a *menu gastronomique*!' Rising, he goes to the bookcase and returns with a substantial volume. 'You know Krafft-Ebing of course? *Psychopathia Sexualis*?' He flips the pages mournfully. 'Even vice has become an exact science.'

'Few can afford an establishment. I was thinking more of self-help. A remedy old as man himself but one that could never be mentioned in print.' Joyce pauses with an air of satisfaction. 'Never until now, that is.'

Proust chuckles happily. 'How did you guess?' Rising, he executes in the air an arc as graceful and strong as a Nijinsky leap. 'A shimmering jet arched forth, spurt after spurt, as when the fountain at Saint-Cloud begins to play. I felt a sort of caress surrounding me. It was the scent of lilac blossom. But a bitter smell was mixed with it. I had left a trail on the leaf, silvery and natural as a snail track though it seemed to me like the forbidden fruit on the Tree of Knowledge.' He allows his arm to sink slowly, a languid dying fall.

'I meant *myself*,' Joyce snaps. 'In *Ulysses*.'

'Ah yes M. Bloom.' Proust resumes his seat with a satisfied air. 'But I was first.'

'*Where*, may we ask?'

'*Contre Sainte-Beuve*.'

'An *unpublished* book,' Joyce sneers, stung nevertheless. 'You'll have to wait for credit. You know all that was cut from the English *À la Recherche*.'

Proust leaps to his feet in hot tears of rage. 'That douche bag Scott-Moncrieff . . . that *salopard*. I knew I should never have trusted him. *Never trust an invert*.' He turns to Joyce in an attitude of supplication. 'You'll have to tell the English. *Tell them. Tell them*.'

Lying back in his chair, Joyce performs a coarse and provocative mime of the act under discussion.

'*Oh!*' Proust cries, looking away in disgust. 'Indelicacy is an *abomination* to me.' Nevertheless he steals another glance. 'Oh *really* . . . this is *too much* . . . you're *common* as dirt.'

So it draws to a close, the night of bizarre and unique détente. Despite his lack of strength, Proust insists on seeing his guest to the door.

'With the memory of these hours of exquisite pleasure I shall build, deep in my heart, a chapel dedicated to Ireland.'

Joyce does not look pleased. 'What has Ireland got to do with it? Dedicate it to *me*.'

Proust bows in courtly submission. 'And of course . . . if there's anything . . .'

'I'd like to say goodbye to Céleste.'

Proust straightens up, in his dark eyes a terrible struggle between hospitality and megalomania. Without a word he goes back into the room and rings the bell.

'Why do you keep her locked up?'

Proust sighs. 'I would wish her life to be as decked with joys as mine is thorny with sorrows. But she has chosen her way. Often beautiful wild flowers like to bend over the abyss.'

'Grant me one more favour.'

Proust stiffens. 'If you wish to be flogged I have trained staff. I can arrange chains . . . a British Navy cat o' nine tails . . . a convicted murderer . . .'

'I just want you to let her go to the altar again.'

Proust considers the request. 'Mass!' he snorts at last. 'Only the fatalism of the Muslim makes sense.' He turns away coldly. 'But as you wish.'

Céleste enters and looks to her master who averts his eyes. She goes instead to Joyce who also looks expectantly at Proust. The master turns away but remains in the room.

'You have been granted permission to go to the altar,' Joyce says. 'Also I'll send you something. A bottle of duchess' scent.'

Céleste stares at the floor in confusion. 'Monsieur is very much afraid of the scent of duchesses.'

Proust has rung again, surreptitiously, and when Henri appears, wraithlike, speaks to him in an urgent whisper out of the corner of his mouth.

'Keep an even closer eye on her for the next few weeks.'

'*Can we meet again?*' Joyce is whispering passionately to Céleste.

She raises her sorrowful eyes to his. 'We shall all meet again in the Valley of Jehosaphat.'

Biting back tears, Joyce takes both her hands in his. 'Look after yourself. Take cocoa every day and fill out a bit. And you know what I said . . . I mean about . . .' – she nods quickly – 'that was all madness . . . *madness.*' He squeezes her hands fervently. 'I am sure they are as spotless as your heart.'

With a grunt of impatience Proust comes forward to take Joyce by the arm. 'I shall see you to the main door.'

'But you're not well,' Joyce says sarcastically. 'It's too far.'

'We must never be afraid to go too far. Truth lies beyond.'

He guides Joyce gently but firmly out of the apartment and towards the lift, only releasing his grip when the cage arrives. Hanging his head, Joyce hums a tune from Donizetti's *L'Elisir d'Amore* – that most heart-rending of arias, *Una furtiva lagrima.*

'Life is for our readers,' Proust murmurs gently in consolation.

Joyce nods sorrowfully. 'We who have nothing will give them the world.'

'We shall teach them to fight their way back to life, shattering over and over again the instantly forming ice of custom and habit.'

Yet as they emerge into morning, the light of common day each has done so much to redeem, both of them stagger back with sudden cries of shock and pain.

Joyce lifts an arm to shield his eyes. 'God, that's *brutal.*'

Proust claps a handkerchief on his mouth and nose. 'The spring, the spring. Dust, pollen, horse hair, horse dung.'

Partly protected, they advance defiantly once again.

'Sure ye'll soon be off to Cabourg and the Grand Hotel,'

Joyce suggests, getting only a bitter laugh in return for his pains.

'The Grand Hotel is full of nothing but Jewish wholesalers now.'

They regard in silence the morning activity of Rue Hamelin – the shops opening, awnings going up, Léon Quinot's delivery boys setting baskets of groceries on tricycles, people coming out on to balconies, going to work, bearing home from the Boulangerie des Etats-Unis bags of fragrant warm croissants and bunches of baguettes.

'What is the greatest sin?' Proust suddenly cries, turning and experiencing the disillusion of the Redeemer in Gethsemane. For the only one who could offer support is fast asleep against the door. After all, Joyce has been up all night whereas it is only Proust's bedtime now.

Proust is faced with the ineluctable destiny of the race – every man has to answer his own question himself.

Directly in front of No. 44 a placid cart-horse pauses in the centre of the street and deposits on the cobbles a steaming symmetrical pyramid like a ceremonial mound of cannon balls. Even now Proust does not withdraw. Instead his waxen features tremble with emotion; tears of exaltation shine in his cavernous eyes. In a near-suicidal gesture of heroism he removes the handkerchief from his face.

'*To be incurious before the spectacle of the world.*'

Roy Fisher

ITEM

A bookend. Consider it well
if that's the way your mind
runs. One-handed

this year at least, and lame,
unable to shift it somewhere better
than where it unbalances

one of the unsafe heaps that
make up my workroom, even I
get driven to consider it,

putting myself at risk of unaccustomed
irony, metaphor, moral.
It's one of a couple. The other's long-

lost in the house and has turned to pure
thought. This one's material,
cut from three-quarter-inch softwood,

deep-stained as oak and varnished
heavily; a few scratches. Made up
of three pieces. The face,

five inches across by four-and-three-quarters,
with the corners cut in at forty-five
degrees from three inches up; two

nails struck through to the base,
same shape, but three by three-and-a-half,
hollowed and plugged with lead. A buttress

braces the joint. The outward
edges all bevelled, and the whole
glued solid. It's professional,

effective as a brick would be
but with less style. No trace
of commercial fancy anywhere on it.

When my life's props come to suffer dispersal
this piece gets dumped, if I've not
done it myself first. Should it get to a junk-stall

there'd be nothing to know but these
its observable properties. All the same
it does have unshakeable provenance – unless I

choose to suppress it. I don't.
I've certain knowledge the thing is fifty-two
years old, manufactured in 1944

at the enormous works of the Birmingham
Railway Carriage and Wagon Company,
the neighbourhood's mother-ship and provider,

her main East entrance
sunk in the bend of the street I lived in.
Set up to build saloons for the world's

railways. Then Churchill tanks. Then latterly
by day and night, huge helpless plywood-skinned
troop-carrier gliders that were crawled out

wingless and blind between the houses,
lacking engines, armour or arms. Lacking
bookends. The bookend maker was a foreman

coachbuilder from the top of the street,
a man of some status, genial; Mikhail
Gorbachev would be good casting if unemployed

when this poem's filmed. My bookends
formed part of a short, non-commercial,
privately produced domestic series

using materials, tools and time stolen
from the Ministry of Aircraft Production
and its contract, and designed as family gifts

for the Friday firewatch team, four veterans
of the Great War who gathered as ordered
by law and played cards in an empty house all night,

never looking outdoors. Against
regulations, but less culpable
than the woodworking: it was forbidden

ever to reveal the sources of one's secret bookends.
The same foreman had an only daughter.
Well-provided: plenty of body, a job

in the factory office, a husband stationed
not far away, a home with her parents. Tapping
into a quiet custom of the time,

she worked out the date of her army call-up,
got pregnant, got herself certified so. Aborted
the foetus at home while the debris

was still small enough for the closet in the yard
to flush it; kept quiet, played for time;
won. Another little knot of illegalities.

As to this bookend, to say that the first
load it supported was a crimson-backed set of miniature
home encyclopaedias, forced into the house

in the newspaper wars of the Thirties by the agents
of Beaverbrook, later Minister of Aircraft Production
would be artistic, ironic, and, just possibly, untrue.

Jane Duran

IN THE PAINTINGS OF
EDWARD HOPPER

May we stop here?
In the filling station
the meter is at zero.

Up and down the laundered
street – it is guesswork
what goes on
behind the open windows.

A face turns from another face
swept into the glare
a small town
dares to withstand.

The eyes could fill with tears.
A wolf could come from the woods
meaning it.

We sap our strength
raking leaves, over coffee,
in a room for the night
or sitting quietly

till daybreak. Houses
take up their old positions
in the wind.

All at once the looseness of fir trees,
the seemliness of our lives.

Elaine Feinstein

PRAYER

The windows are black tonight. The lamp
at my bedside peering with its yellow
40-watt light can hardly make out the chair.
Nothing is stranger than the habit of prayer.

The face of God as seen on this planet
is rarely gentle: the young gazelle is food
for the predator; filmy shapes
that need little more than carbon and water,

evolve like patterns on Dawkins'
computer; the intricate miracles
of eye and wing respond to the same
logic. I accept the evidence.

But God is the wish to live. Everywhere,
as carnivores lick their young with
tenderness, in the human struggle
nothing is stranger than the habit of prayer.

ELAINE FEINSTEIN

BONDS

There are owls in the garden and a dog barking.
After so many fevers and such loss,
I am holding you in my arms tonight, as if
your whole story were happening at once,
the eager child in lonely evacuation
waking into intelligence and then
manhood when we were first *copains*,
setting up tent in a rainy Cornish field, or
hitchhiking down to Marseilles together.

You were braver than I was and so
at your side I was never afraid, looking for
Dom 99 in the snows of suburban Moscow,
or carrying letters through Hungarian customs.
I learnt to trust your intuitions more than my own,
because you could meet Nobel laureates,
tramps and smugglers with the same confidence,
and your hunches worked, those molecular puzzles,
that filled the house with clay and wire models.

In the bad times, when like poor Tom Bowling,
you felt yourself gone for ever more,
and threw away all you deserved, you asked me
What was it all for? And I had no answer, then
or a long time after that madness;
nor can I now suggest new happiness,
or good fortune to hope for, other than
staying alive. But I know that lying at your side
I could enter the dark bed of silence like a bride.

Peter Redgrove

THE LEVEE

*She put on a silver dress and desired that there should be a
street party between the two houses on her birthday. This was
almost the only time left to her. He remembered her fondness
for angels, and hoped that she might become one.*

I

This mirror is now a dress
A glittering sensation
And the face in it
A baby closely attending to her birth.

She holds her levee
In her silver full-length dress
Transforming the enzymes of cancer
Into a great birthday party
Between two houses, a street party;

On receiving this gesture
We have descended as in a lift
Which does not transport us
But which shifts the scenery
As the numen approaches, and everything
Trembles into its alternative

II

The chief party-goers,
Chief doves or
Ministering angels
Like the beating of wings
Cooing and wooing
On the head of a hypnos;

They would strut turn by turn
Into their lady's vestibule,
The siblings, the in-laws,
The sons and daughters,
The remote relatives
With their dusty shoulders,

Would fly in their turn
And perch at the bedside
For some jokes, for some memories,
And bill and coo there
With the silver hostess
Who is to be virginised
When the party is over,
Into a statue;

And bill and coo
In the room full of wings
Of wings rushing like falls,
Everyone turned to angels
Forgetting to tiptoe
Forgetting not to laugh aloud,
Because death is invited on tiptoe,
Everything trembles into its alternative,
Everything is sexualised;

She points with a certain meaning
To the structure of the lanceolated
House-vestibule,

Its running curtains and the
Portrait head of her
Sculpted with a cowl
And set high in the dome,
Its little fountain on its threshold
And the darkened cave within;

We were visiting her home
Now we are among her genitals too
A party laid for death.

Touch the sleeper and the winged heads
Swarm out like flies from the carcass
A carcass that is riches, and the
Knowledge in those faces;
This is a magic touch
And what the sleeper has to say to us
About flesh blood and bone
Made in those steamy cathedrals
We call sleepers

There will be a nubby cowled portrait
Which is alive during the party

And as the fountain gains stature
It becomes wings,
She is being withdrawn
Into the great Angel,
The party-goers hold the doors open

III

By insufflation she smelt the lily
To start the whole process going
To incubate the innocence
Fragrance and clear skin
While the doors are open

311

And the party-goers come and go
Into the death-chamber
To greet with party-laughter
And speak awhile
On the fragrant wings of wine
With the inhabitant
Of the two worlds at once
On the gentle threshold,
Everyone is gentle on this threshold;

And it is the food's task
To be shared in the light of this dress
Between the people in attendance
And others far away
For it is the property of this threshold
To stretch over the whole world;

They share food at this threshold
That the cancer-enzymes digest also
They eat this food together
Much too fast,
They gobble it up,
They cannot digest the whole party away
Which is a work
Of her Great Angel
Drawing her up
On the ladder of the bed
Reversing the Matron
In the silver dress,
Restoring the Virgin.

IV

And some so inspired
By the room of the silver dress,
And the good angels drawing her out carefully
Like a white flute out of its case

Its red plush case,
All the juices of this chamber
Become the wines of the many various years;

To draw her forth
Intact;

There was an occasional interference
On the radio of distant weather.
The party loosened all our souls.

Like whitecaps on the radio
That wing-hiss saying
Let flights of angels
Sing thee to thy rest,
The radio wingbeats in the silver dress.

Suddenly as Death turned
On the pillars of the throat
She slipped into his breath
Which carried her away easily;
Then a virgin was present on these pillows
Not in our modern sense either.

Christopher Hope

POGROM

Extract from a novel in progress

VINCE AND SHIRLEEN de Lange were British Israelites.

The Israelites all lived in Nickleton: an old mining hamlet a good half-hour from Buckingham on bad, rutted dirt roads. A couple of dozen pre-fab miners' houses, a community hall the Israelites used as a temple and three windmills; that was it. They needed somewhere to wait for the world's end, and since they didn't have a date, waiting had to be cheap. Just a trickle of them settled at first. Soon it was an invasion. Provincials up from the coast in rusty saloons, suitcases tied up in plastic bags, hand in hand with bewildered children. Or fancy folk in flight from the big cities, with tales of rape and gunfire in the new South Africa.

Nickleton had no shops or post office and Israelites were sometimes in Buckingham for groceries, or to scrounge firewood and cheap cuts of meat from Mr Bok the butcher at Karoo Choice, and to drop their kids in the new White School, which raised eyebrows because they were always broke and the White School cost big bucks. They'd hang about telling people what they should do to be saved. You'd see them in Sampie's Café; in the bar of the Hunter's Arms; in the farmer's co-op. Bright smiles and guitars and city shoes.

Vince was a big, sandy fellow. The heat got to him. He gave out moistness like steam off a hot road after a summer storm. There was an air of retreat about him. A making off. It was there in his slippery handshake; slide-away sultana eyes. But affable and easy to like. Selling insurance, that had been his game – his neck of the woods, he called it – back in the big world. Before he came to live in dusty Nickleton. Before he became an Israelite.

Shirleen wore a lot of white that set off her dark hair; white leather bolero, white ribbon in her jet hair. The dimple so centred in her cheek you felt it couldn't be real. Bright lips and gales of scent. Where Vince backed off, Shirleen came forward. She was outward, friendly: soft smile and a warm handshake. She'd been on a make-up counter, back in the big world. Before she had her vision. It was hard to imagine any vision persuading her to settle in dusty, stony, pinched, parched countryside, miles from anywhere, being herself so very plentiful, with a roundness she tucked into a pair of white jeans, and high-heeled cowboy boots and the dimple puckered in her plump left cheek like the button in an eiderdown.

Israelites hadn't much to do while waiting for the world to end. They were not Christians and they did not talk about God. It was Yahweh this and Yahweh that. They would be saved by Yahweh. Flood, fire and boils were waiting for those Yahweh hadn't saved. How they lived no one knew, but they were always saying their needs were few. A guitar for making up new hymns because hymns were scarce. And a copy of their second sacred text after the Bible, Pastor Tezer's book telling them of good and bad noses in the Holy Land.

They might have been religious but they weren't old-fashioned. They brought their city ways to the Karoo. Shirleen in her boots and her Walkman and her dark twinkle. Vince and his guitar. Modern people. Out and about people. Streets ahead of khaki shorts and wrinkled lemon frocks, beige safari suits and electric-blue shorts and matching socks, which were high fashion in Buckingham.

That was the thing about the Israelites. The end of the world might be at hand, but they dressed for it.

When people thought about the Israelites at all it was to wonder how they paid the bills. They weren't saying they were good and they weren't saying they were bad; though everyone agreed they were crazy to live in Nickleton where the wind blew high velocity and the sand flew at those little tin-sided old miners' shacks and rattled them worse than windmill blades.

Pascal LeGros at the Hunter's Arms took to Vince and Shirleen. Cognoscenti, he called them. And one hell of a change from the bumpkin factor in Buckingham. Tolerant too. Israelites didn't want their followers to be British. Or even to speak English. And certainly they didn't have to come from Israel.

Vince and Shirleen had been to Mauritius, so they were qualified to talk faraway places with Pascal, who had daughters in Miami. Well-connected, too. As Pascal told it, the Israelites had left the Holy Land way back when and drifted over to England, and became part of the Royal Family. No wonder Buckingham's bumpkin factor didn't like them. But then what did one expect? Minds narrower than needles, two-faced yokels who never set foot in the pub – devil's cockpit, seat of Satan – then hit the bottle in their back gardens. Oh, yes! Like there was no tomorrow. Vince and Shirleen called themselves saved, chosen by the Lord and all that – yet they dropped into the Hunter's Arms for a civilised snifter. He, for one, welcomed that, he told his partners, Mike and Maureen.

Maureen pointed to their bar card, unpaid for months. She'd welcome some cash. Saved they might be; they were also seriously broke.

Some of the curious visited the Israelite temple in Nickleton on the Sabbath and heard Vince tell them about being saved, and to beware of black women who lured white men into bed, determined to steal their genetic codes. That Yahweh voted for separate races and anyone who'd seen the violence and lewdness and interbreeding of the cities since the elections knew the world was about to snuff it. They liked what they heard and signed on.

It pained the new pastor of the Dutch Reformed Church, young Rusty Niemand – brought in to replace Dominee Greet who did a runner. Buckingham already had too many churches. A Dutch Reformed Church for brown people and a

Dutch Reformed Church for white people and a New Dutch Reformed Church for Specially Pure White People.

Niemand protested to Maureen that Buckingham already had a religious war on its hands. Who needed another? Half his flock had swanned off with the mad defector Greet, and taken up residence in the little old deconsecrated Anglican church, beyond the abattoir. Now he was losing youngsters to these Nickleton soul-snatchers who were eating into his remaining congregation like a plague of bloody locusts.

Maureen gave him short shrift. Niemand had discouraged his parishioners from visiting her hotel. She simply adjusted her towering blonde hair-piece, shifted the little parabellum pistol on her hip and said pulling customers was hard for everyone. And started calling him minister of the 'Much Deformed Church'.

Until the Israelites came to town everyone had believed Pascal LeGros was a full one-third partner in the Hunter's Arms and the brains behind the place, full of talk about beating the bumpkin factor and putting Buckingham on the map for the discerning traveller. He was going to theme the bedrooms in the Boer and Bushman myths and magic of the old Karoo. Persons of the world, at home in Mauritius and Miami, would love the newly refurbished Hunter's Arms, where springbok hunter and philosopher, weary tycoon in search of his soul and rural raconteur would meet and mingle over old-fashioned mulligatawny in the restaurant, or stoups of mulled wine in the library. Buckingham must go for quality. The country had changed. It was time it adapted or died.

The way Vince and Shirleen became Israelites was a sign of their quality. It had happened one morning in a sports shop in a town called George while they were shopping for running shoes. 'Nike, if you please,' LeGros would nod when he told the story. 'No tat. My kind of people.'

Vince and Shirleen had been chatting to the saleswoman, as people do back in the big world, about rugby and politics and armed hold-ups and who got car-jacked in their street, when suddenly the saleswoman looks Vince straight in the eye and asks – does he not seek the kingdom of Israel? Leaving their running shoes unbought Vince and Shirleen hurried home, opened the Bible and there it was: Yahweh's order to Moses to seek the Promised Land. Within weeks they had given up their jobs, sold their house, and moved north to Nickleton. It had been a vision. People with vision impressed him, tremendously.

Maureen announced to Mike that she had had a counter-vision. In it Pascal became the big white bwana. And the Big White Bwana was messing up, wasn't he? And to Pascal's surprise, Mike said, yes. Bloody right. Messing up something chronic.

Until then Mike had been hedging his bets. Mike and Pascal went back a long, long way. Back to selling roofing felt and windscreen wipers. And time-share seaside apartments in Margate. Big, round Pascal in his tennis whites. Little dark Mike, slight and sharp. When you asked Mike what he was, he said he was a sidekick. And Pascal was the brains, the business end of the operation that brought the three of them to the Hunter's Arms. But Mike was hitched to Maureen now. Widowed Maureen whose late husband had worked on the copper mines in Zambia. One minute he was there, the next it was toodle-oo, she told Mike, when they got together. Maureen of the big bucks, Maureen of the huge hair and the tiny pistol and the doddering, incontinent old Ridgeback called Brad whom Pascal hated worse than Bill Harding hated his wife's budgerigar. Brad was a walking health hazard and should be put to sleep. Maureen invited him to try and she'd shoot him dead.

But it was Mike who told Pascal that his menus were the pits. Who'd want Sole Bonne bloody Femme in a desert town where they thought good cooking was roasting half a sheep on the fire and pouring beer down your throat while turning the spit with your bare toes?

And it was Maureen who booked the weekend away and, in case he didn't take the hint, told Pascal they were sick of minding the bar while he propped it up with his belly, claiming to be owner and sole proprietor of the 'best damn little pub in a hundred miles'. Sick of Big White Bwana wafting about like a noisy cloud, spouting ideas. He sailed by and they got wet. Doing the stuff. Throwing out drunks; talking staff into staying on when Pascal screamed at them for messing up the flambéed bananas. Poor little brown people, told to pour half a bottle of brandy over your fruit and watching a month's wages go up in flames. There were nasty burns when the sight of good hooch going to waste got too much to bear and they tried to snuff out the bloody flames with their fingers. She and Mike were off to the coast, Friday through Sunday.

Pascal did not take the hint. He felt the break would do him good and hired Vince and Shirleen to mind the hotel. They got close instructions about checking the receipts in the public bar where Henry the brown barman and his predominantly brown customers roistered until the small hours; and they got instructions about the Karaoke machine and to make bloody sure that only respectable persons were admitted to the ladies bar. Brown was fine. So long as it was respectable brown. Shoes were to be worn at all times. No spitting. Anyone effing and blinding could do that sort of thing in the public bar.

Maureen wanted to know how he could trust strangers to keep decent receipts and Pascal replied that if you could not trust a British Israelite, who could you trust? When you've made your peace with the Lord, when you were set for Armageddon, you did not fiddle the accounts. Finesse replaced pettiness. And just looking at Shirleen told him she was full of finesse.

Maureen began telling Mike she felt sure Pascal was sneaking into Nickleton at night and banging Shirleen. Mike asked a couple of guys in the pub if they could picture it. Pascal in his baggy cricket flannels and white jumper rearing over his belly like a wave of milk, from chin to knee, huge Pascal stepping nightly on tiny feet in sparkling tennis shoes down Nickleton's single street, passing the old station, the rusting minehead workings, and sailing invisibly into Shirleen's little tin-sided house. Which was only a little bigger than he was.

Might as well believe the moon grew wheels and waltzed about the sky and no one noticed.

Maureen believed, alternatively, that if Pascal wasn't biffing Shirleen in Nickleton then he was doing it in Buckingham. Which was an even weirder idea – Shirleen in her cowboy boots clippety-clopping into the Hunter's Arms and slipping into Pascal's bed. Maureen had said once that the only thing bigger than Pascal's belly was his opinion of himself. His idea of love would be to go to bed with himself. Yet, still, something told her he was banging Shirleen.

Barney, the ex-crop sprayer, mumbled into his beard in the corner of the bar that it was like hothouse gasses. When Bill the Englishman bought him a beer he explained. People pumped carbon dioxide into the atmosphere. Damaged the ozone layer. Right? Got back bad ultraviolet rays that gave people cancer. OK? Well, likewise the elections. Hot air. Poisoned promises gave people diseases of the head. Dreams of free houses and electricity and phones sent farm workers loopy. Bamboozled them into choosing a brown mayor. Dominee Greet ripping off his toga because ten brown people walked into church. Setting up in opposition to the old firm. The arrival of the British Israelites fleeing the 'horrors of the Great Whore'. At first he'd thought they meant the Great War, but they weren't old enough for the last bloody war. Then Pascal, Mike and Maureen buying the Hunter's Arms, which hadn't made money in years. Some Buckinghamers reckoned the three of them must be sleeping together. Crazy, right? Now Maureen. Let Mike try logic on Maureen. Just ask her this question: if Pascal was doing what she said he was doing, why go away when Shirleen was minding the bar on Friday night?

Maureen screamed when she heard about three to a bed and said she'd rather kill herself. But she had an answer to the question: because Pascal was pulling a fast one, that's why.

In fact it was Vince who minded the bar on the Friday night Pascal, Maureen and Mike left for the coast. Propping a big Hebrew concordance against the cash-register, doling out the beers and doing a gentle sell on Israelite beliefs. No one much liked the religious stuff. But Vince was unpushy and a good quick barman. You never needed to ask twice. And Shirleen was free to mingle. She was easy to talk to. There was about her a directness, turning on the speaker a clear fixed gaze. She really cared about hunting springbuck, or the best way of docking lambs' tails and not getting blood on your boots, or why the dam was empty again this year.

She was a fine audience. Leaned close and listened hard. Her scent was full of flowers. There was something friendly in the creak of her white jeans when she crossed her knees and nodded and leaned, full of understanding. It was a pleasure to explain things. To offer her a drink. Sliding a bill across the counter with a wink at Vince: 'Same again for my friend, here', or 'Give your good lady a refill.' She had this way of matching drinks to the speaker. Sensible port and lemon with Mr de Wet, the inspector for the People's Bank, up on a night's audit, who said he'd never had such a man-to-man talk with anyone in Buckingham; Babycham with Bill the Anglican, who told her jokes about lunatics. Plain beer with Williamson, the new brown mayor, who was a democrat and hated fancy habits and asked if she'd thought of serving on the town council.

When she cried that she simply couldn't keep up with serious drinkers, she'd wait till her thirst caught up with her, thanks all the same, someone patted her arm and said, 'Not to worry' and 'Tomorrow's another day', and told Vince to put the cash in the till for later.

Vince smiled, very relaxed, setting up the drinks with lazy ease, and paging through his Hebrew concordance. How many people knew, for instance, that 'Adam' was an old Hebrew word meaning 'red' or 'ruddy' and referred to the colour pink, as we experience it when we blush? And who were the only people in the world to blush? Europeans, white folks. That's who! They were the original Adamites, children of the ruddy countenance, pink people, the chosen of Yahweh.

And people were impressed. They couldn't recall a Friday night like it. Shirleen listening. Vince reading Hebrew while he kept the beers coming. Even Mr Bok the butcher, who had called the Israelites a bunch of wankers, religious his arse!, probably fleeing their creditors, took a break from telling Shirleen all she wanted to know about slaughter-house techniques, and said maybe Vince had a point. In his experience, black guys didn't blush.

It was Barney, who had shared with Shirleen the story of how, after the war, he and a few friends built South Africa's first iron-lung from spare airplane parts, who summed up the general feeling when he raised his beer and thanked Vince and Shirleen for a wonderful, wonderful evening.

On Saturday night, it got even better. The bar was crowded soon after opening time. The entire rugby team came down after a hard game away, against neighbouring Zwingli. Big boys called Dion and Darryl and Danie with their ears rubbed raw from the scrum, smelling of their showers and Brut aftershave, and planning on an evening of snooker. Normally the older customers kept well clear. The young were inclined to get rowdy after a few beers and dance on the snooker table. Or, after the gymkhana, to ride horses through the swing doors of the bar. Whereupon Pascal in white flannels and cream sweater would rise above the bar, full and fat and furious and wag his finger, spots of darkest red glowing on his cheekbones, and threaten to send them to the public bar where the brown guys drank, but they jeered at him and called him Old Man Moon Rise and Moon Doggie and Fool Moon.

But this Saturday night Shirleen was soon reaching out to the young around the pool table, saying she felt really silly not being able to play, but she simply couldn't learn. After that she and the boys got on like houses on fire. Pressed to the pocket lip, she leaned roundly over the cue, shining in her white bolero, with Danie or Dion putting their arms around her shoulders to steady the shot. Cheering when she potted her chosen colour. Happily stumping up for her next Campari and orange. And when she cried that she simply could not keep up with them, they said 'Not to worry', or 'Night's young, isn't it?' and told Vince to put the money on ice till Shirleen's thirst caught up with her.

On Sunday night Vince and Shirleen opened the bar. Something Pascal never did because, in the old days, Sundays in Buckingham belonged to God and you didn't even go for a walk and old habits died hard. But the bumpkin factor faded when Vince opened that Sunday night. People came who never set foot in the place. Farmers from miles about. Stranger still, some women came with their men. Normally, no respectable woman walked into the Hunter's Arms bar – not by the front door, anyway. Maybe the women came because they'd heard tell of Shirleen's natural friendliness.

But they soon put their doubts aside. Shirleen gave her attention to everyone, without exception. She was working hard, trying to be pleasant. Like a really professional hostess. She was much nicer than Maureen who never left the bar, always packed her pistol, sometimes drank more than the guys and her perspiration loosened her hair-piece and you could see her thin grey hair beneath.

The place was humming. You could hardly see across the room. It must have been pretty late in the evening before anyone began to register that, from time to time, Shirleen – who'd been listening astonished to the rocketing prices of good bull semen – suddenly vanished from the room.

She was never gone long. Maybe ten minutes. Sometimes no more than five. Then she'd be back, slipping effortlessly into place to hear about the days when wool sold so high that you drove around the veld pulling scraps off trees; or why you could never tame a Bushman. It took a further little while to realise that when she disappeared, so did whoever she had been listening to last.

They all got it at more or less the same time. Everyone except Vince, busy pouring shots for customers or collecting the price of drinks waiting on Shirleen's thirst to catch up with her. And saying happily that if you were an Israelite your needs were few and Yahweh would provide.

Everyone began chewing over the space between their ears. Men wondering, was *this* how Yahweh provided? Women trying to recall where their husbands had been all night. Everyone knew the Israelites were broke. Groceries and school fees and firewood had to be paid for somehow. But *this* broke? A lot of men looked around for someone to blame. It was a bloody mess, that's what it was. It could hardly be worse. Especially if you hardly ever set foot in the pub. And when you do, you're hobnobbing with a woman who goes upstairs with men and sells her body.

It got worse. They were the men she went upstairs with.

Vince went on talking in the silence. Pass the blush test and join the British Israelites. Vince gave his shy, affable grin. Yahweh would provide.

Once more, it hit everyone around the same ghastly moment. Vince approved! This wasn't a bloody scandal, it was business. Vince had been marketing Shirleen. Each guy, as he slipped from the bar, had believed himself specially chosen. Easy enough to fix. The Hunter's Arms had plenty of empty rooms – white candlewick bedspread, clean sheets – and every one an identical set-up.

Yahweh not only provided, he doubled your money. While Vince banked the bucks for Shirleen's untasted drinks in the bar, she was rolling the customers upstairs.

It was Mr Bok the butcher, draining his beer and downing the glass with a firm slap on the counter who spoke for all of them: 'Me? Join a bunch of Jews. No ways!'

Shirleen reached for her Tia Maria and studied the ceiling. Vince flushed and said he could not allow that remark to pass. It was a lie. The Israelites were not Jews.

Bill the Anglican, who had gone upstairs with Shirleen first, wanted to know: if not, then what?

Shirleen crossed her knees and said 'British actually.' The creak of her white jeans sent shivers around the room when she added, 'Through and through.' She talked about how the Queen of England descended from Abraham. Beneath her throne reposed the Stone of Scone, which was actually the Tablet of the Law Yahweh gave to Moses.

Barney, who had borrowed to go upstairs, was mad as hell. If British Israelites were the real thing, who were the guys in Israel? Fairies?

Vince began hurting. Sweating. The others in Israel were

fakes. Semitic interlopers. They seeped into the Promised Land. 'Look guys—' he held up Pastor Tezer's book of noses. 'Check it out. Ours are straight. And we blush.'

So they ought, someone yelled from the back of the room and got a big laugh.

Mr Bok said, if they weren't Jews then they gave a bloody good impersonation. And stomped out.

People were leaving. Fearful men watched closely by frowning women. Dreading the interviews to come. Wondering how long it would be before the news was all around town.

Vince started yelling about the ire of Yahweh scorching those who mocked his Chosen People. But no one really cared. Seriously, what more could the Israelites do? The damage was done.

When he got back next morning Pascal found not a lot of love around. Barney told him what had happened. Guys wanted someone to blame. If he hadn't pulled her in. If he hadn't gone off to the coast. If he hadn't been the one who was supposed to be banging Shirleen in the first place. Then maybe none of this would have happened.

Pascal tried to put a good face on it. He said: 'I, for one, refuse to be held responsible for the full-scale adultery of an entire town.' He checked the till and receipts. They'd doubled. Cash accounted for; takings present and correct.

Considering how wrong Maureen had been about him, she might have given Pascal a break. But now she implied that maybe he wasn't up to it anyway. All froth and no champagne, was the way she put it. After all, everyone else had been screwed. The hotel included. Why not him? She scorned his accounts. What about drinks paid for but never poured? What about the mattress money? Vince and Shirleen – Brothel Keepers of Distinction – had made big bucks. The hotel would never see a cent of it.

Mike knew he was supposed to feel bad, for Maureen's sake, but he just couldn't keep his admiration to himself. It bubbled out of him. He went on about a rip-off, a scam, a bloody cheek! Only to start asking, again, did the Mayor really go upstairs? How many bedrooms did Shirleen use? They'd never filled that number. He worked out the takings, muttering 'Jesus, classy stuff!'

Come Monday lunch-time, bilious silence was settling like fog over the town where people had done what they shouldn't and no one knew how to handle it. That was when the invasion began. A cavalcade of old cars from Nickleton carrying every British Israelite, parents, pensioners, kids, babies, clattered into town and formed up outside the whitewashed, thatched town council buildings in Voortrekker Street. They must have worked all night long to organise the banners: 'True Israel Is Us' and 'Yahweh Rules' and 'Jews Can't Blush'. They'd also made a huge blow-up of the important drawings of Jewish noses from Pastor Tezer's Book. At a signal from Vince, the Israelites tapped their noses to point out how straight they were.

The cops slipped out of the station in Church Street and would have closed down the show but Mr Williamson, the new brown mayor, reminded them of the big change since the elections. We could disagree in public now. It was a healthy sign.

Anyway, the Israelites weren't protesting against the council. It was hard to know what their beef was until the crowd, led by Vince and Shirleen, marched down Voortrekker Street and surrounded Levine's General Dealer. They milled around the front stoep yelling for the Jews to come outside and do the nose test.

That's when Pascal said he had best have a quiet word and explained to Vince and Shirleen that the Levines had sold up and headed for the diamond fields fifty years before. All that remained was the name. There were no Jews left in Buckingham. Old Mr Joffe, the saddler, had been the last and he had been dead ten years.

But they weren't giving up. They marched down to the old synagogue on Leibrandt Street where they began chanting, 'Adamites United Will Never Be Defeated'. The old synagogue had been for decades the Dinosaur Museum, full of dusty fossils and clawprints fixed in rock. When she saw the marchers, Miss Trudie the curator, a timid woman who wore pink, and wife of the school head who had been one of the first to go upstairs with Shirleen, burst into tears and ran out of the back door and all the Israelites cheered.

After that things calmed down. The Israelites went back to Nickleton and got on with their lives. Buckingham did the same. When Shirleen appeared in town, in her bolero and boots and wide smile, women looked at her more closely; men looked the other way. No one said anything. There was nothing to say.

There were a couple of isolated incidents – a swastika spray-painted on the wall of the old synagogue; in the far corner of the cemetery reserved for Jews, behind a screen of cypresses, two headstones dating back half a century kicked over, and yellow paint daubed on the fallen stones.

Buckingham Town Council had abolished traditional opening prayers, after the election, in favour of a multi-faith minute of meditation. Before these incidents were discussed Mayor Williamson asked councillors to meditate on the right of all to protest without giving offence to any section of the rainbow community in the new South Africa. The council then agreed that the swastika be removed from the town museum.

The cemetery was more of a problem. After long debate they reached what the Mayor called the judgement of Solomon – until Mr Moosah, the Muslim member, objected, and they changed it to the judgement of democracy. It was decided to do nothing. The painted stones behind the screen of cypresses were left where they lay, on the grounds that, as there were no Jews in Buckingham, there was no one to offend.

David Bellos

OUR OWN AND OTHER TONGUE

LITERARY TRANSLATION IN THE 1990s

BRITAIN AND AMERICA have long been notoriously resistant to foreign writing. Whilst it is not uncommon for only
moderately successful writers in English to be translated into
a dozen languages or more, it is a much rarer privilege for
foreign writers, even those of great stature in their national
cultures who already enjoy large international audiences, to
gain a readership in the biggest book market in the world.
This long-standing imbalance in literary exchange is a source
of frustration around the world, and all too easy to denounce
as an obvious instance of English linguistic imperialism; but
the narrowness of the door which the English-speaking world
holds ajar for the riches of world literature also makes us
poorer in comparison to French, German or Spanish readers
(for example), who have wider and less belated access to contemporary writing from around the world. Throughout the
twentieth century English language publishers have devoted
only a tiny proportion of their energies to translated literature.
Just two to three per cent of books published each year in
Britain are officially described as being of 'foreign origin',
whereas in most other countries the corresponding figure
ranges from fifteen to thirty per cent. The disproportion is
even more visible in terms of market penetration: it is not
uncommon for half the titles in Italian or German best-seller
lists to be translated works, whereas in Britain it is only
in quite exceptional cases that a foreign work reaches the

top one hundred, let alone the top ten. In this context, literary translation could easily be dismissed as quite marginal to what is going on in British culture, a fringe pursuit barely kept alive by moonlighting academics and foreign subsidies.

Against this gloomy background, small but significant shifts and changes have been taking place in the twenty-five years since Britain joined the European Community. Given the large and ever-growing size of British publishing, even the small percentage of translated books in its total output nonetheless means that about 1,500 translated works from many dozens of languages now appear each year in the UK. Of these, a high proportion are new translations of literary works of already recognised merit. This is by no means an inconsiderable contribution to the literary universe of English-language readers. As many of these translated works will stay in print for many years, the cumulative effect of the new wave of literary translation is out of all proportion to its apparent share of publishing activity. The result is that today, as never before, the fiction shelves of major high-street bookstores allow the browser something approaching a world tour of near-contemporary as well as of classical writing. In my own local bookshop, which can hardly be untypical, recently translated thrillers from Spain and Denmark (Arturo Perez-Reverte, Peter Høeg) stand alongside historical novels from Estonia (Jaan Kross) and Albania (Ismail Kadare) as well as family sagas translated from Basque (Bernardo Atxaga) and Turkish (Yashar Kemal, Orhan Pamuk); works by writers as diverse in manner and language as Bufalino, Eco, Bitov, Dombrovsky, Popov, Oz and Saramago are all available in paperback. The European bias of this almost random sample is probably not coincidental: although there are also translations from Japanese, Korean, Arabic and other so-called exotic languages in print, the new wave of interest in the foreign is led and still dominated by writers in major and minor European languages. So whilst it remains true that the British book world is proportionately less open to the foreign than most others, it is no less true that, compared to the 1960s, the 1990s seem like a golden age for literary translation, especially of fiction.

The first great wave of translation into English in the post-war period was associated with a particular publisher – Penguin – and with a broadly educational ambition. Under the general command of E. V. Rieu and Betty Radice, Penguin Classics aimed to make available to the common reader the great books of the classical, medieval and modern European traditions in versions that were accurate in a scholarly sense and also fluently exprèssed in what then seemed an approachable English style. The project was based on a firm conviction, made explicit in many a preface and introduction, that for most texts and most sentences in any language, a compromise between accuracy and fluency could be found by skilled and learned translators. Those now dog-eared, red- and green-edged translations of Homer, Dante, Balzac, Dostoevsky, Mann and many others did a huge service to the reading public; even if they all speak a now dated and rather stuffy kind of Home Counties English, they created a large new readership for otherwise inaccessible literature, and annoyed some perverse readers sufficiently to make them want to learn foreign languages properly.

The second post-war wave of literary translation began to make itself felt about fifteen years ago and currently shows no signs of weakening. It is not associated with a single publishing enterprise, and has certainly had little support from major imprints, whose role in promoting foreign literature has been spasmodic at best. Translations of literary work are most often commissioned by small and specialised publishers, such as Serpent's Tail, Saqi Books, Atlas Press, Carcanet, Forest Books, Bloodaxe, and – chief amongst them – the Harvill Press. It is a wave that has brought new and recent work into English and through which rather more diverse and inventive translating styles have been able to flower. It has undoubtedly been helped along by the subsidy schemes that some far-sighted governments have set up to assist with the costs of translation (including the Arts Council of England's Translation Fund); but the moving forces have mostly been the uncoordinated passions and convictions of individuals.

Few translation projects are as disinterested as that of Odette Lamolle, who retranslated the whole of Conrad out of enthusiasm for the original texts and for the pleasure of giving them a new French voice, without a contract or even any contact with a publisher; but those two passions (for the 'source text' and for the 'target language', in the curiously mixed metaphors of translation studies) are necessarily present in any successful literary translation. The whole trouble is that, like all human passions, they tend towards exclusiveness. They conflict with each other in principle and make a 'complete' or 'total' translation theoretically impossible. To translate is therefore to negotiate a settlement between conflicting demands. The types of settlements that are reached can vary a great deal between different texts and different translators; but there are characteristic types of settlement for any given language at any given period of time.

The historical and perceived resistance of English to foreignness means that there is a very high demand for making translated texts read 'smoothly' or 'fluently', that is to say to read as far as possible as if they had been written in English in the first place. In the language of translation studies, a discipline which hardly existed in Britain before the 1980s, current translation norms are assimilationist and strongly biased towards 'naturalisation'. That perverse magician, Vladimir Nabokov, took a contrary stand and professed utter scorn for 'paraphrases [that] possess the charm of stylish diction and idiomatic conciseness'. Nothing annoyed him more, or so he said, than to read a newspaper review praising a translator for having produced a smooth and fluent version of a foreign work: 'In other words, a hack who has never read the original, and does not know its language, praises an imitation as readable because easy platitudes have replaced in it the intricacies of which he is unaware.' I have to say that I cannot imagine any current professional literary translator rejecting praise of that sort, or feeling any pleasure whatsoever if a reader or reviewer felt that his work 'reads like a translation'. The preference for fluidity is deeply ingrained, not just in the practice of translators, editors and publishers, but in the whole sense of what it means to write English well.

Nabokov's attack on 'stylishness' in translation is really a defence of his own pedantic practice in the retranslation of one of the foundation-stones of Russian literature. In that specific, reverential context, Nabokov's decision to settle for an extremely literal rendering, with footnotes to explain background and alternative readings, is justifiable; but it is not generalisable to new work that has yet to acquire its first readers, let alone cultural legitimacy, in the receiving language. Nobody needs Pushkin's *Eugene Onegin* to be easy; its place in the literary pantheon is immune to accusations of awkwardness. All the same, Nabokov's implementation of his principle that the only 'true translation' is a rendering of the 'exact contextual meaning of the original' does nothing to give Pushkin new life in English, and his argument for 'literalism' relies on some fairly dubious premises. Lines in prose as well as in verse may resist all attempts to pin them down to a single 'exact' meaning; their function may even be to play on ambiguity, imprecision and imponderability; and as even schoolmasterly Nabokov well knew, English may require things to be said rather differently.

In Stendhal's *The Red and the Black*, the young hero, Julien Sorel, has his prospects of marriage and high office dashed to the ground by a letter of denunciation from his former mistress to his prospective father-in-law. He rushes back to the small town of Verrières and tries to shoot the woman who has brought his plans crashing down. The episode constitutes one of the great scandals of European fiction, though it takes up less than a page of print in Stendhal's unadorned, almost telegraphic French:

> *Julien made his way into the new church at Verrières. All the high windows in the building were draped with crimson hangings. Julien found himself a few paces behind Mme de Rênal's pew. It seemed to him that she was praying fervently. The sight of this woman who had loved him so much made Julien's arm tremble*

*to such an extent that he was unable at first to carry out
his design. I can't do it, he told himself; physically, I just
can't do it.*

Stendhal, *The Red and the Black*, trans.
Catherine Slater (Oxford University Press,
World's Classics, 1991), p. 468

In fact, what Julien 'told himself' before raising his arm to
shoot (and miss) his former lover is even plainer if put into
English word for word: 'I cannot it . . . physically I cannot
it.' Although perfectly comprehensible, the word-for-word
version is unacceptable because it is not what anyone
would say, at any stage in the development of English.
'I cannot do it . . . physically I cannot do it' provides the
grammatical prop needed. For the Nabokovian translator,
that is all that would be needed. But is it? The 'exact
contextual meaning' must include the resolution of such
questions as: how formal or informal are Julien's words
for a nineteenth-century reader? Is he chatting to himself or
making a grave pronouncement? How does he speak in the
rest of the novel, and how consistent are these words with
his habitual manner of expression? Though central to the
overall effect of the novel, the passage is so brief that it gives
less than adequate signals to the translator, who must in the
end *choose* what kind of voice to give Julien in English. In
the recent retranslation quoted above, Catherine Slater has
chosen the less formal, contracted form of the verb ('can't')
– to tell us that Julien is speaking to himself, and speaking
in roughly contemporary rather than nineteenth-century
written English – and has also made a tiny addition in the
repeated phrase: 'I can't do it . . . I *just* can't do it.' That
'just' adds the rhythm of contemporary spoken English,
and also a plausible emphasis that is one of the possible
interpretations of Julien's state of mind. 'Just' is not there
in the French. Its function is not to give the word-for-word
meaning of the original, but to lend to its expression in
English a naturalness that the translator considers both
appropriate for contemporary readers, and her pondered

view of Stendhal's intended effect. For in contemporary translation, as in social life, naturalness is highly valued, but rarely achieved without a degree of artifice.

A different kind of crux occurs at the end of Balzac's *Old Goriot*. Here, Eugène de Rastignac sheds his 'last tear of youth' on the grave of an old man and turns to face the city spread out beneath the hill-top cemetery where he stands, saying, in that inner-outer voice so favoured by nineteenth-century novelists, words which if represented solely by their dictionary meanings in English would be: 'To us two now!' Natural as it sounds in the original, the French phrase allows several different emphases of meaning: it is partly a challenge to a duel, partly a declaration of intent, and has overtones of a seductive challenge as well. It is an inescapable fact that any translation has to privilege one possible reading over another, since there is no phrase in English that lends itself to the same range of ambiguity as the original. The Nabokovian imp that resides in all translators – the desire to leave the reader with at least some of the work to do, and, failing that, to leave him and her confounded by the irreducible difference of a foreign text – has to be kept under lock and key. So what would young Rastignac have declared had he been not a French dandy of 1821 but a speaker of late twentieth-century English, in the double fiction of an English translation of *Old Goriot*? Put yourself in his shoes . . . or put him in your own shoes . . . and the possibilities for linguistic anachronism are as numerous as they are disastrous: 'Let's get on with it, then'; 'The world isn't big enough for both of us'; 'It's you and me, babe'. Happy indeed were foreignising nineteenth-century translators, most of whom left Rastignac with his words unaltered: '*A nous deux maintenant.*'

These two cruces illustrate most of the really difficult issues involved in translating contemporary fiction. Taken to its logical extreme, the wish to represent the foreign and to represent it as accurately as possible leads to the kind of non-translation that we see in nineteenth-century solutions to Balzac's brain-teaser. Less extreme variants of 'foreignising' translation styles leave elements of non-English vocabulary and syntax in place. Taken to the opposite extreme, the 'naturalising' style seen in the translation of Stendhal would lead French peasants, Russian librarians, Albanian intellectuals and Israeli conscripts to speak in the same voice, corresponding to the translator's imagination or reconstruction of contemporary informal English. Most translators would conceive of their task as being the discovery, for any individual text, of the necessary point of balance between these two extremes. And most translators must accept that the more successful they are in finding that balance for today's readership, the more likely it is that their work will come in time to seem dated, marked by the rhythms and forms of a particular moment in the history of English. That is why there is in truth no such thing as an 'invisible' translator whose sole function is to allow the original text to shine through a merely instrumental, diaphanous English shroud. Every act of translation inscribes the current state of the English language, and inevitably also the individual mark of its translator.

The paradoxical result of translators' artful successes in making foreign authors sound natural in English is to allow some foreign books to be mistaken for 'ordinary' ones. F. R. Leavis's careless remark, in *The Great Tradition*, that Tolstoy was amongst the best novelists in the whole of English literature, is by no means a unique example of 'translation-blindness'. Who now recalls that *The Bridge on the River Kwai* and *Planet of the Apes* were both originally written in French? In similar fashion, Solzhenitsyn's *One Day in the Life of Ivan Denisovich* currently figures in the approved reading list for the national curriculum . . . in English literature. In the United States, if Lawrence Venuti is to be believed, authors from Plato to Pasternak are presented on Great Books courses for undergraduates without reference to their having been written in a different language and without any reflection on their translators' acts of interpretation. His academic campaign for making translation 'visible' once again, and to make the work of translators a subject of study in its own right, has proceeded in distant harmony with a perceptible raising of the profile of literary translation on both sides of the Atlantic and by growing professional self-awareness amongst literary translators. In Britain, translators have at last won the formal right to be credited for their work on title pages, though even now not all newspapers and magazines give the translator's name in reviews. A British Centre for Literary Translation has been established at the University of East Anglia, and postgraduate degrees in literary translation have been successfully launched at several universities. Translators now find themselves invited to speak about their work at universities, at conferences, and occasionally on radio; even to write essays about it. And it seems to me that the general standard of competence in contemporary literary translation is much higher than it was only twenty or thirty years ago. Though I have no Spanish, Margaret Jull Costa's magical versions of Marías and Atxaga, for example, seem to me to be on a different stylistic plane from the first English translations of André Malraux, Simone de Beauvoir or Jean-Paul Sartre.

Foreign works come into English in a haphazard variety of uncoordinated ways. There are scouts, of course, who seek out potential international figures on behalf of one or more publishing houses; there are private, governmental and semi-official agencies promoting works from particular countries or language communities; there are of course book fairs, with all their attendant gossip and hot tips, as well as literary agents looking for new authors to represent; but alongside the hubbub of international publishing there are individual readers and translators who sometimes succeed in persuading publishers to take on previously unheard-of works. Although most present-day translations into English are initiated by publishers, many of the most significant contributions from abroad to writing in English began as impossible ideas in a single translator's mind.

Whatever the origin of a translation project – in a scout's proposal or a translator's mind – there are few that are successfully completed without some kind of collaboration. In many cases, copy-editors provide that essential other pair of ears and eyes, identifying passages that don't quite ring true or which give particular difficulty to readers without knowledge of the original language and culture. In other cases, the author of the original text is a willing correspondent, and is sometimes able to be a real partner in the translation. Author–translator teams materialise the underlying tension between 'source' and 'target' in a real-life relationship between translator and translatee. But even the best partnership in the creation of a translated work cannot get round the fact that there is always more than one way to say something in English: the choice of tone and voice is in the end the translator's responsibility.

Even the most professional and versatile of literary translators have authors that they prefer to translate, and try not to take on books for which they feel little affinity or motivation. Barbara Wright, though she has translated a great number of modern French authors, is most especially the English inventor of Raymond Queneau; similarly, Juan Goytisolo 'belongs' to Peter Bush, just as the late Giovanni Pontiero created the English voices of Clarice Lispector and José Saramago. Author–translator teams of this kind have no formal protection and, unfortunately, not all publishers realise how important they are. Consistent pairing can provide an *oeuvre* with a degree of stylistic consistency and coherence in English that it would not otherwise have; and even if there are infinitely many possible translations of any given work, it does not serve the English reader particularly well to have quite different styles purporting to represent the different but connected works of a single author.

New books that are worth translating are almost by definition not quite like any other. The translator is thus inclined to lean first of all towards a 'foreignising' style, to give English readers an idea of what it is that is different and special, and which must lie in the language as well as the motif or construction of the text. On the other hand, there is a real author with a wish, a need and a right to have a readership in the most important book-market in the world – and that responsibility inclines the translator to the other extreme, that of naturalising the language to make the work easily approachable without too much readerly effort. In working with contemporary writers, the tension between the translator's two responsibilities is higher, for the prizes to be gained and lost are immediate and real. A stilted translation that attracts no readers may stop a writer's English-language career in its tracks, irrespective of the merit of the original. Whatever narrow Nabokovian principles may assert, the ethics of translation do not hang exclusively on the representation of the 'exact contextual meaning of the original'.

With the passing of time and the increasing sophistication of translation practice, it is becoming apparent that many of the standard translations of nineteenth- and early twentieth-century European classics are often inadequate. Some publishers continue to repackage translations that are not only more than fifty years old, but slapdash and inaccurate too. Others, notably the World's Classics, are engaged in a long-term programme of retranslation of works in the public domain. As major authors of the earlier half of the century fall out of copyright, there may well be a third wave of literary translation to come, to provide not only more fluent but fuller and more accurate English versions of many standard works. Dostoevsky, Proust, Kafka, Mann and Céline have already acquired new and in some cases startling voices in English.

One of the difficulties of getting a better balance between the 'export' of English writing and the 'import' of new foreign works is that most foreign publishing houses have a sufficiency of staff and advisers able to read English well, whereas few English publishing houses have any staff who can read languages beyond French. The publishing of translated literature in English is therefore dependent on informal networks of specialist academics, translators and advisers, on the one hand, and on the translation of third-language work into French. With the exception of Russian literature, which often comes first into English, nearly every book translated here has previously been published (or is in course of publication) in France. Conversely, translation into English makes a foreign author immediately available for translation into a much greater range of languages. Translation into English, despite its particularity, is part of a world-wide circuit of cultural exchange.

There are often great practical difficulties in finding translators for works written in the so-called minority languages. Nobody could conceivably be a professional literary translator from Basque, or Estonian, or Albanian, simply because opportunities for exercising such a profession may not crop up for a decade or two. Sadly, the range of languages taught in British universities is no larger now than it was fifty years ago, and in many instances even relatively widely-spoken languages such as Italian, Russian and Swedish have disappeared from the curriculum. There are consequently cases where the only way to get a major author into English is to undertake a 'double' translation from one of the major inter-languages, most often French, less frequently German or Spanish. In this respect, too, there are strong and necessary links between literary translators working into the major European languages.

There are as many different ways of coming to a translation as there are translators. In the case of my own first translation, I simply wanted to allow my English-speaking friends and relatives to enjoy a book that had bowled me over. I felt that I knew what that book would have sounded like had it been written in English in the first place. The obvious result is that *Life A User's Manual* has patterns of language that are at least as characteristic of my own writing as they are of Georges Perec. David Coward, when he chose to translate Albert Cohen's massive saga of Sephardic life in pre-war Geneva, *Belle du Seigneur*, had a different kind of problem. Long regarded as untranslatable, *Belle du Seigneur* has extensive passages written in the unpunctuated stream-of-consciousness of a passionate and mildly unbalanced young woman. There are of course English style-models for semi-coherent interior monologues – Virginia Woolf comes to mind, alongside Molly Bloom in *Ulysses* – and in that sense Cohen's device is less 'different' when translated into English than in the original. There's nothing wrong with a touch of pastiche (when you can get away with it), but it is very curious to reflect that what is lost in the following extract is not naturalness, but the opposite, the difference of Cohen's French style from other styles in French:

> *No I shan't go down I won't have anything to do with him I don't care if there is a row oh it's lovely lying here in the bath the water's too hot I love it too hot tumty-to tumty-tum pity I can't whistle properly like little boys do I adore being by myself holding them in both hands I love them I can feel their weight their firmness I'm crazy about them I think deep down I must be in love with myself when we were nine or ten Eliane and I used to walk to school together on winter days we would hold hands in the biting wind put on dirgy voices and sing that song I made up . . .*

Albert Cohen, *Belle du Seigneur*,
trans. David Coward (London: Viking, 1995), p. 167

Poetry apart, the outer limits of uniqueness in the original are reached by those few writers who use formal rules as rigid as those of verse. There is absolutely nothing that sounds like Georges Perec's *A Void*, a novel written without any of the words which contain the letter *e*, and certainly no 'style model' for the English translator to pastiche other than the self-same rule applied to English: to do it with no *e*s. Gilbert Adair – celebrated for his pastiches of Lewis Carroll and J. M. Barrie – accepted the challenge, and produced an English text as fluent, as lively, and if anything even funnier than the original. Precisely because in order to translate this at all Adair had to train himself to write in that special variant of English that includes all of its words except those containing an *e*, he found that he could say more or less anything in this new, one-off dialect of English. Following the spirit of Perec's demonstration of the virtue of 'hard constraint', and following Perec's own practice as the French translator of the almost equally constructed novels of Harry Mathews, Adair decorated his translation with all sorts of marks of his own (translator's) identity. The result is a work that is simultaneously a translation of Georges Perec and a book by Gilbert Adair, a joint work that irritates purists just as much as it represents a real, unhoped-for contribution to literature in English. Ian Monk tackled the 'retern of the e', Perec's later novelette, *Les Revenentes*, which uses only the *e* among all the vowels, in a different spirit. It is of course even harder to write without *a*, *i*, *o* or *u* than without the single vowel *e*; the original, moreover, distorts French spelling progressively to reach a crescendo of cacography that would be incomprehensible had the reader not been slowly trained by the build-up of the whole text. Monk adds nothing apart from his own extraordinarily inventive bending of English spelling rules:

> *Hélène dwelt chez Estelle, where New Helmstedt Street meets Regents Street, then the Belvedere. The tenement's erne-eyed keeper defended the entrée. Yet, when seven pence'd been well spent, she let me enter, serene.*
>
> *Hélène greeted me, then served me Schweppes. Cheers! Refreshments were needed. When she'd devested me, she herd me eject:*
> *'Phew! The wether!'*
> *'Thertee-seven degrees!'*
> *'September swelters here.'*
> *She lent me Kleenexes. They stemmed the cheeks' fervent wetness.*
>
> Georges Perec, 'The Exeter Text', in *Three*,
> trans. Ian Monk (London: Harvill, 1996), p. 60

Such examples underline the fact that naturalness is not the only virtue in translation: translators also invent the language that they use. Whether working with established classics or with the latest star from the Frankfurt Book Fair, the terms of the settlement between the foreign and the familiar, between the demands of the original and the tolerance of the target audience, have to be worked out afresh each time. Which is why translation will always remain a literary as well as a linguistic challenge, and one of the writerly arts.

John McGahern
THE WHITE BOAT

THE RAINS HAD flooded the fields along the riverbank for miles. Trees and the tops of tall hedges stood out in the expanse of water, but the big, white boat kept to the deep bed of the river, travelling very slowly. At the entrance to Cootehall Lake, half-moons of the black and red navigation pans showed just above the water, and as the boat passed between the signs it increased speed. The two boys were talking of girls as they turned by the lake wall and saw the white boat come up the river.

'It's a strange time for a big houseboat to appear.'

'He either knows the river well or has good maps.'

Below the quay the high banks defined the river clearly. The full moons of the pans stood just above the water where the river entered the lake below the priest's boathouse, and as the boat prepared to leave the lake it slowed again. When it kept to the right after passing the boathouse the boys knew that the boat intended to tie up at the quay. They left their bicycles on the bridge and went down the slipway to the quay. An old man in pale oilskins was taking the boat in along the quay wall. There seemed to be nobody with him. He had already dropped tyres over the side, and as the boat churned to a stop he waved to the boys and threw them the ropes which they ran round the metal bollards. He looked small and frail when he stepped on to the quay, with thin white hair. He was neatly dressed. His voice was firm.

'Thank you. Thank you both.'

'For nothing at all.'

'It would have been difficult for me to tie her up on my own.'

Deliberately he took a wallet from inside his jacket and picked two large notes from the wallet. 'I want you to take them,' he insisted. 'I wouldn't have managed so easily on my own. I have a feeling you may have brought me luck already.'

They murmured awkwardly, in the manners of that part of the country, that they hadn't expected anything for the tying up of the boat, and, over and above that, what he had given them was far too much.

'I just want you to enjoy the money.' The voice that made light of their objections had a trace of an English accent. 'You must both drop in some evening when I'm settled.'

Such was the glow of pleasure they brought from the shock of the sudden windfall, as if without warning they had just received long-sought-after praise, that they could have been walking on air as they returned to their bicycles.

'Everything is strange about it – a man as old as that all on his own, the big boat, the amount of money he pulled out, turning up at an empty quay in the middle of winter,' they repeated, attempting to puzzle it all out as they cycled through the village. Old Luke Henry who was rolling porter barrels from the pub, standing them on their ends along the concrete footpath across from the church wall, raised his head to mutter 'Good lads' as they passed. 'Not a bad evening, Luke,' they responded politely.

The next morning the big white boat was still tied up at the quay when they cycled across the bridge. There was no sign of life. Across the river a bale of hay and an old tractor tyre were caught in low-lying sallies, resisting the power of the water to sweep them loose.

'I'd hate to be that old and have to come on my own to a quay in the middle of winter even if I did have a big boat and money.'

'He must have wanted to come. He didn't *have* to come in the middle of winter if he didn't want.'

'How do you know?'

'If you have money you can go or stay.'

'For all the money in the world I wouldn't be in his shoes for a minute,' one of the boys shivered.

'What do you think, then, brought him?'

'I don't know. Something must have.' They were as far away as ever from reaching any satisfactory explanation.

By this time nearly everybody else about the place knew that a big white houseboat had tied up at the quay. All the people crossing the bridge had noticed it the evening before. The drinkers crossing the bridge to Henry's had seen it lit up against the dark quay wall and saw it in darkness when they crossed back to their homes after midnight.

In the barracks it was all the talk during morning inspection. Guard Murphy had been barrack orderly the night before and had seen the boat when he went home for his supper to the big house below the quay which he rented from the River Authority before returning to the barracks to make up his bed for the night beneath the phone.

'You better check it out,' the sergeant said, concealing his own curiosity. 'You never know what types are wandering around these days.'

'I'll dodge over to the quay as soon as I get the breakfast.'

Mrs Murphy had the hot porridge and boiled egg and tea and toast waiting. Because of their eleven children the Murphys were poor. They kept hens, ducks, a pig, a pointer and a red setter in the old boathouses at the back. The field along the river that went with the house had been tilled to exhaustion with potatoes and turnips and cabbage. They lived as much on the produce of the field, the pig, the poultry and wildfowl and hares he shot in and out of season as on the police pay. Though Murphy didn't bother anybody much, he was too self-seeking to be liked. 'You'd think he'd give that little woman of his a rest one of these years,' was all that was ever said against him, and only in a tone of mild irritation.

This morning instead of leading his wife upstairs for a private hour or half-hour he took his cap and greatcoat and went to the quay. As he drew near the boat there was a delicious smell of coffee and he saw the old man reading a book propped against other books on a table. He coughed several times and scraped his boots along the granite of the quay.

'Guard Murphy. Michael Murphy. I'm your nearest neighbour,' so the guard introduced himself after his coughing and scraping had eventually drawn the old man out of the boat.

'Richard Farnham.' The man took his hand.

'Would you be intending to stay long?'

'Is there something wrong? Are there fees to pay?'

'Good God no, what could have put that in your head?' Murphy smiled gently. 'I just thought that if you wanted any messages from the shops, or anything, the children would be only too glad to run them. They often run messages for the tourist boats in the summer.'

'No, thank you. I'm planning to walk to the shops later.'

'Luke Henry's beside the church is the best. Luke has nearly everything you'd want and he's decent and reasonable. Luke's an old Yankee, spent over twenty years in America.' The last piece of information was delivered in a tone that implied that this was certain to be of interest. The guard talked of the rains and the flooded fields and how difficult it must have been to navigate all the way to the quay, how a timber barge from the Oakport Woods had gone aground in the flooded fields the week before. After a time it grew clear that he was doling out all this information in the hope of obtaining further information. He didn't want to ask for it directly.

'I travelled all the way up from Limerick. It's not difficult to navigate if you go slowly and have good charts. I'm retired. I always wanted to do this trip in winter after the other boats had gone. I'm not sure how long I'll stay. When you're retired, all the time is your own.' There was great charm and concentration in the self-deprecatory way Richard Farnham spoke. 'It was very nice of you to call.' He hoped the guard had obtained all the information he required and would take the hint and leave.

'All you have to do at any time is to leave a message in the house if there's anything at all you want,' Guard Murphy said, indicating the big house below the quay where he lived.

He went straight from the quay to the barracks. The sergeant and the other guards were in the dayroom, where they lounged about and chatted before going out on their separate patrols – if the sergeant's morning mood was good. All of them listened avidly to the information Murphy brought. He said that the old man had been polite but reserved. He had been anything but forthcoming about what he was doing on the quay in the middle of winter.

'We'll soon take care of that,' the sergeant said. 'We'll ring Limerick. They'll sort out his reserve. There has to be something behind a man like that coming on his own to an empty quay in a big boat in the middle of the winter.'

'There's a man who's turned up on the quay here in a rich houseboat,' the sergeant explained on the telephone. 'Richard Farnham . . . small and thin with white hair . . . a reserved little man with a touch of an English accent.'

A young guard took the call in Limerick. He said he thought he knew who the man was; he'd find out more and telephone back within an hour. The sergeant was irritated not to be put through to the sergeant-in-charge. The good morning mood disappeared. 'We are as well to check these things out,' he said. 'There are far too many people starting to wander round this country on their own.'

The guards waited around for the return call. They didn't talk much. The silences began to increase in the waiting as showers spattered the windows. When the telephone rang, even though the call was expected, it had a startling effect in the bare room. The sergeant was suddenly deferential as he took the call.

'That was the chief super,' he said after he put down the receiver. 'We have our man all right. I'm afraid it's no Whitehead or Kerry Blue we have. They are one of the most important crowds in the whole of Limerick. They came originally from England. They own a big engineering business. The chief super said he was sending a guard round to the house just in case the family don't know where the boat is.'

'I suppose some of us, anyhow, should be thinking about making some kind of move in the general direction of what's left of the day,' one of the guards remarked, and it broke the heavy, overbearing sense of solemnity that now imbued the sergeant.

Then all the guards except the barrack orderly quickly signed themselves out on patrol. Murphy signed himself out on a long patrol by way of Knockvicar and Crossna. From the barracks he'd go for the shotgun and gamebag and the two dogs. Long before Knockvicar they'd leave the road and head into the hazel and shrub of the Smutterna Hills. There were woodcock and pheasant about the hills and the occasional hare, and when the light started to fail they'd go towards the flooded bottoms across from Oakport to wait for the duck.

Soon after Guard Murphy had set out with the gun and gundogs for the Smutterna Hills Richard Farnham closed the boat and climbed the slipway from the quay. He carried the walking stick he'd brought against village dogs. When he reached the bridge he could see the scattered houses of the village. A short avenue of small sycamores led to the big barracks below the bridge, an interesting archway without gates past the barracks leading to what looked like the remains of an old estate in trees. At the head of a large field bordered by the roads and low limestone walls was a church partly hidden in evergreens, and around the field were scattered shops and bars and a post office. There was no sense of any kind of arrangement or guiding idea: it was as if people had come in from the countryside or off the mountain and built church and barracks, shops and bar wherever they could get a site. They could all have been tree seedlings or grains of wild wheat the birds had dropped. Cold-looking cattle were huddled around a metal feeder in a corner of the field. A church, a barracks, a post office . . . there must be a school and dance hall somewhere, but they were not in sight. He entered the bar-grocery beside the church.

'You must be the man who came in the white boat.' Luke Henry rose from where he had been watching the black-and-white television high in the corner of the shop to greet the man with outstretched hand. There was no trace of an American accent in the voice. He was a big burly man with an emotional face, and he wore a red wig which was at odds with the greys and whites of his natural hair at the sides and back.

'How did you know that?'

'Not too hard.' Luke smiled secretly down on the floor before suddenly looking straight up. 'No car pulled up. No strangers about at this time, and not much goes on unbeknownst around here even in the busy time. No high marks for Luke, I'm afraid.'

Richard Farnham explained he had quite a few things to get and that he wasn't allowed to carry anything heavy.

'The young fellow will run them down to the quay as soon as he gets back from town with the car. That's no bother at all.'

It took a long time to complete the order as Luke had to search about in the shelves for some of the items. He limped heavily as he moved about inside the counter. When he had difficulty finding something he had a habit of smoothing back his wig so that it made a small eave over the back of his head. After he had assembled all the items on the counter, he rang up the prices on the till as he stacked them in a cardboard box. No other customer entered the shop.

'I imagine this is a slow time,' Richard Farnham said.

'It's at night people come in around here, but you have to be here anyhow just in case.'

'It must make for a long day sometimes.'

'I don't mind. The same day has to be put round somehow, no matter what. Seeing it's your first time, you'll have something on the house.' Luke put a spirit glass out on the counter. 'Something from the top shelf – a brandy or a good whiskey?'

'Thank you very much but no.'

'You might as well take a chance.' Luke's face, despite the red wig, which was by now all askew, had great charm when he smiled.

'Well, I'll have a glass of water from the tap.'

'That won't get you into much trouble.'

'I used to be partial to strong drink – especially good wine – but it is no longer partial to me.'

'I'm afraid you have lots of comrades,' Luke said as he poured himself a glass of red lemonade.

As the two men sipped their glasses, Luke talked of the river, the rain, the boat from the Oakport Woods that had gone aground in the fields the week before, and how the school was just outside the village but that the dance hall was a good half-mile further on. Richard Farnham expressed surprise that both of them weren't situated in the village.

'People can't agree. That's the why. When we were putting up the new dance hall the old priest wanted it kept well away from the bars. It didn't stop anything though, and that's no wonder. If the priests got their way with the young it's the world itself would stop. There'd be no people.'

As he was about to leave, Farnham asked Luke to add a bottle of whiskey, some orange juice and lemonade to the order, 'In case I have unexpected visitors.' He bought the extra items more in return for the favour of the drink than any expectation of visitors.

'Don't worry. You'll have callers,' Luke said as he twisted brown paper around the bottle of whiskey and placed it carefully in the box. 'If curiosity could burn and you cracked matches round here there are several who'd go up in smoke.'

When he came out of the bar-grocery he faced the church wall. Inside were tall rich evergreens, the tops of headstones, and before the main door of the church a wire bell-rope dangled loosely. They must have to use cloths or towels to toll the bell. He paused for a while in front of the church wall and then turned away from the river. He passed a shop in the corner of another field, beside a black hall that could have been the old dance hall, and then he came on the school and its playground within concrete walls in another field. Ten minutes further on, beside a crossroads, was the new dance hall, well in off the road in yet another field, a gravelled yard for parking, the hall squat and asbestos-roofed, plainly and humbly ugly, the small high windows and the door painted a Virgin Mary blue.

When they first met, his wife used to talk of the fun of going to dances in these village halls, of piling into hackney cars and going to wherever the Blue Aces or the Melody Makers were playing. She had laughed until it hurt as she recounted some of the more forthright male approaches to the matter which the dresses and ribbons and music and dancing both flaunted and hid. She must have been a Helen of these halls, with her tall figure and sharp, perfect features, the blue-black hair. She could hardly have known anything but triumph. She'd have seen, here, her beauty reflected more excitingly in men's eyes filled with desire and fear than in any mirror. Does nature set up such perfection (since a single woman cannot satisfy many) to drive others to the plainer surfaces that obscure what beauty pedestals? As he stood looking at the small dance hall he saw showers gathering away to the low mountain, and turned back towards the quay.

If he had been a boy from one of the farms around here he'd have had no chance of winning her in these halls. He had won her on his own ground; he could not imagine winning her on any other. He had no illusions about his own looks, nobody had ever considered him handsome – though he had attracted a certain type of woman without too much difficulty. In his eyes she was still lovely, with a rarer, finer beauty, perhaps the beauty of a familiarity that had grown.

They had met at a party in the London hospital where his father was a surgeon and she a nurse. It was a retirement party for a friend of his family, mostly made up of older people. They found themselves standing beside one another. She wore a pale blue dress without ornament, and when she asked him how he happened to be at the party, he told her that he was the godson of the retiring surgeon and the son of Mr Farnham. He could have been accused of pulling rank, he reflected, but all positions looked equally menial to him that evening in the face of her beauty. She agreed to meet him again. There was continual tension and excitement, fear and pride, during those first months. All the meetings merged into one another – no separate scene, not even any of the many films they went to stood out – except one. Trying to remember those weeks now was like trying to look down through deep water.

The evening he had asked her to marry him was as clear as the glaze of a broken plate shining out of the shallows along a lake's edge. He wasn't sure where they'd been that evening but it was the evening he left her back at the hospital. It was late and he knew the Underground was about to shut down. He was taking hurried leave of her on the hospital steps when she said, 'Why don't you come in?' 'There's no private place within.' 'I think I know one.'

They went in by a side door, up an empty institutional corridor, and as soon as she pulled the door open that led down bare concrete steps to a big heavy door he knew where they were: the hospital boiler room. Four huge boilers stood about the big basement room in padded walls of thick grey insulation. Against the nearest one, in the semi-darkness of the panels, they held and fondled one another as they had done in corners of doorways and empty sitting-rooms or in the shelter of the trees of Epping Forest on other evenings. Her face was obscured, but the lean strong excited body held a power more imperious than beauty itself. Suddenly he came within his clothes and she felt him come and pressed on his lips and said, 'What am I to do?' He was surprised by the directness. He had believed that Irish girls were puritanical – in particular in things related to the body. He removed his coat and laid it on the floor and drew her down. As they lay together between the enormous boilers he asked her to marry him.

'What a place to ask such a question.'

'It's as good a place as any.'

'If there was music in the background or birds singing . . . but in a boiler room.'

'That's just convention. I'll be glad though to ask you in the presence of the birds as well. I love you.'

'I'll have to think about it. It hasn't crossed my mind till now,' she said. He didn't believe her but was reassured by her kiss on the concrete steps before she opened the door into the still, empty corridor and showed him to the side door they had entered.

He asked her again a number of times but each time she smiled and said she needed to think about it further. She did not seem displeased and he didn't press. He had already come through one failure. A Sunday came when they were invited to his parents for afternoon tea. They had planned to have lunch together beforehand at a small hotel on the edge of the forest. She asked him to meet her that morning at the hospital gates. As he waited for her he had a feeling of being watched, and looked towards the windows high in a corner of the hospital. He saw girls' faces at several windows and one of them waved. He smiled, waved back without understanding, and turned away in some embarrassment. As soon as they met she took his arm.

'I wanted you to meet me early because we are going to Mass.'

He didn't question the demand though he thought it as strange as the girls waving from the windows. The small blackened church of St Anne's stood at the corner of one of the narrow streets off the Whitechapel Road. Most of the sparse congregation looked Irish. He knelt and stood and sat the way he saw others kneel and stand and sit but he did not bless himself or genuflect.

'What did you think?' she asked as they walked away from the church towards the big Sunday market.

He shrugged. 'I found it moving, like most ceremonies.'

'If we are to be married, you know, you'll have to turn.'

For her he'd turn head over heels, turn his coat, turn cartwheels and somersaults.

'I'm serious. By "turn" I mean you'll have to convert to being a Catholic.'

'That's easy because I'm nothing as I stand.'

'I'd never change my religion for anything or anybody. You'll have to take instruction.'

'If you were as in love with me as I am with you, you'd change. Point the way, then. What am I to do?'

'You'll have to see a priest. And you must be more serious . . . and I haven't said I'll marry you.'

'We'd better go to Victoria Park to find a proper setting.'

'If you'll turn you can ask me.'

'Of course I'll turn if you'll marry me.'

'I will. But you must be more serious for the rest of the day. We have to meet your parents.'

The conversion was easy, a kind of adventure, even a pleasure. His parents had been brought up in loose Anglicanism and only visited the church on rare ceremonial occasions, approving of it as a higher moral hygiene. He had not thought much about it all. For years we grow towards the light, become part of that light for a time, and then the light fails. The child and the old often have more sense of the glory of that light than those in the flower or pulse of their life. He had no illusions why he was turning: he was turning for Mary Pat Meehan, spinster, from the parish of Cill, in South Tipperary.

The priest, Father Cahill, was kind, yet sharp and very alert. There had been a brilliant early career, a doctorate from Rome, but he had run foul of some bishop, and was a marked man after that when it came to any preferment. He scraped a living from various chaplaincies and small offices around the East End, and wrote for a number of radical Catholic publications. On the first evening they met, he asked the priest rather stiffly if he should read *The Imitation of Christ* or any other book he could recommend during the course of instruction. Cahill laughed for a full minute. His little speech must have sounded extraordinarily pompous.

'My dear Richard, you are becoming a Catholic not a religious thinker. All a Catholic needs is to acquire a bottle of Lourdes or Knock water and do and believe everything the Pope tells him. You will be allowed a conscience but it is your duty to inform that conscience and to bring it in line with papal thinking. To take works like *The Imitation* seriously would only get you into trouble. I speak with the voice of experience.'

That was the beginning of his instruction and because it was a hot summer most of it was conducted in the Blind Beggar across the road. Not much was drunk, a few pints of weak bitter, and nearly all the talk was of religion in the deepest sense and often lasted well beyond the set hour of instruction. Cahill was a remarkable man. He saw that clearly now, though he had forgotten most of what had been said. He wished he had kept notes: 'Place was the symbol of the sacred in the ancient world, and the day the symbol of the eternal. By building a church in a certain place and ordering the Sabbath on a Sunday, the Church institutionalised both the Sacred and the Eternal at one stroke,' came back to him. 'You are converting – do not contradict me yet – because of beauty. I did not think so once but I am beginning to think so now, that it is as permanent as truth.'

'Yet, you remain a priest?'

'I was brought up to it. When I look around me I see nothing better that I could turn to.'

'Do you have no regrets?'

'None. If it wasn't this it'd be something else. I'd be the same. Life goes . . .'

After all the seriousness and humour of the hours they had spent together, it was with great gravity that Father Cahill received him into the Church, and with an even deeper gravity a few weeks later he conducted the ceremony in which Richard Farnham and Mary Meehan married one another till death do them part.

Her parents were too old, she said, for the crossing and frightened of the strangeness and human tumult of London. Her brother, who later became his friend and eventual fore-man of the Limerick boatyard, gave her away. His parents offered to host the reception but she would not hear of it; as well, a grand wedding would only create distance and strain between her and the other girls in the hospital. He remem-bered going with her to inspect the room she had booked for the reception above the Red Lion and seeing a notice that the monthly meeting of a club which kept racing pigeons was to be held there later the same evening. As planned, the wedding was small. Only a few close friends and his immediate family attended, all of them of the English middle class. Some of them found the reception amusing, even exotic, but their efforts only highlighted the unease of their patronage.

Her friends were young girls from the hospitals, with their husbands or boy friends. They did not notice any distinction of class. They were too embroiled in the adventure of their youth. What he remembered most was a little band of girls at a table by themselves, all of them nurses who had worked with Mary, all in their early flowering. They stamped their feet and cried out their dissatisfaction at the chaste kiss above the wedding cake and would not stop until they kissed again, a lingering simulation of a kiss of passion, which won their noisy approval. Before the dancing and drinking began, his father, who was very popular with the nurses, made a short speech, which was greeted with almost as much jubilation. Father Cahill made a short and witty speech. They never saw him again. They had been busy with their new lives. A few years later, when they tried to contact him, it was too late.

On their honeymoon he met her parents. All the night and day they travelled to the small Tipperary farm she was tense. As soon as he saw them he understood why they did not come to the wedding. It was as if they belonged to another world. They met the young couple in hope of gaining approval. They had put aside their own bedroom. To Mary's eternal honour she would not consider it. They must keep their own room. Her old attic room was where they would sleep. Even today it was heart-breaking to remember them standing at the wooden gate in front of the modest stone house in the middle of the fields as supplicants of the young couple getting out of the big car with the English number-plates.

'Do you think Mother and Father are all right?' Their daughter corroborated that very act of supplication as they lay awake together in the attic room under the sloping boards of the ceiling.

'They're far more than that. They're wonderful people. They're too good for this world.'

'Father maybe, but you'd soon find a difference if you stepped on *her* toes. It's a manner. It's not at all as it appears.'

'Few things are. I feel it's more than a manner. It's a whole culture.'

'I know it well, then, if it is. Its time has gone.'

She was wrong. Culture, manners, gentleness . . . Their time is never gone.

The light of the summer night was in the room in spite of the curtain on the small window so that all the lines of the white ceiling boards were sharp. They appeared close enough to touch with a raised arm. When her silence stood for a long time like obstinacy in the room he drew her towards him. 'Not here.' She kissed him a firm goodnight. 'We'll have other times and other places. I hope you sleep well.'

He remembered the joy of the next morning, the doors open in the kitchen-livingroom so that the fragrance and insect hum and colour of the small front garden and fields were part of the room as they had breakfast, the weight of the whole summer pressing on their lives. Later, through his children and their grandchildren, he felt that he had been allowed to enter more fully into that world, and though he would never be part of it in any sense of belonging, he held it to be a privilege to have been allowed to draw so close.

The next summer he saw the opportunity of starting the business in Limerick. How much of life is chance and luck? How much of chance and luck is what we set out to find? Mary had not opposed the move to Ireland but she was not keen. Perhaps she thought the venture would fail and they'd return with a few spent dreams to their life in England and concentrate thereafter on the easy and practical. She could never be accused thereafter of having stood in the way of that dream. He could still feel his dismay as he looked about the sheds and engines, the dereliction of the quay, the evening after signing the lease . . . He had stood there amid the poor sheds, in the stink of the low tide, the alien huddled roofs of Limerick and its many spires rising to the sky in the distance, and he thought of all the hopes and dreams he'd ever had, and thought in disbelief and anger, 'Is this, now, to be my life?' What else could it ever have been but his life? It had turned out very differently to the way it had been imagined and felt on that dismaying site. In many ways, it was a life that had been steeped in luck. And it was an older but the selfsame life that now stood before this poor country dance hall in light from the low mountains that had summoned up Mary's youth and the luck of their meeting.

He began to walk quickly back towards the quay. Cattle still stood around the feeder in the village field. Small birds fluttered about between the backs of the cattle and the feeder's rim. The long stone walls by the sides of the road were blotched with lichen. This too, amazingly, had become part of his life, its solid setting. He looked at it with deep interest, even involvement, since it was what his eyes saw that caused him to cry out once, 'Is this to be my life?' That necessary vanity had long been burned away. But it was still all that his eyes saw, all that was hidden or remembered and felt . . .

He walked past the school, the crossroads, the shop, the black hall, the church in its evergreens, Luke Henry's, another house that must also be a small shop because of the packets of tea and bars of soap on display in the cottage window, the barracks. Raindrops started to spatter his coat, and by the time he reached the slope that led from the bridge to the quay it was raining heavily. He felt no dismay at the sight of his present home on the quay. He was now grateful for anywhere. Promise and disappointment had both gone. He must be, in all the implications of the phrase, what is called a finished man.

An hour later, a car came slowly down the slope and drove alongside the boat with its headlight on. Luke Henry's son left the car running and the doors open as he got out and took a cardboard box from the passenger seat. Richard Farnham came out of the cabin and thanked him as he took the box.

'For nothing. Thanks yourself,' the young man said, looking fixedly at him as for some sign, and when there was none he said abruptly as he turned away, 'It has all the makings of a bad night.' The car backed carefully out from the quay and climbed the slope to the bridge.

Late the next morning the Garda sergeant called at the boat to pay his respects to the important man from Limerick. He had polished the buttons and stripes of his uniform. His black boots shone. The thinning red hair was combed carefully. That he had been a handsome man was still discernible. Dressed up and shining in the early morning he felt free. He had slipped his marriage and children, his rank and years; it was as if he were walking again towards the excitement his good looks and energy had created about him when he was young. There was no stir of life round the big white boat. Through the glass window he saw an old man's head fallen over a book, dead or sleeping, he thought, and rapped sharply on the cabin roof. Richard Farnham had slept fitfully the night before, listening to the surge of the water against the boat as he slipped in and out of light sleep. Now he woke instantly and got to his feet as if he disliked being caught sleeping. Slowly he put on a jacket and took his time emerging. The first thing he saw was the snow-white handkerchief the sergeant had stuffed up the sleeve of his tunic, the three silver stripes on the dark blue cloth, the tunic clasped at the throat, the handsome, eager face.

'Good day, Sergeant.'

'You're very welcome to our part of the river.'

'Thank you very much.'

'Guard Murphy was telling me you sailed this boat all the way up from Limerick.'

'Yes. That is true. I sailed the boat from Limerick.'

'You'd not be from Limerick originally?'

'No. I'm English.'

'I've always liked English people. My experience is of a very mannerly people. Unfortunately, the same cannot be said of many of our kind.'

'I have found the Irish often have quite beautiful manners.'

'Very two-faced,' the sergeant said firmly.

Richard Farnham disliked the emphasis with which the sergeant demanded attention for his words, seeming both to ingratiate himself and to bully: the man must be very vain. He had taken a quick dislike to him. He saw that an invitation was expected, and was determined not to allow him into the boat.

'I like to take an interest in everything that happens in my area,' the sergeant said after a long bout of fencing that covered the river in winter, the flooded fields, the timber barge that had gone aground the week before.

'It was very kind of you to call, Sergeant,' Richard Farnham closed the meeting.

The sergeant walked angrily away from the quay. Richard Farnham did not watch him go. He let himself quietly back into the boat. Only the closing door made any sound. He disliked turning the sergeant away but he did not feel he had time any more to waste on people he didn't like. He had been polite. Even so the meeting had made him restless. After a light lunch he decided to walk into the village. On the bridge he glanced across at the barracks and archway and saw to his relief that neither the sergeant nor any of the guards was about and that the roads were empty. He found Luke Henry in the empty bar exactly as he had found him the last time, sitting on a stool inside the counter watching the television high in the corner. As soon as the door opened he abandoned whatever he had been watching with what looked like pleasure and bade his customer welcome. Matches, paper towels, a fruit cake, a fresh loaf, an expensive tin of biscuits were bought. He didn't need any of these things but he felt he should buy them to justify the expedition, repay in a small way the friendliness Luke had shown. The items were light and could be carried easily.

Not long after he got back he heard a low knock, to find the two boys who'd met the boat the first evening on the quay. 'I'm delighted you came,' he said. He showed them the boat, then made tea, and they sat and talked. For more than two hours they talked, the darkness no longer deepening when they left the boat, a broken moon far above the bridge casting a grey metallic sheen on the rushing water. The night was cold. They were more bemused than ashamed at how time had passed without their noticing. What they had spoken about was already blurred – their studies, their hopes of what they'd find in life, obstacles they saw placed against those hopes – and they had spoken about the river.

Their host listened intently to everything they said, and they found themselves describing things to him far more eloquently than they imagined they could. In return, he told them he'd been an engineer, urged them to think about it as a career. 'It's hard to describe since it has its own vocabulary: once it's tried out it either works or doesn't work. You have to have an aptitude for maths, and then an interest, and then some luck.'

The two boys were not worried about the lateness. Their families were proud of their schooling because they were the first in their family as far back as the generations could be recalled to have gone to school past the age of legal requirement. They would not have to face any questions, but each was shamefaced that time had slipped by unnoticed, as if they'd been tricked out of their own watchfulness to express themselves too freely, as if a strange spell of charm and attention had been cast to turn the couple of hours into a few minutes.

Richard Farnham felt lifted by their visit. He invited them to call to the boat any time they were passing. It was suggested they might take a trip upriver together in the better weather. He told them he'd show them properly how the boat worked any time they wished. They said they'd call after Second Mass the following Sunday.

Late the following morning Patrick the postman's battered Ford drove on to the quay. Richard Farnham was taking the air between showers and waiting by the car when Patrick pulled himself out from behind the wheel in his postman's cap and crumpled black uniform. Patrick's face was red beneath the peaked cap, humorous, intelligent, and the large sharp nose gave it the look of a lake bird or cormorant.

'You've a fine boat there,' he said as he pulled the grey calico bag from the passenger seat and offered Richard Farnham his hand. 'You are very welcome to this part of the country.'

'Thank you.' He was surprised by the sudden apparition and the friendliness. 'You must be the local postman?'

'Will you look at the state of me? What else could I

be?' Patrick laughed at the very idea that he could possibly be anything else. 'There's a letter for you. A registered letter.'

'I'm sure you must be mistaken. Nobody knows where I am.'

'*Richard Farnham. The Quay*,' Patrick said as he took an envelope from the bag. 'If that's yourself, then there's somebody who knows where you are. This is definitely the quay.'

'I'm Richard Farnham,' he said as he took the letter.

He recognised his wife's handwriting. Quickly he tore open the envelope. The letter ran to three pages. He stood completely absent as he hunted through the words for their general meaning. Patrick watched him with intense interest as he read. If he had moved he didn't think the man would notice. He must be a nervous class of a man, Patrick thought.

'I'm sorry. I'm so very sorry,' he said when at last he lifted his eyes from the words and saw Patrick standing there. 'Please forgive my bad manners.'

'Naturally you wanted to find out what is in the letter. I hope there was no bad news.'

'No. No. But my wife is upset. The guards called to the house to report my whereabouts.'

'No one likes to see the guards call.'

'I'm sorry to have kept you. Won't you come in to the boat?' he offered in disarray and almost by way of apology.

Patrick accepted the offer simply. Richard Farnham tried to blank the letter from his mind as he showed Patrick around the boat. All the time he found himself losing the thread of what he wanted to say, his real attention on the import of what he'd read. Patrick did not seem to mind that he said little, and looked at everything in the boat with interest. Despite his battered car and rag-tag uniform the postman was a wealthy man. He owned the post office, which his wife ran together with a small supermarket, and they had a large farm. All their children were capable and handsome.

He was shrewd, even worldly, but unusual in that by nature he was both emotional and generous as well. Women were fond of Patrick. As much out of easy liking as in apology for the distracted way he showed him the boat, Richard Farnham offered a whiskey when they found themselves again in the cabin.

'Isn't it a bit early in the day?' Patrick asked in a tone where acceptance was held with perfect tact against its appropriateness.

'The bottle hasn't been opened. If you don't take a glass it may have to remain unopened since my time here appears to be up.'

'Aren't you going to have something yourself? You look as if a little something might do you no harm at all.'

'Perhaps a little, then. For company.' Richard Farnham poured a whisper into his glass. He poured Patrick a large measure.

'Hold on,' Patrick said.

'I'm sorry. I'll pour it down the sink if it's too much.'

'I can see you're not a drinking man. I'd let it kill me before I'd pour it down a sink. Your good health.'

'Cheers,' Richard Farnham said as they drank.

'Why would the Limerick guards want to call on my house with news of my whereabouts? I'm not a criminal,' Richard Farnham said angrily.

'Nobody likes to see the guards coming to the house,' Patrick said carefully.

'Why would they call?'

'I'd say they called because they heard from the guards here. Did you give any of them your name or address?'

'I gave the guard who lives in the big house over there my name. I told him I'd been in business in Limerick but am now retired. He asked.'

'That's Guard Murphy. Murphy is mean but he's all right. I'd say it was the sergeant.'

'The sergeant was here today. He didn't say a word about calling the Limerick guards.'

'Of course he didn't.'

'Couldn't he come here and ask me directly for the information he wanted?'

'There are certain people who can't stand it when things are simple and straightforward. They need to twist them round. You must know that by now.'

'I'm afraid I took a dislike to the sergeant.'

'That makes us a pair. The sergeant calls me Mister Sly. People tell him that I mimic him from time to time in Luke's. He often tries to listen outside the bar when it's near closing time.'

'And do you?' Richard Farnham laughed for the first time.

'It wouldn't do to start incriminating myself at my age but anybody as full of themselves as the sergeant needs a touching up from time to time. I better be going now before I say too much.'

'I'm going to have to telephone home. Where would I find a phone?'

'Where else but the post office? You'd be unlikely to try the barracks after all we've said. We can drive to the post office now.'

'I'd prefer to phone this evening.'

'Any time you want. The phone will be there.'

'Would seven be a good time?'

'Seven is perfect. The post office will be shut but the key will be in the front door. I'll be there myself but I'll have told her as well that you are coming.'

After Patrick left he read the letter a number of times. She had every reason to be upset by the sight of the guards coming to the house. Only for their son Michael she would have driven there and then to the quay but he persuaded her to write.

She would see his life in a boat on this quay the way others would see it, and how it must appear in a compromising light. His wife believed in appearances. She it was who had changed houses three times in their life in Limerick to keep their appearances in accord with the family's increasing affluence. She had furnished and decorated these three houses with care. He used to tease her about it, as he did about the various charities and organisations she attached herself to as soon as their children started school. The teasing had always been affectionate, a careful expression of the strong feeling that drew them together and set them apart in their different needs. Left to himself he would have stayed in that first house. He had opposed the moves but came to enjoy the luxury and space she created with their new money.

Their children turned out well. They had been lucky in that too. They all had been bright and confident, more confident than he had ever been. What had they to go on as they started out but the appearances she had provided and the constant, even care they received. She had been the more practical – and always the more honest throughout their sexual life, and her interest in that life outlasted his even though both were old. The dark beauty he married had grown into the handsome woman he never tired of looking at. He had been steeped in luck. If it was possible, he was still in love, and far more deeply attached to her than when they were young.

While he worked, so much of his life had been taken up with his work that the enormous change that had happened to their lives over the years was hidden. When he retired it was a shock to notice how far apart their inclinations had separated them. He had gone into his work. She had gone out to others. How many people he had failed to notice until he had the whole of every day to himself. He found it an effort to get on with other people; by comparison, he had no difficulty with being alone, but it made her unhappy to see him alone.

As a way of escaping the dislocation of his new life, he went back to the yard to design and build the white boat. He was careful to stay away from all the other work of the yard, which his sons now ran, unless they asked, which was seldom, and when they did he suspected it was as much out of courtesy as any need. Long before the boat was completed he had talked about going on the river in winter, when the pleasure-crafts had gone. He did not think she ever took the idea seriously until the boat was built and he was making preparations to leave. Then she opposed it with all her considerable force.

She seemed to view it as a criticism of herself. It had been useless to repeat that nothing could be farther from the truth. Fortunately all their children had supported the idea. It wasn't as if he were going up the Amazon. Ireland was a small country. No part of it was more than a few hours' drive from any other part. He had given ready assurance that if at any time he became the cause of the slightest anxiety he would leave the boat wherever it was docked and return home. He would keep that promise now.

After he rested he took out his one good suit and dressed as carefully as he used to dress for important business meetings. To do so had always given him a feeling of well-being and strength, a detached alertness, a calm that was the opposite of relaxation. The night was very dark so he left all the lights on in the boat before leaving for the post office a few minutes before seven.

A light shone above the front door. Before he could knock Patrick opened the door, his face creased with welcome. In the large living-room he was introduced to Patrick's six handsome children, most of them young men and women. Their mother was warm and energetic, with a face that was a mixture of open kindness and clear-eyed shrewdness. He was also introduced to two workmen who were eating a meal at the big table. Then Patrick showed him into the sitting-room where he left him with the telephone. With its shining unused furniture, the photos and trophies on the sideboard, the sitting-room was like some mummified symbol of respectability. To simplify any dealings, he had the charges reversed. His wife took the call. He kept it as simple as possible. He was ready to go home at any time. He told her that there had been no reason for the guards to call at the house. The local sergeant here had caused the enquiries to be made out of busyness. He told her that he loved her, was anxious to see her, and would tell her everything that had taken place when they met. It was arranged she'd call for him at the quay around lunch-time on the following Wednesday. When he returned to the large living-room, the two workmen had gone.

'The charges were reversed,' he said by way of explanation.

'You'll not be going like that ... You'll have to have something,' Patrick demanded.

He protested that he had already taken up enough of their time but when he saw that Patrick was adamant he asked for a cup of tea.

'You'll have something proper to eat, then?'

'I've already eaten. A cup of tea ...'

As he sat and talked for a half-hour he thought how pleasant and full of life the big untidy room was with all the children and the warmth and the long littered table. Compared to the rooms he had grown up in, the rooms they had brought up their own children in, and the beautiful plain rooms of his parents-in-law in that house in the middle of the fields, this room was more like a crossroads between the needs of private lives and the busy, bustling world where all political importances happen. The atmosphere had touches of the excitement and untidiness, the constant improvisations of a market. How like an unused altar the other room was by comparison, the room he'd telephoned from, an altar to some god of respectability, waiting there in its polished emptiness for formalities everybody hoped would never happen.

Patrick walked him all the way from the post office to where the lights from the white boat lit the slipway down to the quay. As they walked he wanted to ask, 'What is it in people's nature like the sergeant's that drives them to make trouble needlessly?' He didn't ask. He felt it would only be putting social pressure on Patrick and that it would be much more useful to study the question within himself.

On Sunday the bells for First Mass rang at eight and again at eight-thirty. They were like a call to joy and celebration in the still silence of the water. Richard Farnham checked the times and found them reasonably accurate. Between the bells, cars and some voices crossed the bridge. A little more than an hour later a scattering of the same voices and cars crossed back over the bridge. The first bell for Second Mass rang just before eleven. Voices and cars started to cross the bridge and gradually turned into a steady stream. When a number of cars crossed the bridge together they made a hollow sound. Most of the voices were on bicycles. All the cars and voices had ceased when the second bell rang out close to a quarter to twelve. One car driven very fast suddenly disturbed the settling silence. The silence of the village was intense. No dog barked, no cock crowed, a single cow mooed somewhere. He began to make sandwiches. After a long time, motors starting up around the church broke the silence; came closer; crossed the bridge. The voices followed. They sounded more animated now than the voices on their way to Mass. In the middle of this traffic the two boys appeared on the quay. They wore dark Sunday suits, which made them look older and more awkward.

He took them into the boat, uncovered the engine and explained how the parts and the different controls worked. They were interested in everything. He decided to go out on the small lake, reversing the boat down past the boathouse. Once they were on the lake he gave the controls to the two boys, showing them how to reverse, turn up the throttle, slow the boat to a crawl, turn it around. 'Out here you don't have to worry about making a mistake.' When they got back to the quay and after they had the sandwiches, fruit and tea, he noticed their restlessness. Everything had been tense and watchful; there had not been the abandon of talk and listening as on the previous evening. 'You probably have some place else to go to?' 'We're sorry but there's a football match at three.' 'Then you just have time.'

He told them he was leaving on Wednesday but hoped to come back round Easter. He asked if they'd be interested in looking after the boat until then. All they'd have to do was check the moorings from time to time and let the engine run for a half-hour every two or three weeks. Naturally he'd pay them. He wanted them to think it over. He did not want them late for the football match.

'We'll take care of the boat and we don't need any payment,' they said.

'Sleep on it. If you're of the same mind tomorrow we'll come to an arrangement.'

As they were leaving, Guard Murphy came down the slipway wheeling a bicycle. The pointer and the red setter trotted behind. He spoke to the two boys before turning in towards the boat. Richard Farnham was standing by the boat, seeing the two boys away.

'I see ye took the boat out on the lake for a spin,' the guard said.

'They were interested in how the boat works.'

The grey string bag that hung from his shoulders looked plump with game.

'Those boys are bright. I wish my crowd were more like them.'

'I believe you must have been the cause of the Limerick guards having to call on my house during the week?'

The guard was visibly discomforted by the tone. 'It was the sergeant rang up,' Murphy said defensively.

'Why didn't the sergeant come to me for whatever he required?'

'We're not used to boats coming to the quay this time of year.'

'I'm not blaming you, Guard; I'm not blaming the sergeant either but I'd be grateful if you'd ask him why he telephoned the Limerick guards without first coming to me.'

'I'll ask him, then,' the guard said without any enthusiasm. 'I'm sure he thought he was doing it for the best.'

'I'd be grateful.'

When Guard Murphy returned to the barracks he found the sergeant alone in the dayroom, writing a report into the patrol book. He was relieving the barrack orderly, who had gone to the football match.

'I called to the quay,' the guard began carefully. 'The old boy over in the white boat seems to have a bee in his bonnet about us calling up the Limerick guards. He thinks we should have gone over and asked him first.'

The sergeant stopped writing and looked the guard straight in the face as he made the slow short speech. After he finished he continued looking at him until it was clear he had nothing more to add and then went back to his writing. The guard knew better than to pursue the subject. He would not be turning up on the quay again for some time.

Whatever hope of quiet or reflective happiness Richard Farnham had come in search of had now gone. What had he come for? He wasn't sure. A whole new generation that included his sons and daughter had grown up, who now worked to take over what had been his world and was now increasingly theirs. He did not mind being pushed out on to the margins of this world. It was in the nature of things, and in many ways he was delighted with his new freedoms. Had he come to try to experience his new situation more fully, to try to see it more clearly? Perhaps because his life had been so busy and full he had always been drawn to the idea of going to live for a time on a river in winter. To be alone, to live in his own mind for a time, to be on the empty water, to try to see his life whole. At that he had to smile grimly; as if any life could be seen whole, since each life reflected so many lives other than its own, and yet in the midst of it all each life was also alone. He would never be certain now what he'd come for. Would he be more certain if he had been able to remain for months in the boat along this quay? We are born in night and travel through an uncertain day to reach another night. Nobody who lived on earth was in a different situation.

He wanted to be away. He would go now but for the arrangement he had made on the telephone.

The two boys came the next evening a little earlier than expected. They said they'd be glad to mind the boat until he came back in better weather. He already knew their answer and had monies for them in separate envelopes. They were excited by the prospect of taking charge of the boat. He showed them again all over the boat, not because they needed the knowledge but because he saw that they were keenly interested, already proprietorial.

'There is never a serious business arrangement without money.' They accepted with a mixture of embarrassment and pleasure, which they tried to hide, and pocketed the envelopes with self-conscious seriousness. Over tea the talk turned to their approaching exams, and he saw their anxiety. They understood clearly how much their future lives would be affected by that single throw of the dice in the coming days of May and June. Unlike the rich they could not rely on any second chance. 'Come to me,' he said, 'if you think of engineering. You'll have a better idea by Easter, and we can look at it in a more practical way. Anyhow I hope something comes up that you'll like and enjoy.'

'The important thing may be to get anything at all,' they said as they took their leave.

The next day, in bright blustery weather, he walked to Luke's to buy bread and milk, to thank him, and to say goodbye. 'Seeing you're leaving the boat here I'll not say goodbye,' Luke said. 'You'll be back in the summer.'

He had always noticed how reluctant people here were to say goodbye, as if it echoed too close for comfort each final parting.

'I hope to be back before the summer,' he took Luke's warm handclasp in his own. 'Before the crowds come.'

'You'll be back in the good weather, then, but gone before the crowds?'

'That's the general idea.'

'It'd not be too far away from my own if I was ever to travel, to be about in the good weather and gone before the crowds.'

He met Patrick's car a little way from Luke's. Patrick offered him a lift though his car was going away from the quay. He invited Patrick to the boat for a glass of whiskey before he left. 'Otherwise the bottle will just be standing there.'

'I'll wait till you come back. It'll taste better then,' Patrick laughed. 'Unless I have to bring you another letter.'

'I'm not expecting any more letters,' Richard Farnham said, and both men laughed.

He walked past the little avenue of sycamores that ran to the grey bulk of the barracks, the glittering water above it that was not the flooded river but a lake they called Oakport, the bare trees of the wooded island standing blackly out in the water, the boathouse, the long paddocks that stretched to Oakport House against the dark woods. He thought he saw a guard looking out on the road from the barrack window but could not be certain as the evening light and the distance turned the rectangle of glass into a dark depth like water. In the boat he made tea and sat looking out at the rushing river much as he had often sat as a boy looking from his parents' windows into Epping Forest. A dream of girls on the edge of the forest carrying hockey sticks came into his mind. Another dream of a girl with a polka dot headscarf that he had followed for part of an idle Saturday. The low cry in the darkness, 'What am I to do?', as they embraced in the hospital boiler room.

The two boys would certainly dream of girls. He could imagine them talking together, of taking girls out on the river, doing wild things with them in the boat. They'd then rest like kings at riverside towns such as Athlone or Portuma. They'd be shocked to discover that the girls might have roughly the same dreams. Their girlish talk would be just as fanciful, but much more practical, softer, more humorous, being the more securely rooted, knowing more fully that the wild things led to the child in the distance, the house, the school, and the lawn. If they were as lucky as he, they'd realise their dreams, the realisation far more rich and complex than the dream itself because it was the beginning of work, that idea outside ourselves that we go toward and follow for a whole life long though we know it cannot ever be realised. The realisation was in the work and was lost in work.

Here on this quay by this river there was such richness of water and light and stone and church and tree and people and all they reflected of life that he felt he could continue looking on them for ever. They could not be exhausted. In the same light he saw a familiar-looking black Mercedes cross and turn uncertainly down towards the boat and the quay, his wife at the wheel. They had come through all that time together and they were as separate still as on the day they'd first met. He waved, going towards her in welcome, feeling both intense excitement and dismay – at wanting to go back and having to go back to a kind of work he had never even attempted with any seriousness in the whole of his life up to now.

Kathy Page

BEES

WE LOOKED LIKE what we were. If there had been an office worker or a housewife at the bus-stop, they'd have kept clear of us: a sort of thing which used to piss me right off. Now I think, why blame them? A person's qualities aren't visible from outside. For example: I know, because I did some tests once for a bloke at the polytechnic (they paid a tenner), that I've a very good memory for detail – total recall, more or less – but no one on earth could spot that just from looking at me and that's an obvious thing, not a complicated one, such as: I think sometimes that I see things the same way an artist does. Or I can imagine myself leading a revolution, or stealing a famous painting just to keep it in my living-room, or jumping out of an aeroplane with only the silk of a parachute to keep me safe. From the outside, no one would guess any of this, not in a thousand years. They never have and maybe I wouldn't want them to.

We were waiting for the 159. I wore my blue T-shirt and my smarter buff trousers with the crease: clean, but they didn't particularly go. Belinda had on my white T-shirt, a flowery tie-round skirt, plimsolls. She was trying to grow her hair but it just got thicker. She looked about fifteen; I looked about forty. We had the shopping trolley between us – just the metal frame, you get more on that way.

For weeks I had been looking out for a fridge and I had a feeling that morning that I would find it. It was more of a seeing than a feeling. I could picture the kind of street. It would be smart, but not so smart that the neighbours complained if you left something outside. Fresh white paint. Plane trees. The houses would have small patches of garden in the front, where people kept their bins behind a hedge. The fences and walls would be low. Some of the houses would be split into flats, some would have converted attics. Wrought-iron gates, window-boxes, new roofs, entryphones, burglar alarms, Residents' Parking. You get a nose for the right kind of place eventually, just as you can roughly tell by looking at it whether a cast-off electrical appliance will work or not: *Daley is a practical person, useful, optimistic and a good contributor to any team.* I had that written on a reference once by Mrs Ossotto. People often patronise someone in my situation but you learn to sift the wheat from the chaff and that one is true.

A bus came, but it was a 3. I didn't let it get to me.

'I hope something happens today,' Belinda said. She was fidgeting a lot and her face was ghost-white from lack of sleep.

'It will,' I said, thinking of the fridge, 'so cheer up.'

We'd met about a month before. I was passing and I helped her to break down the door of an empty flat on the Estate. Then I came inside to see if there was anything else needed. Right from the start she didn't like the place, but I said: think carefully. Later on you can find something better, but what you need right now is a roof over your head and a door you can bolt. It was clean, the plumbing still there: it would do her for a while.

I went to buy a new lock, and on the way back I saw a cooker in a skip. Next day I found a bloke who took the electric from the corridor for four quid. Meantime I found a rug, a kettle and a not bad mattress so I took them over too.

We got talking. She says she's not told anyone before, but her uncle had interfered with her when she was a kid, which seems to be the case with half the world these days. She says I'm a good listener, which I've often been told before. I tell her I can sympathise because I've not had much what you'd call positive sexual experience myself: just once with an older girl at the Catholic home, when I was twelve. A member of staff found us and I got shut up on my own for a week.

It was late when we finished talking so I stayed. We wore our clothes in bed and I'd made sure not to touch her at all and knew it had to be that way. When I woke up, I made tea. 'Don't go,' she said. So I went to check out at Dempsey House. The warden told me that they wouldn't automatically take me back again if it didn't work out. But I didn't care. I hadn't had the chance to live with someone out of choice before.

I thought it would be paradise. But Belinda never took to the flat. She felt shut in and she couldn't get her mind from going round in circles. So I said we should scout around and see if there was anywhere else, and at the same time, I thought, I can keep my eye out for a fridge and that's how come we were there waiting for the 159, which you wait for a lot.

'Daley,' she said, 'I want a garden when we move. I've gotta have space – ' She has no idea what's on and what's not on. Sometimes she acts as if you're going to hit her; other times she acts as if she doesn't care if you do: like the weather. So I said I didn't see why we shouldn't have a garden, then she put her arm around me, which by then meant I could do the same to her. I knew how to treat her from being in the Group. They encouraged you to get it out of your system, even if you didn't know it was there: bashing cushions, running around on all fours screaming. I thought Christ! when I started, but it was more embarrassing not to and after a couple of weeks I was in there with the best. Sometimes my throat ached for days afterwards, and I'd have this strange, empty feeling as if I'd just arrived from Mars. One time the bloke who ran the group, Ian, took me into his arms and hugged me to his chest; it really stirred me up at the time. But the fact is that kind of professional person only cares about you so much. It is not the same as an actual relationship.

'Backing on to a park. I'd be OK then,' Belinda said.

'Sounds good,' I said, although I knew there was sod all chance of us finding a place like that unless it had rotten floors, no windows, a rodent problem. Even then it would be someone's investment, biding its time: they would get us out, just like that.

Belinda yanked her hand out to stop the bus. We went top front. As we set off, I put my feet on the ledge and thought more about our fridge. How it would be standing at the edge of the road ready to be taken away – a big fridge with a separate freezer at the top. It would fit just so on the trolley. If the conductor kicked up a fuss I would walk it back and Belinda would meet me the other end. Once we had a fridge, we could go on the number 2a and do a bulk shop when our cheques came through. I saw Belinda and me pushing a trolley round a huge supermarket, stopping to decide how many tins of tomatoes to get, the aisles stretching out in front of us. Tea, Dairy, Tinned Goods, Butter and Spreads, Delicatessen, Hot Bread Shop, Fruit and Veg, Pasta, Juices, Condiments, etc. The freezer cabinets, giving off steam. Six cod fillets for two-forty-nine, two-kilo bags of peas, chips all cut for you ready. I would have a list, meals planned out – but occasionally we'd buy off-the-cuff: some strange kind of sausage or milky-fruity pudding thing or spiny-looking fruit that made your mouth wrinkle but it was worth finding out or you'd always hanker after knowing.

I've never gone truly hungry and I'm not greedy but I do have an appetite for making decisions. This above that, have this and wait for that. Two of these, three of those and none of that, thanks. Which size? Which colour? Good value? *Daley is happy to take on responsibilities*, the woman from Social Services once said. Well, true, and good old Daley – but I know now that there's more to me than people like her ever saw.

The picture of us among all that food gave me a lump in my throat. Somehow I imagined that we were smarter dressed and I was a bit younger and she was wearing lipstick, though for the life of me I don't think she ever will.

The fridge would just fit into the niche on the left of the kitchen, I thought. I would load it up from the supermarket bags, fitting everything on the shelves just so. I have a certificate in food hygiene, with distinction, not that it's proved as useful as they said, and I would keep it clean. *Everything he does he does thoroughly and with care*, the teacher wrote on my leaving report and again, it's true.

Belinda gave me a dig in the ribs. She said how if we got a house with a garden we could grow vegetables. Live off the land like the people we'd seen in a programme on TV. She doesn't like vegetables, as a matter of fact.

'All the rubbish could be returned to the soil,' she said. 'I wonder how much land you need to be self-sufficient?' She looked at me as if I would be bound to know.

'A lot,' I said.

'So we'd have to buy flour and stuff. But in a big garden, we could grow vegetables and have a goat. We could make the milk into cheese . . .' People don't have goats in cities. I heard of a woman once who kept a rabbit in a flat and it died of eating carpet. Also goats stink and so does the milk and it would probably eat the garden soon as look at it. How would you get hold of one anyway? I just couldn't see it. But I kept quiet.

'Open fires,' she went on, 'we could collect wood from skips. Be nice, wouldn't it? We could cook on them too.'

'The chimneys would need seeing to, then,' I said, 'and cooking on an open fire is not easy, unless you want to get food poisoning.' I could see I was being a wet blanket so I added that some kind of solid fuel range would be better.

'OK. Candlelight,' she said. 'I don't want electricity.'

'What about the TV?' I asked. We had one in the flat – another thing I'd found. A big Sony in a mahogany cabinet. 'The TV would need electricity, and the fridge-freezer.'

'I don't want a fridge,' she said then. 'I'd rather have things fresh out of the garden.'

'You can't live on greens,' I told her. 'What about meat?' I said. 'That's what fridges and freezers do, keep things fresh, otherwise we'll get salmonella!'

'No. They just keep things *longer*,' she said and I started to get tense, which I hadn't in a long time. A pulse beat in the back of my eyes. I shut them, and all I could see was the fridge, almost new. I could hear it hum.

'We'll be vegetarians,' I heard her say, 'though we could have chickens for the eggs.' My head began to hurt.

'You don't know what you're talking about!' I said. The bus was stuck in a jam. Everything smelled of diesel. I kept my eyes tight shut. 'A vegetarian diet is complicated. You need to get the balance right. Proteins, minerals, vitamins. I know. And what are we supposed to do in winter, living off this garden, if we can't freeze things?'

'They managed before there were freezers,' she said, 'they bottled things.' I opened my eyes.

'Who the fuck is going to bottle things?' I said. I never swear.

'Me,' she said. It struck me for the first time that since we'd been sharing, Belinda hadn't lifted a finger.

'Oh, yes?' I said.

'Anyway, we haven't got a fridge, or a garden,' she said, 'so this is stupid.'

'But *I* want one,' I said, turning to her, jabbing my finger at my chest to underline the words. I could feel my face go red.

'You always want such ordinary things,' she said then, in a bored voice. The bus was still stuck in the jam. Something was going on in the street ahead and she stared at it, ignoring me.

'No I don't!' I said. 'Nothing feels ordinary to me. I would have thought you would understand that! And what's wrong with ordinary? You're pretty ordinary and I want you.'

'Oh, fuck off, dickwit,' she said, pushing past me to get off the bus.

I watched her cross to the opposite pavement. She didn't look back. I sat there, running the conversation through in my head to see where it had gone wrong. I thought I had gone as far as I could with her garden idea, but it wasn't practical when you got down to it. At the same time I had to admit that the feeling I had about the fridge had swayed me. The fridge was almost human the way I felt about it and that wasn't right. It was stupid to care so much about something that didn't exist; then again we both did it. We both kept pictures in our heads. And kept adding to them. I could see that now. In fact, it was the thing that joined us.

I got off and started to run after her. I had to slow to a fast walk because of my heart banging in my chest. I could just see her. I had forgotten the trolley but never mind.

'Belinda!' I shouted

It might half-work, I thought. Even suppose we stayed in the flat but got hold of an allotment – people do. She'd do the gardening, grow as much as she could and I'd do what I'm good at to make up the difference. When we had everything we needed I'd start selling on. Appliances are one thing; the real money these days is in antiques. Glass lampshades, doorknobs, patterned finger-plates, letterboxes, bell pushes, bits of wrought iron. There's plenty of empty private houses, you can't squat them but they're stuffed with things like that – all you need is a screwdriver. A stall. A van. Then I could go for the bigger things – fireplaces, cast-iron baths, panelled doors. It might half-work, if she could accept that. I might even end up with a shop.

'Belinda, please stop!' I called as I saw her hesitate then disappear into a big crowd that had gathered by the railway bridge. Maybe she'd meant it when she said she'd do the bottling and so on. Why not? Maybe she wanted to pull her weight. What had I done? Squabble over a fridge. It wasn't even true about her being ordinary. I thought how she might just wander off and then I'd be back to square one or worse, just as they'd warned me at Dempsey House.

I knew that's how she'd go, if she went. She wouldn't warn you. She wouldn't announce it. No discussions. She'd wander off and all I'd be left with would be an ache. She had wandered off from somewhere when I first met her and I didn't even know where from.

'Wait, Belinda!' I shouted, 'Wait!' I pushed into the crowd. People were turned in a kind of circle; I squeezed my way through. Everyone seemed big and solid. I couldn't see what was going on: some kind of fight. I don't like violence. Christ, I thought, I'll never get out of here.

But there she was on the other side plodding on down the

street. The lot of traffic coming towards us was stuck as well and a police car zoomed up on the wrong side of the road. One or two people had got out of their cars and were going up to join the crowd and look at whatever it was. I caught up.

'Belinda,' I said. She kept walking but she slowed down.

'What pisses me off is that the things you want are easier to get than the things I want,' she said. She still wouldn't look at me. She was chewing her lip. 'Most of the things I want aren't possible. It isn't fair. I feel things'll never go my way.'

By then we'd got to another bus-stop and the traffic was moving. I had a pain in my side. We sat down and I told her how I had thought it through. I'd added bits by then, for instance I told her that I thought we might well be able to keep bees, even here in the city. I'd read of it somewhere: that there are more flowers in city gardens than in the whole of the countryside put together. It was a day for seeing things and I saw a white wooden hive. I saw them, fat stripy bees buzzing and crawling on a sticky comb and I saw the honey dripping into a big glass jar. It was the colour of strong tea before the milk goes in, a dark, reddish brown, glowing. I told Belinda everything, until I ran out of words. Then she kissed me on the mouth. It was as if she was turning me gently inside out to look for something she had lost.

'Let's go home,' she said.

Jon Silkin

THE OFFERING

With a day's leave I tapped at my aunt's sash window –
the slender breast of Swansea bay. Her father said,
'soldier, don't come this way again.' Honeysuckle
was my childhood's visiting, her smile disremembers.

At six, I disturbed him and father. About my waist
he scissored his thighs, for my stillness. I hardly
breathed, father silent. What can the Psalms provide?
What, but death? no no, never think it, falling
off the stairs in my father's house. But he lingered,
and with the fingers of a mechanic the Shekhina,
her great wings pinned back as the hair with a headband,
    undid the soul.

I must kiss wet lips, taste of sugared lemon,
the top lip a white bristling. 'Kiss grandfather,'
mother said. All that the child did lacked generosity.
Like the drive-belt on a nineteenth-century loom
relatives, from the distaff side, move in line
and ask for love, such as I have not to give.

The gates of the Psalms open, I hoping I may
be blessed, that I may bless. In these unlocked spaces
with black crew-cut fur and violent teeth, property
of the Hebrew kingdom, one pads with a sign from his neck,
'close the gates, your aunt is washing her hands and feet.'
On the toiletry of women I have not intruded –
but find what you have not given, and offer it
with strength that does not countervail delicacy
and put a small blue flame of rosemary
in flower into her hand.

Rebecca Swift

THE END OF THINGS

September came heavily, heralding the
End of things; you, for example
And the bitter apples on the tree
We collected loyally but which sat in
Paper bags endlessly until decay
Loved them more than we ever could.
September fell heavily, monsoons in
Haringay, torrents over tiny bridges
Sprouting madly, unsound roofs let
Water in (I noticed, oddly, now that we're
Selling the garden with the apple tree).
Winter grew heavily; and as sharp days
Darkened, we negotiated an ending
Quietly (endlessly) in curtained-again rooms;
Your thick drape threatened terribly to
Hold me and make me feel warm –
Whilst quickly now, no longer wanted apples
Fell from trees and rotted silently in the uncut grass.

Lavinia Greenlaw

WHAT WE CAN SEE OF THE SKY HAS FALLEN

Luke Howard 1772–1864

Born into a lost fortune (the wrong royal attachment
in your *land of reasonable freedom*), a third-generation
Quaker, excluded from the military or church.

A childhood marked by freak weather – roused
from your bed to see the night lit by a meteor, dim days
of what was found to have been volcanic smog.

Knowing your expertise and expertly knowing it to be
of the moment – chemistry was *business*, you insisted,
industrial secrets. (The debate around the role of your
factory

in the manufacture of ether whispers on.) You slipped once,
crushing a bottle against your wrist which cut so deep,
the arsenic (*al-zarnik*, orpiment) gilded your veins.

Those weakened hours filled with the ellipses and
questionmarks
of science – *ideas*, you insisted, eager to admit
your amateurism, excess Latin baggage and poor maths.

Your ninety-two years held three kings, a queen, two
planets,
Faraday and the first photograph. Somewhere between
Income Tax and the Battle of Trafalgar

came your essay on clouds: cool distillations
from your observations' heat. Not giving shape, you found it
and found yourself ever after sky-bound, abstracted,

frightening the grandchildren with your carnival of
                                  apparatus
and unfashionably forceful speech. *People say I am
weather-wise, but I tell them I am very often otherwise.*

Raising thousands for relief of the war-tattered continent,
you disembarked in that half-drowned country
where the language like the rye bread scoured your tongue.

Taking notes on a stork's dance, its nest's construction,
Dutch kindness to cattle, how they walk beside their
                                  horses,
the Napoleonic roads. The itch of continental quilts,

your infant German, half-grown French, the patchwork
where you took each meal in a different principality, amused
by borders, pub signs stuck in a hedgerow or ditch.

Scrutinising evaporation at a salt works, able to see
banks of snow lift away from a mountain,
how the water of the Rheinfell is nothing if not boiling
                                  snow . . .

You heard of Goethe's *inclination to sing the Praises
of Thy Theory of Clouds.* He was avid for the *true
observation of a quiet mind (and such reasonable beliefs!).*

Goethe's request, you first thought a hoax. Reassured
– *one of their very celebrated Poets of Weimar (I think)* –
you sent your life in ten pages. He wrote at least

twelve thousand letters and received eight thousand more.
His effusive note promised a full reply of which there is
no trace in the seven volumes of his life

(something known of every day). You carried a mirror
into the light, insisting you had less to tell than Franklin,
less to pass over than Caesar.

RED RACKHAM'S TREASURE

In the last room we found the merman
crouched in a tank of dust,
fiercely articulate but too far gone
for either air or water. A pastiche
of dog's teeth, cat's claws, paper,
the stale fur of fox or rabbit,
and the desiccated tail of a deep-sea fish.

We took the fifty dentists' chairs, the toy
illustrating the evolution of the wheel,
the false weights and measures,
brass plates from surgery doors,
the doctors' walking sticks, the mortsafe
and the charms collected in the field
from the bodies of German soldiers.

Matt Thorne

THE HONEYMOON DISEASE

AN APOLOGY TO God, Evelyn said. Two weeks of absti-
nence to atone for all the times before they were married.
For all the times on Evelyn's sofa, in Evelyn's bed, in the
back of Michael's car. For all the times in the churchyard,
the car-park, the fields behind her parents' house. She made
the announcement casually, as if suggesting something that
would benefit them both. She made the announcement on the
seventh day of their honeymoon.

But it wasn't the timing that upset Michael. What upset
Michael was that it didn't seem fair. All those times had been
for Evelyn, not him. After she'd told him that since being born
again she considered it a sin to take the pill, he'd been happy to
limit himself to the pleasures provided by hands and mouths.
He was terrified of Evelyn's parents, and knew he would be
punished if he got their daughter pregnant. So every time he
felt Evelyn undoing his trousers and sliding her underwear to
one side, he drew back, only for his girl-friend to redouble her
affections and grind herself against him. He knew that if he'd
followed the *Christian Relationships* handbook they wouldn't
have got into heavy petting in the first place, but even more
frightening than getting Evelyn pregnant was the possibility
of her seeking satisfaction in someone else's arms.

Evelyn was naked when she made the announcement.
Michael tried not to look at her, unnerved by the sensation
of being simultaneously cross with her mind and pleased with
her body. He knew she was waiting for him to respond, so
he said:

'I love you, Evelyn, and as we've got eternity ahead of us, I'm happy to do whatever you think is right.'

Evelyn pulled up her coral-coloured knickers and straightened the elastic with her thumbs. Michael could see himself reflected in the mirror behind Evelyn, a pale midget next to her giant brown back. She stared at him.

'You're not cross?' she asked.

'No,' he said, 'I'm not cross. Should I be?'

'No, I mean, I'm glad that you're not.'

Michael wondered what had prompted Evelyn's decision. The room was getting claustrophobic, but it had been her idea to go to a West End hotel. She had made it sound so erotic, forget the trimmings and concentrate on the sex, but now he thought she had always had this in mind, and had refused to go to a tropical paradise in case he abandoned her for a passing maiden.

'So what do we do now?'

'Don't be angry,' she said.

'I'm not angry. It just seems pointless to stay here. And we can't move into our place yet.'

'We could go to my parents.'

Her parents. He should have known that was coming. It had been a mistake to bring her to London. She'd spent her entire life in the country, and this was the longest she'd been away from Balsham. He accepted her suggestion, and they caught the train at King's Cross.

'Can we do other things?' he asked, leaning across the table.

'I don't understand.'

'Instead of sex.'

'Like what?' she asked, smiling at him. 'Shopping? Gardening? Going for walks?'

He laughed, despite himself. 'No, stop it, you're being cruel.'

'Let's not talk about it.'

He hated it when she said that. He looked out of the window, and let his arm drop loose around her. She noticed his irritation, and tried to catch his eye. He looked away, but couldn't help noticing her smile. When she smiled, her lips thinned at the corner, making the bulge in the centre look soft and enticing. 'We can do some things,' she told him, 'but nothing serious. And not inside the house.'

Although he hadn't had a religious upbringing, Michael had always been intrigued by Christianity. At senior school, his teachers had boycotted the Gideons' visit, and he was one of the few to attend their assembly. They gave him a New Testament bound in red plastic. He referred to it throughout his adolescence, and when the time came to choose an extra O level, he favoured RE over History. He didn't think about Christianity between leaving school and meeting Evelyn, but once he started going to church regularly, he found himself wanting to ask the members of the Brethren questions they'd discussed in school. But every time he entered into a theological conversation, it would have to revolve around whichever hobbyhorse the speaker was obsessed by. Like miracles, for instance. Ah, they'd say, you wouldn't worry about that if you believed in miracles. *Do* you believe in miracles? It was like trying to prove the existence of the sea by asking him if he believed in fish.

Evelyn's mother was waiting for them on the platform. It was raining and she was wearing a blue raincoat. Mother and daughter had similar taste in clothes and when something didn't fit her any more, Christina Herbert passed it on to her daughter. Unfortunately, this tended to be underwear, and Evelyn gleefully enjoyed informing Michael whenever she was wearing her mother's bra or knickers.

Christina smiled at them. Evelyn had inherited most of her facial features from her father, sharing his high forehead, wide chin and brown eyes. From her mother, she had inherited a stocky body and dry hair. Christina had been taken out of school when she was fourteen, and Michael thought that Evelyn's effete father had been forced to marry her to get some strong peasant blood into their line.

'I didn't expect to see you two children so soon,' said Christina.

'Mum,' Evelyn protested, 'we're married. That disqualifies us from ever being children again.'

'He knows I don't mean it. I'm just pleased to see you.'

They walked to the Rover, the smallest of their three family cars. Michael knew he would never be able to compete with his father-in-law on financial terms, and had felt embarrassed when he told him he wrote a property column for the *Peterborough Gazette*. But Anthony had been kind to him, telling Michael he hoped God would bring him good fortune and keep him strong.

Christina mouthed a quick prayer to St Christopher and slipped a tape into the stereo. She told them it was a piece she had to learn for a performance in a fortnight's time, then chatted with Evelyn about the other people in the orchestra. Michael tried to follow what was being said and laugh when appropriate, but Evelyn started giggling whenever her mother mentioned a musician's name, so it was hard to hear the details of each story.

He gave up and looked out of the window. The journey to Evelyn's house was a relaxing one: a smooth ride through the country with the last light of the evening guiding their way. Michael had left his own car at his parents' house in Peterborough, and he disliked being without it. Evelyn put her head on his shoulder. He noticed Christina's eyes in the rear-view mirror. He was constantly observed in Evelyn's house, as if he was the key to everything the Herberts didn't understand about their daughter. Now it would be even worse, with each family member trying to solve the mystery of the aborted honeymoon.

When they arrived at Evelyn's house, her dog, Bentley, trotted across the gravel driveway to take his place by her side. He was a remarkably prissy dog, a golden retriever who had learnt not to approach Michael. He felt a flicker of repulsion when he saw his wife hold out her hand for the animal to kiss, and wondered if this mutt was the real reason they'd come home. Even Christina tutted when the dog started licking her daughter's face, and she asked her son-in-law:

'Are you hungry, Michael?'

'I am,' said Evelyn.

'Well, there's a surprise,' said Christina, stroking her daughter's head.

One thing Michael couldn't complain about was the quality of the food he was given at Evelyn's house. Even for this late supper, there was a choice between chicken pie, some grilled trout left over from dinner the day before, or ham sandwiches. Michael chose the pie. Evelyn's father, Anthony, arrived home just as Michael was about to tuck into his meal.

'So you've come back to steal my food, have you?' he asked, and Michael felt embarrassed.

Anthony was carrying a burgundy briefcase and Michael wondered if he was returning from a session with a client. There was something not quite right about Anthony. Living in Peterborough, Michael had met lots of Cambridge men, and their defining characteristic was their reluctance to talk about their success. With Anthony, the money showed, and it was most evident in his choice of luxuries. He was more worried about having expensive ice-cream than books or art, and the only things hanging on the walls were family portraits, at least one in each room. Michael didn't know if it was Christianity that made him like this, but Evelyn had told him her father was a grammar school hero, the first of his family to go to a university of any sort.

Anthony asked his wife to fetch his post and sat down at the table with Evelyn and Michael. He made small talk, but kept getting distracted by his letters. Whenever one of the women said something ill-considered, Andrew raised his eyes to Michael. Midway through the meal, Evelyn's sister, Anna, came down from her bedroom. She looked at Evelyn and Michael wondered why she didn't seem surprised to see them.

'So now you've seen her, back to bed,' said Christina, looking to Anthony for support.

'She's going to be around for a while,' he said, 'so you'll have plenty of time to catch up.'

Anna stared at Michael. She was wearing a lumberjack shirt as a night-dress and her hair was pulled back into a pony-tail. Anna's features were comically masculine, and Evelyn had told him that Anthony felt no embarrassment about treating her as he would a son. According to Evelyn, Anna had never had a boy-friend and she acted as if she had no interest in finding one. She was a huge fan of American television, especially *Buck Rodgers*, and her room was filled with model spaceships.

She turned round and went upstairs. Anthony took the kettle from the kitchen and retired for the night. This was the first time they had been left alone in her parents' house, and Evelyn looked nervous. Michael felt trapped, and regretted going along with Evelyn's decision. As much as he loved her, he'd had a liberal upbringing, and hated being restricted. Even as a child, he had done as he pleased, slipping out of the house after midnight and going for long walks around the surrounding streets.

Evelyn took his hand and led him into the lounge. She pushed him into one of the large leather armchairs and sat on his lap. Then she took the remote from the coffee table and turned on the TV. There was a documentary on the films of Pasolini. Although he wasn't an expert on anything, Michael had a knack for picking up little bits of information about famous names, and liked talking along with the television. Other girls had been impressed by this knowledge, but Evelyn found it patronising, and had made him promise to stop explaining things to her. She told him that she didn't know about these things because she didn't want to, and resented his implication that being a Christian made her ignorant.

There were several flies in the room, and one kept returning to Evelyn's bare foot. The insect drew Michael's attention back to his wife's body. Before now, Evelyn had got cross if he looked at any part of her for too long. He had hoped she would lose this self-consciousness once they were married, and wanted to spend long hours in the bath with her, memorising every part of her anatomy. But now he thought she would always be shy with him, and saw no way to break this barrier.

The fly moved down into the gap between Evelyn's first and second toe. He was transfixed by the insect's progress, and felt himself growing hard beneath Evelyn's weight. She reached down to flick the insect away and he put his hand around hers, stroking the soft pad beneath her toes. He remembered reading that there were points in the sole of the foot that could produce sensations in every part of the body. He wished he knew more about this science, and could find the spot that would weaken his wife's resolve. He considered trying to trick her with a slow seduction that would last all night, starting with the underside of her foot and covering every inch of her body, relying on Evelyn's lust to kick in at the crucial moment.

'Shall we go to bed then?' she asked.

'Where am I sleeping?'

'In the second guest room. Mum's even started calling it Michael's room.'

'Great.'

Evelyn looked at him. 'Come on, Michael, you've been wonderful about this so far.'

'You don't even think about it, do you?'

'I'm going to bed,' she told him. 'We'll talk about this tomorrow.'

So these are my conjugal delights, Michael thought as he carried his suitcase to the spare room. He'd drunk two cups of coffee with his supper and he was scared he wouldn't be able to get to sleep. He cleaned his teeth and washed his face, hoping these routines would dull his alertness. Then he sat on the edge of the bed, watching himself in the dressing-table mirror. He felt frustrated, and knew he would have to do something to break his mood. He undressed in front of the mirror and stared at his erection, telling himself he wasn't going to feel guilty about wanting his wife. The Herberts had left a Bible out for him, and he knew Scripture would endorse his feelings. He closed his eyes and let the book fall open in his lap. Then he picked out a line with his finger. It was from Psalms, a passage about the qualities of a noble wife: *In her hands she holds the distaff, and grasps the spindle with her fingers.* Exactly. Evelyn should be here, holding his distaff. He considered getting into bed and grasping his own spindle, but he was sure Evelyn's mother held his sheets to the window every morning.

He clambered across the king-size mattress and slipped beneath the sheets. The pressure of the bedding against his groin concentrated his frustration into one unscratchable itch. He turned out the bedside lamp, and pushed his back against the mattress, determined to get some rest.

Minutes passed. Country darkness. Being here frightened him, and he couldn't understand why people felt safer among these black plains. He lay upright on the bed: alert, aroused, scared. The first time Evelyn had taken him to church, he'd been amazed at how little control these people had over themselves. So many prayers for strength. Were they all so sure they'd go astray? Until now, Michael had never once been afraid of himself. But staying in this darkness, unable to satisfy his desires, he could understand how it was possible to lose control.

He had to get out of this room. He dressed and walked out on to the landing, excited but also scared. He paused outside the Herberts' bedroom, then moved on to Evelyn's. The Herberts made their daughters sleep with their doors open and Michael could see his wife's leg where she'd kicked off the duvet. He paused, wondering if she'd wake up if he darted across to kiss her there. Then he remembered Evelyn telling him they couldn't do anything in the house. OK, then. He moved on to her sister's room.

A man stared at him. Michael jumped, then recognised the face of Buck Rodgers, smiling out of the life-size poster on Anna's bedroom door. What would she do if he climbed into bed with her? He would have to cover her mouth, whisper reassurances about it being their secret. He had always resented that his wife wasn't a virgin when she met him, and this seemed as close as he could get to turning back the clock and experiencing what his wife's unfucked cunt had felt like. Plus, it would even the score.

He turned away, ashamed of himself. This was a stupid lust, no good could come of it. He went downstairs and walked through the dark house to the lounge. He would watch TV, that was the answer. He moved quickly, and didn't stop until he felt his foot coming down on a cushion of soft fur and hard bones. Bentley growled and started barking. Before he could silence the dog, Anthony was already coming down the stairs. Ashamed, Michael mumbled a child's excuses. Anthony stared at him, as if trying to work out how a grown man could be so foolish. Michael blushed. They both returned to bed.

At six o'clock the following morning, Michael was awoken by the song of a wood pigeon. It was a sound he despised, the aural equivalent of dull pain. Waking so early made Michael feel sick. His eyes stung, and he spent the next hour trying to get back to sleep. As soon as he'd managed this, Evelyn climbed into bed with him. She was wearing her black satin night-dress, its short length complementing her stocky body.

'Won't your parents come in?' he asked.

'We've got a few minutes. I told them I was waking you up.'

Evelyn climbed on top of Michael and kissed him. His morning erection grew even stronger as it pressed against his wife's underwear.

'Go on, take them off. Just for a *second*,' he begged.

'Michael, we agreed. It's for God.'

He rolled over. 'Get off me then.'

'Don't be like that. I still love you, and it's only a matter of time. Thirteen more days, that's all. Just pretend we don't have an agreement. Imagine it's only being here that stops us.'

He pushed her away and moved to the other side of the bed. Awake now, he wanted to get dressed and go somewhere, but he knew they would be spending Saturday at home.

'I hope you're not going to be like this all day,' she said.

'What's for breakfast?' he asked.

'It's up to you. Mum remembered how picky you are so she just cooked extra of everything and if you don't want it, we'll eat it.'

Michael pulled on his trousers and went to the second bathroom. He hated shaving here. There was no space to live in this house. There was constant hot water, but the light carpet revealed every drop slopped over the side. There was an abundance of food, but every mouthful eaten was witnessed by four pairs of eyes.

After his shave, Michael joined the family at the breakfast table. Anthony Herbert was reading the *Telegraph* while his wife made a fresh pot of tea.

'What do you two children want to do today?'

'Christina,' said Anthony, 'I'm sure Michael doesn't appreciate being called a child.'

Michael looked at his father-in-law. Anthony rarely missed an opportunity to correct his wife, but this was the first time he had supported Michael. He wondered if he'd mistaken Anthony's expression last night, thinking that perhaps he understood his frustration with his daughter.

'We thought we'd stay in today,' said Evelyn, 'and go out tonight.'

'So you'll be wanting a lift then?' Anthony asked, fastening his watch around his wrist.

Christina looked up. 'I'm sure Anna can take them.'

'OK, dear,' he replied, his voice rising. 'I was only offering my services.'

'I can take them,' said Anna, ending the conversation.

During the drive, Michael sat next to Anna. He felt guilty whenever she spoke to him, and he was certain Evelyn noticed his awkwardness. Anna drove them to Cherry Hinton and dropped them outside the White Horse. They were meeting Evelyn's best friends, Josie and Graham, who were sitting in the saloon bar. It was early evening and the pub smelt of Pledge.

Graham embraced Evelyn and asked Michael what he wanted to drink. Josie smiled at Evelyn and moved in to kiss Michael. Embarrassed, he drew back, and she rubbed his shoulder instead. Graham bought the first round and Michael helped him carry the glasses back to the table. Graham was wearing a thick grey jumper and his blond hair had been recently cropped. Evelyn asked if she could stroke his head.

'It suits you,' she told him. 'Makes your jaw look stronger.'

Michael was irritated by Evelyn's comment. He knew she didn't mean to make him jealous, but that made it even worse. Normally, Michael felt that he was reasonably attractive, but next to Graham he knew he was lacking. Graham had the body of a swimmer and a strong, calm face. Michael was all awkwardness and odd angles, his jaw too square, his hair too wiry. Graham was Evelyn's previous boyfriend, and later in the evening he swapped seats with Michael so he could have a private chat with her. It annoyed Michael that this was an accepted part of their nights out, and he decided to get revenge by making a fuss of Josie.

He answered her polite questions enthusiastically, encouraging her on to personal topics. He was never sure where he was with Josie, but she seemed to respond to his conversation. She always wore black dungarees and a hat that looked like a purple cushion, and if it wasn't for her lively face, she would be easy to ignore. Her expression grew more admiring as the night went on, and by the end of the evening he felt he could trust her small blue eyes.

Not until he met Evelyn did Michael come to hate Sundays. Nothing could prepare him for the two-hour service at the Herberts' local Brethren Church, and he felt annoyed from the moment Evelyn climbed into bed with him.

'Don't you want me to take my knickers off today?' she asked.

'Why do you have to keep teasing me?'

Evelyn sat up. 'Teasing? I was trying to be loving. Can't you do that without sex?'

'Leave me alone,' he said. 'I have to get ready for church.'

*

Michael and Evelyn sat with Anna and Josie at the back of the church. Anthony and Christina sat further up, in the row behind the elders. Graham played the piano during the service, with his father accompanying him on tambourine and bongos. They were fond of singing here, choosing hymns with clapping and gestures. At one point they had to stretch their arms out and chant, 'Christ has died, Christ has risen, Christ will come again,' a display Michael considered ridiculous. Today's speaker based his sermon around Chapter III of Jeremiah, but somehow still managed to work in references to the impending apocalypse and an attack on the pupils of a nearby comprehensive.

The sermon was followed by a period of open prayer. Michael always used this time to work out who to avoid at coffee afterwards, and just as he was focusing his disdain on a man with blue boat shoes, the entire congregation turned to stare at him and Michael felt certain Jesus had given them the power to read his mind.

'I want to tell you about my husband,' said Evelyn. Her voice was trembling and she clutched the photocopied notice sheet. 'Until Michael was baptised here, I felt angry with him. I needed him to become a Christian, and it seemed as if he was refusing to spite me.

'But I know now that it was a test from God. To be honest, although Michael wasn't a Christian when I met him, his lifestyle was much closer to the teachings of Jesus than mine. I knew I believed in God, but that faith became an excuse for a moral laxity on my part. The reason why I felt so angry with Michael is because I was angry with myself.

'I wanted Michael to believe in the same way I believed. I wanted him to know instinctively that God is there, and to use this knowledge as a way of putting off difficult questions. But he couldn't do that. He needed me to live in a way that he could recognise as better than his own. In order to help Michael find the Christian in him, I had to rediscover the Christian in me.'

Evelyn sat down. Michael took her hand, impressed by her honesty. He felt a second of resentment when he realised this would be taken as a sign that whatever was wrong with the newly-weds was now resolved, then decided he didn't care. Evelyn's words had made up for the banality of the service, and he even felt something of his old love for her as they rose to sing the final hymn.

His good humour lasted five days. Michael relaxed into the luxury of the Herberts' lifestyle, and after lunch every day he took long walks with Evelyn, talking about what they would do when the fortnight was up. He even started forgetting about sex, and imagining himself as an ancient monk. Evelyn read him a passage from a book written by a medieval mystic who experienced great visions after she stopped sleeping with her husband, and this made Michael feel part of a grand tradition.

Then Evelyn told him she wanted to spend an evening with Graham. All his frustrations fed into jealousy, and he was certain Evelyn would sleep with Graham as a way of satisfying herself while still fulfilling their agreement. He had never forgiven Graham for being his wife's first lover, and his mind filled with pictures of Evelyn praising Graham's strong jaw as he went down on her. But once he started arguing with Evelyn, he realised she wouldn't stand for his jealousy, and he had to base his argument around not wanting to be left alone with her parents. She accepted this, and the compromise reached was that while Evelyn was with Graham, he would visit Josie.

'I'm so glad you're here,' she said. 'I really wanted to show you my flat.'

Michael looked at Josie's skinny white arms as she handed him a glass of whisky. He wondered if she always wore the same dungarees or had several pairs.

'Graham hates my flat. He says the only reason he's marrying me is to teach me good taste. But I really wanted to show you my flat. You do like it, don't you?'

He nodded. She smiled. He felt touched that she wanted his approval, and he wondered why she was so nervous. She had called three times that day to ask Evelyn what Michael liked, and had even cooked him a meal. His wife's lack of jealousy made him suspicious, and he wondered if he was at the mercy of a partner-swapping arrangement orchestrated by the others.

So he praised her flat, and ate the peppered steak, and they talked about their tastes in music, film and art. She listened attentively to his gleaned summaries, and never once picked him up the way his wife did. He grew more attracted to her with every drink and became increasingly worried that he would say something inappropriate. Josie remained sober, and when she made a remark that surprised him, he thought it was safest to get her to repeat it. This time she said:

'Don't you think it's unfair that Graham and Evelyn got to sleep together and we didn't?'

'I don't follow,' he said.

'We saved ourselves. We never stopped believing.'

His gaze returned to her bare arms and thin fingers and he wondered how her touch would differ from his wife's. As he stared into her blue eyes, he felt a tension in his stomach, and realised Josie had already made the choice and for her any anxiety was either past or waiting ahead.

'I think,' he began, 'morality is more complex than people imagine. I think the reason it exists is because sometimes it's psychologically necessary to do wrong. I think knowing when to sin is an important part of being a Christian.'

'I agree,' she said.

He looked at her. 'It has to be a secret. For ever. I like being married.'

'I know,' said Josie, 'and I want to be married too. And even if Graham left me, I would never do anything to risk my friendship with you and Evelyn.'

She kissed him. He tried to respond calmly, but couldn't control his shaking. He felt nervous and awkward, but he sensed Josie's desire would be strong enough to see them through.

'That whisky's really gone to my head,' he said, trying to stand up. Josie unhooked her dungarees and they fell around her feet. She stepped out of them and stood there naked apart from black lace underwear and a purple hat. She pulled off the hat and her black hair fell across her face. She unzipped his trousers and pulled him down with her. He looked at her muscular legs, fascinated as he stroked them with the palms of his hands. She unbuttoned his shirt and kissed his chest. Pulling down her knickers, she sat over him and he pushed himself up against her, hands pressed against the carpet and his feet stretched into points.

The next morning, Michael and Evelyn went for a walk in the fields behind her house. It was an important place for them because on their first visit there they had made a yellow indentation in the grass that had stayed for several summers. For a while they looked for the square again, but they both knew it was gone. They found another place to lay out the blanket and Evelyn said:

'I'm sorry.'

'What for?'

'This whole thing. I've been lying to you and it was wrong of me. I know I've made you feel insecure and I'm sorry. You'll probably laugh when you hear how petty the reason is.

'The thing is, I've had this problem for a while, but I was too embarrassed to tell you. The reason why I wanted to stop having sex is because I've got an infection. I've had it before, but it was really bad in the flat, and it's embarrassing because it's called the honeymoon disease, and to get it then made me think there was something wrong with our marriage. I thought it was a sign. I know how stupid that must sound. Please forgive me.'

Evelyn was crying so Michael held her. He felt her weight against his chest and he remembered the first time they had come here. They'd had a row and Michael had caught the next train home. On the journey back, he realised he'd been in the wrong and spent two frantic days trying to call her. Since then, they hadn't had any serious problems and tried to finish their rows as quickly as possible. This was the longest there had been any ill-feeling between them and

Michael was glad it was over. He held Evelyn and told her he understood and that everything would be fine. When she stopped crying, they made love in the long grass and walked back to her house.

Hwee Hwee Tan

THE GAMBLING MAN

NIGHT AT THE Jalan Besar Stadium and the punters swung into action, wheeling and dealing, five-figure digits rolling off their tongues. The referee glanced at his watch, and the punters knew. Only ten minutes left, time for final bets, last chance for any transactions.

Beepers vibrated against belts, spurred their owners to death leaps, taking four steps at a time, down the stairs, racing for the three empty phone booths. Handphones rang their frantic rhythm above the shouts and crackle of Hokkein. The bookie activated his black phone with a slick snap – 'Geylang win 5, I give you half a ball. Okay, one hundred thousand dollars. I on you.' One hundred thousand dollars, that's half a year's salary, but the punter bit the bait. Those unequipped with modern telecommunications equipment used their hands, flicking fingers in the air, shouting over shoulders.

The market closed, the trading floor wound down. Everyone sat down on the yellow benches, jaws clenched, tapping the *Lianhe Wanbao* newspaper on their knees. The stand became a shrine, as prayers rose with cigarette breaths, that grey incense, pleading favour from all the major deities, from Guan Yin to Jesus, from Buddha to Vishnu. After all, Singapore was a multi-religious society.

The stand positively buzzed with the thrill of illicit activity, but Inspector Koh could do nothing but watch, powerless to arrest. For it was all words and fingers, deals sealed by the tongue; the punters would never testify against each other in court. Without any written evidence, without letters hammered in type, Inspector Koh never gathered enough evidence to win a conviction. He could only watch and wait. Over the years, Koh saw the punters prosper, observed how they replaced their striped Crocodile polo-shirts with ones from Valentino, how they graduated from Goldlion buckles to Dunhill belts, progressed from white sneakers to Testoni loafers.

All the successful bookies ultimately upgraded their crew cuts to 'helmet heads' – all-over hair perms. You see, any poor sod could get a straight back and sides from a cheap Indian barber shop round the corner, but perms were bloody expensive. And if you could afford to perm your whole head, well, that showed that you were in the big time, baby.

Koh's big break finally came when *he* appeared – the *ang mo*, the red head, the foreigner, that solitary white face in the sea of Chinese ones. Pale like marble, with wisps of red hair, fine, fragile features and eyes full of bright blue innocence, the *ang mo* would have looked terribly pre-Raphaelite, but for the freckles and glasses. In his late twenties, the *ang mo* looked like a university lecturer, with his beige cotton shirt, softly padded jacket and old-fashioned Oxford shoes. Typically, like all geeks, as proof of his latent 'outrageousness', he sported loud yellow socks, and a Swatch watch patterned after designer vomit.

The *ang mo* sat in the stands, scribbling notes.

Maybe he's a lecturer, Inspector Koh thought, maybe he's doing research.

The referee blew for full time.

'Manchester United versus Wimbledon?' the *ang mo* shouted. 'Next weekend. Win 7.'

A man in the crowd below turned around. 'You let me half a ball?'

'You're on,' the *ang mo* said.

A shout from above – 'Twenty thousand dollars, win 7. You on me?'

The *ang mo* stuck up his thumb and nodded.

Koh's knuckles whitened as he tightened his grip on the stair rail. The *ang mo* wrote down all the bets in his filofax. This was what Koh had been waiting for, that filofax – a record of names and numbers, bets inked in black and white.

'It was so embarrassing, and you didn't even know.' Mei Mei frowned at her husband. 'Chris, are you listening? Chris.' She tapped his tuft of red hair. 'Earth calling Dr Chris Huggins, can you read me?'

'Sorry – just thinking about class at uni. Teaching Defoe tomorrow. He can be, really, uh, deep.' Chris shook his head and blinked a couple of times to clear his head. 'Right, I'm with you now. "Justice is always violent to the party offending, for every man is innocent in his own eyes." Marvellous quote from *The Shortest Way with the Dissenters*.'

'You weren't thinking about Defoe or justice,' Mei said. 'Don't think you can smokescreen me with all that literary crap.'

'I *was* thinking about Defoe!'

'No you weren't. It's the same every Sunday night. You lie in bed, practically catatonic. When I jerk you to attention you always insist that you were ruminating about Updike's latest novel, or the Bosnian peace process, or the Tory party conference at Blackpool, but I know you're lying. I've seen that glazed look before. You're replaying the winning volley by Mark Hughes in the FA Cup semi-finals. You can disappear into your own little fantasy world for hours. Your mind's like a VCR on perpetual re-wind.'

Chris raised his palms in surrender. 'You know me too well.' He sighed. 'I started off thinking about Defoe, about justice, then I thought about how everyone thinks it's unfair that Man U win all the time, and before I knew it I saw the Sparky smashing the ball in mid-air.'

'Mentally, you've never developed beyond puberty. You're twenty-seven going on twelve.'

Chris stuck an imaginary knife in his back, twisted and turned his body, his face contorting in mock agony. 'That was a completely unprovoked attack, but I know you love me anyway, dear.'

'I never could resist little boys.' Mei first met Chris five years ago, when she left Singapore to study for her Master's in law at Oxford. She worked part-time at Blackwell's on George Street, and one day, while stacking the shelves in the Literature department, she saw a red head staring at the novels with innocent awe. His face looked so fragile – skin white as fine china, as if one touch would shatter it into a powder of dust. With those plump cheeks, curly red hair and brilliant blue eyes, he looked like a baby angel, full of boyish innocence, a face empty of guile, filled with pure naïve joy. One look at him and Mei knew that she had to marry him, dedicate her life to protecting that innocence, preserving that purity, sheltering him from an evil and cunning world. Even though the red head towered a foot above her, Mei felt a deep need to go up and pat him on the head. She suppressed that urge, asked whether he needed any help, and things exploded from there. Before she met Chris, Mei's master plan was to join Tan, Lim & Associates, biggest law firm in Singapore, then start her own practice, and perhaps write a few award-winning plays on the side. But after meeting Chris, she suddenly wanted to get married and spend the rest of her life being barefoot and pregnant. This reaction embarrassed her. Her waspish comments, she reasoned, were a just payback for the feelings Chris engendered within her.

'I know I keep nagging you about this,' Mei said, 'but one day your obsession with soccer is going to get you into trouble.'

'I'm not obsessed.'

'Yes you are. What's the name of the wife of the coach of the goalkeeper of the England team?'

'Bob Wilson coaches Arsenal and England goalkeeper David Seaman. Bob's wife is called Meg.'

'And you say you're not obsessed. Which brings me back to what I was scolding you about before you went into your dream world. You know who Meg is but you can't remember the name of my niece.'

'*Zhen Chou, Zhen Cai* – it's not that big a difference. It was an easy mistake to make.'

'There *is* a big difference. *Zhen Cai* means "genuine fortune". *Zhen Chou* means "really smelly". I don't think my niece appreciated being called "stinko" at her birthday party.'

'Oops.'

'Oops indeed.'

'I can't help it if you've got such a big family. Fourteen aunts, twenty uncles and millions more nephews and nieces. It's difficult to keep track of names.'

'*I* remember the names of *all* your relatives.'

'Considering that just includes my mother and father, that's hardly a serious mnemonic challenge.'

Mei remembered the first time Chris brought her to meet his parents in London. Chris announced that he was going to marry Mei, move to Singapore and work as a senior tutor at the National University of Singapore.

'Why don't you move to Singapore with us?' Mei asked Huggins and his wife, Marge.

'Yes, why not?' Marge said to Huggins. 'We've been married for forty years and you've never taken me anywhere.'

'Well, I'm doing an epochal case of unpaid VAT on disposable plastic forks at Sunderland next week,' Huggins said. 'You're most welcome to come.'

'I want to go to a place with palm trees, pineapples, and sun-drenched beaches,' Marge said. 'There's nothing in Sunderland except rain and industrial decay.'

'I can't abandon my clients,' Huggins said. 'They need me.'

'I think your burglars and molesters could survive without you,' Marge said.

'Don't worry, Marge, we'll visit you every month,' Mei said.

Later, after they had left her future in-laws' place, Chris asked her, 'Why did you promise my father that I'd visit him every month?'

'Why not? Your father obviously adores you.'

'My father thinks we get along a lot better than we do. You saw how he kept telling stories about all these great "adventures" we had together when I was a child, but usually I have no *idea* what he's talking about. I hate it when my father keeps going "Remember this, remember that?", and I can't remember a single thing. I just have to sit there with a fake smile like some retard.'

Mei realised that Chris and his father suffered from selective memory. They shared the same experiences, but extracted different recollections. Memorable episodes for Huggins senior meant nothing to Huggins junior; fundamental affairs for the son were considered frivolous by the father. Walks in Hyde Park, bedtime stories, lunch at McDonald's, these burned like stars in his father's mind, bright points of light and love; but when his father talked about stars, Chris recalled nothing but black gaps, blank vacuums.

During another of their monthly visits, Huggins asked Chris what was new in his life, and Chris said that he had been 'born again'.

Huggins laughed, but then he saw that Chris wasn't smiling.

'Oh I'm sorry, I wasn't laughing at you – I thought you were joking.' Huggins spread his hands apologetically. 'I never understood religion. I remember going to a Billy Graham rally once. I spent the whole evening wondering how I could get up and go to the loo without the counsellors thinking that I wanted to make a commitment.'

In the car on the way to the airport, Chris said to Mei, 'Why does he keep doing that? Everything I care passionately about – soccer, literature, Jesus – he always thinks it's "just for fun" or "just a phase". He just treats them like some short-term disease like the measles. Ignore the problem and it will disappear in time.'

Huggins collapsed on to the muddy brown sofa, a sofa which had the same scruffy consistency one associates with teddy bears that have been loved too much.

'So what did you get up to today?' Marge said. 'Murder, robbery or rape?'

'I spent my afternoon engaged in a spot of indecent exposure before Judge Davies. He was rather shocked,' Huggins said. He touched the radiator. 'I think my hand is in danger of getting frost-bite.' He looked at the blanket wrapped around Marge's shoulders. 'We could save on heating if we went to bed earlier. For example, before lunch. What's the point of staying up after ten to watch Jeremy Paxman sneer his way through *Newsnight*?'

'Ten o'clock is the watershed, you old fool,' Marge said. 'The sex and violence only comes on after ten.'

Huggins took out his Legal Aid cheque and waved it in the air. 'Our ticket to the high life, our passport to prosperity has finally materialised. Consequently, I took the liberty of splashing out on a few luxuries like – ' Huggins took the products out of the brown paper bag. 'Cigarettes, bog paper and the *Evening Standard*. All the equipment one needs for an entertaining hour in the toilet.' Huggins removed page five from the newspaper and gave it to Marge. 'While I'm enjoying my marathon bowel movement, you might want to read this. It's an article about "Integrity First". I could never understand why Chris joined them. According to the article, they're obsessed with honesty. New members have to make restitutions for their "crimes", like returning typing paper and biros that they took from the office. One member actually returned a thousand quid that the tax man gave him by mistake. Their sixth commandment is – "Thou shalt not jaywalk".'

'They're just trying to do what's right,' Marge said. 'You wouldn't understand that.'

'Of course I understand. Life is divided between what is right and what is fun,' Huggins said. 'Personally I prefer the latter.'

'Inspector Koh, CID, Gambling Suppression Branch.' The man ID-ed himself and thrust a piece of paper in her husband's hands. 'This is a search warrant. Please co-operate with us. We will conduct the search in your presence.'

An officer came out of her bedroom and handed Chris's filofax to the Inspector. 'It's all here. Names, dates, amounts. It goes back for more than a year.'

Mei wanted to say, 'What are you doing? This must be a mistake. I must be dreaming', but the words stuck in her throat, for when she looked at Chris he did not look back, and when they cuffed him, led him away, as his shadow grew smaller, she heard a small noise that sounded like 'I'm sorry'.

Mei poured herself a glass of orange juice and sank into the black leather sofa. She did not touch her drink. The water vapour condensed, ran down her glass and left a rim of liquid on the table. A cluster of ants scurried across the wooden table, and waded into the wet rim, looking for sugar. Red blades of light filtered through venetian blinds, then darkness.

She did not know how long she sat there, how long before she reconciled herself with reality. The facts – Mei and Chris Huggins, two church-going professionals who would never even dream of parking on double yellow lines, had just been the recipients of a full-scale, no-kidding, yes we have a legal right to flip through your bras and panties police raid. Raids usually reserved for drug smugglers and secret society members.

She was a lawyer, she knew the drill, the bail process. But still, the police station shocked her. Police stations in Singapore always shocked her. After watching countless American cop shows, she always expected police stations to be dark and menacing, the air heavy with heat, assaulted by grime, noise, cigarette smoke and paper blizzards. But this station was so clean and bright, so unexpectedly cheerful, it was unnerving. With pink floor tiles, lime green walls, air-conditioning, and an assortment of potted dumb canes and money plants, the station looked more like an accountant's office than a sin bin.

The duty officer sat beneath a framed Snoopy jigsaw puzzle. He heaved the bail bond book (which was the size of two Monopoly boards) before Mei, and smiled. After she signed the book, she sat below the 'Charge Office' board, next to the fire extinguisher. Some resourceful person had created a make-shift container for the marker pens and duster by wedging a soap dish between the wall and the extinguisher.

In the corner, through a Panasonic stereo system, Technotronic exhorted everyone to work their body. The duty officer, in his mid-twenties, took Technotronic's advice to heart and gently rocked his head to the dance beat. On the top of the left stereo speaker, a gold trophy proclaimed this station the winner of the 'Most Courteous Report Room Contest'.

Mei could see part of the lock-up from where she sat. She expected bars of steel, but instead a wire mesh fenced in the cells, mesh reminiscent of the ones used for the chicken coops at her aunt's kampong.

Chris finally emerged from his cage, his shoulders scrunched, twisting his fingers.

They walked out of the police station, silent. Surrounded by flats painted in bubblegum purple, pink and green, the police station looked like it had been planted in the middle of buildings designed by Disney. Everything was so strange, so surreal, so removed from what Mei expected life to be.

'Tell me this isn't happening,' Mei said.

'I'm sorry,' Chris said.

'How did it start?'

'Every month, after we visited my parents, while you shopped at Oxford Street, I dropped the bets off at William Hill.'

'You knew it was illegal?' Mei said.

Chris nodded.

'How much money did you bring across in all?'

'About one or two . . .' Chris cleared his throat. 'Million pounds.'

Mei frowned.

'I was doing a good deed, collecting those bets,' Chris said. 'I didn't make any money out of this. I'm just a courier. You see there's this charity – the Bryan Gunn Leukemia Appeal. Gunn's the Norwich City goalkeeper, his baby daughter died of leukemia, so he set up this scheme. He recommends a bet at the bookkeepers, and if you place that bet, ten per cent of it goes to fund medical research. Just think about it –

I've brought over a few million pounds in bets, and that's over a hundred thousand pounds to charity. My betting pool helps save leukemic babies, for heaven's sake. How bad can that be?'

Mei shook her head.

'You're really pissed off, aren't you?' Chris asked.

'Don't worry, I'll do a Tammy Wynette.' Mei smiled wryly. 'I'll stand by my man.'

'So what's going to happen to me?'

'I've got good news and bad news.'

'Bad news first,' Chris said.

'The maximum sentence is a fine of two hundred thousand dollars and jail not exceeding five years.'

'Ouch. And the good news?'

'The minimum fine is twenty thousand dollars, and one month's jail.'

Chris flinched, jerked his head back like a turkey. 'That was the good news?'

'Sorry, I lied,' Mei said. 'What do you expect – I'm a lawyer. I should have said – I have bad news, and bad news.'

'That's a whole year's salary down the drain. It's a lot of money.'

'Masses. Gobs. Heaps.'

'Jail . . .'

'Is compulsory. One month, minimum.'

'Oh dear.'

'I'll visit you.' Mei took Chris's hand. 'I'll bring cookies.'

'Jail. Why? It was just for fun. I didn't hurt anyone.'

Mei rolled her eyes. 'It was just a "guy thing", I suppose.'

'Exactly.'

'You expected a spanking rather than a kick in the teeth.'

Chris spread his hands helplessly. 'It was just a *game*.'

'So are you going to plead guilty or not?'

The next morning, Mei read out the headline from the national newspaper, the *Straits Times*. '"Visiting Oxbridge Lecturer Is A Bookie." However, that's not all. Look at the other goodies I got from MPH.' Mei slammed a stack of British newspapers on their dining-table. 'You've made quite a big splash in England. "English Professor Arrested For Gambling In Singapore," that's from *The Times*. Of course my favourite is from the *Sun* – "Busted! Red Devil's Don Caught In Betting Scandal."'

Later that day, Mike Lampert, Chris's pastor, paid him a visit to perform some emergency damage control.

'People don't believe in right and wrong any more,' Mike said. 'Everything's relative. The only thing that matters nowadays is whether something is fun or hip. But "Integrity First" tries to be different. God chose *us* to live by his perfect standards. And that's tough. The world is watching us all the time, Chris, it's like a siege. Everyone is waiting for us to make one wrong move so that they can go "nea-yeah, nea-yeah, look at that bunch of hypocrites."'

'I'm sorry,' Chris said.

'You're one of our high-profile members. Thousands of students look up to you. But now everyone from Los Angeles to Timbuktu would have read about your crime in the news. This scandal is a big crisis for "Integrity First". I hate to see the name of Jesus dragged through the mud. So what are you going to do?'

'I don't know.'

'You're obsessed with soccer, and the devil has used that obsession to ensnare you. Acknowledge your sin, Chris, destroy it. Confess your guilt before God and man.'

'You have any *idea* what's going to happen if I plead guilty? They could lock me up for *five* years,' Chris said. 'I'm scared, Mike. I'm an academic. I'm supposed to be a weedy, all-spectacles, helpless nerd type. I can't cope with *jail*. What about my job? The university is not going to want to employ a convicted felon. I have to clear my name.'

'You *know* you're guilty, and if you plead innocence, you'll be lying. You might get away with lying in the court of man, but when you die, *God* is going to judge you.'

'For heaven's sake, keep still, or I'll stab you with my needle.' Marge put down her knitting.

'They gave a drunk and disorderly six months,' Huggins said. 'That's what the justice system is like in Singapore. If they gave six months for heckling a night-club singer, imagine what they'll give Chris. And you tell me to sit still.'

'I suppose you think that bouncing off the walls like Speedy Gonzales is going to persuade the judge to reduce Chris's sentence.'

'And I suppose that *you* intend to send all the twenty sweaters that you've knitted in the past three days to pacify the judge,' Huggins said. He walked around the room even quicker now. 'You fret in your own way, I'll fret in mine.'

'At least *my* knitting isn't aggravating enough to stir any latent psychotic tendencies. Why don't you just go to bed?'

Everyone always sent him to bed, tried to put him to sleep, as if he was a stray dog. The last time Chris visited, Huggins began the account of his glorious triumph in Regina vs. Arthur Simms, but Chris cut him off with a smile.

'We all remember that case, Father, wasn't it in all the newspapers?' Chris said.

'Yes, three inches,' Huggins said. 'Every newspaper, from the *Telegraph* to the *Evening Standard*, all of them ran columns that were at least *three inches* every day of the trial.'

'You look tired,' Chris said. 'Why don't you go to bed?'

Huggins looked at the clock. It was only nine. 'I'm not tired,' Huggins said.

'Sleep is a marvellous thing,' Chris said, '"knits up the ravell'd sleave of care, Balm of hurt minds, chief nourisher in life's feast." Shakespeare.'

Huggins went to the bedroom, while Chris stayed up to talk with Marge. While he was around, the conversation had been full of awkward gaps, but once he'd left Chris and Marge to themselves, they yabbered about the most trivial things – Emma and Ken breaking up, the price of bread at Asda versus Sainsbury's, and the eternal puzzle of where birds keep their VCRs if they didn't have homes.

The laughter, the flood of words, filtered through the paper walls. Huggins pulled up his blanket and stared at the ceiling. Overhead, a solitary bulb swung from its cord.

It wasn't always like this. When Chris was young, Huggins and Son were a dream team, constantly creating schemes to outwit the tyrannical Marge. Once, when Marge banned Chris from eating chocolates (citing some lame reason about tooth decay), Huggins rummaged through the rubbish and found the perfect hiding place for the chocolates – a soiled, crushed cardboard box.

'The best way to conceal something from someone is to follow Dupin's principle in "The Purloined Letter", that is, to put the object right under their noses,' Huggins told Chris. 'Now see, this box absolutely emanates unimportance. It looks like something you wanted to dispose of, but forgot to. Like a country vicar, it has the air of something that knows that its sole purpose in life is to be ignored.'

Huggins placed the box on Chris's desk, right next to his school books. From that day on, Chris munched happily from the box of chocolates on his desk. Whenever Marge raided Chris's room for contraband, she always checked under the bed, looked for false bottoms in drawers, secret compartments in the floor, but she never thought of examining that tattered old box.

A bright light woke him from his dreamy recollections. The moon filled his window, perfectly round and bright, like a searchlight, flooding the room with white. Usually, the moon glowed sullenly, dim and yellow like his teeth, but tonight it shone like the sun, lit up the streets so it looked like day.

Underneath his balcony, shoppers scurried past, puffing under the weight of their Tesco bags. Undoubtedly, the most famous Tesco bags belonged to Arthur Simms. They contained the head, fingers, breasts and toenails of Mr Simms's wife. Simms had chopped her into bits, after which he phoned the police and confessed to killing her.

So with all the evidence stacked against his client, Huggins rose to cross-examine the chief witness for the prosecution, Dr Mackey.

'Dr Mackey, you think that my client, Arthur Simms, attacked his wife with a chopper? That he chased her around the house, hacking at her mercilessly?'

'The forensic evidence would support that scenario, yes,'
Dr Mackey said.

Huggins looked at his client, who sat in the dock, shaking
his head. Small, balding and bespectacled, Simms looked more
like Woody Allen than Hannibal Lecter.

'You found scratch marks on the defendant's chest?'

'Yes, I think they were made by the victim's nails,' Dr
Mackey said, 'when she was trying to fight him off.'

'Now the scratch marks, they were one and a half inches
long, and half an inch wide?'

'That's correct.'

'But those measurements don't match the measurements of
the victim's nails. The marks on Simms's chest are wider than
the width of the victim's nails. Isn't that strange?'

Dr Mackey kept quiet.

Huggins swooped in for the kill. 'Now fingernail scratches
are distinctive, wide at the top, tapering off at the bottom?'

'I suppose so.'

'But the scratches found on my client's chest are straight,
regular, almost parallel. More like the marks made by a chopper. Isn't it possible, Dr Mackey, that my client's wife attacked
him *first*, hitting his chest with the chopper? My client then
tried to defend himself, wrestled the chopper away from his
psychotic wife, and accidentally hit her, in self-defence. When
he discovered that she was dead, he panicked, and started
hacking up her body. But after he had come to his senses, he
rang the police and told them about the terrible accident.'

The judge stopped his scribbling. He looked at Dr Mackey,
who was silent. The jury leant forward in their seats, waiting
for Dr Mackey's response.

Finally, Dr Mackey said, 'I suppose that might be possible.'

'I suppose that you're dreaming about one of your murderers again,' Marge said as she slipped into bed beside
Huggins.

'Not really,' Huggins lied. 'I was thinking about . . . the
moon.'

The moon blazed like burning magnesium, burned like a

vision, a revelation. It lit what was hidden on other nights, like the pale blue flowers emerging out of the damp wood in the roofs below. Huggins saw what he never saw before. Suddenly he heard light-bulbs clicking, lasers crossing, beams converging – all his recent briefs, they were so trivial – postal workers accused of pilfering envelopes, housewives who left their cars in parking spaces reserved for the handicapped. He respected his clients, but they were all strangers. Now he had a chance to defend his *son*.

'What are you staring at? Why don't you go to sleep?' Marge said.

'How can I sleep, when my boy is all alone in a foreign country, facing five years in the chokey?' Huggins jumped out of bed. 'When Chris was young, he always relied on me to outwit any opposition. He needed me then, and he needs me now. I have to defend him. It's my duty as a father, and a lawyer. It's my destiny.'

Huggins barged into the apartment, shoving his suitcase into his son's hands.

'Don't worry about not having a spare room, I can sleep on the couch,' Huggins winked at Chris. 'Much practice with your mother.'

Huggins laughed at his own joke. Chris did not laugh. Instead, he stared at the suitcase, stared at his father and stammered.

'What Chris means to say is,' Mei said, 'what the hell are you doing in Singapore?'

'I've come to defend my son.'

'You know nothing about Singapore law,' Mei said.

'You can brief me on Chris's case.'

'I'm perfectly competent to defend my own husband.'

'But you specialise in civil law. You spent most of your time in London poring through bills of exchange and charter parties. I, on the other hand, am an expert on criminal law.'

Huggins took out a packet of Marlboros. 'Anyone care for cancer? No? Good choice. Smoking's a filthy habit.'

He lit his cigarette, inhaled, then blew out the smoke with great satisfaction.

'But you don't have a licence to practise in Singapore,' Mei said.

'Of course I'm aware of that,' Huggins said. 'I intend to make a temporary application to the Attorney-General's office.'

'They won't grant your application. The permit's only for cases of public importance, *and* if you're going to argue a special point that's never been argued before.'

'Which is precisely what I intend to do. I came to Singapore to rip apart the Betting Act. I will find some special point that will free my son. Don't forget, I was out saving defendants from the death penalty while you were still an embryo in your mother's womb.'

Huggins extinguished his cigarette on the coffee table.

'I don't *want* you to dig up some special point,' Chris said. 'I'm going to plead guilty.'

Huggins flinched, doing the turkey head jerk that Chris always performed when shocked.

'See, there's no justification for a special permit,' Mei said. 'Chris will plead guilty, I'll make a plea in mitigation, and the judge will sentence him. End of story. Nothing a local lawyer couldn't handle.'

'I'm not going to change my mind,' Chris said. 'I talked to my pastor, and he's right, I have to plead guilty.'

'Your *pastor*?' Huggins said. 'What does he know about the law? I suppose he found some reference to section 5(3) of the Betting Act in the Second Epistle to the Corinthians.'

'I'm not the old Chris you raised as a child. I've been born again. *God* is my father, and he wants me to tell the truth, and the truth is that I'm guilty. I don't want you to go to court and twist the truth to try and get me off.'

Huggins locked eyes with his son. Mei stared at the clock and watched the second hand tick a quarter of a way across the round face.

'Is that what you really think of me? That I spend my whole life trying to set criminals free?' Huggins said.

'You don't care if a person is guilty or not. The law's just a game for you – the more you can get away with, the more fun it gets.'

'If my goal in life was to get crooks off the hook, I wouldn't still be a lowly junior barrister. No, I would be out helping Mammoth Oil Incorporated evade taxes and throw Greenpeace protesters in jail. I'd be rolling in piles of Queen Elizabeths, rather than wondering where the next cheque for your mother's Persil Power is going to appear from.'

'But all your clients *are* criminals. Murderers, shoplifters, muggers – '

'Little people, Chris! Underdogs. Postal workers, road sweepers, waitresses, little old ladies, black youths stuck in ghettos where the only way they could ever get a pair of trainers is to steal them. I defend them against the racist police, against stroppy judges, defending the poor individual against the entire resources of the Crown. Society would like nothing better than to dump my clients in jail for as long as possible, to flush them down the toilet bowl, these supposed dregs of society, instead of thinking of ways to help them. While the rest of the world bays for blood and justice, I am the solitary voice in the desert that cries for compassion.'

With that, Huggins launched into an account of the Simms case. 'That's the kind of person I save. Postal workers, who without the benefit of my counsel would be five feet under by now.'

'That's what I used to think,' Chris said. 'When I was a child and you told me all those stories about fingerprints, dodgy confessions and the burden of proof, I thought you were the most brilliant lawyer alive. So when the Simms case came up, I decided that I really had to see you trying one of your cases "live". But when I saw what you were really up to, it made me sick. For the first time in my life, I saw what really happened, and not just what you chose to tell me. You never tell the full story. Sure, you always tell people about your brilliant chopper cross-examination, but you never tell them how in real life Simms looked like a thug but you got him to cut his hair, and wear glasses even though he had perfect vision, so that he would look nice and meek. You never tell them about how his wife went to the police station every week, beaten and bruised, begging the police to protect her, but they couldn't do anything. I know what really happened. Simms was like me, he knew he had done something evil and wanted to confess, but you talked him out of it, you told him, "I can plant reasonable doubt in the mind of the jurors. I can help you get away it." '

'That wasn't what happened at all,' Huggins said. 'I've cursed the law, argued my way round, above, underneath the law, done all I can to change it, but I've never broken the law, nor helped any of my clients break the law. The first commandment of Huggins's religious faith is that the law is sacred. Simms was innocent and I proved his innocence.'

'You didn't prove his innocence, you just planted reasonable doubt,' Chris said. 'That's what you've done all your life, it's your job, planting doubt. I'm guilty, and that's that. I don't want you to shed doubt on that, I hate grey areas, I want everything written out in black and white. I want life to be crystal clear, transparent.'

'If you say you're guilty, then you have to plead guilty. I won't persuade you otherwise.' Huggins forced a smile. 'But all is not lost. I can help Mei with your plea in mitigation. I'm the master manipulator of judges. If Mei uses my arguments, the judge will fall in love with you. By the end of the hearing, he'll be blowing into a stack of Kleenex; he'll want you to marry his daughter and bear his grandchildren.'

'Why can't you just leave things alone? I don't want you to have anything to do with the case.'

'Why won't you let me help? It wasn't always like this. Don't you remember the good old days, we were the dream team. Don't you remember how we outwitted your mother, your teachers – '

'That's exactly why. What kind of father teaches his son to deceive his own mother? At first I didn't realise how serious it was, but then I joined "Integrity First". I always thought all these little sins – white lies, cutting corners, going behind other people's backs – weren't a big deal. Then I met the people at "Integrity First". They just blew me away. They're just the most downright, straight-up, honest people ever. Totally transparent. They're people you can trust completely. People who you know will always do the right thing, big or small. People who never compromise. I had never met anyone like that. It was so refreshing. What you see is what you get.'

'Why won't you let me help? Do you really think I'm so incompetent?'

'I'm sure you'll be brilliant. That's the problem. I know what's going to happen if you help Mei with the mitigation. You'll think up excuses, wonderful excuses no doubt. But it was excuses, rationalisations – pretending that doing something for charity gave me the right to break the law – it was excuses that got me into trouble in the first place. I've got to stop making excuses, take responsibility, and accept the punishment. The buck stops here.'

'So this is what you see.' Huggins pointed to himself. 'An amoral monster, a tempter, a morally corrupting influence.'

Huggins sank into the sofa, silent, weighed down by his son's contempt for him. He opened his mouth, but he couldn't think of any arguments that would lift the weight that crushed him. The overhead fan kept time, the blades creaking with each slow turn. Occasionally, it shuddered from its exertions, but then, with a wheeze, it continued its stroke through the thick air. Time turned slowly; the sweat thickened around his neck.

'I'm tired, jet lag and all that,' Huggins said. 'I think I'll go to bed.'

The moon woke Huggins again. It wasn't as dazzling as the night before, but it was bright enough, casting light on old wounds, waking him to the twilight sound of crickets, immense; waking to empty spaces in the throat.

He walked to the balcony. Mei was there, her fists tight against the green rails. He told her about his vision of the moon, how he was sure that it was his destiny to rescue Chris.

'The moon you saw, it must have been during the Mid-Autumn Festival,' Mei said. 'It falls on the fifteenth day of the eighth lunar month. That's when the moon shines at its brightest.'

'What does the festival celebrate?'

'There was once an emperor called Hou Yi. He did slavery, summary executions, high taxes, mass starvation, the usual despotic things. He obtained a magic elixir from the Queen of Heaven which would enable him to live for ever. Chang-E, his wife, stole the potion to save the people from eternal tyranny. After she drank the potion, she floated to the moon. If you look at the moon – see that wisp of black that floats against the moon's smooth canvas – that's Chang-E, the maiden of the moon.' Mei touched his arm. 'Why don't you go back to sleep? You've got an early plane to catch tomorrow.'

'I can't sleep, I keep thinking of all my trials, all the lost causes, all the briefs beyond hope, all the cases I've won. And I know that I can save Chris,' Huggins said, 'but he won't let me.'

'A prophet is not without honour,' Mei said, 'save among his own kin, and in his own house.'

That night, Huggins dreamt that he was Chang-E. He had black hair tied in pigtails that dangled from the side of his fat face, and a grey beard. His pink silk dress, soiled with gravy stains, felt tight around his pot belly. He ran to the burnished throne, and grabbed the elixir. The soldiers burst into the room, screaming, waving spears and generally giving out murderous vibes. Huggins gulped down the potion and started floating to the moon.

He arrived at a hotel with a green neon sign that flashed – 'Moon Palace'. At the reception, he rang the bell. Marge came out and looked at him critically.

'What are you doing here, you old fool?' she said. 'There's no room at the inn.'

Lorna Tracy

LIFE IS AN INCIDENT IN A LONG STORY

It will all become clearer when you are immortal.
Byron, *Cain*

AS OLD-FASHIONED AS the sound of rain is the sea falling
upon a long strand.

Things fly past, losing altitude.

The guests in the hotel garden looked up when the shadow
of wings fell across them, inwardly pleading that the creature not come down among them; that it not land where
they were.

And that was strange, because they were there to see
birds.

Miles above was an airliner, tiny in the stratosphere, inaudi-
ble, and translucent like the shed skin of an insect, a ghostly
moult, in which two hundred tourists ate chicken dinners,
watched violence on bulkhead screens, slept unaware of
the rainbow film, universal sign of a cancelled covenant,
shimmering against the thunderhead three miles below them.

Mrs Winterside came up from the sea, carrying her shoes in
her hand, her towel across her shoulders. At the footbath she
rinsed her feet and dried them and went up through the hotel
to her room – her suite – the pair of connecting bedrooms she
shared with Ethel Ormerod. Mrs Winterside peeled off her
maillot and dropped it into the tub. She showered in cool
water, put on a kimono, and went into Miss Ormerod's
room, which was shuttered and dim. Ethel Ormerod was

not there. Probably she was in the restaurant having her pot of tea, her bit of cake.

Mrs Winterside unlatched the wooden shutters and stepped on to the terrace to look for the horse and rider. At five in the afternoon sometimes a grey stallion was exercised on the beach – impassive rider caracoling, mount's neck arching till the head almost kissed the chest, rider and mount making a single creature enclosed within the rhyme of the black tassel tossing on the horse's forehead and the tassel-shaped tail. Mrs Winterside hated to see a docked tail. Hated any nip or tuck inflicted in vanity. Would a naturally flowing tail have spoiled the impression? But there would be a reason, a tradition, an ancient why of it. There always was. The Spanish and their horses: all drama and proud display. The art of pain is a very Spanish art.

In front of the terrace, separated from it by a kerb and a three-bar iron railing, was the flat roof of the restaurant which Miss Ormerod believed made her bedroom vulnerable to unlawful access. Mrs Winterside had pointed out that it would require a very long ladder to reach the roof. No one would bother, she said.

'Well, you don't know who might be in the next room, do you?' said Ethel. 'They could get in from their terrace. Just by climbing over. Anyone could come in.'

It cut no ice with Ethel Ormerod that in the next room were Mr and Mrs Hookpit, fellow bird-watchers, members of her own group. If you couldn't trust *them* who could you trust?

The first day, as Ethel had havered between which room to take, Mim Winterside, who had no dread of intruders, finally volunteered for the room with the risk. She would like to have that room. The sea view would be ever so nice. The inner bedroom looked out on to a whitewashed passage, a blank wall. In the end, though, Ethel risked it. If she kept her shutters locked and the draperies drawn at all times she *might* be safe.

As Mrs Winterside stood on the terrace to look for the horse and rider her attention was arrested by something on the restaurant roof. The strong sun, an hour from setting, gonged off the white surface. Mrs Winterside wasn't quite sure what she was seeing. Someone had dumped a great mound of rags in the middle of it; a tall untidy heap of brown and chamois-coloured rags out where the room notice asks guests not to go, *por favor*.

And something was sticking out of the top. The long white woolly extension had a head and a beak and an eye . . . And the eye was looking at her.

Mrs Winterside thought: ostrich. Then: ostrich is not a bird of Andalusia.

The bird on the restaurant roof was a vulture. An eater of the dead.

There indeed was the fearsomely hooked beak capable of ripping through horse-hide and tearing the carcass into gobbets. What was a lone vulture doing out here on the restaurant roof? Vultures lived among mountain crags, sharpened their talons on rocks. They were sociable birds and very idle – soaring, feeding, sleeping. They had the life, all right. Only yesterday in the mountains behind the hotel they'd seen them – griffons like this one – coming down on to something behind a ridge. They had not climbed the ridge to find out what the attraction was but from the road they had counted fifteen, seventeen, twenty, twenty-five birds gliding down to the meal, a donkey probably, or a cow. The huge birds went down behind the ridge and they stayed down. Whatever it was, it was something worth their time. Good carrion.

'It came down right over the garden. We thought it was going to land by the pool. We thought maybe it wanted to drink. But it went on to the roof. Can we come up and look?' Everyone seemed to know there was a vulture on the roof. So everyone trooped through the suite and on to the terrace and looked at the vulture – all the bird-watchers, the hotel staff, even some of the other guests who had seen the bird planing down.

The bird-watchers had been in the field all that day, in a scorching, scouring wind. As soon as they'd got back it was off with boots and socks smelling of pickled beetroot and into the pool. Only Mrs Winterside had gone to bathe in the sea and missed the arrival of the vulture.

Mrs Winterside did not mind everyone coming into the room. She felt honoured that the bird was out there. But having a vulture practically on the terrace unnerved Ethel Ormerod. She believed it meant to come in. Just the thought of a vulture in her bedroom started an anxious flutter around her cardium. 'It's a vulture, Ethel,' said Mrs Winterside, 'not a house cat. It doesn't *want* to come in. It's a wild bird.' She said if Ethel wanted to go down to dinner she would stay on the terrace and make sure the vulture did not try anything.

It was a beautiful vulture, Mim thought, and she wished she had seen it come down, as the others had, on those plank-like wings. Except for mute swans, she had never been so near to such a big wild bird before. The vulture was smaller than a swan, larger than an eagle. Like the swan its head and neck were covered in downy white. Looked clean as a whistle. Cleaner than a swan's mucky neck. The plumage was full of sombre sienna tones and the dry ochre and tawny colours of the Spanish earth. She reckoned the bird's style accorded with the early seventeenth century. Its jizz was dumpy. The ruff – a circle of narrow, decurved buff petals – would become white when the bird was older, said the ornithologist. The edges of the coverts were richly patterned in fulvous browns and buffs and laid down in fish-scale scallops like skirts over a black petticoat.

'He' – everyone seemed to think of the bird as 'he' though not even the ornithologist knew its gender – 'He has kind eyes,' said sentimental Mrs Millwood.

No one could explain the vulture's presence on the roof. It must be hurt or sick. It could hardly be lost. The mountains, though fifty kilometres distant, were in plain view. Nothing had seemed amiss with its huge wings as it descended. It was gliding like a hall carpet, said the ornithologist, just the way it should. He thought perhaps it had been poisoned. It showed little fear, so it must be feeling poorly.

Depressed by its fame, the vulture put its head down. Awkwardly bundled in the burdensome wings, shaggy black flight feathers sticking out all around it like a fringe of stiff tatters, it more than ever resembled a heap of rags.

It looked very unhappy.

Mim waited with the bird until darkness fell. She missed her evening glass of fino and was nearly late for dinner.

At bedtime, short Miss Ormerod got tall Mrs Winterside to manipulate the levers that locked the bolts at the very top of the terrace shutters, and to fix in place the iron bar across them, and to draw the heavy draperies over the lot in case the vulture should make an attempt on her room.

Something in her mattress ticked all night. She did not sleep. It was her heart.

She *thought* she did not sleep. She did sleep. In fact, a thin skin of uneasy dreams lay over Miss Ormerod's sleep that night – a skin that a vulture's terrible beak could easily tear, going for the rotted meat in her *id*, wanting everything rotten that was in her, all the time staring straight at her with that one full-frontal eye like an ancient Egyptian.

In the morning Ethel Ormerod again called upon Mrs Winterside to deal with the shutters, to open them very carefully and tell her whether the vulture was still there. 'Oh, I couldn't sleep at all,' she said in her plaintive way. 'Is it still out there?'

'Yes, Ethel.'

'Is it doing anything?'

'It's sleeping.'

In the night the bird had moved to a sheltered position against the hotel wall. Its head lay hidden in its feathers. Now Mrs Winterside could see what thick short legs it had, like pillars of ice or salt, covered to the toes in white lambswool. And the toes! Huge, naked, with iron talons. Toes thick and dry and bare as a cow's teat coming at a flat right-angle directly out of the woolly, clean-looking legs. A really big man's hand might have such a span.

When Mrs Winterside had got the letter about the arrangements for the trip and learned that she would be sharing a hotel room with a Miss Ormerod it had flashed up immediately, a memory: *Ormerod, Miss, Her Hostility to the Sparrow*. W. H. Hudson's books sometimes had that curious kind of index entry. Mim had not supposed that *this* Miss Ormerod would be hostile to the sparrow. Vultures, though, were clearly another thing. The vulture was now practically on the terrace, complained Miss Ormerod after breakfast. 'I'm very worried that it will come into my room. I had to leave the terrace doors open – they're so hard to close – and I'm afraid the vulture will get in.'

Mrs Winterside bit back the advice that if threatened by a rapist one should either faint or urinate. She wondered if Ethel had ever read D. H. Lawrence on swans:

> *But he stoops now,*
> *in the dark*
> *upon us; . . .*
> *he . . .*
> *furrows our featherless women*
> *with unknown shocks . . .*

Mrs Winterside climbed over the railing on to the forbidden roof and approached the bird. The vulture swung its neck from side to side like a lever to watch her. A metre away from it she stopped. 'One does not meet oneself until one catches the reflection from an eye other than human,' wrote Loren Eiseley. But the unhuman creaturely eye is unreflective. To it the world is given and accepted unpondered.

Man is the pondering animal. Sometimes he is.

To a vulture a human being is only another feature in the landscape, like the crag it roosts upon, the thermal it floats in, the stink it seeks and follows for its food – except that a human being is of less interest than any of those things.

Sulkily, the vulture shifted its fulvous cape around itself, turned its back on Mrs Winterside, and raised a pale wrinkled cuticle over its Cyclopean gaze, troubling her. The closed eye too much reminded her of a dead nestling's.

Sometimes Mrs Winterside was still bemused to be among bird-watchers, to be – late but in earnest – a bird-watcher herself. Most of her life she'd thought of bird-watchers as benign idiots. Then in the youth of her old age her eyes were opened after a summer week on the north Norfolk coast and revelation streamed in. A couple of adult education courses later and here she was in the 'Spanish funnel' observing the great autumn migration of the passage birds of northern Europe.

A few days earlier, the bird-watchers had met one another for the first time at the dazed hour of half-past five in the morning in the departure lounge of a provincial English airport. 'The VUP lounge,' muttered Mr Hookpit to his wife after waiting two and a half hours for the delayed charter to Malaga. 'Very Unimportant Persons.' The flock wanted to fly. Everyone was dying to kill time. Shifting impatiently in her plastic seat, Mrs Hookpit watched a stewardess in a smart uniform brisking through a door marked NO ENTRY with her little wheeled plaid suitcase following on a lead like a wee Scottie dog wearing a wee plaid blanket.

Mim Winterside sat by herself smoking. The group might as well know from the beginning that she had bad habits so that later on they could be impressed by what a considerate smoker she was. She knew no one around her. She had identified, but not yet introduced herself to, Miss Ormerod. Miss Ormerod in mac, oxfords, hairnet, scarf, canvas hat, tweed skirt, white blouse, cardigan and windcheater was wearing as much of her wardrobe as she could to reduce her luggage. She had something indefinable about her that reminded Mrs Winterside of bloater paste sandwiches and the war. The rest of the group, except for the ornithologist who was the leader, were in pairs, male and female. Experienced nesters by the looks of them, heads grey or bald – or bald and grey in patches together. Even the ornithologist had grey hair, though at fifty he was by a decade the youngest of them all.

Finally they were allowed to board. There they waited again. The passivity of the long-distance passenger. Using the PA system like a confessional, a wailing female sang of some misery she had, an extremely intimate sorrow. She employed direct address. Mrs Winterside felt as if she were party to a crossed line and couldn't hang up. *I really do not want to know this woman's sufferings. Spare me this blueness.*

By the time the breakfast trolley came the plane was above the occluded south coast and an unidentified shining object appeared in the sky. It was the sun. As usual, England would not benefit by it. Mrs Winterside in her window seat put on a pair of plastic dark glasses with black and white frames as boldly striped as a roadblock, and offered the sausages on her tray to the woman sitting next to her. The woman was fat as a beetle and concerned about this.

'I went on that new Health Studio slimming diet for two weeks last month,' she admitted, declining the sausages.

'Really! Two weeks. How was it?'

'I lost a lot.'

'How much did you lose?'

'She lost eighty-five pounds sterling,' said her husband in the aisle seat. 'I'll have those sausages if you don't want them, Frances. You can eat my mushrooms. You're all right with mushrooms. No more calories in a mushroom than in a paper box. Looks like my wife is about to have another fat attack.'

'Well, I did. I lost nine ounces on that diet.'

Not even half a stone, thought Mim. Just a few bits of gravel.

Earlier, in the departure lounge, Miss Ormerod had noticed, with resigned disapproval, the fumarole that was Mrs Winterside's smoking mouth. The ornithologist observed this too. He it was who had paired up the two 'senior maidens' – 'senior maidens' being what they call the old bitches in his native Cumbrian dog circles. Miss Ormerod he knew from experience was a vacuous slow-drip complainer, implacable as a healthy peristalsis, who made a speciality of being helpless. Of Mrs Winterside he knew nothing. From caution he had assigned them the hotel's best available accommodation, the suite with the sea-view terrace. In case they didn't get on they could at least shut a couple of doors between them. The married couples in whatever state of accord would have to share the four walls of one room.

Mrs Winterside knew nowt of senior maidens, but even as a married woman she had always thought of herself as single. She was a single woman not because she was unmarried but because, married or not, she lived alone in a world of her own. She had the character of an old maid and she believed that an old maid was a fine thing to be. Kernels of popcorn that refused to blossom into cottony structures were called 'old maids'. 'Old maids' were hardened and discoloured from exposure to the heat. They were the surplus, eaten last if eaten ever. But they had a fine nut-like flavour and challenged the teeth. Non-conformity, not collapse, inhered in 'old maids'. They might be unfulfilled as popcorn and nothing in the human dentition could break some of them; people with tender or faulty teeth detested them but Mim Winterside enjoyed thinking of herself as a tough, resistant old maid, contentedly lurking intact in the heat at the bottom of the popcorn pan of life.

Mr and Mrs Winterside's marriage had always been an adversarial relationship. When Sam Winterside got particularly angry with his wife he would describe her as an anti-Semite. She hooted at that, for it suggested that she loathed Jews so much that she had married one for the sole purpose of ruining his life. Surely this was a most subtle refinement in the expression of racism! As for Mr Winterside, his brains were in his pants, she said, and said no more.

Recently, when she was still only half-divorced, if someone happened to ask her whether she was married, she'd look puzzled and say, 'I'm not sure.' At that time Mrs Winterside felt like the shipwrecked sailor who couldn't think what to do first to improve his situation. He started countless projects, finished none and finally lay down to bask on the beach 'until he was saved'. This seemed perfectly to describe her own state, except for that bit about basking, and getting saved. She was not going to get saved. Not now. It was much too late. And despite global warming, North Sea beaches weren't getting any baskier. The sun in England was a candle in an ice-house.

Then, one day, she thought: There's nothing left now but life.

It seemed to her a wonderful thought. A novel thought. And more than a thought. An opportunity. Like that moment when she fell in love with birds in Norfolk and confirmed it with a September morning blackbird chuckling in her laden plum tree – that shadow behind the leaves and fruit, when it was too late in the year for any more singing. How Creation must have enjoyed making the birds.

After the lump sum settlement, Mrs Winterside became a toddler in the jungles of finance where independent financial advisers waited behind every tree that was not already the lurking place of a tied salesman with a bank or a building society. Charities seemed to regard her as a source of monthly pay cheques. She began to read the *Financial Times* and await enlightenment, but not with unreasonable patience. Promise, large promise, being the soul of advertisement, she learned to seek out the tiny asterisks and daggers in the large print of inducements referring to the fine print of reality where it was admitted that things can go down as well as up. Investment was exactly like gravity, Mrs Winterside concluded, and was no more to be feared, if one treated it respectfully. She toddled on into the dark with greater confidence, radiating the naïve charm of fifty thousand free-floating pounds.

She had to make a will. Advice on this was to get professional assistance, not a form from the stationer's. Professional assistance in writing the will would give her, as the solicitor put it, 'Come-back if things go wrong after the event.' And Mrs Winterside had thought: Come-back? Come back *after the event*?

Back all the way from the dead just to cause a barney, Mr Winterside would have said, knowing the woman the way he thought he did.

It was an intriguing thought, though.

The taste underlying the scent of 4711 cologne is blackberries, Mim realised, dabbing her face before going down to dinner, at the same time noticing how, even between closed lips, that front tooth set at an angle to the others still gleamed out like a misplaced eyeball . . . She was not reconciled to that tooth, not even after sixty years. On the other hand, Mrs Winterside coolly accepted the decline in her attractiveness as commensurate with nature's plan. 'I'm sixty-three. I don't mind people knowing how much mileage I've done.'

As she did not have 'good hair', she did tend to envy women who did. Mrs Winterside's hair always resembled a corn circle or an old dipper's nest. Miss Ormerod had strong, thick hair with a natural wave in it. When Mrs Winterside complimented her, Miss Ormerod pulled a reluctant smile tight across her dank teeth. Not someone who holds out both hands to life, thought Mrs Winterside.

At fifteen Ethel Ormerod had parted that hair, which was then chestnut, brushed it back, and held the shoulder-length tresses off her face with two side-combs in the style that had served her for the next fifty years. Ethel was like that. She lived all her life in the same house in the same town, where she taught the same geography lessons year after year in the RC girls' school until she retired. She had the best maps of Spain anyone had brought on the trip.

Mrs Winterside longed to ask: Where on your *secret* map, Miss Ormerod, is Utopia? Someone once said that every map must locate Utopia, even though no traveller is ever likely to arrive there. On Mim's map Utopia was just beyond Terra Incognita, in the vicinity of dragons. Not that Miss Ormerod thought to ask. It is hard for the self-absorbed to be curious.

You can go there. Magic words. Modern travel. Mrs Winterside had become a paradisiac. *You can go there. But the cost to the planet will be far greater than the price of your ticket*.

You can go there. Mrs Winterside was aware, if somewhat dimly, of the fatal and ubiquitous rainbow. One could not go there without the aeroplane or the motor car. One could not sail between the Pillars of Hercules as John Keats did two hundred years ago, haemorrhaging on board the *Maria Crowther*, on his way to Naples to look for his health. Which hadn't been there, nor in Rome, but his grave was in Rome or near its walls and he was buried after dark, outside them, as Roman law prescribed for aliens and Protestants.

You can go there.

She signed up for Spain and paid her deposit.

Starving, sweating, dressed for autumnal Britain, stuffed along with the luggage and Miss Ormerod into the back of a minivan, exhausted, dozing, Mrs Winterside had her first sight of the Atlas mountains and sprang awake with wonder. Across the Straits, perhaps magnified by water, in the unmisted light of mid-afternoon, dowsed in pink sunlight, huge bare mountains and rearing cliffs of seemingly fresh, unweathered rock. Africa! Primeval light upon primeval land. It seemed, looking at it, that all the last ten million years were still to come; as if nothing else familiar to a human being had been brought to life yet. The gap between that era and the present age was no larger than the one between Morocco and Spain, or the finger of God and the hand of Adam on the Sistine Chapel ceiling. But Africa seemed very far back in time – like starlight. As if one had followed a beam of starlight to its brilliant source.

Dry white clouds floating their shadows on the sea ... blue skies full of raptors and flocks of bee-eaters ... Mrs Winterside forgot she was hot, tired, and hungry. Mrs Winterside was enthralled.

All along the mountain highway across the bottom of Spain the wind farms strung Mercedes-Benz badges on towers along the ridge tops to turn in the Atlantic gale, in the bright winds of trade. Hundreds of them twinkled along the contours, bringing the bullfights to the *haciendas*.

The coastal plain was rolling, water-shaped and barren. The farmers were farmers of tiles and rubble. White towns topped low hills like clamshell middens. At a distance they looked like snow on a brown winter landscape. Bare fields were already combed with harrow and plough in the hope of winter rain that had not come for years. Other fields, equally desiccated, contained thousands of thin, bored, fighting bulls, shoving their noses into the dry earth. There was no grazing. The land was in extremis. But the tourists got their showers and pools and golf-courses. The Guadalquivir still had draught enough for the pleasure steamers. *So that's all right then.*

There was a persistent smell of sewage boiling in the drains, but Mrs Winterside expected that. That was just how it was in southern Europe.

Mrs Winterside soon learned that her room-mate was one of those people who have trouble with doorknobs, and hotel coathangers – those impossible ones that have to be separated from their hooky part and then re-attached when you wanted to hang anything up. The bar they hung from was too high, anyway. Ethel couldn't reach it. She just couldn't. Mrs Winterside had to hang up all her clothes for her, and get them down when she wanted anything. And even if Ethel had been tall enough she couldn't have got the two bits of the hanger back together; it was like threading a needle. She could not work the terrace doors, open the shutters, draw the curtains, turn on the shower or set the air-conditioning. She could not slide open the minivan door or attach her seat-belt. Yet she lived alone. How did she manage? Mrs Winterside removed the hangers, turned the key, opened the shutter and closed the draperies, set the air-conditioning, while Ethel grunted and sighed. 'Oh dear, I can't – ' Her tone was mild, hopeless and enormously complacent. She had perfected a useful sigh that began with a little clutch of breath at the glottis, to express how obstructive and unreasonable the material world was.

Mrs Winterside had arrived with some useful rules. HOW TO EAT IN SPAIN: Draw soup towards you, not away. Never cut an egg with a knife. Keep both hands on the table. Eat the dessert fruit with knife and fork. If the fruit is an orange, cut the poles off, stand the orange upright on the plate, holding it with a fork, and peel it on a north-south orientation. Cut the peeled orange in half, then into bite-size pieces. Peel an apple or pear in the same way. Peel a banana with your fingers, then lay it on a plate and eat with knife and fork. She looked around the table. Ten English people were drawing soup away from them, and she was spitting out the ham bits.

A green and mottled brown pear reclined on her dessert

plate like a seal on a beach – neckless, bald, pin-headed. Did she dare? Did she dare to eat a pear?

Mrs Winterside watched her room-mate eating. The blankly staring eyes, unsnecked from the brain, the little frown that appeared between them as the fork approached and the jaw unhinged itself to start the feeding process. She had a potato nose and narrow suspicious eyes the colour of hard rain, set slightly aslant, as a mallard's are, out of which she glanced sidelong into her neighbours' plates. Tonight well-tanned thighs of *poulet* in a foetal crouch lay there, next to little piles of french beans. (The meal looked like a dismembered body murdered in a woodlot, thought Mrs Winterside.) She was the only vegetarian in the group. On her plate were beans, two boiled potatoes and a grilled fish. The night steaks were served she had said to everyone in a general way: 'Your entrée has been goaded to death; the bullrings are the abattoirs of Spain.' She mentioned an American, who, thinking to give her a special treat, served her a rare steak. It tasted like a nosebleed. It was the last time she ever ate meat.

Behind the bird-watchers' communal table were the Germans at theirs. Mim could not see how they drew their soup. Maybe they drank it straight from the bowl like tea from a saucer. Almost all females, they were noisy as starlings. German speaking German unto German. They say Berlin is beautiful again. How *could* it be with *that* language filling the air? Their laughing and shouting, drinking and quacking would go on into the smallest hours in the hotel bar and they would pile out raucously again at dawn to go off horse-riding. It was a singles club, the hotel owner's large-eyed sister explained to the ornithologist, who thought: *Three drakes and thirty ducks. She has the Spanish eye, all right, does the hotel owner's sister. The Spanish eye: blue-brown metallic iris. Oils seem to be swirling just under the surface.*

Every night after dinner there was a little meeting to list that day's birds, the habitats, hear the next day's drill. The ornithologist felt satisfied with his little flock of feather-less bipeds – everyone keen, but not a twitcher in the lot, thank God. They were settling nicely into the routine: early nights, early starts, long days in the field. The hotel's packed lunches were something of a trial – thick dry sandwiches that dislocated your temporo-mandibular joint if you attempted an encompassing bite, and disintegrated if you didn't, and being stuffed with fresh tuna, drew clouds of flies whatever you did.

'Look at him,' said Mr Hookpit, nodding towards the ornithologist. 'So keen on his subject that he's trying to *become* a bird.' The ornithologist was standing in a dusty field discoursing on the Andalusian Hemipode that with great good luck they might see but probably wouldn't. Unconsciously as he spoke, he slowly flapped his arms, clapping his thighs on the downstrokes. 'Grey-crested, double-breasted, with pale blue irides, green cap and pink legs,' said Mr Hookpit, with a wink at Mrs Winterside. 'Quite a handsome bird!'

The first thing Mrs Winterside would do after returning from the field was to see how the vulture was. She dreaded to discover that he had left them to know the secrets of eternity. The bird's head was usually down – so down sometimes that only the woolly white pate was visible. The ornithologist waited for it to defecate. He waited two days. It produced nothing. It did nothing. Truth was he expected nothing. It remained on the restaurant roof, not eating, not shitting, not drinking. Mrs Winterside wanted him to eat something. She considered the impropriety of offering a bird a hard-boiled egg she'd saved from the packed lunch. She wanted to see him open his wings.

Miss Ormerod was hoping the ornithologist would look in her room for her when they got back from a trip in case the vulture had got in. 'I'm afraid it may come into my room, you see, with the doors being left open. The maid leaves them open while she cleans.' She really wanted him to tell her the dreadful bird was quite gone away. Just the thought of Griff – someone had started referring to the vulture as 'Griff' – right outside her door was destroying her whole peace of mind.

The ornithologist quite enjoyed imagining the great griffon vulture flat-footed on the headboard, its wings spread wider than the bed, waiting to ravish Miss Ormerod in her maidenly sleep.

The ornithologist began to feel a little concerned about Mrs Winterside, that she might be bonding with this vulture. Crazy ladies were always a risk on these trips. He'd had his share, but he'd never had one who bonded with a bird of prey.

'She'll just stand there looking at it,' reported Miss Ormerod. 'For *hours*.'

Mrs Winterside laughed and said she had come here to watch birds and Griff was one hell of a bird to watch.

Mrs Winterside was surprised on the whole at the attitudes of these bird-watchers. Their relationship to birds seemed to involve a great deal of aesthetic distance. They might have come to Spain for the birds, but this bird was too much and it was too close. This bird was a scavenger. Innocent had nature made it, but this bird was *disturbing the peace*. The Hookpits drove the vulture off their terrace when they found it there. Dismayed, Mrs Winterside watched the vulture hopping sideways, like a competitor in a sack race, shuffling on the huge flat feet, struggling to ascend the kerb and force its bulk through the railings as it retreated on to the roof. There it leant back on its short black tail, looking like a bollard knocked askew, and withdrew its head into its shoulders.

The bird had done no harm on the Hookpits' terrace. Probably it only wanted the shade the terrace wall afforded. Very shocked, Mim realised that the Hookpits regarded Griff as a *wog*. A dirty foreigner. They were not afraid of him, as Miss Ormerod was, but they recognised his otherness and did not like it. The bird was God's spy flying about in search of sinners like its cousin the black vulture of Chile, Neruda's *Coragyps atratus*.

Tender-hearted Mrs Millwood was still insisting that Griff had kind eyes and Mrs Winterside was still arguing with her that kindness was unavailable to creatures. 'No animal can be kind, not in the way you mean, and that's simply because each animal is kindly. I mean, it is of its *kind*. No animal can be "kind" except – very occasionally – man. Even among mankind a kind man is exceptional.'

Strange, that cruelty is not numbered among the seven deadly sins. Perhaps because it is the very mother of sin, no one dares name it.

Behind Miss Ormerod's shut connecting door and her bolted and barred shutters which Mrs Winterside had bolted and barred, and the draperies drawn across them that Mrs Winterside had drawn for her because Ethel was too short to reach, she dreamed she had to get all her food from a vending machine that looked like those Underwood typewriters they used to have in lawyers' offices when she was a girl. By following the instructions meals would come out of it. Of course, for Ethel, they did not. She could not see how the machine was meant to work. She was hungry. On the left side of the machine a lever projected made of a blue examination book folded into a cornet. On the spine were the words: I LIKE MY DINNER   YES   NO   with boxes to tick. And nothing provided with which to tick them. She wanted her pot of tea. She wanted her piece of cake. Her pockets were empty. The cafeteria was deserted. No one anywhere who could help. She wanted someone to work the machine for her. She pictured the food she wanted. She clicked her glottis and sighed her exasperation and no one came to help her. She could never make things work. How could she have her nice pot of tea? How could she get her cake?

She woke briefly, recalling her many brothers, but they were all dead now.

Then she dreamt of something like the lean horse of the Apocalypse with a long, long blue face, skeletally thin, like Bewick's unbearably sad engraving of a great racehorse in its last days, a discarded champion, starved and neglected. She was in Harrogate, having a little holiday. The horse was blue and pink, bald and scabby. Holes were in its skin. The horse had come to her back door seeking food but this back door was not hers. She was not in her own house. She had no food for it. The horse turned away into the street and stretched out dead upon the cobbles.

When Sunday morning came Ethel turned up the collar of

her mac against the boiling wind, tied on her headscarf and walked half a mile to the village to have a bite of Jesus. She was a strong walker, but always moaned and grunted as she bent over to lace her shoes, as if the task were impossible, the effort hopeless, the enterprise out of the question and beyond her energies. But when she was finally off she went lickety-split. She could go mile after mile along the salt-pan berms, up the mountain tracks, back and forth along the beach where the sanderlings rushed, stitching the sea to the shore like demented sewing-machines. 'A sanderling weighs half an ounce,' declared Mrs Hookpit. 'You could post one anywhere in the EC for twenty-six pence.'

'She means a stint. A stint could weigh half an ounce,' said Mr Hookpit. 'A sanderling's heavier than that.'

On the third afternoon after his arrival Griff was nowhere on the roof. Ethel rejoiced; Mim grieved. When Mrs Millwood came into the hotel to report that Griff was down at the footbath *drinking*, Mrs Winterside rushed to be sure. There he was! No one had observed him fly from the roof but everyone took it for a good sign. 'He's feeling *much better*,' said Mrs Millwood authoritatively.

How do *you* know? thought Mrs Winterside jealously. Vultures are rather stupid birds whose vocal compass amounts only to disputatious grunts and hisses when there is food or space to be shared. Griff was a bird with no conversation, one of nature's mutes. Silly Mrs Millwood thought he had kind eyes! And she imagined she knew how he felt!

In Griff's silence was enormous presence. It was a commemorable vulture.

The ornithologist looked for droppings, found none. The difficulty of asking the hotel kitchen for bits of rotten meat without giving the chef offence was somehow overcome (for freshness would have curdled Griff's iron stomach) and parts of a suitably tainted chicken obtained and put out in the sun among the sand reeds near the beach path where Griff was. He did not eat them. Then half a cat, a road kill, was collected and presented a little further from the hotel. The ornithologist found modest droppings. The bird dipped his ancient head and drank again at the footbath, lifting up the long neck to let the water down, bowing and stretching till he had had enough.

Mrs Winterside liked to take her post-meeting brandy into the deserted garden where the pool glowed and the hotel cat came rubbing. The Germans never seemed to go out there in the evening and Mim liked to look up into the sky, at the white house of the moon. No discoloured urban night here. And that very bright shiner – could that be Venus, where an astronaut if he ever landed would be crushed, roasted, suffocated and corroded all at the same time?

These indeed were nights in shining armour. Here she could reflect sometimes that she was a woman without a shadow, without an image, without a husband, without a child, without a lover, without a family. How could she be so constantly happy? But she was.

Mr Winterside adulterated their marriage, so he *had* to demonise Mrs Winterside. He made her a redundant wife. She imagined a robber holding a knife to her husband's throat and demanding: 'Your money or your wife!' How quickly Mr Winterside would say: 'Take my wife and you can have the money for nothing.'

It had simply turned out that it was impossible to love her; no one could ever do it.

That person was singing in the bath again – the barbarous warbler, she dubbed him.

She had not responded in the expected way, people said, mentioning the pain of divorce, the sympathy one owed to both parties, the tragedy of miscarriages, the childless years. People rushed to say these things, thought Mim Winterside, but they were all things she herself had never felt. She had not craved motherhood. If it had been her lot she would have done her best, but as it had not she was relieved. It was not possible to speak of these things, particularly not to Mr Winterside. He was always in denial. Still, people meant well and she could never be so ill-mannered as to throw their sympathy back into their faces and say honestly how little she regretted anything that had happened, anything that had not happened. She had never seen a child she wished were hers. She was a sterile woman – a *happy* sterile woman. It was a scandal. It was unnatural. She simply preferred her selfishness. And so far, her selfishness had not been punished. Except by marriage to Mr Winterside, perhaps.

Some sanctimonious person had declared once: 'We cannot be only ourselves.' Oh no? And why not?

For now the planet was quietly breathing in the Atlantic tide. The moon was full and the sea, drawn by it, appeared to her a pure, clean, transparent menses dropping high up the foreshore all night. The sea was always to be heard from the hotel. She thought of Griff out there in the night now, on the other side of the garden wall, among the sand reeds, in the hotel floodlights, experiencing what? Real sleep? Or some dull, wakeful, primitive patience.

As the Chinese photographer says: Wash the birdie!

Then she knew what Miss Ormerod reminded her of: a Ross's gull, the Arctic bird that flies *north* in winter to sit for months in the dark on the ice floes. A relic gull. The last of her kind, escaping the struggle with coathangers, seat-belts, sliding doors, bolted doors, locked doors of all kinds, air-conditioning units. Air-conditioning in the Arctic was permanently out of control. She had many siblings once, but they were all dead now, like her mother and her father and her aunts and her uncles. She had told Mim about them and had not heard Mim's murmured response: My parents had almost no children . . .

We English, Mim thought, are a people who have never had enough and are always afraid of asking for too much.

English life: all ashes, no phoenix.

Why, there are even birds that have given up flight, that have retreated from that peak experience.

When Mrs Winterside looked at Griff she felt she was looking at the truth. The truth of an indifferent eye. Between Mrs Winterside's gaze and the vulture's the only mediator was Mrs Winterside's self-deceiving human nature. Griff was not a photograph or a sculpture or a computer-generated image of a vulture; to himself he was not even a vulture. He was not anyone's *idea* of what nature is made of – the Great Commodity Lie everyone lives now, without thinking about it, without even knowing they are part of it – the lie from which it follows that life itself can be bought and sold and that it *should* be. Griff was the unrepresented substance, a part of the material world, and nobody's *image* of it.

Mim stood before the bird's resistance to Mrs Millwood's assertion – her well-intended lie – that its eyes are kind, and recognised the irony: she herself was lying in the very act of seeing this bird. If she so much as looked at it she was already telling lies about it. To see the bird with her human eye, to think about it at all, was to use the bird, depict it, manipulate it, make it other than it is, and false. She reduced it to an image and a lie. Whatever Griff saw when he looked at Mrs Winterside it was not an image or anything by which a bird could profit in any way at all. It looked at the truth because it could not do otherwise: it did not know that truth existed. Mrs Winterside could no more have done that herself than she could soar on the thermals with nothing but her own body – though in the lies of her dreams she could do that, too.

And so she was condemned, both self-condemned and condemned of the whole natural creation that excluded human-kind from the truth. What a price to pay for consciousness! There was simply no way in the world of her existence by which she could become honest. Or enter into honest relations with the rest of creation. She could not look straight at anything; everything she saw was through a smear of lies. And it had to be so.

Griff kept his soul. She'd lost hers. Or been born without one. Lost before she was born. And there was nothing she could do about it, being human. That was as close to the truth about Mrs Winterside as she could ever come. A million miles away. An astronormous distance away.

Mrs Winterside did not sleep well that night. In the morning before breakfast she wrote the postcard she'd promised to send to the neighbour who was feeding her tomcat: *I'm fine.*

Are you fine? Hope you are enjoying Mr Bones. I've dreamed that he put on a green sweater and jumped out the attic window. But I'm fine. I really am. And so is Mr Bones.

The excitement before breakfast was the news that Griff was trailing two or three metres of blue rope attached to his leg. Someone somewhere sometime had knotted several lengths together to make a crude jess. When the bird escaped, the jess must have become so completely tangled in his feathers as to be invisible. He'd finally picked it loose except for the knot around the leg. Now the ornithologist knew exactly what to do. Hookpit stood by with a kitchen knife while the ornithologist leapt aboard the vulture with a flying straddle, riding it like a broomstick. At the same time his arm shot out to grip the neck just below the head. The bird grunted a strangled syllable. Hookpit cut away the jess. The ornithologist leapfrogged over the bird's head and jumped clear. The vulture did not move.

The ornithologist was now covered in feather lice. In his room he stripped off all his clothes and hung them over the balcony railing while he showered, then collected specimens in a bottle he later filled with gin. There were people back home who would want them to study. One didn't get a lot of chances at a vulture's feather lice in England.

Soon they would return to a country where it would be autumn, that consumptive among the seasons, growing thinner and thinner with ever-increasing thinness, its hectic cheeks and haunting beauty.

The evening sky was covered in flakes of high cloud like a soft mail of feathers. Mrs Winterside looked down the sea towards where the sky liquidates its stars. *You can go there . . . you can go there . . .* A rack of dry grey cloud stood out over the sea at the horizon. A slot was in it where the sun inserted itself like a coin and bought them one more Spanish night.

Ethel woke up well-rested. No vulture. No dreams. She was quite keen to get back now. She was missing the grey light of her native town where the sun, when you could see it, was like a frantic eye behind the blowing nets of North Sea mist.

She liked that.

In the adjoining bedroom Mrs Winterside was still in her dreams, driving in reverse gear with one foot on the accelerator and one foot on the brake.

John Tusa

ALL THE CHANNELS IN THE WORLD

'NEVER BELIEVE ANYONE who prophesies – especially about the future.' It might have been Sam Goldwyn and how right he was. Forecasting is a hit and miss business, often relying on straight-line projections of what we already know, and making too little allowance for human behaviour, the cyclical nature of development, and sheer accident in determining the difference between life today and life in a generation's time.

Forecasting, especially in its futurological guise, misleads in another sense too. It confronts us abruptly with the possibility of absolute change in our lives, conflating the gradual evolution of life into a blunt contrast between what is and what will be. As Albert Einstein noted: 'I never think about the future. It comes soon enough.' Alvin Toffler, the father of Futurology, warned us of the phenomenon of 'Future Shock', meaning that a stark confrontation with the future is bound to bring us up short as we face the scale of the changes to come, without reference to the timescale within which they will occur. For, as we look back over a generation, the first impression is that life is not so different from what it is today – an impression made possible only by the fact that it has happened gradually, and that on the whole we have been able to manage our own involvement in it. But the second impression – the one that strips out time, that ignores our ability to come to terms with change – is perhaps the more accurate and revealing. In this perspective, the changes in the last generation have been huge.

In the world of broadcasting thirty years ago, there were only two national TV channels, one for BBC, one for ITV. There was no commercial radio, and no local radio either. There was no colour TV; there were no video recorders, no cables, no satellites, no worldwide television. In fact, it was thirty years ago that the very first transmission of TV pictures took place across the Atlantic featuring, among other things, the inauguration of President Lyndon B. Johnson. Now it is an everyday instant, meal-time occurrence. More remarkable still is the fact that most of the big changes have taken place in the last decade of the three. Change is taking place fast: but the pace of future change will be faster still, and that is an essential element in the perspective of the future of broadcasting.

Not long ago, the Dean of Engineering at Yale, Alan Bromley, formerly Chief Scientific Adviser to President Reagan, spoke of the changes he had witnessed in his field during his lifetime. When Bromley graduated as an engineer in 1948, television and antibiotics were laboratory curiosities; the backbone of transportation was the twin-engined DC3; polio stopped the playgrounds each summer and there was no cure or vaccine in sight; a portable communication unit was still the sort of thing that Dick Tracy played with; man in space was the purest science fiction; and the computer was a good idea that had been around for more than twenty years, occupied cubic yards of space, generated large quantities of heat, and needed twenty-five engineers to do what a pocket calculator can do today. So things change, hugely, and they will not change more slowly in the future.

At one level, forecasting the future of broadcasting is comparatively safe. There are already many developments under way which are bound to happen. The technology exists, the capability exists, the commercial imperatives exist, the governmental will exists. With those elements in place, consumer demand has little choice but to follow. (One of the modern triumphs of technology has been its capability to be massively innovative and to anticipate our unvoiced needs.) What are the changes that are virtually bound to happen? There will be more: more of everything. More terrestrially based digital TV channels – eighteen new ones, according to the Heritage Secretary, Virginia Bottomley, marking what she called a change as significant as the move from black and white to colour TV. More satellite channels beaming into your dishes. Africa expects twenty-four satellite channels within two years, covering the Atlas Mountains to the Cape of Good Hope. By the end of 1997, the global forecast is for 150 channels of digital TV to be available world-wide, with no fewer than 500 available across Europe.

There will be more cable channels running past your home, and probably therefore coming into it. There will be more radio stations, through the air, on studio quality digital networks, via cable. There will be more advertising, more sponsorship and more pay and subscription to pay for these channels. There will be more commercial television. There will be more TV on demand, perhaps on dial-up systems through telephone lines, more films and far more sport. More single activity specialist channels. There will be more personal relationship programmes, more sex channels, with – judging from the just published schedules of Britain's first Playboy TV channel – programmes such as *Playmate 6 Pack*, *Masseuse 2*, *Babewatch* and *Sex Under Hot Lights* (the word 'adult' has been redefined in relation to such channels). There will be more shopping channels, more people participation shows, more human disclosure shows, more money competition shows. There will be more news on the move; more police patrol car TV; more live accident TV; more television that aids and enhances mood changes. Ever since 1987, a cable network called simply 'Landscape TV' has been available. In the estimated 800,000 homes that have it, it offers soothing pictures of the natural world with classical and contemporary instrumental music playing over the top. Some have called it a 'low stress channel', others a 'channel to pull teeth to'. Others have noticed that it is very popular with Ecstasy-energised young clubbers, chilling out after an all-night rave.

Not all this viewing will be passive. These aggregates of access will allow interactivity from home to office or business as it has never been known before. There will be information about consumer services from shopping to banking. In an experiment in interactivity in West Germany more than a decade ago, a man was seen dialling up his bank account and investment valuation last thing at night, and retiring to bed reassured with a sweet sense of security.

There will be more zapping from channel to channel. Zapping increases in geometrical proportion to the number of channels available. Increased choice will place a harsher premium on instant viewability, with a programme that fails to deliver virtually immediate gratification finding itself punished by the zap button. Discontinuous viewing will carry a new meaning, the discontinuity applying to the leap from channel to channel. In fact, the number of people whose viewing over fifteen minutes will be made up of rapid grazing through various channels, a blur of sport, studio, news, movies and ads, will grow rapidly. An attention span of five minutes will look positively extended, a gratification span of fifteen seconds may increasingly become the norm. There must be a high degree of confidence – as they say in the City – that some broadcasting world like this will happen. And this is before any attempt at guessing the impact of entirely new and undreamed-of technologies.

In 1968, Michael Frayn wrote a novel called *A Very Private Life*. In this look into a fully wired future – a phrase itself unknown at the time – no one leaves home at all because all knowledge, all sensation, all entertainment, all human contacts take place through a network of pipes, tubes, wires and electromagnetic beams. Frayn's technical terms sound thirty years out of date, but his imagination, of a life where, as he puts it, 'our wishes go out along the wires and electromagnetic beams, and back by return will come the fulfilment of them', has an increasingly plausible ring. In this electronic dystopia, the home has become the means of fulfilling people's dreams, as the ultimate exaltation of the private over the public. Public life has become increasingly dangerous, disagreeable and disorderly, and has required increasingly authoritarian measures to control it. But in Frayn's imagined futuristic world, the response has been the exaltation of the private.

Whoever could afford it built a wall around himself and his family to keep out society and its demands ... All over the world, each family with the intelligence and energy to manage it built its own castle into which nothing, whether food, air, information or emotion was admitted until it had been purified and sterilised to suit the occupiers' needs.

And the home holovision – which replicated all external perception and sensation, from friends, family, to the countryside – is the instrument by which Frayn's private life of the future has become possible. Thirty years on, that picture looks less simply fanciful than it did in 1968. But in some respects it looks distinctly unambitious in relation to what is about to happen. Great fantasiser as he is, even Frayn could not foresee 'Landscape TV'.

Faced with this immediate cornucopia of television and radio, a further question arises. It may appear contradictory or even nonsensical. If there is to be more of almost everything, will there be less of anything? A guess can be hazarded that there will be fewer state broadcasters; fewer channels paid for by state levy or licence fee; fewer networks of mixed programming; fewer owners; fewer programme-making centres; fewer single documentaries; fewer major documentary series; fewer contemporary and experimental dramas; fewer extended news bulletins; and all of it conditioned by one overriding economic reality: less money.

On these assumptions, the outlook for broadcasting could be expressed in a series of antitheses. The future of broadcasting could mean more choice but less diversity; more information, but less knowledge; more action but less news; more gratification but less satisfaction; more viewers but fewer audiences; more entertainment but less engagement; more immediacy but less depth; more in the present, less in the past; more up to the minute, but less tradition; more on demand, less to wait for. If those antitheses were truly to reflect the future pattern of broadcasting, then television and radio would have largely ceased to be media of expression and communication as we have come to know them, and would instead have become more like any other public utility. TV and radio on tap; programmes on demand; running hot and cold information, entertainment and education. Films or programmes are watched exactly when the viewer wants, not when a TV network or channel scheduler decides. Gas, water, electricity, the media – all will be just a question of guaranteeing a safe, reliable and massively increasing supply at ever-decreasing cost.

Or the antitheses can be posed differently and more positively. The new world of broadcasting will provide choice, not control; profusion, not scarcity; range, not limitation. One can only paraphrase the joy of Shakespeare's Miranda in *The Tempest* at seeing human beings other than her father or Caliban for the first time and say, 'Oh brave new world, that has such channels in it.'

There are at least three possible reactions to such outcomes. One is to say that the march of technological progress is so insistent that it is idle to question it. Another is to say that to question scientifically based advance is morally wrong because it would be tantamount to denying the right of science to think for itself and to act on the consequences of its discoveries. The third is to marvel at the scale of the likely changes and to address the questions raised by them.

Serious questions about the future can be raised in four principal areas. First, what will happen to patterns of ownership and accountability? Second, what effect will these changes have on the presentation and flow of news nationally and internationally? Third, what effect will they have on the body of knowledge traditionally valued and taught in schools and universities? Fourth, what effect will they have on societies and the way that they relate and interrelate with individuals?

A look back at the way in which ownership has evolved in the international media offers little room for encouragement. A handful of proprietors dominate the skies and the cables, either merging with one another, or doing deals with one another, and elbowing aside smaller players in the global scene. The names of the new media moguls are well known: Murdoch, with Sky in Europe, Star TV in Asia, Fox TV in the United States; Turner with cable football interests in the United States, and his CNN news network, national and international, now merged into a major conglomerate with TimeWarner. They confront equivalent giants such as ABC/Capital Cities/Disney. Also in the field are companies such as MTV/Paramount/Viacom, not to overlook Britain's Pearson group and Germany's Bertelsmann. They all have the satellite and cable channels on which to put their programmes; the film library, or video library of golden oldies to form the spine of their programming; the subscriber base from new films and sport to allow ever larger bids to be made for sport that was once available to all viewers of the public broadcasters for only a minimal charge, and, as they become ever bigger, so their capacity to deter entry into the global market by newer, smaller players becomes ever harder to overcome.

Globalisation is an important, maybe the all-important, economic strategy for companies. It is, according to the chief executive of Granada, Gerry Robinson, a message currently being lost on the leaders of Britain's other commercial TV companies. In their fragmentation, they risk missing the ability 'to think global, act global and be global'. He may well be right in offering that as a piece of sound business advice. But it does not follow that globalisation is a strategy that will lead to the greatest viewer and listener satisfaction, still less that it is designed to do so. Where – apart from price – are viewer needs allowed for in a scheme of things where economies of scale in production, the most widespread distribution of the product, and the lowest production costs are the most important considerations? Where are quality, diversity and range to be fed into these calculations, and how are they to be accounted for? Why should a few individuals and their institutions control so much of human expression at a time when one of the great achievements of the twentieth century has been to fight and resist political domination and thought control in the name of the individual's right to be free?

Why, having overcome political tyranny, should we accept it so easily in our leisure pursuits?

It may well be that the question of the globalised control of our mass entertainment, culture and values by a small number of media owners will be one of the key issues for the next century. The dissemination of a homogenised view of the world, of life, of behaviour, of clothes and lifestyle, is a form of ideological persuasion. Those that present and advocate it have a vested interest in persuading the viewers that these are the new norms and they are in a strong position to be persuasive. Accompanying these values is an open belief that modernism in almost any form is preferable to what has gone before, and that consumerism, as delivered by the market, is a guarantor of both economic and, by extension, political freedoms. These are powerful arguments, representing heady forces. But they are so powerful, so possessed of the means to persuade, that this new orthodoxy may well not be recognised for what it is – a new ideology with all the dangers attendant on any ideology.

The conventional defence to such challenges is that large media conglomerates are neither innately nor necessarily dictatorial because they have diversity built into their fabric and their nature. We are safeguarded by their very nature which is to make money and, as Dr Johnson observed to Boswell, 'There are few ways in which a man can be more innocently employed than in getting money.' If there is money to be made out of cultural, political or social diversity, then it is in the interest of a global enterprise to meet that demand – at the appropriate cost, of course. The enterprise may be politically inclined to the right, as in Murdoch's case it certainly is, but if he judges that there are readers to be won and money to be made by publishing a newspaper of the left, then he will do so. On this view there is no clash between ownership and expression, because it is in the interests of ownership, almost its job, to make money out of reflecting diverse expression. On this interpretation, the very idea of diversity is safe in the hands of the few, for they have a commercial interest in delivering it to the many.

They may have no obligation to do so, better still they have an interest.

For some, that is neither a beguiling, still less a conclusive argument. To enjoy freedom and diversity of expression because it is a convenient way for a media proprietor to make money reduces supposed basic rights to a matter of somebody else's commercial opportunity. Our freedom becomes dependent on their whim, not on an absolute right belonging to us. It is qualified by the need to make money, and by the fact that once it fails to do so, there is no guarantee that the right will not vanish. That is no basis for genuine, properly secured freedom of expression which must be that we can publish, view and hear what we need to as well-informed citizens, not because someone else decides to afford it on our behalf, but because political rights include such a right and have designed the systems of regulation capable of delivering it. Freedom and diversity of expression must be an expression of conviction, rather than just another stall in the market-place where a right can be afforded provided it is marketable.

In the arena of international entertainment, the outlook is 'Hollywood and bust'. No one can do anything but marvel at Hollywood's ability to create a series of world myths and images that appeal to children of all ages and every nation around the world. No one can challenge Walt Disney's ability to say to visitors to his theme parks and viewers of his films the phrase used by Jesus Christ, but subtly modified, 'Come unto me all ye that travail and are heavy laden, and I will reassure you.' Reassurance is fine and we all want it from time to time. Make-believe is necessary and enjoyable as a relief from the relentless pressures of reality. But make-believe and reassurance as a philosophy of life hardly meet the needs of a world in its present state of turbulent transition. It is a deception to pretend that they do, but that is the collusive pretence in which we all take part at the heart of the Disney bargain.

But the objections to a Disneyfied, Hollywoodised world view of life go further: not so much a Pax Americana as a Pax Mickeyana. They are exactly the same as those to a world where biological and ecological diversity are threatened by economic development. You cannot risk losing biological forms or local ecological systems; the balance of the global biological and physical eco-systems needs them. Equally we cannot risk losing cultural diversity and variety under the impact of an overwhelmingly American-based set of cultural values, whether they are on film, TV or in the world of pop. It is surely the ultimate arrogance of such media owners to say that the superiority of their products is demonstrated by their success commercially. They are impossible to challenge. It is hard for local media to resist the sheer commercial power of the global giants. But is the existence of that power some kind of absolute validation of their right to do as they like? This is the challenge for national governments. Can they devise regulations which strengthen local diversity and the authenticity of national cultures and variations, or are they content to watch over a globalisation of culture to one standard, as a welter of channels leads to a homogenisation of human experience? It was an American comedian, Jay Leno, who once joked, 'We're going to ruin your culture, just like we ruined our own.' But is it a joke?

On the news front, the soon-to-be-crowded international scene presents a somewhat different set of dilemmas. Many, perhaps a majority, of world governments, restrict the flow of news and comment within their own countries. This is unlikely to change until the governmental systems change. For two generations now, international broadcasting – first radio, then more recently television – has broken through governmental barriers and allowed citizens to hear for themselves what their governments would prefer they did not. I can think of no reason for justifying such censorship, and see the arrival of international television on the scene – CNN, BBC World Service, Sky – as an unqualified improvement to the flow of news to citizens denied it. Some governments try to justify their continued attempts to keep out news on grounds similar to those used against cultural infiltration. Yet the cases are very different. Certainly interpretations of events may vary, but the basic facts of international events do not. Governments who try to prevent their citizens seeing and hearing the news invariably have something to hide.

Will the new multi-channel broadcasting environment make things better? Not unless two things happen. First, that one or more competitors of equal standing and power increase the competitive choice on offer. In some parts of the world, there is no competitor to CNN. In many, the only real competitor is BBC World Service. In a few, Sky is a competitor. The world's viewers need more choice than that, need more variety of coverage, more diversity of opinion, a broader range of views. But the commercial basis of these services – the BBC included – automatically limits the ambition and extent of the coverage. Their financial base does not begin to match up to the real costs of providing full international coverage of the world. The future proliferation of channels by itself is no solution to the question of providing independent news, diversity and variety to the world as a whole. It is like having ever more and more printing presses, but no idea of how to earn the money to write the papers to be printed on them.

There is a further tension between the objective needs of the audience and the ability of television companies to meet them. On the face of it, satellite channels are the ultimate breakers of censorship. Beam in your signal of free information and leave it to the ingenuity of the individuals to receive the signal. It does not work that simply. If the Murdochs and Turners are to make money from anything like a mass audience – say in China – then they must get on to cable systems on the ground. Here the governments – often no friends to free information – can set their own terms. As gatekeepers of their cable systems, they will only allow in those networks that play along with the official view of the news that their citizens should see or hear. Given that companies must rely on governments to justify their investment, can they afford to offend those governments?

Recent experience suggests that they cannot and will not. They render unto Caesar not only the things that are Caesar's but things he might not dare to ask for in the first place. The most notorious instance of this came in 1993 when Rupert

Murdoch bought Star TV from the Hong Kong magnate, Li Kaishing. Star had acted as the pioneer for putting up BBC World Service Television in Asia where one of its footprints covered the whole of China. Murdoch first boasted that satellites could overturn governments. Then he realised that governments did not like the idea of being toppled, and that this role might conflict with his more immediate aim of making a return on his huge investment in Sky. When the Chinese authorities, his new potential partners, told him how much they disliked the BBC for constantly 'harping on' about the Tiananmen Square Massacres, Murdoch found he could satisfy both his commercial needs and his instinctive dislike of the BBC by throwing BBC World Service TV off the beam covering China.

The moral of that event is that the future diversity of channels is no guarantee of freedom of communication unless regulatory frameworks create greater diversity and competition among those supplying programmes and creating networks, and unless governments see the creation of such diversity as a priority. Technical profusion is a means, not an end in itself. If profusion is also to mean increased availability of news and information, then a different set of questions have to be answered. How can we harness that profusion to the diverse needs of the viewers without handing over the viewers to the power of the proprietors? If the commercial proprietors are to be the essential providers, how are we to introduce true accountability, apart from the threat of commercial failure or mutual predation?

But questions arise elsewhere about the impact of the multi-channel environment. Ever since television and radio started, the networks in which they presented themselves to the public have been mixed in their character. Since there were so few channels, they had to have a broad remit, and a broad appeal to as much of the audience as they could get. In fact the aim of the two land-based popular channels in Britain – BBC and ITV – is still to attract half or more of the total available audience. This broad social and interest base to the mixed network should not be taken for granted.

The assumption behind it is that there is a large audience available not only for the programmes that you can predict they will watch – comedy, sport, natural history – but also for those that they may be tempted or induced to watch. There is a crucial concept in programming called the 'inheritance' factor, namely those viewers who do not tune in because they are determined to watch programme X, but those who stay tuned because they can be beguiled, engaged to watch. But the social assumption is even more important. It is that we viewers, we citizens, have broad tastes, and we cannot be compressed into the neat categories of marketing, where income and taste and choice are the determinist prisons of the consumer market. We are ready to be involved in a general television network, because we define ourselves as individuals more broadly than market categories are designed to allow. On this assumption, there are opera lovers among football fans and vice versa. It is a socially cohesive, integrative view of society and of human beings, believing that there is more to the individual than being defined as a consumer, and that human curiosity overleaps consumer categories.

When channels proliferate, the mixed network vanishes. In its place, the specialist network – sport, comedy, documentaries, nature, shopping. Such networks are very different in nature, and they are crucially different in their approach to the individual and society. For whereas the mixed network emphasizes what viewers have in common, the single issue channel emphasizes what separates them from others. The viewers are increasingly defined by the very specific and particular interests that they are known to enjoy, and that market research is designed to identify. But it follows that it is less likely that they will stray from the once-established pattern and networks of their primary choice, and impossible for them to stumble across something they might know they would find interesting.

We know what we gain from single subject channels – a vast supply, perhaps of every single first division football match played in England. But what do we lose from this proliferation? A sense of sharing with others? A possibility of surprise? A sense of being part of a collection of individuals who all through separate choice make up the mass television audience, and find that sharing in the mass act of viewing becomes a valued social experience? How often is the question, 'Did you see?' a conversation starter, part of the social glue of everyday exchange, an integrator, not a separator. It is inevitable, as the mixed networks come under greater commercial pressure from their single subject rivals, that this element in social life will be less significant than it was, and could disappear altogether. Will the proliferation of channels act as a further atomiser of social interchange? Are we ready to give up altogether the cohesive contribution to society that the more limited number of necessarily mixed channels have made? Whatever the answer, let us not pretend that the proliferation of choice, of viewing, does not carry a social price with it. Individualism was the great, bursting child of the sixties' revolution of the left. Now it has been taken up by the driving nineties' commercialism of the ideological right. Is that what the class of '68 would have wanted? Will the new world emphasize what sets us apart from one another or what unites us? On present indications, the former seems the more likely.

Other questions follow. What will the sheer weight and volume of impressions flooding from hundreds of channels do to our awareness of the past and our sense of historical continuity? Of course, with so many radio and TV channels available, some will be dedicated to education. But these are likely to be of a comparatively specialist kind, increasingly tied in to formal learning, associated with schools and universities, or other institutions of continuous education. The problem lies elsewhere. The TV screen, or the computer screen for that matter, are overwhelmingly instruments of the present, screens for presenting the immediate, ideal for conveying and reinforcing images of the here and now, and adept at conveying a modern lifestyle that crowds out anything but the present.

These media are so successful at presenting, processing and adapting information, the information presented is itself so rich that the question arises whether it is not in danger of crowding out knowledge, the transmission of knowledge and any sense of continuity in our analysis of information. If the manipulation of information has become so rapid, so probing, how good will it be at including any sense of the continuities, the traditions that form the essential background of knowledge to our store of information? How good will media of the 'now' be at including any sense of, or attributing value to, an understanding of the 'then'? Knowledge will be stored, but unless the new proliferation of media include that store as part of their everyday presentation of reality, then it will remain dry, dusty, unused and moribund. Is the past to be consigned to a distant computer dump, little used and less valued? Why will we need a memory of the past when the present surrounds us in all its glory? As Keynes observed: 'I do not know what makes a man more conservative – to know nothing but the present or nothing but the past.' There is little danger of the latter, but rather more of the former.

The questions can be expressed like this. What happens to knowledge when it is transmitted visually and orally, and not on the page or in a book? What happens if the style of the presentation of information becomes not only more alluring but more influential than the substance? What happens when the new proliferating channels create images of the present so intense that they command attention and loyalty, and then reflect and replay those images so insistently that they crowd out most of the alternatives?

Society and politicians may consider them, and decide either that the consequences will not be as described, or that they are perfectly acceptable. What is not acceptable is to suggest that the questions should not be asked, or that the process of change to a multi-channel environment, managed by a small number of global players, is so obviously beneficial that it should remain beyond question. We know that the future of broadcasting will deliver more – of almost everything. But the more is so much more that it will be different as well. We should not let that occur without asking and considering the precautionary question: what might we lose in the process?

Michael Hofmann

METEMPSYCHOSIS

Your race run, the rest of us,
mother, sisters, sisters' boyfriends,
ran repairs. Trimmed the hedge,
whited the walls, weeded the stones.

The place looked five years younger –
you might not have recognised it.
It took you dead to harness us,
give us some common, Tolstoyan purpose.

It was the day the ants queened themselves,
or whatever they do. Got to the end,
and came back all self-conscious with silver wings,
folding stuff they hardly knew what to do with.

Like the Ossis in Berlin, they got everywhere
(a run on cuckoo clocks). The clever ones
would go far, to be in position for
the next pedestrian incarnation.

ZIRBELSTRASSE

(for my mother, and in memory of my father)

She's moving out of the house now, the sticky sycamores
one after the other struck by lightning outside the picture
                                                    window
that my father struck by lightning liked to keep curtained
before the lightning came for him a second time early one
                                                    morning

460

and he lost his balance, his speech, and last of all his
mischief,

the high pines that gave the street its name chopped down
by the new people, only the birches left standing
whose thin leaves and catkins reminded me of her copper
silver hair,
the old woman upstairs with all her marbles and mobility
put in a home by her Regan of a daughter who sold the
house

over the heads of my parents, sitting duck tenants,
bourgeois gypsies, wheeled suitcases on top of fitted
wardrobes,
the windows where my sister's criminal boyfriends climbed
in at night,
over the hedge the pool where the dentist's children screamed,
the old couple next door, *Duzfreunde* of F. J. Strauss,

the patio stones with their ineradicable growths of moss,
the weedy lawn where slugs set sail of an evening and met
their ends
like Magellan, sliced up in the salty shallows of their own
froth,
the potatoes my father bestirred himself to grow one year,
gravelly bullets too diamond hard to take a fork,

moving with all the books, the doubtful assets of a lifetime,
the steel table only I had the wit to assemble and left my
feet on,
the furniture and lamps picked up in border raids to Italy,
once austerely challenging, now out of date *moderne*,
too gloomy to read by, and sad as anything not bought old,

the Strindberg kitchen with the dribbling Yugoslav fridge,
the Meissen collection we disliked and weren't allowed to
use,
the *démodé* gadgets for making yoghurt, for Turkish coffee,

the turkey cutlets not so much cooked as made safe in the
frying pan,
the more cooking cut corners and dwindled and became
rehash,

my off and on kingdom in the cellar, among the skis and
old boots,
my father's author's copies and foreign editions,
the blastproof metal doors, preserves, tin cans and
boardgames
of people who couldn't forget the Russians, the furnace
room
where my jeans were baked hard against an early departure.

Maureen Duffy

WASSAIL

Off to bury Ivy I run through the platitudes, close
cousins to those doldrums where a ship founders or's
                                        becalmed.
The tube shuttles me from West to East, present to past
an unpaid bill trolleying across Button and Clemoes
outfitters, under two thousand years of London embalmed
above, around me; a century of it ours. Upcast
at Bethnal Green each stop's a grey felted scrapbook page:
snapshot Bow where I was first schooled to read and write;
                                        Plaistow's chest
clinic whose Little Titch doctor told me to eat my greens.
Beyond Barking's pot-bellied gas retorts my glass cage
looks out on almost country till Dagenham's soiled quest
for *urbs in rure*, flat fields slicked back with rain where the
                                        wind keens
and I'm almost there. You didn't suffer like some; had all
your marbles unchipped: a string of clear beads or the
                                        flawless
glass jewels we ricocheted down the gutter, ruby, sapphire
emerald or crystal with a twisted skein in the middle;
had fourscore years and then a bit of a cold or less;
nothing to worry about, a case for aspirin and camphor.
But everything happened to you at Christmas: married,
widowed so it's somehow right that we're here again, three
                                        days
to go, the kings on their way, the Sally army oompahing
through the shopping mall and none of your cards sent.
                                        Harried
by a rain bitter as old men's dewdrops, in saffron clays
that clog our boots, we stand with smart plastic grass
                                        cladding

463

the indecent mounds, learning all sorts of things. You came
here every week for twenty-six years bringing children and
then
grandchildren so they should know and there'd always be
flowers
to his name. There's a gap on the stone where a discreet
flame
can burn your reticence between husband and brother again.
Your middle-aged children hang on to their lovers
as though they might slip and teeter in where the family plot
lies wetly agape. And it's Christmas I hotly recall
with us coming on Boxing Day through mist and snow to
where you were
living then, with a stop for rum and coffee at some grotty
station buffet before the chill, always downhill stroll
to welcome: the crates brought out; roast, sprouts and spuds
and beer;
the games and singing and dancing to a lone piano
till it was time for aunties two in a bed, a small
cousin sandwiched between. Whispers we played, musical
chairs,
pass the parcel. Then it was each in turn to sing solo:
Danny Boy, I'll be your sweetheart, take you home, my
lover, my all
while you and your Roy in the kitchen were stoking us
up stairs
in cups of tea loose laced with gin. And suddenly I'm stormed
by all the things I wanted to ask gone with you into the
family plot
sucked down by those wet lips: the last repository
of ways pre-war; in service, first you then him, uniformed
by scratchy serge battledress, cock's-comb forage cap. 'It
was hot
as hell. But I learned to drive a truck though I was
jittery
at first.' Lord of his milkfloat smashed to bits on Christmas
morn.
And after that your mufti years of Xmasses alone.

When I get back indoors I find wedged in the tread of
                                                my shoes
thick tears of clay I can't just scrape off, chuck in the bin.
I get a knife, a potted-up plant, pale refugee grown
leggy, attenuate with winter blues
that the first November frost forced me to bring in.
I prise their earth from my soles and tamp it down.

Maura Dooley

OUR LIVES AND OURSELVES

Mam, I want you to know
I made this the old way
with paper and pencil,
rough copy, fair copy,
a child at my elbow
and not enough sleep.

I wanted to tell you
the parlour still smells
of snuff and of polish,
of musk roses, soot,
the chill Northern wind
and the dampness of spring.

On Sundays while Nellie
and Clem are at Chapel,
I sit setting down here
my heart's smallest secrets,
in ways I could never,
when life was your shroud.

A mother, a daughter,
the rough and fair copies,
I never could tell you
our own little story
of soot, of musk roses,
our lives and ourselves.

I want you to know, Mam,
it's your hands I gaze at
spread over these letters,

as if to protect them
from words and from meaning,
from something as simple

as just making sense.
This silence between us,
has made the keys blurry,
the way this 'g' trembles
on a word I once fought
that now fits like a glove.

A BLANK FILM

On Assateague and Chinquateague
the wild ponies we watched for kept hidden
and the astonished faun who came upon us,
as we listened to the strange songs of strange birds,
was a blank when the film came back.

The Cape Henlopen lighthouse sought
through narrow lanes, picturesque on my tea towel,
had slipped under waves half a century before,
washing up here tonight, in those moments,
when questions go unanswered,
when eyes open on darkness, emptiness, silence.

I wipe my hands and spread the tea towel to dry.
I could recite from it for you, the names of all
the lighthouses of the Eastern Atlantic seaboard,
Sandy Hook, Castle Hill, Brant Point,
West Quoddy Head, the Isle of Shoals.

Their lights are a stranger's cry across the water,
a gasp or a sigh, breaking up ice,
each beam like turning a page,
flooding the darkness for a single moment
and then another moment and another.

John Burnside

KATE'S GARDEN

THE DAY TOM Williams came back I was still working at
home. The good thing about freelancing was that I got to be
alone all day, in an empty suburb, just me and the cats and
the blackbirds, and an occasional heron, standing motionless
in the reeds, down by the river. I liked that feeling: I never
tired of raising my head, halfway through a piece of work, and
noticing the light at the window, the still gardens, the empty
gravel paths and lawns. It was a world where nothing had ever
happened. Time had passed – I would know by glancing over
at the clock on the mantelpiece – but the movement had been
so fine it was imperceptible. On those warm spring mornings,
I kept having privileged glimpses into limbo: a state, not of
suspension, but of infinite potential.

My study was upstairs at the back of the house. I'd placed
the table so I could see the Williams's garden, rather than
my own: ever since Tom had left, eighteen months before,
Kate had worked out there every weekend, digging, planting,
weeding, pruning, sowing. She was a fine gardener, with an
excellent eye for colour and texture, and what had been an
attractive plot before Tom disappeared was now a work of
art. Kate was a slight woman, pretty and nervy, with tiny
birdlike hands, but she extended the patio herself, and she
carried large, soggy bags of mulch or compost from the front
yard, where the delivery men left them, and dug them in
herself, working through every Saturday afternoon and all
day Sunday, intent on what she was doing, single-minded,
utterly absorbed. I think, for the first time in her life, she was

truly happy. Making that garden may have been her therapy, but it was also her joy.

On weekdays, I got to admire her handiwork. The other gardens could look odd, sometimes, for being deserted all day: I had a sense, occasionally, of something missing there, but Kate's garden was all the more beautiful when she wasn't in it. It was as she intended, I think: a home for the plants she'd chosen and nurtured; a refuge for birds and hedgehogs; a breeding pool for frogs; a lure, in the early morning, for hungry deer. The only sign that the garden was meant for human use was an old wooden bench that she scrubbed and oiled every spring, and put away in the shed in October. There was no lawn, no drying area, no barbecue. Instead, she filled the space with lilies, junipers, irises. She had rare alpines and a rose-covered trellis to hide the shed. At the centre of one flowerbed, she had placed a large, amphora-shaped pot. I waited weeks to see what she would plant in it, thinking it was rather beautiful as it was, standing empty, filling with light and rain. It was some time before I understood that that was exactly what she intended.

It's no exaggeration to say that Tom disappeared. In some ways, it was no surprise, either. Tom was a strange man. I remember, when we first moved in, Kate came round to introduce herself and invited us to dinner. All through the meal, Tom barely uttered a word, keeping himself busy with passing plates and serving bowls, clearing up between courses, or opening bottles of wine. Kate ignored this pantomime: the conversation rolled along naturally without Tom's participation, ranging from where to buy furniture through gardening tips to what I was working on at that moment. Then, halfway through the sweet course, the talk came round to an article about twins that Janice had read in a magazine, about how twin births occur more often than is generally known, only one of the twins is absorbed by the other, or dies, in the womb. Tom listened intently.

'I should have been a twin,' he said, when Janice had finished.

My wife turned and gave him her best interested look. 'Really?'

'Yes,' Tom said, softly. 'I don't have evidence, nobody ever told me, but I know it's true. I had a twin once: maybe he died, maybe he's hidden inside me – I don't know what happened to him, but I know he existed.'

I glanced at Kate. She was staring out of the window at the darkening garden.

'But how do you know?' asked Janice.

Tom shook his head softly and gazed at her. For a moment I thought he was going to cry.

'Because I miss him,' he said. He smiled immediately, sensing he had taken the conversation too far.

'Anyway,' he continued, 'I've always thought there ought to be someone else like me in the world. Someone who sees things from my point of view.' He smiled again, to let us know he was only joking, and offered Janice more cream; then, after an awkward silence, Kate asked Janice something about her work, and the conversation continued as before.

Tom barely spoke another word for the rest of the evening.

For a time, we had the usual neighbours' arrangement with the Williamses. We took turns issuing invitations for dinner, about once a month, always leaving a loophole for excuses. Then, one late summer afternoon, Tom went out in his shirt-sleeves and never came home. Kate called the police, then the hospital; she wrote to Tom's sister in Jersey. There was no sign of him. It was as if he had vanished off the face of the earth.

I don't know what I would have done next, but it seemed to me that Kate gave up too easily. I could imagine searching for Janice for ever, if the same thing had happened to us. But Kate seemed almost relieved. She kept going to work – she only had one day off in those first few weeks of Tom's absence – and she spent the weekends in her garden; whenever I saw her, she greeted me as if she hadn't a care in the world. She seemed so contented, I was too embarrassed to ask if there was any news of Tom.

I could never imagine being with anyone but Janice; I

could never imagine wanting anyone else as I have sometimes wanted her, with the sheer vivid physicality of desire that grips me unexpectedly, even now, when I watch her applying her lipstick or fixing her hair in the mirror, or when she comes in from the bathroom, wrapped in a clean towel, with drops of water still glistening on her shoulders. I could never imagine feeling for anyone else what I feel for my wife, yet I think I fell in love with Kate Williams a little, during that first year when she was living alone. It was something about the clothes she wore: the green duffle-coat, the red and cream tartan scarf, the black woollen hat that she kept pulling down so it almost covered her eyes. I would catch myself wandering out into the garden for no reason on a Sunday afternoon, just so I could talk to her. I can't explain the sensation I had, when she put aside her rake, or hand fork, and stood chatting to me, her hands moving all the while. I was fascinated by her hands. She never wore gloves, so her fingers would usually be crusted with soil, or scratched in places where she'd caught herself on a briar or a thorn. It wasn't desire I felt, but it wasn't only compassion; it was a pure, dizzying love. Sometimes when I went back inside, after talking for a while, Janice would look at me strangely.

'What is it?' she'd ask, as if she'd read some unexpected tenderness, some unwarranted concern in my face – even though I knew my expression was quite non-committal.

'Nothing,' I would answer, casually.

'Were you talking to Kate?'

'Yes.'

'Ah.' She would pause a moment. 'How is she?'

'Fine, I think.'

'Any news of Tom?'

'I didn't ask.'

There would be another short silence then, so it would seem she was thinking of what she was about to say next for the first time.

'We ought to invite her over,' she would say, and I would agree immediately. We would tell ourselves it was the least we could do, we would look at our diaries later and set a

471

date and have her round, for dinner, or a drink. Then we would forget all about it. For different reasons, neither of us wanted her in our house. She made us feel awkward for being together, even though she seemed happy by herself. It was an assumption we made, based on our own lives, that any woman whose husband had left her must be lonely under the brave façade she maintained for the rest of the world. Or maybe it was an assumption Janice made, an assumption I was obliged to share. I wasn't altogether sure what Kate felt but, though she had never once talked about it, and even though she hadn't much liked him, Janice was certain, deep down, that Kate was waiting for Tom to come home.

I had been working all morning. The book I had just begun translating was well written and engaging, a literary biography of the poet, George Seferis. It was the culmination of a lifetime's study, a labour of love, and I felt privileged to be working on it. I had been utterly engrossed for some time: I might never have noticed Tom if I hadn't heard a flutter of wings and looked up. A bird had almost flown in through the open window, then veered away at the last moment. I barely saw it but, looking down into the sunlit rectangle of Kate's garden, I saw Tom quite clearly, sitting upright, with his arms folded, on the dark wooden bench.

He looked much as he had the day he left: his hair was a little longer, but he was wearing what looked like the same white shirt, the same light-green trousers, the same boots. It had been almost two years; now, here he was, sitting quietly in the garden, as if he'd just stepped out to take the sun. I could scarcely believe it. He looked too substantial to be a ghost or an apparition yet, at the same time, there was something unreal about his being there, in the ordinary daylight. It took a few moments for me to work out what it was about him that looked out of place, but when I did I understood how much he had changed.

The kind of people I know usually dismiss any talk of auras as mystical mumbo-jumbo, but I don't think there's anything supernatural in it. Every human body gives off a light of some kind. There are days when Janice is perfectly golden; she's someone who attracts light and adds to it a touch of her own buttermilk-yellow warmth. Other people are subtler, or more subdued: they reflect greens or blues or crimsons, depending on their mood, on how happy or tired they are. That morning, when I saw Tom sitting in his wife's garden, he was wrapped in blackness – only it was more than that, there was a kind of luminescence to his body, what I can only describe now, remembering it, as a black light. I had never seen it in him until that moment; yet, at that moment, I knew I had always suspected it was there. I've never seen it in anyone else. It was the only time I have ever encountered a tragic figure, and I knew, without hearing his story, that tragedy had somehow overtaken him, either on the day he disappeared, or sometime later, when he was lost and trying to find his way home.

I couldn't be completely sure, but I guessed he hadn't seen me. He seemed not to see anything; he simply sat stock still, with his arms folded over his chest, gazing straight ahead. I could have left him there; I could have gone back to work and pretended I hadn't noticed him. It was none of my business, after all. It wasn't as if I'd ever liked him much. As far as I was concerned, he was a bit of an oddball, a man who had casually walked out on his wife, without a word of explanation, without even a postcard to let her know if he was alive or dead.

I could have left him out there, but I didn't. I assumed he'd gone away without a key to the house, and he was waiting now, for Kate to come home and let him in. He must have known he'd have a long wait. It was a warm morning, but I wasn't sure it was warm enough for him to sit out there all day in his shirt-sleeves. I'm not sure if any of this is what I was thinking at the time, though. In the end, it was probably curiosity that made me ask him in. Or perhaps it was something more. Perhaps I was already harbouring the suspicion that what had happened to Tom and Kate could happen to anyone: that any love affair, any marriage, however passionate, however satisfying, was an invention of sorts, part good luck, part imagination. I knew, at the back of my mind, that there were times when I had to work to keep my idea of Janice intact. If that was the case, there would be times when she had to work just as hard. At one level, it was really nothing more than a conjuring trick and I was already wondering what it would take to break the spell. Perhaps that was what passed through my mind, as I walked downstairs and opened the back door, to ask Tom inside.

He didn't respond at first. He looked up and stared at me for a long, unsettling moment; I'm pretty certain he didn't recognise me: he'd forgotten who I was and, from the look on his face, I could tell I wasn't all he had forgotten.

'Would you like a cup of coffee?' I called over, in as matter-of-fact a voice as I could manage.

He stared at me in silence for a few moments longer, then shook his head.

'It's no trouble,' I said. 'Kate won't be home till later. You might as well come in for a while.'

All of a sudden, without my knowing why, I felt it was important that he come in. It had never occurred to me before, but at that moment I was aware of a kinship between us, a likeness. Perhaps he was aware of it too; or perhaps he only responded out of politeness, or sheer passivity, but he stood up then and walked over to the fence that divided the two gardens. He looked puzzled, as if he hadn't expected to find a barrier, though the fence had always been there.

'Come around the front,' I said, quietly. 'I'll put the kettle on.'

When I remember that day, I think of Tom as a ghost, a phantom who sat silently at my kitchen table, and drank three cups of coffee, one after another, like a man dying of thirst. I made small talk for a while, and he listened, with his eyes averted, nodding or shaking his head from time to time, or making small, unintelligible sounds. I talked about myself, about Janice, about people in the village, but for some time I didn't mention Kate, and I didn't ask the one question he must have known I wanted to ask more than anything. It was odd. I had to know why he had left – it wasn't my business, and it didn't really matter, one way or another. He could answer, or he could simply refuse to speak. I had nothing to lose by speaking out. Finally, I gave in to the impulse – to the real need to understand what had driven him away.

'What happened to you, Tom?' I asked him. I was aware of how quiet my voice was, of how gentle I had managed to sound. He looked up at me: he seemed quite mystified, as if he hadn't understood the question. Then, after a long pause, he sighed and shook his head.

'Nothing happened,' he answered, just as quietly. 'Well, nothing I could tell you about. I just went for a walk that day, and realised I couldn't go home. It wasn't right any more. It wasn't fair on Kate.'

'It wasn't very fair to go off without even letting her know where you were,' I replied, a little more sharply than I had intended.

He gazed at me. He seemed stunned, and I realised, even before he spoke, that Kate had lied to us – by omission, no doubt, but intentionally, nevertheless.

'Did Kate tell you that?' Tom asked.

'Well,' I said, in as conciliatory a tone as I could manage, 'not in so many words. I suppose we just assumed.'

He nodded. 'Of course.'

He spoke as quietly as ever, but there was bitterness in his voice. 'I telephoned her,' he said. 'And I wrote, four times. I couldn't tell her where I was, but I wanted her to know I was all right.'

He set his cup aside and stood up. 'I'll be going now,' he said. 'Thanks for the coffee.'

I stood up too.

'Kate won't be back for hours,' I said. 'You can stay here if you like. I'll just be upstairs. Make some coffee. Keep warm.'

He smiled slightly. 'That's kind of you,' he said, 'but I'm not waiting for Kate.'

He moved towards the door.

'Then why did you come?' I asked.

'I was happy here,' he replied. 'That was a long time ago, but I still think about it.'

I didn't speak. I couldn't think of anything to say and, for a moment, I thought he was on the point of telling me his story after all. Then the moment passed and I knew he would never tell anyone why he had left, not even his wife. He couldn't.

'The garden looks nice, don't you think?' he said.

I nodded. 'It's beautiful.'

He looked down at his feet and I thought he was about to cry. 'I just wanted to see,' he said at last.

He smiled again and made his way through the hall to the front door and stood waiting for me to open it, to let him go back into the nothing from which he had come.

'Where will you go?' I asked.

He shook his head slightly. 'I don't know,' he said. 'Anyway. Thanks.'

He made a slight gesture that made me think he wanted to shake hands, but before I could respond, he turned and walked away, a man in his shirt-sleeves, out for a walk in the empty suburbs.

A few nights later, I couldn't sleep. I decided to get up and work for a while: it's something I do from time to time, to get me through the insomniac hours. I work well at night, and I enjoy being alone, listening to the owls as they flit back and forth along the river bank.

I had gone through to the study, as usual, to avoid disturbing Janice but, before I could switch on the lamp, I caught a glimpse of white, moving in the dark, beneath our apple tree. It was only the ghost of a movement and, when I looked again, there was nothing; yet I was sure, without knowing why, that Tom was there. It was an absurd idea: even Tom couldn't disappear like that, in a single movement, melting into the darkness, crossing back into the limbo to which he now belonged. Yet I was convinced that he had returned, as a ghost returns, for one more look at the garden his wife had made.

I didn't tell Janice that Tom had been in our kitchen and, of course, I didn't mention his late-night visit. I didn't say anything to Kate, either. There was no point. Tom had come home for his own reasons, and now he was gone. Kate continued in her garden and I still admired her handiwork, but only from a distance. I no longer invented excuses to go out and speak to her; I think she must have noticed the change, but she didn't seem bothered by it. She was happy that Tom had gone. There was something offensive about that happiness, but I didn't want to spoil it by telling her what I knew.

Yet perhaps there was another reason why I didn't want to talk about Tom's visits. I'm still not quite sure what I felt then, or how I feel now, but to speak at all would have been something like an admission of guilt, of thinking the wrong thing and so putting my faith in danger. It would have meant admitting to my suspicion that love is an act of faith. It may come by chance, it may begin as something else, but it continues only by a deliberate and sustained effort; it doesn't endure of itself, it has to be maintained, by strength of will and the force of imagination. I wasn't sure what Janice believed, but I had no intention of tempting providence by discussing Tom, or Kate, or how fragile I knew our lives were. We could grow apart, or we could take one another for granted; we might meet other people and drift into something easy and fleeting; I could look up from a newspaper some spring morning and find myself gazing at a stranger. If we had ever stopped to think, we might have seen all the possibilities. Part of the game we were playing, part of the act we had to sustain, was pretending the danger wasn't there. As far as we were concerned, we believed we would exist for ever in that house; we would never die, or if we did, we would vanish together, without a sound, leaving no trace behind. That was the superstition by which we lived: what we didn't recognise wouldn't find us. We assumed the bad things would happen to other people and went on living, with our eyes averted, moving from one day to the next, with no obvious purpose; but all that time, in complete secrecy, we were working to maintain the fiction we had to believe, in order to carry on.

E. A. Markham

SAFE HOUSE FOR PHILPOT

PEWTER STAPLETON

IF THE LETTER was confusing the tape was more so, and I seem to have spent the entire weekend reading myself into a tangle. OK, Castine was on the island. The island was now recognised by CNN, no one could doubt its existence any longer. Furthermore – and the tape made the claim seem credible, there were lots of voices, many of them French – at one time there had been as many as fifteen hundred people on the island of St Caesare, evacuees from Montserrat, courtesy of the French air force. The French had also dropped tents and rations for 1,500 people for three days. But they changed their mind in mid-operation and re-evacuated to Guadeloupe and Antigua. They left rations and 600 tents on the island, now in possession of Castine. With Castine was the Commander seeking asylum which, in my name, Castine had granted. We were to address all correspondence to *The* Castine. Barville Post Office. St Caesare. West Indies.

I couldn't be bothered to work it out; another of Horace's jokes; Horace not taking his tablets; Horace feeling neglected by those of us abroad getting on with our own lives. I was in the middle of editing a book of plays and I wanted to make use of the Easter break – no teaching, no students – and was determined not to be side-tracked, despite the flattery. Castine was a literary invention of mine, oh, over two decades ago; but as my projected literary career stubbornly failed to take off, Castine wasn't exactly a household name.

So I quietly accepted the compliment and tried to get on with my editing.

It was odd, though, that the volcano should bring into existence an island that I'd more or less created. And in the right place. Uncanny. Though I could live with that; because the island may not have been *exactly* in the place where I had put it: what seemed to have moved the argument on was Horace's claim of having given the Commander asylum. Horace had slipped into his role of Governor, of Priest; *the* Castine. The Commander was a sort of reproach to me that I dreamt about, relieved I hadn't had to encounter him in recent years. Earlier, he had grown used to my support, and when I tried to distance myself he accused me of something unpleasant. You had to remind yourself not to be fazed by this, for the man was a bigamist, a member of the Kreuger gang and a murderer: you could withstand the charge of moral cowardice coming from Commander Philpot. But Horace couldn't have known much of this. So, they were on the island, my island, a madman and a murderer. Or have I got it wrong again?

On with the editing.

THE HISTORY

I remember years and years ago having a conversation with a friend, a historian from Montserrat; he had written a 'History' of Montserrat including all the usual stuff about Columbus naming it on his second voyage in 1493, naming it without landing because his Arawak guides told him the island was uninhabited. (Though he also didn't land on Antigua and other islands that he had named on that trip.) We had several conversations on this subject.

A hundred and thirty years after that Columbus afterthought the Irish stumbled on the same uninhabited island of Montserrat, which bore traces of habitation everywhere. When I pressed my historian friend for an answer to the vanishing population – documented information which he didn't challenge – he reminded me that these were hurricane islands, earthquake islands, but that without studying the archaeological evidence, and maybe taking on board the anthropology of the Mesoamerican people, he couldn't speculate. Well, these weren't my disciplines, so I was prepared to speculate.

I'm speculating now: It's 1492, early in the year, before the arrival of you know who; the region is *pre*-Isabella, *pre*-Ferdinand. So, this is *not* Guanahani, this is St Caesare, hot and guilty, fresh up from the sea, wisps of smoke – not yet named, of course. The Great Man comes by a year later (what the world calls his Second Voyage) and *misses* it because he comes up on the wrong side, the Montserratian side from Dominica going north. The guides didn't tell him the twin island had cooled down enough for patches of vegetation to appear, a place possible for their friends to camp out as the priests had divined that Montserrat was due to blow in three days. Though it was a bright morning, the Italian took the cloud of smoke hanging above Montserrat as mist, and diverted himself by naming Antigua to the east and Redonda straight ahead as he sailed on.

So there you have it. Taking risks the historian couldn't, I had the new island warming up enough in the mid-1620s to deter the Irish dissidents, expelled from St Kitts by Governor Warner: they gave the unnamed mountain wide berth (granting it a few choice Cromwellian epithets) and settled on neighbouring Montserrat, unaccountably still uninhabited. Then the French got into the act, came by and named it. 1660s. A Cartesian joke, probably, calling it Caesar's island; a place from which to keep watch on the English (and Portuguese and Spanish and Dutch and anyone else they could think of); a smugglers' nest and a place later proposed, and rejected, for an Emperor's exile.

After centuries of colonial neglect it became *my* island in 1972 when, in Sweden, I needed to attend a conference, a UN-sponsored conference on the sea, and my advisers said that being ambassador of somewhere obscure would help: what are uninhabited islands for (with the Arawaks long gone) but to have you represent them in calm and grown-up places like Stockholm?

Our HORACE/Our CASTINE

In the seventies Horace had briefly held a post with an international agency in Europe and this, despite everything, made us inclined to give him the benefit of the doubt. But that was a memory more or less erased now. The letter was redirected from my London address to Sheffield and got here the day before Good Friday.

The St Caesare postmark made me suspect more than a joke because just over a fortnight ago my sister had rung from London to say that she'd received a package for me. From St Caesare. It was obviously from Horace, playing the fool. And – she was a wicked wit, my sister – she congratulated me on having secured my own island at last, complete with Post Office. She wanted to know if I had sent out the stamp machine to Horace: so when were we all going to go and settle down on my estate, sort of thing. But after the knockabout she revealed her real concern for the people of Montserrat where the volcano was threatening, yet again, to blow: how could they bear it? We had family there, too, who were old and sick; no one knew where they were camping out: you couldn't contact anyone who had been evacuated, and they didn't think of getting a message to you. Then there was this funny report by CNN that there were people on St Caesare! I had told her to hang on to the parcel because I would try to get down to London over Easter. But after getting Horace's letter I rang and asked her to put the parcel in the post.

It didn't help; it clearly was a joke, but that didn't help. There was no stamp as such on either letter or package (which turned out to be a tape) but a franking machine had been used – why did it cost the same amount to send both letter and package overseas? And why was it in French francs, as it would have been in my version of the island? The letter said that Castine was in post, that things were calm, that his little Latin and less Greek had grown rusty so he had stopped labelling the island vegetation, and would pick up that aspect of things when I arrived to help out. Meanwhile, he would continue to secure the family lands. That was the letter. If there was too little information in the letter there was too much on the tape.

There were lots of voices on the tape, voices in French as well as those that were clearly Montserratian, following Horace's self-conscious 'The isle is full of noises' introduction. People sounded tired and subdued rather than panicky. They told stories of endurance and rescue, breaking off to send messages to friends and family that they were alive and OK. Apparently, a couple of people had been drowned and a few injured but on the whole everything was OK, though with the ash and sludge everywhere, even if homes survived intact, everything would be spoilt. God was good, good in mysterious ways. There was universal praise for the French who had kept them warm and dry and had supplied food, as well as mounting the rescue effort. One or two even sent prayers and blessings to me and my family (my mother, now dead), clearly thinking that I had had something to do with it.

When I checked with my sister again she said it was CNN who had told the people they were on St Caesare; and when you're tired and traumatised you'd believe anything. She thought maybe they had taken the evacuees to nearby Redonda and realising there was nothing there, had then moved them on to Guadeloupe and Antigua.

So how did she account for Horace thinking he was on St Caesare? And the St Caesare postmark?

Oh, Horace was a sad case. And didn't I hear the latest? The British were sending out infected beef to the islands as part of their aid effort, so Horace was clearly the first one to come down with the mad cow disease. But it wasn't right, it wasn't right for old and sick people to be moved around like baggage, one day here, another day there, not even knowing what island you were on.

I called various people who, like my sister, had Sky-TV, and tried to piece together the information. No one could make much sense of it though the feeling was that the French were putting energy into the operation to claw back some credit, their public credibility after the nuclear tests in the South Pacific and their dodgy operations in Africa and the

Middle East needing some sort of lift. That's why they had dropped all those tents on an uninhabited island in the Eastern Caribbean.

But there's no doubt they had established a massive refugee camp on the island. The BBC, apparently, had confirmed this, but not the name of the island – though the BBC had continued to tarnish its reputation for accuracy by repeatedly referring to the Dominican Republic instead of Dominica as the place where the British Government, under Saudi pressure, had wished to send Saudi dissident Muhammad al-Masari into exile. The *Guardian* had, in the same issue, referred to Montserrat as a British colony (true) and as a Spanish island (false) and to St Caesare as a nearby French dependency. Both the *Financial Times* and the *Spectator* mentioned evacuees having been taken to St Caesare. Because I'd been busy with my editing I hadn't been watching the news or reading the papers, so I hadn't come across any other reports.

But the Montserratians had been taken off St Caesare island. Horace's figures had been confirmed: 1,500 people had been involved; 600 tents had been dropped with rations for three days. When they were re-evacuated after only a day the tents and rations were left. And it seems that the Castine and the Commander were now the only inhabitants of the island.

There was a mischievous message on Horace's tape that the Commander sent his best to me, and said he'd never doubted that I'd deliver. (Philpot getting in a low blow.)

THE CASTINE

Framingham. Nr Boston. USA. Dr Ruth Krim looks at the time and sighs; it'll be too late now to do anything. What's the point in having a night off if you can't even get it together to go to a movie? Is she growing pathetic in her old age? A woman past forty living like a student? But without the car, going into Boston is out of the question. But it was right right right to go back to school even if it meant you didn't have a life, even if it meant debts you didn't even want to think about and being holed up here, still, in Framingham. She doesn't have anything against the Portuguese, it's just Framingham; not that she wants to go back to Boston, to Brookline – way out of reach now, anyway: maybe she'd take up that offer to share an apartment in Weston – a bit far out but maybe safer; security, security. Something flares inside her that life has to revolve round *is it safe, is it safe?* as if she's some Nazi criminal in a Dustin Hoffman film. Ah, well, she's too tired to go out anyway; and too depressed. Workdepressed. Lifedepressed. Come on, girl, pop something into the microwave and *eat*; pretend to have a normal life. See if there's a video worth watching.

Why is it that turkey no longer tasted of anything? Or is it Framingham? Or having a TV dinner on your own? With the prospect of years of the same coming up? She doesn't want to think about work. Lucky to have a job, they say, but she doesn't ever want to go near burns victims ever again. Or stroke victims. Victims don't cheer you up. She needs a personal comedian, that's what she needs. Maybe she's just more tired than she thinks, for when she turns on the video and sees some foreign army doing heroics on an offshore island and hears the name St Caesare, she panics and thinks things must be getting to her.

SHEFFIELD

Twenty-four years ago I invented the character Castine. I was travelling in Sweden with my partner, Ruth. Ruth Krim. We'd had a bad experience on the outskirts of Stockholm and were more or less rescued by a couple in the Tampax business. Olga and Matz were a Danish-Swedish mother and son whom we contacted, and they set us up in a flat in the middle of Stockholm free of charge. They were only friends of a friend whom we'd met in London at a poetry-reading venue, so their generosity was appreciated. They adopted us partly for their own mildly voyeuristic reasons (which we didn't mind, particularly) but also because of our 'spirit': they claimed the outsider's privilege to be bored by Swedish Volvo dullness and lack of imagination. They found us small jobs giving poetry readings in the Old Town; and we also gave the odd performance to the American draft-dodgers (there were reputed to be 40,000 of them in the city) when we could. The Tampax daddy had been an airline pilot (and his wife flew planes as a hobby) but he also ran a small business making herbal tea; and we were initiated into that, a messy job but well-paid, and convenient because the herbs and berries for the brew were kept in the basement of the building.

Largely to live up to their expectations Ruth and I decided to gatecrash the UN Conference of the Sea being held in Stockholm. It was Olga who had casually remarked that if we were writers of imagination and short of money we might consider it an adventure to turn up at the conference and bluff our way in as official delegates. After all, there were people from all over the South Pacific, from islands no one had ever heard of, so it shouldn't be difficult. It was, in a way, inviting us to sing for our supper. So within two or three days I had transformed myself into Castine, 'native' representative of St Caesare (what today we'd call 'First Nation' representative) in the Eastern Caribbean, with Dr Ruth Krim, anthropologist and linguist, the beautiful American, as my official interpreter.

FRAMINGHAM

Ruth is impatient, excited; she's on the phone, enunciating to show this is long distance.

'The little creep,' she says, not unkindly. 'So where's he got to now, he still in Manchester? . . . I expect he's married with lots of kids. Oh. Let me just get a piece of paper. I guess Sheffield's the place where you get all that steel, uh?'

She's writing down the telephone number and maintaining the conversation.

'OK, OK; I'm good, I guess . . . And is 0114 the code for Manchester, sorry, Sheffield? Right . . .'

She listens for a bit, then. 'Oh, I suppose it's just going back to school and sort of losing touch and. So how're you folks doing over there? . . . Well, thanks for the number, say hello to everyone, I don't know if you're in touch with people like Simon and Gunda. OK. Well . . . Oh, one last thing before I sign off. *Don't*, I mean, on any account, eat British beef, that's official.'

She kills the tone and immediately starts dialling; stops. 'The little creep.' She puts down the receiver but continues talking to herself in a normal voice. '*I* took the risks, you creep. I was the one to do the last-minute dash to Oslo to sort out the language. He just had to dress up and be colourful. And teaching in Sheffield certainly beats fucking Framingham any day.'

This time she does dial.

PHILPOT

I knew Philpot before he was the Commander and that makes me sentimental: we are dangerous, sentimental people, we sacrifice the individual to save humanity. Rubbish. And we say rubbish when you tell us this. Rubbish. That, they tell me, is my problem. OK, so I can safely stop worrying about failing eyesight and of dreaming about my hygienist in other circumstances, her mouth open instead of mine: I can treat nagging thoughts about unpaid bills and debts and overwork and lack of fame and being raped by a man and editing a book nobody's going to read – I can treat all of these to a local anaesthetic: these things are nothing compared to my problem which is sentimentality.

But Philpot is an important part of my life. He belongs to that going-with-ideas strand of my life. Whether that's unfinished business or abandoned business I leave to others to tease out. I don't want to be bothered now by Philpot; I don't have energy for Philpot, I want to get back to my editing; there'll be serious questions there, enough, and we can call them aesthetic ones; then we'll come up roses.

OK, I give up. Philpot: *This here island's too small for the both of us*. Philpot and I came over on the same boat in 1956. From Montserrat. Of course I was a schoolboy and he a man deep into his twenties. We seemed to be about the only two people on the three-week voyage who didn't get sick. So we strutted a bit, the young scholar and the man of the world who had done the usual things: labouring on government works projects all over the island – building the new grammar school, the hospital in Plymouth, the new jetty after the '54 storms. Here were we setting out on conquest; I would be the General, he the troops. I would command, as the ancients did, in Latin and Greek; Philpot would be the new boys, the Russians and Americans *combined*. 'Watch this hand,' he'd say, holding up an arm; 'I coming for you, women of every shape and size in London, England. Feel this muscle. This is man who cut cane, work cotton ginnery, grind cassava; you ever see Englishman with muscle like this?' On the boat we sealed the pact with Italian wine which, after the second day or so, we were the only two 'tourists' in a position to drink.

True, we more or less parted company in England. He went to live somewhere near Finsbury Park and we settled in Maida Vale, and 'England' intervened, really. Then I remember that strange winter of '62–'63 when I was holed up in Wales, at Lampeter; and if my memory serves me right the first man through that Russian landscape was Philpot. He had come to Wales to ask my advice considering I was a scholar and that my subject was philosophy. The problem? Maureen, the woman he lived with, was about to have a baby and Philpot wanted me to look through my books, my Plato and Aristotle and the logic of things Greek, to come up with a suitable name for it.

This created a difficulty; apart from other things I hadn't actually got to Aristotle yet, apart from background stuff like Russell's *A History of Western Philosophy*, and I suspect Aristotle may have been the one most likely to name babies. But we had a go; can't let the troops down. I remember taking down a book from my shelves: Voltaire's *Philosophical Dictionary*. So, starting at the start, how about Abraham? Or was that too tame. Though Abraham was a Big Daddy of a name in several cultures. Asia Minor. Arabia. And it must have been Voltaire who suggested the international possibilities for Philpot's child – Thoth (Egyptian), Zoroaster (Persian), Hercules (Greek), Odin (Swedish), etc.

Nothing there. But we had time, the baby wasn't due in weeks. After Sunday lunch, at which Philpot pronounced himself satisfied with the Latin grace which went well with the gown, we thought of being up-to-date and robust, something German, perhaps. But Philpot thought that would threaten the English, reminding them of the bomb-sites all over London, and they would probably kill the child as a war criminal to prevent it moving into the middle classes where it belonged.

So it was back to the classics for a name that would fit. There'd been a programme on television on the Shah of Iran's 'White Revolution', and that gave us Cyrus and Darius and Xerxes. But you couldn't assume the child would be a boy so I had a look – seeing we were in Wales – at the *Mabinogion* to see if some Welsh Queen would come through. But Philpot objected. We should stick to boys' names. Even if I came up with something girlie from the *Mabinogion*, the book was too hard to pronounce and a man shouldn't make a fool of himself by not being able to pronounce the source of his child's name. Furthermore, he liked a good, strong name that would suit either boy or girl. When the child was born, a girl, they called her Nigel.

Philpot came back to Lampeter, down the old A40, to see my play the following year, and to apologise for allowing himself to be overruled by the women who had made him change Nigel's name for something girlie. The child, he felt now, would always be ordinary. But we had a good time after the play, talking philosophy, chopping logic.

THE MURDERS

Murders start out as things innocent as words. Philpot at

the supermarket in some northern town he's not used to, explaining why he has to take action against the assistant who refused to wrap his cheese. Philpot on his coach deep in the country, middle England. Behind him, schoolboy beating up schoolgirl. Everyone on the coach relaxed about it. Philpot pulls up, threatens to shoot the boy dead, to, well, just take him out unless he got his shit together. But the passengers take exception to the language of the coach driver, for this is middle England not America; and the driver shrugs and drives on. *Again*, Philpot on the phone asking about his telephone bill. The account is closed, the voice at the other end says. The account is not closed, Philpot says, I've got it in front of me. The account is closed, the girl says, using one of those voices you want to push back down her not-really-expensive throat. Can you put me on to the Manager, Philpot says. Why, she says. What d'you mean, why, I want someone who knows what he's talking about. *I* know what I'm talking about, she says. No, you don't. Don't talk to me in that tone of voice, she says. Don't *you* talk to me in that tone of voice, I'm the customer. What tone of voice, she says. *That* tone of voice, that *illiterate* tone of voice, despite the accent. You're the one that's illiterate, she says, and hangs up. So a man can't win with language; so a man will have to *act*. A man will have to accept that this is America; he might have to poison the entire water system to get redress for that voice.

This is nothing; this is old Philpot.

I suppose I detected a change in the late seventies when we came back from abroad, from Germany, with Ruth deciding to go back to America, a lowish point for us; and I have a memory of Philpot turning up in uniform. He had lost a battle at school over his daughter. Not *that* daughter, another daughter, another family. One had been deprived of her name and now this; he would not let his children subside into becoming anonymous 'black youth'. There was a war on. First they divert you; they divert you into the foolishness of getting rid of one of your families: why? Did he beat his women? He did not. He used to, but for a long time now he did not. Doris Day's husband beat Doris Day; Philpot did not beat his women. The law should come down on the husband of Doris Day and give Philpot a break. In the days when he beat women he thought he was the scum of the earth, though he acted otherwise. And all the other wife-beaters knew they were scum. Now it's different. Evidence is that there is no grand lady, no queen or princess that hasn't felt the back of some man's hand. Or worse. So don't talk to him doing his best to keep two families going. So here we were again, the soldier and the scholar. Of course there were those who said you had to be both, soldier and scholar, though that's unreasonable to expect. He'd met a fellow who claimed to be both, but the man was a fraud. Though he did write a good essay on the necessity for fraudulence; had I come across it?

There were things going on in my life which made me not entirely receptive to Philpot so all I could say was no, I hadn't come across the essay, though it reminded me vaguely of Machiavelli.

No, that wasn't it, the man's name was Kreuger.

Good name, we both agreed.

FOUNDING PERSONS

'Is that Sheffield?'

'Yes, this is Sheffield.'

'Come on, Pewter, what're you doing in Sheffield, is it the middle of the night in Sheffield or something?'

'No, it's just . . . you know, it's just . . . Sheffield, I know that voice, let me guess.'

'I hope you're not thinking of Hillary Rodham Clinton, you sound very British.'

'Ah, gets to you, gets to you. Incidentally, if anyone asks, Hillary and I are just good friends. So, Ruth, fancy hearing from you. I mean, good, *good* to hear from you.'

'You get my card?'

'Your card? No, I . . . Oh, your card! I got a card about two years ago, three years ago . . .'

'So you got my card.'

'. . . saying you were going back to school.'

'You never answered my card, creep.'

'There was no address on your card.'

'There was, too.'

'There wasn't. Otherwise . . .'

'Well, the address is a closely guarded secret. National security, and all that. So what's going on on our island?'

'Oh, you've heard about that. Weird.'

'I reckon if we've got our island then everyone's got it wrong. For years they've been getting it wrong. You know what that means? It means that old McGovern must have beaten Tricky Dick way back in '72 and that Eleanor must be out there on our island hanging out, waiting to be taken out to dinner. Remember Eleanor?'

'I remember Eleanor.'

'Remember how Eleanor complained that George was so depressed after the defeat that he wouldn't even take her out to dinner!'

'Well, Nixon won, so he got the chance to take Eleanor out. So how're you, Ruth; have you graduated? Is it Doctor Krim?'

'We won't talk about that; I'll send you my graduation photograph, if you give me your . . . Sheffield address.'

So we talked about St Caesare, with Ruth reminding me it was her island too, bringing each other up to date, though that didn't get us far; so we hung up while there was still a lot to say, giving us the excuse to ring back.

An hour later Ruth rang back. What was I doing?

I was actually in the middle of reading Ionesco's *The Killer*; so I said, nothing much, just reading the paper, doing a bit of editing. Ruth was thinking of old friends: was I in touch with Simon and Gunda?

No, I hadn't seen them in years.

What of Josh and Ginette?

Yes, but they're in France.

Do they live in France now?

No, but, you know.

And how're they doing?

Oh, you know.

And who else was there? Simon and Jo.

Yes, yes. Of course I don't get down to London that often. Well, I do but, you know, I don't stay over that often. And Simon and Jo have got their own place now.

What of Hanz and Karen?

Oh, I'm not in touch with Germany.

OK, who do we know in England? The Leanings in Manchester, are they still alive?

Wouldn't have thought so; they were, what, fifty-six, when we knew them, sort of late seventies. Mid to late seventies; and she had angina and was in and out of hospital. Though *he* wasn't ill, no, he must be around somewhere, though probably not in Higher Openshaw.

Ruth liked the Leanings.

Yes. Maybe I'll . . . Yes.

And talking of Sweden. Any news of Matz and Olga?

We must contact Matz and Olga. Because St Caesare is their island, too. Olga was sixty, which means. No, she's only mid-eighties. Now about Matz, we're not so sure.

So who else was there?

Oh . . . How about, let's see . . . Kate and Hernandez?

Who are Kate and Hernandez?

No one, I just made them up.

I see your jokes haven't improved; your jokes will be banned on the island.

PHILPOT

He pointedly didn't blame me for the break-up of his marriage, his marriages. Philpot had one family in Finsbury Park and another in Scotland (in Paisley) which was convenient during the years he was a long-distance coach driver. He wished to maintain both families openly, as aristocrats do, and asked me to advise, from my reading, on how best to present the situation to the simple-minded and the morally timid. I had failed to do this, so first one then the other of his marriages had collapsed, leaving his children with more than unsatisfactory names.

Then one day he materialised to say that a friend had killed a man in order to teach others a lesson. This friend from St Vincent, a postman, had killed a man. (I noted his tact in suggesting that the 'friend' was from 'another island'.) Anyway, this was the situation.

A postman?

Yes, a postman.

So, this man was a postman and he had a sense that there was something funny about one particular house where he delivered the mail. It was clear that the woman of the house was being knocked about. Nothing as obvious as black eyes and that kind of thing. Once, when he heard whimpering inside he went round the side and looked through the window and saw her bent double easing herself up from the lino on to a chair. But some things aren't your business, you're not paid to mind other people's business in this country. And he put it out of his mind. Time passes, you have to attend to your own life. So with the Vincentian. But then he gives up his job as a postman because of the weather and takes on a job as a school caretaker, but then has to give that up because of the violence. He tries to get his old job back at the Post Office but is out of luck because the technology has changed. (Even the Post Office has changed its name.) So, to cut a long story short, he gets out the old uniform and becomes a postman again for the day.

He seeks out his old patch just to see how things are getting along. (Will they recognise him or is he just another anonymous threat?) He knocks on a familiar door with a mock-registered letter and a prepared story – you know, wrong number, wrong name, something like that. There's no answer so he goes round the side, and what he sees is not pretty to report. But the same man and woman, torturer and tortured, are demonstrating that nothing has happened in the world since he last passed this way. The neighbours, the police, God and Allah are asleep. Even the woman's stamina doesn't know when to say 'enough'; she can't be expecting rescue, she doesn't even look that much worse than before. And the man is calm, a perfumed man, in his element, smiling; he invites the postman in, prepared to have a little chat, not bothered about the concentration camp in his kitchen. So the Vincentian does a bit of sign language as if he's an idiot, smiles, and withdraws, not for him to intrude on the people's thing. But that night he comes back with a friend, and they persuade the torturer to go for a drive to a place you don't need to know about, and they let him understand that this thing won't be quick.

The Vincentian was a follower of a thinker who called himself Kreuger, though we suspected that wasn't his real name; and this was the phase of preventive action; and this was a service that more and more bruised and scarred women were beginning to call on.

HORACE

I never quite understood the term 'Ur-Shakespeare'; but I fancy this is Horace's phase. Not for him Gonzalo's *The Tempest* speech; he would admit traffic, he would be magistrate, etc. On his island 'letters', in both senses of the term, would be known. He would take care of management of the family lands, castigate idleness and not necessarily insist that island women be pure. And he would make himself spiritually responsible for the Commander.

The last time I saw Horace was after the 1989 hurricane, hurricane Hugo. I'd flown out to Montserrat as part of the relief effort; and we landed on the offshore island, courtesy of the smugglers. There, we waited for the ferry to Montserrat. Horace's sister Margot, who was a government official, was expected to meet us there, but she was engaged elsewhere, and instead we were met by a little group headed by Horace. He looked like a priest down on his luck, but what I'd taken to be a dog-collar was just the top of a white T-shirt underneath the rest of the costume. The rains had continued after the hurricane and even such clothing as was saved was

impossible to get dry, so Horace was taking advantage of the
general dress spree before the Red Cross hand-outs imposed
the more conventional look of have-nots.

Scorning to dwell on his own predicament, he made gentle
fun, I seem to remember, of my greying hair. Even then he presented himself as Margot's representative: Horace was your perpetual stand-in. He was irritating, he embarrassed us, he looked
after our interests in ways we wouldn't have sanctioned even if
we knew what he was doing. (He had escaped to France once,
via Guadeloupe, and through exploiting friends and family,
managed to erect a couple of benches in the Alpes Maritimes
to a great-aunt of ours who had apparently died a heroine.) You
could be angry with Horace, but it was an effort.

Maybe he was the right Governor for the island.

FOUNDING PERSONS

'So you're not married with children and . . .'

'Afraid not.'

'. . . making the world more crowded.'

'Nah. And what of you?'

'Oh, men are . . . difficult propositions.'

This was getting awkward, so we talked about St Caesare.
'Can you remember your Castine speech?' Ruth asked. (It was
early evening and I was trying to calculate the right sort of
tone to adopt for America in the middle of the afternoon.)

'Course not, that was twenty years ago. Twenty-five.'

'*Uuyeewang moro wiinong iikanabairong.* Got that?'

'Ridiculous.'

'Remember what it means?'

'Oh. I'm sure it's something like: ME BIG CHIEF. ME DRINKY
MORE COCONUT WATER THAN LITTLE CHIEF.'

'Yes dear, very funny. "Upon everybody bestow that which
is good." Got that? Remember that? Though I hope you're
not still talking in translation.'

'I think you're making it up. You know I just thought of
a use for our island. We could rent it to the BBC for all

those people they send to desert islands. It'll be groaning with Bibles and Shakespeare, but think of all that music; we could sell some of the classical stuff and keep the Dylan and the jazz.'

'That sounds a bit stressful.'

'We can always get rid of the Bible.'

'Yes, dear, but what do we do about your jokes.'

'Talking about jokes, I heard a good one by Norman Mailer.'

'Oh no.'

'No, really. He's in this downtown restaurant. *Elaine's*. Manhattan.'

'That fool.'

'He's having dinner, and this English reporter comes up with her microphone, because, you know, *Elaine's* is the place to be if you're a writer or. And she says. "Are you Norman Mailer?" And he says, "Yes, I'm Norman Mailer," surprised that anyone should recognise him and. And quick as a flash he says: "I'm getting to be so old I live in Massachusetts. Er."'

'Fool.'

'It sounded better first time round. So we won't have any Mailer jokes; what else?' (I was thinking we should have Andrea, the hygienist at my dentist's, but I wasn't going to own up to that.)

'It'd be nice to have everyone come to visit, maybe once a year. But you know what I'd really like?'

'What's that?'

'A really good chemist. Stacks and stacks of stuff, never running out. And maybe a reflexologist.'

'A reflexologist! Someone mucking about with your feet!'

'I knew you wouldn't be ready for the island.'

And we talked about being ready for the island, the most comprehensively stocked desert island with Shakespeare, Bibles and luxuries, and above all, music. Add to that – a large, benign animal that was not a carnivore. (We took it for granted that among the luxuries was a strawberries-and-cream plant (strawberries-and-no-fat-cream plant) and a statue of Muhammad Ali.) There'd be no place, repeat no place for Bob Dole after the débâcle of '96. But, talking politics, a luxury could include the voice of Irish President Mary Robinson, acceptable to both parties, like soft Irish rain, warm and health-giving; also a pastrami sandwich place like the one on the corner of Arlington and the main street, though Framingham must never be mentioned. Instead of Framingham, the second town or main village should be called McGovern (or maybe even Dakota – not quite Omaha – but maybe something like Sioux Falls, though not Badlands). Or just call it McGovern. Or George 'n Eleanor. And what else? Definitely no bicycles on a mountainous island (a reference to Ruth's difficulty in riding a bicycle in flat Stockholm in 1972); certainly no pressure to ride bicycles. Granted. And the luxury of luxuries: a troupe of players as in Shakespeare, better still in Jonson, dwarfs and mountebanks, fat men with high-pitched voices and women who could play Lear; and they would, of course, do Molière and Chekhov and Soyinka and improving speeches from Emerson.

Don't shoot, don't shoot, this isn't a plague of locusts, these are tuneless songbirds migrating from the English country-side. Wrong again, I'm bleeding something other than blood, and my eyes are open: that's what comes when you go to bed thinking of a woman visiting campus with her baby; or thinking of Ruth creating a language; thinking of the hygienist; thinking of Audrey, the cleaner, ten years your senior while reading a few pages of Henderson the Rain King. *Seamlessly, the woman with the baby comes across a big tree sawn off at the root: the flesh-like wound causes her to turn the baby's head away. The experiment with the cleaner, ten years your senior, hasn't worked, doesn't buy credit, doesn't serve to extend your life: her cheerfulness relentlessly closes the ten-year gap between you; she recommends having all your teeth out, and a seaside holiday. The next cleaner must be ten years on the other side of you. A moral issue? Ruth is over forty now, who's to blame for that? Framingham? Time to count sheep.*

It's raining, the tents have an eerie feel; I miss them, though I

know they're there. I'm dashing from tent to tent of this ghost
city and bump into Professeur Croissant, an old teacher from
the village in Montserrat, long dead: he looks the same as he
always did, maybe that's why I know he's dead. Without
surprise he points out the burial-ground (ah, he changes into
the Commander, but never mind): he points to the place where
Horace, in his robes, is reburying a member of the family,
disturbed by the earthquake in Montserrat. When I realise
that other members of the family, long dead, are piled up
waiting reburial, I wake in panic, in relief. And reach for
the book.

Strangely familiar, while I'm trying to figure out where the
landmines, which were definitely in the dream, fitted in.
Strangely familiar because I'd picked up the wrong book,
the Ionesco, which I'd just finished reading; not really finding
a justification for murder; though the Architect and Berenger
seem dated, childhood figures, 'Their Radiant City', a seventies
title, a book long-read. It's true, isn't it, that both Mill and
Kant justified capital punishment. And there was some clown
on the radio recently going on about suttee. Good thing for
women of eighteen, bereaved. I'm thinking that I would provide Philpot a safe house in Europe, live up to expectations,
come through, accept my historical responsibility.

I'm reading Bellow, but reading doesn't distract you, except
to make you vaguely superior to the bulk of England asleep
and vulnerable. Matz and Olga's basement in Stockholm
would do, then he could make the herbal tea, be useful.
Or bring him to Manchester, Higher Openshaw: rewrite
the Leanings into history. Though again, Germany at the
moment seems tempting before it settles down to order.
(Which is more dangerous, civil order or disorder? Discuss.)
Billet him on our old friends the Moogs out in Buckfost. Herr
and Frau Moog, one son and one daughter – bright child,
the daughter ('I want to do my homework, I want to help
to make Germany strong again'). Or maybe we should ease
up on Philpot, take him across the river to Ebertplatz, our
old stamping-ground, Aquinostrasse, where Ruth and I had

problems with the Turks, and with the Köln police, seriously big and cigar-smoking (or that may have been the taxi-driver, the night in question). Whatever. The Commander is a man with cane-cutting skills, a follower of Kreuger.

It's too late to ring Ruth. (On the island it would be useful to have one of those fellows from *Gardener's Question Time*, with his Latin, to help Horace out with the plants, the one with the accent which doesn't grate too much: a castaway would have left Pliny's *Natural History*.) Bellow promises too many pages. Tomorrow, I'll ring my sister and ask if it's true that the volcano has disturbed the family burial-ground.

Once, a long time ago, Philpot asked me a question which I thought might be philosophical; it had to do with the nature of *time*. Precisely: *Where does time come from?* I thought I'd work on this, a chance to shine. But he quickly put me right. He was into being domestic, doing the cooking, and noticed that *thyme* had disappeared from the shelves round his way, even in the supermarket: what was going on there? What Third-World thyme-growing country was being torched to impair his cooking? As a scholar I should know. I might put my mind to that now (for you can't, seriously, justify editing at this hour of the morning); and really, Saul Bellow is such an odd name for a man, don't you think?

Adam Thorpe

TYRES

MY FATHER STARTED the business in 1925, the year of my birth. It was a good business: roads were rough and tyres were punished. In those days, there was the inner tube, and the outer casing of hard rubber. I always saw these as the body and the soul. Don't ask me why.

The main road is very straight, and always has been: Roman, they say. In those days there wasn't much traffic, although at the time we thought it was busy. Life would go by us, and now and again stop. We were proud that M. Michelin was a Frenchman: for once we had invented something useful, instead of making a lot of noise about nothing. No, really, I am proud of our business.

I started helping my father as soon as I could stand upright, just as he had helped his father, who was a blacksmith, hammering hot iron tyres to wooden rims. I was at first scared of the hiss of the compressors, of the great blade that took off the rubber, peeling it like an orange. I learnt to see a tyre as sad, when its chin lay flat on the ground, melting away – and when it was fat and full and bounced, it was happy. My father could roll the tyres like a man I once saw in a circus that came to the village. The worn, sad ones lay leaning each upon the other like old men one side of the yard: my father would roll another so that it fell exactly into place against the end. He called this 'playing his accordion'. Some of the farmers would take these old tyres away, for use on the farms, where they would have a second life under a trailer, bouncing behind a horse or perhaps a donkey over stony fields. In very hard frosts, they would heap up the old, dead tyres at the ends of the fields, so that the evil smoke would scare the frost away from the vine-buds. Not everyone did this: it was my father's idea, I believe, and they didn't like to think he could tell them things, a man who had turned away from the land.

My father would tell me, when I was old enough, how one must never fall short of the highest standards, in this job. The road was getting busier, and the future looked rosy. But, he said, if you fall short of the highest standards and start 'cutting corners', or grow sloppy and let a man drive away with a set of tyres unevenly inflated, or with an inner tube that – from the very kindest of intentions – you have pretended to yourself is passable though frayed in one spot, or with a tread that is smooth as here (he'd smack his furrowed brow), you might be sending that man to his death. Every time we heard of a local accident, our hearts beat faster, and not only because this unfortunate occurrence might have involved someone dear to us; many, if not most, of those running around on the roads at that time were putting their faith in our rigour and honesty and skill. Even I, a pimply young lad handling the bicycle trade (how much more considerable it was in those days!) knew that my hands were capable of bringing injury or even death, if I let my attention wander, or felt too lazy to triple-check a pressure or a repair or a bolt or the depth of a tread.

The blessed Trinity, my father called it: the check, the double-check, and the Holy-Ghost-check. Who was a Protestant through and through.

Even the local *curé* would use us. My father and he drank together, in the little office with its Dunlop tyre-clock, talking about Verdun or other things closed to me, while I dealt with the *curé*'s battered old bicycle – a Raleigh, from his time in Flanders. M. Dunlop and M. Michelin: these were my father's gods. I would like to say that my father was like the Michelin man, but he wasn't: I was always, from maturity, bigger than he ever was, but he was never fat. His face has always had an emaciated look, perpetually sucking on its dead cigarette, glossy with grease and seamed with dirt. Tyres pick up the filth of the world, they are not fussy. In their treads I have found the hair and blood of small, hapless creatures. In the great chasms of a giant truck's treads I once found a shrew, intact but quite lifeless, its tiny paws folded as my mother's were on her death-bed, in the room smelling of camphor and candles.

So the road passed by us in a blur, and now and again would come the tell-tale sounds of tyres turning into our yard, scrunching over the grit and dust, and we would lift our heads to look, squinting in the heat and glare or rubbing our hands in the cold.

André Paulhan et Fils. That sign was painted in 1942, when I was seventeen. I was very proud.

The next day, we saw our first German limousine. We had seen German trucks before, passing through the unoccupied zone, on their way to elsewhere, but never before had we seen a big, black Mercedes, with a little flag fluttering on its bonnet, and motor-cycle outriders. It did not stop. There was much less activity on the road, after the country was defeated, but my bicycle hands were kept busier. Our old tyres were soon used up, and new tyres were only fitfully available, until my father came to some agreement with the local powers in the town. We had no family there, except some distant cousin of my mother's: we are all from further up, in the mountains, the Paulhans. There is a tiny village in the chestnut country, about ten kilometres from where we lived at the time (when we weren't sleeping on the job, as happened two or three days in the week), which is mostly bats and ruined walls, and a simple church. That was our village, once. At least, the *mas* was ours, and the *mas* was well nigh a village in itself. I won't go into the reasons for our dispersion, or we shall be here all night. Suffice to say that it was not for wanting to see the world, or the descent of the Holy Spirit one Pentecost! We go at each other hammer and tongs, still, the Paulhan clan, until we are threatened. Then we hold as fast to each other as one of my tyres to its rim. We don't meet much, these days.

One time, in March or April 1943, my father came back from town one day, looking very pleased with himself. He was scrubbed clean and in his best suit. He had left very early, before I had even shaved. He had spent the morning in the gendarmerie, he told me. 'There are a few new faces I don't know, but there is Jules, getting along fine, with his own office. He is in charge of regularising.' 'What is he regularising?' I asked. (There were no clients about, I might add.) 'The STO,' he said. My heart came into my mouth. By this he meant the latest bad idea of Laval's, the *Service du Travail Obligatoire*. Jules – an old schoolfriend and card-playing companion of my father's – did no more than type out lists and send out letters, but he had a certain control over things. Jules had shown my father round, 'and I shook a few hands'. Just as well he had scrubbed his own, as best he could. That is why I escaped the fate of certain others of my age, amongst them several friends. When I was twenty, I spent a few not unpleasant months in the Vosges cutting wood and gathering charcoal and getting very cold with some young people from places like Lyon – smart, educated people, who had never cut wood in their lives before. But I never went to Germany.

Whether it was because of this visit, and his odd evening with Jules playing for small money and drinking, I do not know – but the Germans used us. That is to say, they used us when it suited them, for they seemed to have their own mechanics, even their own tyre people, just as they had their own newspapers and their own films and their own language. Maybe they would have used us anyway, in that case, but my father saw it as his doing. The odd thing is, he hated the Germans – they had, after all, given him his limp, in '17, and the itch would come back with heat. When the *maquisards* really got going, he didn't turn them away, when they came as clients. He served them and pretended that he didn't know, but somehow those boys never paid, only shook hands. But he said to me, one day, after the famous 'Petit Ours' (tall and elegant) had had a tube repaired on his motor cycle one evening, late: 'Don't get mixed up in all that. These boys, they are free. You are not. When all this is finished with, and those bastards are back in Berlin, that sign will have your name on it, and your son will be *le fils*. I will be the old fellow who stands watching the world go by, and getting in your hair, and proving, at ninety, what a damn good grip I still have at the expense of your clients' knuckles!' He laughed uproariously at this, but I think he was nervous, inside. I suppose he was playing a delicate game. He was a man who could never take risks. It was moulded into him, it was part of his job.

When old Mme Renouvin slid off the road in her little blue Peugeot, in 1938, and was found dead as a log in a wild rose bush, where she'd been thrown, and the report in the local paper blamed it on a 'blow-out', my poor father did not eat for days, like a fast of repentance. The fact is, Mme Renouvin was the worst driver anywhere, and in those days you could smooth out a tread in months if you took corners poorly, the surfaces were that gritty. But she was a client, and the last man to have dealt with her tyres was my father. Surprisingly, there was no decline in custom. That, as I said, came with the war, when the road traffic died away to near silence, and everyone went hungry. If we hadn't had the chestnuts, in our area, I think we might have starved to death. So my father's visit to the gendarmerie certainly put things straight.

I was in love, if there is such a thing. It was a girl who passed by on her silver bicycle every morning and every evening. She was a clerk in the silk-works, further up the road. She would work all day in the roar of the river-race and the typewriter clicking away like a mad nuthatch, and I would work in the hiss of the compressor and the clatter of my tools and the intermittent gossip of our clients, dreaming of Sunday, when I could walk in the woods and mountains, and breathe good air, and forget the war. I noticed her first as a very young girl, just coming into womanhood, when she arrived in the yard with a tyre in ribbons, and caught her ankle on the pedal, walking the bicycle towards me. She was nothing much to look at then, except for a mass of beautiful, glossy black hair, but she spoke in a very sweet, soft voice, and had a winning smile. She hardly looked at me, and (both being shy, I suppose) we exchanged only a few commonplaces. But some dart must have wormed its way in, for when I saw her pass on her way to work (as I surmised, and soon confirmed) I recognised her immediately.

This must have been just after the war broke out, in '40. I remember poppies between the vines, and the white asphodels that came up always (and still do) in the good-for-nothing field at the back, and the poplars on the river glittering like fountains in a wind – so it would have been late spring. The dust was on the road; the last of the big rains had passed a few weeks earlier. The whole stretch of the road, either way, was empty (just before all those refugees from the north trudged past, with their wheelbarrows, in June); the poppies thinned into one crimson thread of silk either side, and the plane trees dappled nobody but the birds, alighting while the 'coast was clear'. Rubbing my hands on a rag, taking a moment's break between two jobs, I saw coming up from the west, from the town, a dark-haired figure on a bicycle. I stepped back as she drew nearer: I am naturally shy, as I have said, and in the long time it takes for a bicyclist to pass us from first sighting there is much that can happen in the head, and many possibilities for difficult exchanges of regard. As I recognised her from my slightly retracted vantage-point, I have to say that I blushed; she was already hot in the face from the ride – but anyway, her skin was so 'olive' that one never saw her blush. My skin is from my mother's side; my mother had red hair, which everyone claimed was from German mercenaries a thousand years ago. What rubbish people speak!

I nodded as she passed, busily washing my hands over the pail. There was a wealthy client, a local meat-supplier, talking with my father, coming out of the big shed. He showed me a three-inch nail that had just been taken out of his nearside rear tyre. I indicated my admiration and commiseration, as one always has to with these bores, and then looked after the girl, who had now dwindled to a dot. I forgot to say that as she ticked past, just before the bore opened his mouth, she glanced at me and smiled. Her lips fell into an open pout as they automatically described a *bonjour*, but mine stayed frozen. They are like that: the muscles of my face have a will of their own, at times. It is because I am shy with people, unless they are clients. Also, it was because my voice had only just broken, and still threatened to be all at sixes-and-sevens.

It was after this that my father gave me a lecture on treating clients as if they are the most interesting people in the world, with their tedious, repetitive histories of three-inch nails and roads full of sharp stones.

You cannot fail to strike up some relationship with those who pass you at definite times six days a week, but it took two years before I had reached a sufficient maturity to wave at her as she passed, and shout some innocuous greeting (I mean, more than *bonjour* or *bonsoir*). The final 'breakthrough' came after three years when, pedalling towards me at the time I just 'happened' to be wiping my hands on a rag at the edge of the road (which is also, of course, the generous entrance to our yard), she wobbled and wandered a little towards the middle. Seeing, as I could, a large military vehicle bearing up behind her at considerable speed, I waved my hand and shouted at her to keep well in. The military vehicle swirled the dust so much that I was not certain for a few moments of her safety, but she emerged from the cloud, hugging the verge, with a somewhat shocked expression, which did not preclude her look of gratitude as she pedalled past me, thanking me very much. A look which I responded to with a clownish shrug, making her laugh.

On her way back that evening, when I just happened to be washing my hands in the pail under the old Michelin sign, with its tyre-man pointing potential clients in, the ticking slowed and stopped before I had time even to look up. 'Thank you,' she said. I stood, wiping my hands on my overalls (normally I would shake them dry, on such a fine day, because my overalls were of course greasy, but I could not shake them free of moisture with her so near). 'That's all right,' I said. We couldn't think of anything else to say for the moment, but it didn't matter. I was aware of my father hammering in the shed, and of a sleek black Milice-type car shooting past, and of a couple of motor cycles stinking of some home-made fuel – dung, probably – struggling to overtake a horse trotting with a cart full of hay and sun-blackened, nattering kids, but it was not to these that I attended with anything more than unconscious instinct. Yet I recall them all very clearly

– along with the loveliness of her form and the sweetness of her face, her legs held either side of the bicycle, very straight (I imagined) under the pale blue dress, propping the rest of her body while she could think of nothing to say. What is there to say to someone you have known as a reliable face and form for three years, but with whom you have never exchanged more than a greeting? Someone you know you will see at a certain precise point twice a day, as one sees a tree or a house or even some discarded piece of metal rubbish in a ditch, too jammed in even for the floodwaters to snatch away? Someone who, if suddenly no longer there, can leave a hole in your heart, and a feeling of doom until the moment he or she reappears?

This is all very well, but it is recounted in the warm (oh so warm!) glow of hindsight. Look at me there, in the yard, still the boy who knows nothing of the world, or keeps mum about it if he does. I was filled, let's be honest about it, with a sense of helplessness and near-panic, for this might be the only opportunity I would ever get. Once I had seen her in the market, when my father had heard of an exceptional delivery of Normandy apples and sent me off in a client's 'borrowed' car to grease the vendor's palm. But it was so odd to see her then, standing like anyone else on the ground, and not on two spinning wheels, ticking past, that I failed to do justice to the occasion by positioning myself next to her with some joke at the ready, as many a lad of my age might have done. A few other times I had reckoned I had seen her, at a distance, in one of the streets or on the main square of the town, but she had never come for repairs, or a new tyre. That's what it was like, during the war: people dealt with their own problems, their own repairs, more than in peacetime. Everyone 'cut corners', from necessity. It was a difficult period.

So I was glad when she pointed at the nearest pot-hole and said, 'I was avoiding one of those.' This gave me an opportunity to open up. 'It's the military vehicles that do it,' I said. 'The roads can't take them. The surface is battered stupid by all the trucks.' (This was about six months after the German invasion of the southern zone, by the way.) 'We are all battered,' she said. She looked sad, then, and I noticed how her face had thinned over the three years I had watched her. If she lived up in one of the villages to the north, she must bicycle a lot of kilometres each day, on a diet of boiled chestnuts or whatever. There was something sinewy about her, though, that one could trust. I nodded. I was conscious of my father in the shed, and how he'd told me to keep my mouth shut. 'Petit Ours,' she said, all of a sudden. I felt renewed panic, inside. I frowned. She looked at me, thoughtfully, as if reading my face. Then, because I didn't say anything more, she set off into the distance.

'Chatting up the skirts, then?' yelled my father, from the shed door. 'Hey, young Raoul's picking the cherries as they pass!' There was no one around, and his joke was lost to the air, after echoing as usual in the shed's cavern behind him. I told him to piss off, under my breath. I was exhilarated and at the same time very upset that the girl (whose name I didn't even know) was involved in some way with the Maquis. It never occurred to me that she might be working for the other side: that possibility might have been suggested by my feigned ignorance, but that was an automatic reflex. You've no idea on how many levels one's mind worked, in those days: isolated compartments of body and soul, with a lot of soft rubber in between.

I was upset not only because her existence might suddenly be perilous, but also because she had not stopped just for me, or for her feelings about me. In the end, I never knew how deeply involved she was, but I reckon it must have been on the simplest level of message-carrying, like a lot of kids and teenagers in those times. My position, on the main road, with the cover of the business, would have served the Resistance well. That was obvious. But I was not the one to make that sort of decision alone. Maybe my father did more than just give the *maquisards* 'God's credit', as he used to call it; but if so, I never knew about it – and trust between father and son would mean nothing, in that case.

The Germans – and, naturally, the Milice – started to furnish us with increased custom as the war dragged on and things became more and more difficult. Since many of our clients were paying us in blackmarket goods, the honest cash of the occupiers was very welcome. One day, I was sitting in a café on a Sunday morning (the place in the tiny square this side of town), when a man in a peasant's overalls (but not, somehow, a peasant's bearing), sat down next to me and said, 'Try a nail or two. Otherwise we'll be thinking you are collaborators.' With that, he got up and left. My hands were shaking so much I spilt my drink. I imagined the other, mainly old, men in the café were looking at me. The wine tasted sour (it probably was). This was about a month after the girl had stopped to thank me.

I decided to do something clownish, to make her stop again. My heart thumping like a drum all night, I rose early and started work before my father had shaved (we were 'sleeping in', that night, in the little rooms above the office). I had never missed her in the morning, but I wanted to be absolutely certain. The advantage of the morning encounter was that my father always did his paperwork until nine, and the thick net curtain across the office window obscured the view of the yard sufficiently to waylay any casual glance – even that of my father's. At a quarter to seven, with the sun laying broad stripes across the white road, so that vehicles seemed to appear and disappear as they approached, I saw the girl in the distance . . . to my relief, I have to say (nothing can be relied on except death, and so forth). There was nobody else on the road. I stepped out into the middle with a bucket full of stones and earth and started to pour it into the pot-hole, the subject of our former exchange. I was so nervous I nearly dropped the bucket, for my arms were very weak all of a sudden, but I was already stamping the stuff down by the time she stopped. 'You've no right to do that,' she said. I paused in my work, and my prepared grin froze into what must have been rather a stupid-looking grimace. 'You'll be arrested for overstepping the mark. *Les Allemands sont corrects.*' With that last familiar phrase, I knew she was 'having me on', and my grin restored itself. 'It's for you,' I said. 'I know,' she replied. She giggled (no, not quite – but there is no other word to describe such a sprinkle of delightful, teasing merriment) and pedalled off. I was left gazing after her, empty bucket in hand, little stones caught in my boots. If a truck had not blared its horn, I fancy it would have run me over.

Of course, all doors were open now. My father wondered at my whistling gaiety that day. His eyes narrowed over lunch – which we'd have, on those summer days, at a little table set under the plane tree in the corner of the yard (the road is too noisy for that, now). He poured himself a generous quantity of wine and eyed me suspiciously over the tumbler. His face (no more nor less emaciated than it was before the war, just a little sharper) gleamed with sweat and grease. I smiled back, innocently. Despite the heat, a bird was singing in the branches above us. Or perhaps I imagined that. There was a noon stillness, otherwise – though the Germans never respected our hours, and would shatter the holy quiet at unpredictable moments. I saw the wine go down his throat as I had seen it go down for as long as I could remember, and the throat always glossy and dark. He wiped his mouth and set the glass down more energetically than usual. 'Wipe that bloody stupid grin off your face,' he said. 'Or I'll think you're up to something.'

There was no doubt that the game he played was a strain on his nerves. I have no doubt that men like my non-peasant in peasant's dress had approached him in recent months, when the bolts were turning tighter on our world. He must have felt cornered, in some way. He wouldn't have liked that.

But if he didn't like what was happening under his very nose, then he never said so. That evening she waved with a merry laugh as she passed, and my father was in the yard, jacking up a big white Delage (the one with the electric gearbox that belonged to M. Coutaud, the footwear fellow). I didn't turn to look at him, but neither did he wolf-whistle, or yell something about cherries. The next morning was a Sunday, and I spent it roaming the hills around my family's village, making myself giddy from too much exercise combined with a lack of proper nourishment. We never talked about the war as such around the table: only the lack of food.

Now and again the Germans trundled up the little main street, knocking plaster and even stone off the corners of the old buildings, matching their exaggerated wheelbase against the donkey-cart dimensions of the village turns, but otherwise the war was something that went on either far away, or in the subterranean parts of the mind and the land – places one only entered at one's peril. Certainly – let me assure you of this – the Paulhans were never regarded as one of those *salaud* families who put all their eggs into the enemy basket. Many were the folk around us who looked upon the early days of Vichy as times of redemption for the poor, ground-down countryman, but they tended to be Catholics, who didn't even mind very much when the Jews (including a few of our clients, most of whom I had never even thought of as Jews) were taken away. My father disliked Catholics with a two-hundred-year-old force flowing in his veins. Thus he had no time for Pétain. Apart from anything else, he had put all his eggs into the basket of progress, which he saw as intimately connected with the automobile. Now we were living as people had been in his father's time, or even his grandfather's. To my father, the war was a personal attack on his business. Thus he felt no compunction in screwing what he could out of the enemy.

Do I make myself clear? There is nothing obscure about what followed. I will set it out like a spread of cards, as stained and smeared as my own, but no less honest. I lost, I lost more completely than most men lose . . . but let me go on. The girl and I, we slowly discovered each other; her name was Cécile Viala, she came from a small family that farmed in a simple, modest fashion two valleys west of mine, in a village I had never visited – yet we decided that we must have crossed each other's paths at numerous moments during our lives, if only at fairs and festivals, when we were to each other only another strange face under the trees.

She never again mentioned 'Petit Ours', or anything in connection with the Resistance, or even the war, very much. Twice a day we would talk, and she would arrive earlier and earlier, so as to talk for longer. She shook hands with my father, and my sisters soon learned of my 'affair'. They teased me about it, but I was happy to be teased. They said I should invite her over, for they had learned how pleasant and pretty she was from someone who worked on the machines in the silk-works – and how clever she was, too, and what a fine hand she had, and what a head for numbers. Far too good for a dolt like me! One morning, I said that I would be walking in her valley. (The idea popped into my head, just like that – really, it was not so far as the crow flies, but I am not a crow!) She looked down, shyly, and said, 'I can be walking there, too.' So we worked out a place to meet, in very sensible tones, as if we were talking about prices, or bent wheel-spokes – and as she pedalled off I realised that I had made my first secret assignation with the one I adored. I felt giddy, and even a little sick. I spread too much grease on the wheel-rims, and dropped a ring spanner on my toe. I had to sigh, as real lovers do – as if someone had taken a pump to my mouth and overdone the foot on the pedal. Each hiss of the tyres seemed to express my own impatience with the ordinariness of things: no young man could ever have been in love as much as I, I considered. Where my palm had rested on the warm leather of her saddle, lay the cold arc of a jack's brace. I turned it with a ferocity that my father happened not to see, or he would have cuffed me on the ear, as in old times.

We met under a certain, ancient chestnut tree already dropping its life-sustaining fruit, on the path that eventually winds up to her village. We avoided the shepherds and their tinkling goats as best we could, and made our way deeper into the woods. Neither of us said much, I remember. Without the long road, the yard, the trucks and bicycles, cars and horses, the dust or the puddles, the regularity of the moment twice in the day and the knowledge that it would not be extended beyond ten or so minutes, we were a little lost. The world was suddenly like an immense garden in which we could wander at will. Before a fine view of the higher mountains to the north, blue fold upon blue fold, I took her hand. Yes – we had not yet held each other's hand! Hers moved in my light hold like a little rabbit, and I thought I was going to explode. I sighed as silently as I could, and then I said, 'You make me very happy. I would like to do this every Sunday, even in winter, until I'm so old I can no longer walk.' 'What an odd thing to say!' she cried. I felt very disappointed: I had rehearsed it all the way up the slope. Then she said, very quietly: 'Me, too.'

Oh, let's get on, let's get on to the inevitable horror, after God alone knows what happiness of embrace and gentle kiss up there in those lonely, lovely hills. It will bear only brief telling. First, a big truck – a Latil, huge for those days, six cylinders, a 12- to 13-tonner diesel – passed us one morning, six-thirtyish, at a hell of a lick, scattering grit and clouding the yard in dust. Moments later, two German armoured cars shot past, clearly in pursuit, and I heard a terrible tearing sound, which I believe was some kind of machine-gun fired by the Germans at the truck. My father and I ran out into the road, only to see the Latil swerve as if to turn – in fact, it slewed to a halt in a great vortex of white dust and the Germans did likewise, if only just in time. A figure leapt from the truck and ran off into the vines, with the Germans following on foot, firing like mad. We saw, over some obscuring trees, black smoke rise up in puffs and heard several loud bangs. These, I assume, were the grenades later reported in the local paper as having been thrown at the driver (who escaped, for he still lives to recount it). The truck was full of dynamite, which any one of the many bullets fired could have set off at any moment – and it was near enough to us to have taken our shed clean away. My father and I kept our heads down, as the Germans by this time (early in '44) were very nervous and shot at anything that moved, if they felt it threatened them. But I wanted to warn Cécile, who was due to pass at any minute. To run up the road would have attracted fire, and even to go the back way, through the vineyards, would have been assumed suspicious by the Germans. So I walked up the road.

'Where the hell are you going?' yelled my father. 'For a walk,' I called back, and then kept going, keeping by the verge, with my hands in my pockets, looking as ordinary as possible but with terror beating in my mouth. I had, I think, a fifty-fifty chance of attracting fire, but none came. When I saw Cécile, I waved, and she stopped. 'You're going to be late for work today,' I said. She held my hand. She was quite startled to see me out of my usual place. She took the long, winding back route and arrived safely. My return was easier: the German guards, looking minuscule against the Latil, hardly seemed to look at me. There is nothing worse than facing danger with your spine.

That evening (by which time everything had been cleared up), Cécile thanked me with an open kiss. My father called me 'a bloody fool' and gripped my hand. He was proud of me, for once.

Then the village, one Sunday, was crossed with the darkest shadow of war – that of blood. We were sitting down to eat when the rumble of a convoy sounded. 'Bloody Boche,' murmured my father, followed by something ruder, in patois. A few minutes later there was shouting, and sounds of gunfire from the northern end of the village, near the little crossroads. There was lots of banging on doors, and we were all told to pay a visit to the *Mairie*. In the larger room, on the big table there used for the meetings of the *Conseil Municipal*, were laid three bodies. Their guts were literally looped and dripping almost to the floor, ripped open by that brief burst of gunfire. One of them was a local man, the son of the butcher, a little older than myself. The other two I did not know. They looked surprised in death, and it was said later that, though all three were members of the Maquis, no one knew why they had taken that road slap-bang into the German convoy, and then reversed in such panic. I know why: because, for all their bravery, they were mortals, and felt mortal fear. I was sick in the gutter, immediately afterwards, to my shame. We all – the whole village – filed past the bodies and came out silent and pale. A few of us cried. I had never seen anything like it before, the only dead person I had ever looked at being my poor mother, at peace in her bed.

The following week they looped a rope around the long neck of 'Petit Ours', whom they'd caught in a botched raid on the gendarmerie, and pushed him from the town bridge – over which the schoolchildren were forced to walk class by class in the afternoon, while the body swayed in the wind. The Mayor had to give a speech, thanking the Boche for keeping public order and so forth. The atmosphere was terrible. It crept up the road and cast my father and me, and most of our clients, into a deep gloom.

But some of our clients, of course, were Germans. One, in particular, was a large, friendly man – and probably the very chap, as an officer of the Gestapo, keeping an eye on things out here, who had ordered the execution of 'Petit Ours'. His huge, soft-topped Maybach (of which he was very proud, and with good reason) needed a change of tyre, about a fortnight later: a sharp stone had finally wormed its way in, on his way to the town. Both spare wheels, carried on each side of the bonnet, had been stolen, but we found the right fit. I remembered the words of the fellow in the café, and the ripped stomachs of the three good men, and the swaying body of 'Petit Ours', three days after his death, sending foul whiffs of gas up the river. In a shadowy corner of the shed, out of the bright sunlight, I took a brand-new inner tube and quietly (though my father was in the office, talking with the fellow) shaved its rubber with a small steel file on a certain spot, until it looked frayed, but still just airtight. I placed this inner tube in the new tyre. The officer's chauffeur and some other armed minion watched me fit it on to the wheel – the nearside front one – but I could scarcely stop my hands from trembling. In those days we tightened the bolts by hand with a box spanner, not a gun, so there was no risk of over-tightening, but I kept dropping the tommy bar with a big clatter. Anyway, I was giving the disc chrome a little polish by the time the big man himself stepped out of the office. I saw him, in the mirror-finish of the chrome, advance towards me, all distorted, looming over my shoulder like a big bat, and I composed my face and stood up. He pumped my hand and boomed at me about the state of the roads, and my father handed him the bill, which startled him.

The fellow patted the bonnet and began to discuss the

future of the automobile, while the two minions leaned on the sweeping mudguard and smoked. His black gloves did a little dance while he talked. He must have been some sort of technical engineer before the war, for he was full of this idea that would avoid 'grovelling in the road' with a jack and getting your knees dirty: some sort of crowbar lever that would work a fitting under the bonnet, and put up either set of wheels as desired, and bring the whole car into suspension with a final twist. (A few years later, in about '48, a British couple in sunglasses stopped for a puncture-repair in a 1¼-litre MG, and laughed when I searched for the jack. It had exactly the same system as the Gestapo officer had described, and I all but burst into tears. They did not understand my upset: they said something about the French having 'a different sense of humour' – which really means none at all, perhaps.)

While the man was boring us stupid with his broken French, booming from under his glossy peaked cap, his boots as polished as his coachwork, his jacket and breeches as black, I heard the ticking of a bicycle . . . but it cannot be Cécile's, I thought, for there is a grating sound behind it. I glanced at the road – and there was, indeed, Cécile, coming to a halt at the entrance to the yard. She looked tired and worn, as we all did, after the events of the last few weeks. When she saw the Germans, and the big car, she made to go – but thinking only of how suspicious they were, and unpredictably sensitive and vengeful, I made my apologies and went over to greet her.

'You should be ashamed,' she murmured. 'Don't worry,' I said. 'It's not as you think.' Her face brightened, and then looked intense and questioning, and then spotting something over my shoulder, she as quickly disguised her interest behind a soft laugh. The officer had evidently been staring at her, for he then boomed his own greeting: 'And might a fellow take a lift on the saddle from a pretty damsel, like a stick of bread?' – some such tripe. She shook her head, adding: 'No. My chain is loose.' That explained the grating sound, and I offered immediately to mend it. We were nearly six kilometres from the town, and more again from her village.

I noticed how sinewy her calves were, to the point of being wasted by effort and lack of proper food. She shook her head and pedalled away, without so much as a blown kiss or a wave. 'Till Sunday!' I shouted after her, recklessly. 'Till Sunday, Cécile!'

There was a banging of doors, and the Maybach purred like a black, evil cat out of the yard, and turned to drive towards the town. It was at that moment that I saw Cécile, in the distance, apparently shudder to a stop. Her head bent down and I could just make out her hand between the wheels. Clearly, the chain had come off at that moment. I began to run towards her, my father shouting after me. The Maybach got there first. As I ran, an ominous sense of doom came over me: a kind of terrible chill, that made my heart slow, though it was pumping hard to keep my speed up. With a hundred yards to go, I saw the luggage locker opened, and Cécile's bicycle placed in it. She appeared to be in conversation with the officer, for I spotted his black glove waving through the side window, like a little black snake's tongue. The long and the short of it is that she was forced – I can only think that the appropriate word – forced by circumstance (my belief is that she hoped to extract something useful from the enemy in that brief drive into the town) to accept his offer of a lift, gallant gentleman that he pretended to be. (Or perhaps was, in another airtight compartment of his brain.)

I was left coughing in a dust-cloud, for they accelerated away at great speed, as was typical – dwindling to a dot and out of sight in no time. I had not even had time to turn on my heel when there was a distant bang and clatter, as of heavy pots and pans falling off a shelf, and smoke began to drift above the plane trees. I ran as fast as I could, in the silence, but could not finally approach the spot for all the uniforms ringing it already, waving their guns – like excited kids around the blazing effigy of the *Petassou*. For myself, though, it was the beginning of winter, not the end. I leave fresh flowers every year, on the anniversary. The terrible scorch marks on the trunk have been long rubbed away by the rain and the sun and the wind, and the dent has grown out. The tree is well again – for we crop the branches close, here, as a matter of course.

I tried – I still try – to explain to people her presence in the car, but I am not sure, now, anyone really cares, or even remembers her very much. When my father 'retired', in '69, I did no more than touch up *André Paulhan et Fils*; I could not change it, I could not paint it out. Well, I have had no sons, of course, staying unmarried – and anyway, he still hangs around the yard, getting in my hair (what little I have of it left to me), and showing clients what a firm grip he has, at ninety-odd. The road is very busy, of course – business could not be better. But something went out of the job, when it all went tubeless, to my mind. I don't suppose I will miss it. You'll see the flowers on your way in, to the left, tied to the trunk. When they begin to fade and wither, I replace them with the plastic type. To be honest, no one knows the difference – shooting past as they do, these days.

Marina Warner

CANARY

WHEN HE FIRST came to London from some small town
in Delaware, one of those American states most people in
England can't place on the map, the word was that he was
sexy. He had thick hair which corkscrewed; even then, when
he must have been in his late twenties, the Heathcliff-like
grimness and metallic blackness of this pelt was lightened
by little twists of silver, and his jacket was dusted with
loose scales of dandruff. Close up, he sometimes smelt of
zinc-rich shampoos with which he tried in vain to control
it, and he would dash an impatient hand at his shoulders;
women frequently flicked at the scatter of flakes from his
scalp absent-mindedly. You could tell who he was sleeping
with when they showed this unconscious intimacy, touching
the traces his body left.

Selden had been to Vietnam. Though almost everyone
who met him then was against the war and had been on
the Grosvenor Square march and even bound their brows
in headbands of torn muslin in emulation of Viet Cong
mourning rituals (so it was believed), and although these
protests were not exactly insincere and even consumed time
as well as energy, Selden's career as a grunt was terrifically
interesting to almost everybody who heard of it; it, too, made
him sexy, to men as well as women. Pinch used to throw quiet
looks at him with those funny pale parrot eyes of his, which
are baggy above and below and show the whites all round
the iris; he was studying him, like an actor picking someone
to imitate for a part. Pinch was – is – much more active than

Selden when it comes to numbers, but he felt then that he was short of style, I think.

I first saw Selden in a half-lit backroom at an artists' party – I forget where, or which hostess it was. But I first remember half-lying, half-sitting beside him on an Indian mirrorwork bedspread spread on a low couch, both of us suffused by that aroma of patchouli cut with grass which you still sniff around stick-thin beggars working the tube. Selden seemed very grown-up: he is in fact a little younger than Pinch, but older than most of his other friends in that gang, all of whom had coincided at the College in different ways. He never did talk about the war. But he did talk about brothels and prostitution in far distant places and he had a provocative theory about casual sex and its pleasures and its costs. People always demurred, of course, but wanted to hear more. And if you were a woman, like me, who thought that sex for free (I'm old enough to call it 'free love') was a sign of liberty and that liberty was civilisation, you were outraged. But you didn't forget Selden. Or the shiver of jealous inquisitiveness his experiences produced. His defence of the bordello was an insult to Us, but it implied secrets that tantalised: that bought women are better at it, better at giving head, at displaying, at crying out, at squeezing and scratching here and there – these were the pictures that came up in my mind's eye as if I was in the mean white room with the Madonna on one wall and the girlie calendar on the other that Selden described having visited in Da Nang.

That night however he was talking about Gutenberg, and about Wittgenstein and language setting the limits of the world; he was chuckling that experiences which escaped the net of words could not have happened.

Greer was sitting close, on his other side, wearing a feather necklace and had his hair dyed blue in homage to Andy Warhol's silver; he was already celebrated then. He'd even sold out his degree show – a sequence of oil paintings about the hero Gilgamesh's drunken rampages and his passion for the wild man Enkidu, all set in grey rainswept streets of an L. S. Lowry smokestack cityscape and terraced miners' cottages.

Selden tapped his friend on the thigh, and said, 'Do you think queerness doesn't exist if there aren't any words for it?'

'Of course it does. It happens.' Greer spoke slowly, in his Northern accent that managed to be simultaneously blunt and drawling. 'In silence, in the dark, you don't need words, or pictures. There's a kind of knowledge that's got roots somewhere else. Skin remembers. My skin does.' The younger artist closed his eyes under his crown of blue. He was short-sighted and when he looked at Selden again, his pupils were very open: 'The rest's a load of rubbish.'

'Slang dictionaries,' Selden went on, 'show mankind's inexhaustible inventiveness when it comes to sex. But even so, I bet that most people learn from what they hear – and read – and pass on experience in that way. Art runs ahead of life.' He raised his head to address the room. 'Don't you want to have all the lives you read about? To be Jack Kerouac one day, Stephen Dedalus the next? Polymorphous! To escape the plan that's written there, in your DNA, as we've just been informed.'

He was working on a series of prints at the time: portraits of Famous Men for the Long Gallery in the *musée imaginaire* he was assembling, he said. He was going to make a miniature version in a box, and sell it as a multiple. But even while he was laying out his high plans, I couldn't help seeing him in the jungle of Nam and working the peepshows and whorehouses of Da Nang, and this is what happened, I think, to almost everyone who sat down near him, couch or no couch, mirrorwork bedspread or no.

'Can I think beyond what I can say?' Selden was holding his hands out in front of him as if speaking with them. 'Does it really hurt me when a man says to me "I'd like to see you dead"? Why do women shake and tremble when a man whispers obscenities at them down the telephone? Or curses them from a car for failing to indicate a turn? "Fuck you, asshole!" Why does that make my pulse pick up? When a critic writes, "This man isn't an artist, everything he touches is hideous" – does something actually happen? Am I wounded? Do I bleed? Words . . . –' He went on stabbing the air like the punctuating top line from the trumpet when the melody's unfolding below, in the low thrum and throb of the bass solo. You felt – I felt – that sex was the inevitable outcome.

But in my case it turned out it wasn't inevitable at all, because I was friends with Jessica, whom he lived with, then married, and we eventually became close, though not as close as she wanted, I think. This was partly because I wanted to keep the door to Selden ajar – I should admit that when I saw Jessica (which was far more frequently than I saw Selden) and as I began to sit for her I kept on hoping that I would see him and that we would talk and I would be able to tilt my friendship towards him rather than her. Or that he would like her paintings of me because they were of me, or that I looked especially fascinating, as if I were one of those dowered princesses whose images were sent to possible bridegrooms in the courts of Europe, and were unveiled – the curtain drawn aside – and the prince gazed upon the face and was captured. (I am trying to be honest, and honesty frequently means owning up to the sentiment and banality of one's desires.)

I sat for Jessica for days on end, over two or three years, it must have been, but intermittently, as I didn't have time to go daily. Like all the artists in that group, she always had several canvases going at once, so that when one model was available she could resume that painting, and so on. (Pinch had made so much money he had different studios on the go, too, with different models, and, it was said, different lives with them in each.) I would take the Number 31 bus to her studio – which was in a large ground-floor flat with duck blinds floor to ceiling on the front bay. In their ideal pristine state these blinds had a pale silver crinkled glow on them like Japanese rice paper or like that common biennial, honesty, which can set miniature full moons softly radiating in the flowerbeds of damp spidery London gardens in October. She had two sets of them so she could send one to be cleaned, because the smuts from the traffic load outside slipped through the window frames, past the outer sash and through to the gap between the double glazing, where they accumulated and from where they seeped into the interior of her painting space, tingeing the cool selvedges of the blinds with grey dust.

The studio was seductive; it separated you from all other concerns, and sitting for Jessica emptied your world of everything but her and you, together, one opposite the other. She talked a little when she was painting, often of the paints themselves, their character, their quality. She sometimes squeezed them straight on to the canvas and then dipped and spread them from there; she loved the slide and give of the brush in the pigment, she said, as she dragged an outline into a blur.

In the first portrait, which was called 'Anya, West London', I looked oddly cheerful, I thought. Nudes are serious, on the whole, unless they're Beryl Cook butterball belles. But I was lying on a couch, on a quilt, gazing straight out of the frame – trying for a kind of Olympia look: Jessica was an open admirer of Manet. My body was slightly swaggering in its nudity, and my face didn't show a trace of that inward rapture of self-absorption that the female nude traditionally communicates, in Old Masters and centrefolds alike. There was a touch of Third Reich naturism about it, I thought privately – a kind of pink healthiness and physical assertiveness which I didn't feel had much to do with me. But it had impact, in its disavowal of any anxiety about middle-aged flesh in the buff. It was festive; celebratory was beginning to be a buzz word at the time – and Jessica's paintings were indeed just that.

But that was the trouble with them as well. I told Branko as much: 'Jessica is so insistently upbeat about everything. It gives her work a kind of fake sunshininess. In that painting of me, I feel like an outsize apple in a supermarket, displayed under a pink bulb and sprayed every now and then to keep it glossy.'

Branko was indignant, and it was probably stupid of me to criticise Jessica at all to him. He was Jessica's most constant concert-going companion, as Selden often worked late and didn't want to interrupt a painting to hear live music. 'There's absolutely nothing faked about Jessica's sunniness,' he almost shouted at me. 'She *is* happy. When she sees happiness in others, she doesn't feel her innards contract with envy the way we do. God, how can we all be so twisted that even sunshine has to be ironical? Or some kind of a cheat? For Jessica, a sunshiny day is a sunshiny day and she rejoices in it. But you've just become cheaply cynical and brutalised – like me, like the rest of us.'

His forehead was slippery with sweat as he burst out with this; yet Branko of all the group was the artist who painted the most forbidding images of all: cross-hatched thickets of lead white and lamp black for familiar parts of London as sites of ongoing atrocities (he had been born in the Balkans, he had racial memory, he said). But Jessica was soothing, even to someone as hackled as Branko.

As I say, Jessica paid attention to the present moment and its immediate offerings of rewards: that delight in the ooze and squidge of the paint from the tube, that mother-of-pearl capsule of her studio. She had a large, clear look, wide eyes under a high, unlined brow and rain-coloured hair which swept back and down in a soft springy fall; the kind of formal harmony of face and figure that could be showered on, windswept and dishevelled and only emerge enhanced, like beach pebbles, like sorrel under woodland cover in spring, like rollered lawns. But she was kind with her beauty, and never pressed her advantage. I know this, because she liked Ian quite a lot and wanted us to sit for her together, and when we did so – only three times, as art isn't his scene, and he felt awkward stripping down in front of a woman painter – I fancied I could hear her calling to him with her brush. She painted his cock so lovingly, I was surprised when I saw the results that it hadn't risen up then and there to the squeeze of the paint and the dab and push of her brush strokes.

Ian is twenty years younger than me, and I think it embarrassed him to become a spectacle, a partner in an ill-matched couple, like in those cautionary images of a warty old lustbag and his beauteous paramour (with her hand in his purse). Jessica wanted to celebrate us, she said: 'You're an example to us all, Anya,' she'd cry, 'none of this giving up on life and love at the age of fifty . . .' Personally, I welcomed the chance to lie with Ian for hours because his body had properties for me as crystals do for New Era adepts, or multivitamins for health addicts or taking the baths for my grandfather's generation back in Austria. He has a kind of fresh briny smell as if he had been swimming in some sea before the motor car was invented, before the industrial revolution, when the word pollution merely meant ritual defilement, menstruating girls in temples, not soapy poisons frothing on the tideline and the river banks. His body hair's soft, and in the studio light, I could see its springy spirals fringing his edges against the milkiness of the interior lighting. This all sounds OTT, so I'll add that he was one of those men who are much more appealing at very close quarters than dressed – he's an ordinary thirty-year-old coffee-coloured Londoner from across a room, with twists of scrappy hair on his head and a tendency to puffiness about the eyes and waist from the statutory quantities of beer that media boys and girls have to put down after hours (Ian's a photographic technician in a studio I use for colour processing and other jobs).

I really enjoyed lying still, curled up against him for one of Jessica's paintings of couples – she posed him so that he was spread-eagled, legs making an upturned V centre front so that there was no avoiding his genitals as the focus of the composition. I was an incidental form to his glory, and though as I say, I half hoped that all these images of my body were going to be appreciated by Selden when he finally got to inspect them, I could see that I had to take second place to Ian's dark young prodigality of flesh.

By the way, it proves how wrong that old idea is – that old excuse – that a man's cock has a mind of its own. From our position prone on the bed, we couldn't see Jessica; she was concealed behind the canvas and only became visible when she hooked her head round to scan our joined skins more closely. An erection isn't involuntary in the same way as sweat or bruising, whatever St Augustine thought and everyone after him believed about unruly concupiscence and the primal curse. The signal has to pass somehow through the brain: I'm still enough of a disciple of free love to think that sex is an act of intelligence and that it's stupid to think otherwise.

But was Jessica really an *ingénue*? She seemed so. When she wasn't wearing overalls to paint, she favoured dirndls with embroidery and rick-rack. Branko had given her an original antique one from his part of the world, and the heavy cloth, when it swung against her limbs, revealed a girlish, slim neutrality of flesh – edenic in its simplicity. She spoke in a soft slow voice on the telephone, and her manner was subtly cajoling, so that agreeing to her invitation or request was like settling back on pillows plumped and patted for your head in a children's game of Hospital and having bandages tied with soft fingers around make-believe injuries. The same feeling of a game came over me when Ian and I were posing as lovers for her – that we were playing Mummies and Daddies, as my brother and I used to do, lying together on the bed pretending to do what grown-ups do at night but not knowing what the mystery was or how to enact it for real. This was disturbing – here was a woman in her forties who could make you think thoughts that you quelled, blushing, in deference to her childlike innocence of manner. Yet how was that possible? When she liked to paint her models naked, and spread-eagled in close-up?

As I see it now, it was because I am devious and cynical – though not more so, I think, than anyone else – that I didn't trust the simplicity that shone from Jessica's mouth and eyes and murmured in her gentle voice. I suspected she was up to something.

Her parents had been sixties flower children – she had been brought up on a retreat inland from Big Sur in wilderness forest; they were both therapists, who used hot springs, hallucinogenics, Gestalt psychology, Masters & Johnson's sex findings as well as a vegetable garden and glasshouses filled with crisp white mooli and hairy okra and cherry tomatoes that burst on the palate like grapes; they had a cage for raspberries soft and dimpled as babies' toes, and a small orchard where the fruit could be picked from the branch and where wigwams were pitched for special meditation sessions in solitude. (This is how Jessica described it – I never got to go there.) They treated patients on long weekends or short-term courses, and they were highly successful all through the seventies and early eighties: rock singers with custody cases, actors with a cocaine habit, record producers whose most lucrative group was insisting on breaking up, couples who wanted to raise the temperature in the marriage bed, came to the farm and helped to cook and serve the communal daily meal at the table where Jessica's genial white-haired, white-bearded father presided.

She had had a very happy childhood, she always said. Everything had always been explained in a level tone of voice; nobody ever lost their temper; when they did feel angry, her father told them to use the anger positively, to turn it into energy for good – towards work, towards others, towards sex, towards providing for self. The housework and gardening the patients did was part of the anger management training. It was highly effective, too. For the kind of guests who came to Swallow Hill were used to having servants, and the chores were a kind of game, not an interminable sentence of drudgery; they were playing Houses, if you like.

But Jessica's craving for art wasn't fulfilled by this life, and when she wanted to leave, the parents gave her a bit of money to live in London and study. There was still a lot of Northern California about her: she liked drugs – smoking dope, mainly. Again, this seemed rather a youthful taste, compared to my Irish malt, Ian's bitter or Selden's vodka.

They had an open marriage, Selden and Jessica. It was well known. Brothels still figured in his conversation as the supreme testing ground of the male libido. When he started in on the subject, Jessica simply bent over her cooking more intently, as if her hair could stop her ears as well as hide her eyes when – the last time I saw him before her death – he set off on a dithyrambic hymn to the Rue St Denis. 'The whores are real whores, no half-measures, no camouflage. In nothing but their bra and knickers and lace-up boots, right out on the street, letting it all hang out right there on the pavement: not the sweet sentimental rag-and-bone shop of the heart, but the charnel house of lites, of the gut, cunt and cock, naked, no pretences. They're fat and old and still juicy, those Paris whores – oh, the ballsiness of it. That's a real trial of a man – getting it up faced with all that. It broke my heart when they cleaned up that street. Nobody comes clean about anything any more, about the inalienable darkness deep down in all of us. That's lust, that's the pity of it, the truth of it – no quarter. That's the severe discipline that you find in the greatest metaphysical writers: in Dante, in his Inferno, with the sinners grabbing and gnawing each other in the ice.'

Jessica revered him. I wondered sometimes if she was like one of those mystics who insist on wrapping themselves in a pox-infested blanket, but remain untainted and unharmed, their inner purity proof against all contamination. I was drawn to Selden's brutality because I was one of his kind, using my camera as a shield to go into experiences for that rush of pain that makes your body palpable to yourself, that undoes the everyday numbness. But Jessica didn't seem to see that aspect of his character. When she talked about him – and she did, often – he was a tender, vulnerable, older man, rather frail, a genius who depended on her strength and her calm to bring out his full potential. The possibility of her infidelity (with all those models) kept up a steady and subtle threat, and the brothel talk a loser's way of retaliating. That much emotional management Jessica had certainly learned from her father and mother on the farm.

'Do you feel possessive? Of your lovers?' she once asked me. We were walking across the Park together, on our way a summer or two ago to a show of Paula Rego's at the Serpentine Gallery. It was one of those London evenings when motes fly gilded on the breeze under the broad-boughed trees and the voices of children and strollers and others float and mingle.

'Well, sometimes, I do, yes.'

'Is Ian faithful?'

'I don't ask.'

'Have you been faithful to him? Because you want to be?'

'Oh, Jessica!'

I wanted to say I didn't get that many opportunities, as in my world, almost all the young men are gay. But I restrained my impatience. She was also childlike in this prurience she admitted so casually – she wanted to poke in and look underneath matters adults usually keep quiet about. She and Selden did have that in common, I suppose, though their styles were different.

'*We*'re not, you know.'

'I know.'

'I like sharing. It makes me feel close to all the people I love.' I realised that under the guise of handing me Selden as a present, she was asking permission to sleep with Ian. And I knew that it wasn't up to me to accept my side of this bargain, as Selden preferred to pay, and pay for them fat and juicy and naked on the street. That was when I withdrew from the closeness that was developing between us.

But I am forgetting something. As if in one of her paintings, I'm looking at Jessica in close-up and I'm failing to give a sense of the position she and Selden occupied in the larger view.

In one of the portraits of me, I'm holding a photograph – Jessica had thought of including a camera but she didn't like the thought of it near my bare skin, she said. The image would suggest my career without violating the conventions: it was a group photograph I'd taken of the boys' gang – Selden and Greer and Ivan and Branko and Cosmas and of course Pinch – which had been published in *Vogue* in the sixties and since then had been republished any number of times in histories of those days, and, just recently, reprinted in an issue of the *New Yorker*. The magazine asked me to shoot the gang again, but it proved impossible to muster them – Greer was in Santa Cruz and Cosmas was too frail now to come up from the beautiful old monastery in Gloucestershire he's bought.

The artists in the gang all painted in the traditional way, in oil on canvas, from the model, or from observation elsewhere, but because they were bad boys, poking about in newly distempered parts of *la vie moderne*, they weren't like stuffy RAs painting the English garden – though many of them have become RAs. The group took as their motto, 'To be with art is all we want', and they came to be known, rather grandly, as The School of London (some of us dubbed it Fog

& Snog). There was debate about which of them was the greatest living painter now that Francis Bacon was dead, but nobody disputed Selden was the brains of the group. Most of them commanded higher prices than Selden, however; Greer, who was of course still the youngest, had always been the most popular with the public, and has remained so, though he's fallen under the influence of Jeff Koons and taken to painting portraits of his cats in pink bows in the style of Fragonard.

Although Jessica met all the criteria of the 'School', she was nevertheless held in an undefined exclusion zone. The many articles written about the group usually mentioned her ('Jessica Bernice, also an artist, married to Selden Finestein'), but she couldn't cross the invisible barrier into the boys' club. Like them, she painted from life, she explored forbidden areas imperturbably. They loved her – and not just Selden and Branko either. She was successful, too, in showing her work, in getting commissions, in selling, in having her pictures reproduced and distributed. One of her paintings of lovers in a London park was taken by the Tourist Board as a poster, then became a T-shirt, a souvenir mug, the cover design on stationery, and so on. But she wasn't one of the group.

She didn't complain. When I think of her now I see her in a patch of light, like the bright yellow streak she used as highlights in the scatter of sun and shade on the ground in her paintings of the park, and her head is on one side as she listens to the men, and she's smiling, gently, at what they are saying; but I can see that they are wrapped in murk, and their voices are breaking up, like a lost station on the radio. She doesn't notice this separation between herself and them; she continues to sit quietly, delighting in them, approving them. It's a cliché, I know, but Selden could do no wrong in her eyes.

In the last days of that summer, Jessica had the show I found too sunny. It included two paintings of me – the double one with Ian, and the single full-length holding the photograph.

Selden stood by his portrait to be photographed for the Sunday papers – not by me. Afterwards, at the dinner, the talk was mostly about his forthcoming retrospective, which was to fill the new Gallery of Modern Art, in the immediate

wake of a big Philip Guston show. This was going one better
than Pinch, whose most recent exhibition had been held in the
old Tate, and who had not (yet) been offered a full survey in
the magnificent space of the new GMA. Selden was planning
to fill it with his *musée imaginaire* in which he was going to
pay homage to all the influences on him – 'the *Upanishads*,
the *Odyssey*, *Finnegans Wake* – and, of course the Cabbala,
the Torah, and the Tanakh, as we Jews call your Bible'. He
laughed, genially. And looked around the table at the faces
smiling with him: his grand manner amused his friends, none
of us shared his cultural aspirations. Pinch had left school
at thirteen, and had the handwriting of a window-cleaner,
and those of us who had been educated valued education
far less than Selden. He had done a correspondence course
in philosophy after he was shipped out of Vietnam; he'd also
been going to weekly classes in Hebrew for years – and
made Jessica go with him. He was making slow progress,
but Hebrew ciphers appeared with more and more frequency
in his paintings.

'The show will be thematic,' he was saying. 'In three parts
– "Silence, Cunning and Exile". I'm going to embed my
pictures in context in each of the sections, with quotations
from the Masters. It's time we stirred people up a bit! To the
possibilities! To a new canon out there – this country is still
pig-ignorant.'

I think now we failed him – no, we failed him and Jessica
– because we let him run on, and didn't issue any kind of
challenge to him or suggest restraint. We didn't warn him not
to antagonise all those pig-ignorant guardians of culture. It's
strange, but Jessica's total tolerance of him silenced any move
on her friends' part on his behalf. Her acquiescence drew us
in like a contagion: she didn't raise a voice to say, How can
you talk like that about prostitutes, when I'm right here? She
didn't get angry with his failure to include her as a fully fledged
member of their group. She'd learned too well to channel the
energies of frustration. And their double attraction over us all
paralysed us in reaction: I was maimed, I must admit, by my
continuing fascination with Selden, and a spark of jealousy

about Ian burned low; so I failed to champion her. She was an innocent, good and sweet and beautiful and talented, and that's a lethal cocktail: underneath the most loving friendship, there remains a deep pull of mortal envy.

But perhaps my weakness didn't arise from this rank ground. I remember once being on a beach in Italy, and a couple with a small child were about twenty feet away. They began tormenting the child, who was playing in the sand next to them. They were lying on a towel and together they pulled the boy – he was naked, about three years old – towards them, and shouting at him, the mother began slapping him on his bottom and then the father whacked him over the head, screaming at him. The child began to wail and try to pull himself away, but the father lifted his arm and said, 'If you don't stop that now, I'll shut your mouth.' My heart was bumping under my ribs, I wanted to rush up and grab the child and wrap myself around him, like a human shield in a hostage film, so that they couldn't touch him without dealing with me first. But then I had an inspiration, and I grabbed my camera out of the polythene bag in which it was wrapped, screwed on the long lens and stood up to take their photograph.

The clicks shut them up. But I didn't know if I would have simply driven their violence behind doors; if next time, they'd slap the child around in private so nobody could shame them by looking.

But I never said to Selden, 'Do stop being so fucking overweening, so fucking self-aggrandising.' And I never said to Jessica, 'Selden is a monster, and, besides, my darling, you're the truer artist.'

I'm not blaming myself, or anyone else, as there are limits on friends' intrusion into privacy and a marriage is a sacred space, whatever degradations it has suffered, in which visitors take off their shoes and bare their heads and join in the liturgy as performed by the celebrants, rather than impose their own ideas.

Nevertheless, Selden plunged headlong into an exhibition of himself while Jessica stood by, gently acclaiming him at every stage. And when the blows came raining in on him, it was she who took the brunt of them; she was the personal assistant in the ministry who opens the letter bomb, she was the canary who is carried in a cage through the terror-stricken streets of a city after an unknown cult has poured liquid gas on the pavement to poison the air.

Selden Finestein: The Musée Imaginaire was a huge show; its opening marked the high point of the artistic year. He selected the work himself – he is very autocratic, and people, as I say, are scared to give him advice, even in professional matters. That was the first miscalculation. The second was that he insisted on giving sources in the original language, with translations: the wall captions included Greek and Latin tags, German gobbets from Kant and Heidegger, Danish for Kierkegaard and even Chinese and Japanese for various lines from Chuang Tzu and Zen. He intended a déliberate provocation: Selden included an enormous painting of the Death of Keats, in which Keats was a self-portrait. The wall caption read: 'Artists who have wisdom and are ahead of their times are never recognised by the philistines who set the standards of the day. My work and I have always enraged art critics. This painting is an allegory of art's inextinguishable vitality and a memorial to the poet John Keats, who was killed by a review.'

The painting showed Keats in a space superimposed on a photograph of the steps of Trinità dei Monti in Rome. The dying poet was wearing Selden's trademark red-and-white check work-shirt and braces and was surrounded by figures who – as the key on the wall explained – represented contemporary artists in the guise of their precursors. So Shelley's recognisable delicate features were given to a body holding a palette and brush with a beribboned cat on his knees (Greer). And so forth. Various newspapers and magazines were lying tattered and stained underfoot, crawling with lizards and flies and a rat or two. At the private view, Selden was helpful with explanations: 'Lizards don't do anything but lie in the sun, like our contemporary art commentators, fat on their salaries and so lazy that it's usually necessary to poke them to see if they're actually alive.'

The Gallery of Modern Art should have stopped him, could have stopped him, perhaps. But he is obstinate and hard to gainsay. The critics could have laughed – at the sheer effrontery of it. He was like a drunk picking a fight with them, and they could have ignored him, and looked at the work. But they didn't. An eminence in the art world delivered his verdict: 'Finestein has the best brains of a golden generation of British art. But as an artist, he can't draw a figure that doesn't look as if it's falling apart.' Even those papers which never usually cover art leapt in: 'Go back to the US army, Selden! or didn't they teach you to look down the end of a pencil?' *Buzz*, the television late-night arts show, summed up: 'A has-been, a no-talent, a wannabe Wittgenstein, the grand old man of transatlantic art, Selden Finestein might as well go down to the Job Centre. That's the verdict in the London art world today.' In *The Times*, an investment adviser warned: 'Contemporary art can be an invigorating risk, but in the case of Selden Finestein, the Bungee rope is liable to snap.'

Selden withdrew into his studio and shut the door. Jessica had to call him on the intercom from the front door to talk to him and he didn't always answer. She was sick with worry, and she asked us, she wanted to know. Why had they attacked him so ruthlessly? Was Selden right that the English hated foreigners, especially Americans, and ever more especially Jews? Greer told her that it was like the old U.S. adage about the blacks: 'In the North they say, "We don't mind them going high as long as they don't get close", and in the South they say, "We don't mind them getting close as long as they don't go high." Selden riled them, he went too high and he's got too close. That's why I left England, do you see that now?'

It was while Selden was in retreat that Jessica died. She opened the mail about ten days after the opening, and found the weekly papers' notices, including a review by a critic whom they had counted on. It was no better than the rest, and it hurt more, because he was a friend and had changed his mind in public without saying so in private.

When Selden did appear that night, for some food, Jessica told him she had a bad headache. He wanted to know what the weeklies had said, if the picture was improving at all. She told him it wasn't. He picked up the journal and read his friend's condemnation of his work, and went back into the studio.

The funeral was arranged before she was buried, because the need for an autopsy meant delays, and that is contrary to Judaic rite. In the synagogue, her male friends were each given a little paper head covering. I had never heard a cantor sing live before. His laments were beautiful, throaty, and I cried when I saw Selden on the other side of the room looking so haggard and wild-eyed and thin, and when the rabbi said Jessica was like the moon, reflecting the sun's light back on earth in kindly, silver rays from heaven. Pinch came in late and stood awkwardly to one side, his pouched eyes drily glittering. Greer read a poem Jessica had once illustrated. Jessica's father flew from San Francisco, though he is very old; he said afterwards that there was maybe a strain of something in the family: his great-aunt had died suddenly of an embolism, too. But he shook his head, and added, 'These strokes are of the spirit, and the body is just the spirit's vessel, which cracks with it. It was the malice she couldn't bear. Jessica believed in human beings, in love, in kindness, in goodness and she believed art was all these things. We brought her up like that. But London's no Swallow Hill, and she found out she was pretty much alone here with those beliefs. I guess it killed her.'

The interviews began again soon after, and Selden told the journalists, 'They were gunning for me, but they got her. I have work to do, and when I've done what I was put on this earth to do, I shall kill myself.'

I rang him up once or twice; but it was hard to connect to him, and I stopped trying. When I bumped into one of his studio assistants recently, she told me he's coping.

BIOGRAPHICAL NOTES

Dannie Abse was born and educated in Cardiff and studied medicine in London. Of his nine collections of poems, the most recent is *On the Evening Road* (1994). His *Selected Poems 1950–90* were brought out by Penguin who also published his autobiographical novel, *Ash on a Young Man's Sleeve*. He is a Fellow of the Royal Society of Literature.

Simon Armitage was born in 1963 and lives in Huddersfield, West Yorkshire. His latest publications were *The Dead Sea Poems* (1995) and *Moon Country* (1996). He has written extensively for radio and TV and is currently writing a play for the National Theatre.

Isobel Armstrong has been Professor of English at Birkbeck College, University of London, since 1989. She writes on nineteenth-century themes, including a study of glass and its cultural importance as a material in the period. She has published work in *Navis*. This poem is one of a series on windows.

David Bellos has translated (from French) several of Georges Perec's novels, notably *Life A User's Manual*, (from German) essays by Leo Spitzer and (from French translations) the Albanian novelist Ismail Kadare's *The Pyramid* and *The File on H*. He has written studies of Balzac and articles on nineteenth-century French fiction. His biography of Georges Perec (1993) was translated back into French and won the Prix Goncourt for biography in 1994.

Edwin Brock was born in London in 1927 and lives in Norfolk. His first collection of poetry appeared in 1960, since when he has published about ten collections in England and America. He has been poetry editor of the literary and arts quarterly, *Ambit*, since shortly after its inception in 1959. He worked as a writer with various London advertising agencies and is now retired.

John Burnside was born in Fife, Scotland in 1955 and has published five books of poetry, including *The Myth of the Twin* (1994, short-listed for the T. S. Eliot Prize) and *Swimming in the Flood* (1995). A new collection, *A Normal Skin*, will be published in May, together with his first novel, *The Dumb House*. He is currently writer in residence at the University of Dundee.

Ron Butlin, born in Edinburgh in 1949, has published five books of poetry, most recently *Histories of Desire* (1995), and a novel, *The Sound of My Voice*. His work has been translated into over ten languages and he has given readings in Mauritius, Nigeria, France, Switzerland, Eastern Europe and North America. His new novel, *Night Visits*, will be published in 1997.

Julia Darling lives in Newcastle-upon-Tyne. She has published a collection of short stories entitled *Bloodlines* and several of these and other stories have been broadcast on Radio Four. She is currently working on a novel and a second collection of stories. She also writes for and performs with *The Poetry Virgins*.

Louis de Bernières was born in 1954, and is now a full-time writer. He is the author of *The War of Don Emmanuel's Nether Parts* (Commonwealth Writers Prize for best first novel, 1991), *Señor Vivo and the Coca Lord* (Commonwealth Writers Prize, Eurasia Region 1992), *The Troublesome Offspring of Cardinal Guzman* and *Captain Corelli's Mandolin* (Commonwealth Writers Prize, 1995).

Maura Dooley won an Eric Gregory Award for her poetry, and both her collections, *Explaining Magnetism* (1991) and *Kissing a Bone* (1996) have been Poetry Book Society Recommendations. She is editor of *Making for Planet Alice: New Women Poets* (1997) and is currently editing *The Honey Gatherers: Love Poetry* and *How Novelists Work*, both for publication later in the year.

Nick Drake was born in 1961. His publications include *Chocolate and Salt* (1990), *The Poetry of W. B. Yeats* (1990) and a section in Faber's *Poetry Introduction 8*. Translations include Griselda Gambaro's *Putting Two and Two Together* (Royal Court, 1992) and Lope de Vega's *Peribanez* (Arts Theatre, Cambridge, 1997). He won an Eric Gregory Award in 1990 and is completing his first collection on a Wingate Scholarship.

Maureen Duffy has published five books of poetry, fifteen novels, six plays (and work for radio and television) and six non-fiction books, including biographies of Aphra Behn and Henry Purcell, and a play about Purcell, produced at Southwark Playhouse. She is Chairman of the British Copyright Council and the Copyright Licensing Agency. She is currently working on a new novel.

Ian Duhig was born in 1954. He worked for fifteen years with homeless people and has since been Creative Writing Fellow at Lancaster and Leeds Universities. In 1987 he won the National Poetry Competition; his collections, *The Bradford Count* and *The Mersey Goldfish*, were shortlisted for the Whitbread and T. S. Eliot Poetry Prizes respectively. 'Nominies' is the title-poem of his third book.

Jane Duran was born in Cuba and brought up in the USA and in Chile; she has lived in England since 1966. Her poems have appeared in a variety of magazines and anthologies, and a selection was published in Faber's *Poetry Introduction 8* (1993). Her first full collection, *Breathe Now, Breathe* (Enitharmon Press), won the 1995 Forward Poetry Prize for Best First Collection.

Elaine Feinstein's first book of poems appeared in 1966. She has written twelve novels, several radio plays and has translated the poems of Tsvetayeva. In 1995 she was chairman of judges for the T. S. Eliot Poetry Prize; she is a Fellow of the Royal Society of Literature and Hon. D.Litt. of Leicester University. Her *Selected Poems* came out in 1994; her new collection, *Daylight*, appears in March 1997.

Tibor Fischer was born in Stockport in 1959 of Hungarian origin. His first novel, *Under the Frog*, was shortlisted for the Booker Prize in 1993, when he was listed among the Granta Best of Young British Novelists. His second, *The Thought Gang*, appeared in 1994. His third novel, *The Collector Collector*, will be published in March 1997 and he will co-edit *New Writing 8*.

Roy Fisher was born in Birmingham in 1930 and is a writer, jazz musician and broadcaster. He has published ten collections of poetry, of which the most recent are *Birmingham River* and *The Dow Low Drop: New and Selected Poems*. He has worked collaboratively for many years with the artist and book designer Ronald King, and also with Tom Phillips, Derrick Greaves and Ian Tyson.

Penelope Fitzgerald won the Booker Prize with her third novel, *Offshore*, which was based on her experience of living with her three children on a houseboat on the Thames. Two later books, *The Beginning of Spring* and *The Gate of Angels*, were also shortlisted for the Booker Prize. Her most recent book was *The Blue Flower*. In 1996 she was awarded the Heywood Hill Prize for her achievement as a writer.

Michael Foley was born in Northern Ireland in 1947. He has published three collections of poetry (*True Life Love Stories*, *The GO Situation* and *Insomnia in the Afternoon*), a collection of free translations of French poetry (*The Irish Frog*) and two novels (*The Passion of Jamesie Coyle* and *The Road to Notown*).

John Forrester is Reader in the History and Philosophy of the Sciences at Cambridge University. Among his publications on psychoanalysis are *Language and the Origins of Psychoanalysis, the Seductions of Psychoanalysis, Freud, Lacan and Derrida* and, with Lisa Appignanesi, *Freud's Women*. He is preparing a cultural history of Freudianism in the twentieth century.

Lavinia Greenlaw has published two pamphlets of poems (*The Cost of Getting Lost in Space*, 1991, and *Love from a Foreign City*, 1992). Her first full-length collection, *Night Photograph*, was published in 1993 and *A World Where News Travelled Slowly*, her second, appears in autumn 1997. In 1996 she was Writer-in-Residence at Wellington College.

John Harvey studied at Cambridge University where he now teaches English Literature. His first novel, *The Plate Shop*, won the David Higham Prize in 1979; his second, *Coup d'Etat* (1985), deals with military dictatorship in a European country. His third, *The Legend of Captain Space*, appeared in 1990. His non-fiction writing includes *Victorian Novelists and their Illustrators* and *Men in Black*.

Philip Hensher's novels include *Other Lulus* and *Kitchen Venom*, recently in paperback. His stories have been broadcast on BBC Radio and published in various anthologies, and will be collected as *Zuleika Dobson in the Great War*. He wrote the libretto to Thomas Ades' opera, *Powder Her Face*. He writes on a wide selection of topics for several newspapers and magazines.

Michael Hofmann was born in Freiburg in 1957 and lives in London and Gainesville, Florida. He has published three books of poems; a fourth, *Approximately Nowhere*, is due in 1997, along with a book of essays. Among his numerous translations are novels by Franz Kafka, Wolfgang Koeppen and Joseph Roth, and by his late father, Gert Hofmann.

Christopher Hope's last novel was *Darkest England*. He is a past editor of *New Writing* as well as the author of *A Separate Development, My Chocolate Redeemer, Serenity House* (shortlisted for the 1992 Booker Prize) and *The Love Songs of Nathan J. Swirsky*. He is at work on a book, *Me, The Moon and Elvis Presley* from which 'Pogrom' is taken.

Michael Hulse grew up in Stoke-on-Trent and Germany and works in publishing and TV in Cologne. His poetry collections include *Knowing and Forgetting* (1981), *Propaganda* (1985), *Eating Strawberries in the Necropolis* (1991) and *Mother of Battles* (1991). He co-edited *The New Poetry* (1993) and has won the National Poetry Competition and Eric Gregory and Cholmondeley Awards.

Robert Irwin used to lecture in medieval history at St Andrews University and has written four novels, *The Arabian Nightmare, The Limits of Vision, The Mysteries of Algiers* and *Exquisite Corpse*, and two works of non-fiction, *The Middle East in the Middle Ages* and *The Arabian Nights: A Companion*. His *Islamic Art in Context* will be published in 1997. He is working on an anthology of classical Arabic literature.

A. L. Kennedy has published two collections of short stories, *Night Geometry and the Garscadden Trains* and *Now that You're Back*, and two novels, *Looking for the Possible Dance* and *So I Am Glad*, and has won numerous literary awards. She was listed among the Granta/Sunday Times Twenty Best of Young British Novelists. Her first full-length film, *Stella Does Tricks*, will soon be released and her next book, *Original Bliss*, appears in spring 1997.

John McGahern was born in Dublin in 1931 and is the author of three collections of short stories, of which the most recent is *High Ground* (1983), and five novels, *The Barracks* (1962), *The Dark* (1965), *The Leavetaking* (1974), *The Pornographer* (1979) and *Amongst the Women* (1990) which was shortlisted for the Booker Prize. He lives in County Leitrim.

Shena Mackay's most recent novel, *The Orchard on Fire*, was published last year to great acclaim and shortlisted for the Booker Prize, the McVitie's Scottish Writer of the Year Prize and the Saltire Prize – results as yet unknown . . . ; it will appear this year in paperback. Her stories have appeared in many magazines and anthologies as well as on radio, and most appear in *Collected Short Stories*. She is at present completing a collection of stories and is at work on a novel.

Duncan McLaren's first novel, *Tunnel Vision*, is set in an accountancy firm; its first chapter appeared in *PEN New Fiction 2*. His second novel, *Archie Van Gogh*, did not interest publishers in the least. His third, *Chinese Illustrations of the Path to Immortality*, is so clearly unpublishable that he did not bother to submit it. A questionnaire 'How do I carry on with this book I'm writing about contemporary visual art?' is available from the author.

Paul Magrs was born in Jarrow in 1969. He did his PhD at Lancaster University where he also took their MA in Creative Writing. His first novel, *Marked for Life*, is in Vintage paperback, along with a collection of stories, *Playing Out*. His second novel, *Does It Show?*, appeared in 1997.

David Malouf's most recent novel is *The Conversations at Curlow Creek*, published later this year in paperback. His other novels include *Johnno*, *Fly Away Peter*, *The Great World* (winner of the Prix Femina Etranger and the Commonwealth Writers Prize in 1991) and *Remembering Babylon*, which was shortlisted for the Booker Prize and won the first IMPAC Prize last year.

E. A. Markham heads the Creative Writing programme at Sheffield Hallam University and has edited *Sheffield Thursday*, *Writing Ulster*, *Hinterland* (the Bloodaxe Book of Caribbean Poetry), and the *Penguin Book of Caribbean Short Stories*; his publications include three collections of short stories, *Something Unusual* (1986), *Ten Stories* (1994) and *Taking the*

Drawing Room Through Customs (1996), and six collections of poetry.

Pauline Melville's collection of short stories, *Shape-Shifter*, won the Guardian Fiction Prize, the Macmillan Silver Pen Award and the Commonwealth Writers' Prize for best first book. *The Ventriloquist's Tale*, her first novel, will be published in 1997.

Dorothy Nimmo was born in 1932 and educated at York and Cambridge. She started to write in 1980. She took an MA in Creative Writing at Lancaster University and is now Warden of the Friends Meeting House in Settle. She has published four collections, most recently *The Underhill Experience*, and won a Cholmondeley Award in 1996.

Ruth Padel's poems have appeared in newspapers and magazines, including the *New Yorker*, the *Irish Times*, the *Observer*, the *Sunday Times* and *London Review of Books*. Her third collection, *Fusewire*, appeared in 1996. Her prose books, *In and Out of the Mind* and *Whom the Gods Destroy*, are available in paperback. She is writing a book on myth, song and desire.

Kathy Page has published four novels, the latest being *Frankie Styne and the Silver Man* (1992). Her short stories are collected in *As in Music* (1990). She is now completing another collection, *Paradise and Elsewhere*, and a fifth novel, aided by an Arts Council Bursary.

Peter Redgrove's most recent books of verse are *Assembling a Ghost* and *Orchard End*. He has recently published *Alchemy for Women* with Penelope Shuttle, a practical version of their famous *The Wise Wound*. He has published twenty-four volumes of poetry and ten books of prose fiction, most recently *What the Black Mirror Saw* (1997) and fourteen of his plays have been broadcast by the BBC. He was awarded the Queen's Gold Medal for Poetry in 1996.

Keith Ridgway lives and works in Dublin. He has had stories and poems published in various magazines and anthologies, including *Phoenix Irish Short Stories 1996*. His novel, *The Long Falling*, will be published by Faber in Spring 1998.

Robin Robertson is from the north-east coast of Scotland. His first collection, *A Painted Field*, is published by Picador.

Jane Rogers has written five novels, *Separate Tracks*, *Her Living Image* (winner of a Somerset Maugham Award), *The Ice is Singing*, *Mr Wroe's Virgins* (screened on BBC 2 in 1993 in her own four-part adaptation) and *Promised Lands*. Her TV play, *Dawn and the Candidate*, won a Samuel Beckett Award in 1989. She teaches part-time on the MA in Writing course at Sheffield Hallam University.

Penelope Shuttle lives in Cornwall with her husband, Peter Redgrove. Her sixth book of poems, *Building a City for Jamie*, appeared in 1996. *Alchemy for Women*, co-authored with Peter Redgrove, their sequel to *The Wise Wound*, was published in 1995.

Jon Silkin's most recent collections of verse are *The Lens-Breakers* (1992) and *Selected Poems* (1994). He has recently published a critical work, *The Life of Metrical and Free Verse in Twentieth Century Poetry*. He edited *The Penguin Book of First World War Poetry* and, with Jon Glover, *The Penguin Book of First World War Prose*; also *Wilfred Owen: The War Poems* (1994). He co-edits the literary quarterly, *Stand*.

C. K. Stead (b. 1932) lives mainly in New Zealand and has published nine books of poetry, seven of fiction, four of criticism, and has edited *Letters and Journals of Katherine Mansfield* and *The Faber Book of South Pacific Stories*. Three of his novels, including *The Death of the Body*, have recently been reissued; his *Selected Poems* will appear in 1997. He was appointed CBE in 1985.

Rebecca Swift was born in 1964 and read English at Oxford. She has edited *Letters from Margaret* (1992) and *Imagining Characters: Six Conversations about Women Writers* by A. S. Byatt and Ignês Sodré (1995), and her poetry appeared in *Virago New Poets*, 1990. She has worked as an editor at Virago Press and in 1996 she co-founded The Literary Consultancy.

Hwee Hwee Tan was born in Singapore in 1974 and is completing her M.Phil at Oxford where she also tutors. Her short stories have been broadcast on the BBC and won one of the Ian St James awards. 'The Gambling Man' is based on a drama script which she developed with the Television Corporation of Singapore. She has recently completed her first novel, *Foreign Bodies* (Michael Joseph, August 1997).

Matt Thorne was born in Bristol in 1974 and educated at Sidney Sussex College, Cambridge. He has recently completed an M.Litt. in Creative Writing at the University of St Andrews, during which he wrote a novel, *Tourist*. 'The Honeymoon Disease' is his first published fiction.

Adam Thorpe was born in Paris in 1956. He has published two volumes of poetry, *Mornings in the Baltic* (1988) and *Meeting Montaigne* (1990), and two novels, *Ulverton* (1992) and *Still* (1995). He has written three plays for BBC Radio and his first stage play, *Couch Grass and Ribbon*, was performed at the Watermill Theatre, Newbury, in 1996. He is working on a new novel and poetry collection.

Anthony Thwaite has published twelve books of poems, including a selection in the Penguin Modern Poets series, *Poems 1953–1988* and *The Dust of the World* (1994). He has taught in Japan and Libya, been literary editor of the *Listener* and *New Statesman*, and co-editor of *Encounter*, 1973–85. He has received a Cholmondeley Award and was appointed OBE for services to literature.

Charles Tomlinson's paperback *Collected Poems* appeared in 1987. His work is translated into Italian, German, Spanish and Portuguese (the Italian edition received the Cittadella Premio Europeo). He translates from Spanish and Italian and has edited the Penguin *Octavio Paz*. In 1995 he received the medal of the City of Genoa for *In Italia*, all his poems about Italy with Italian versions.

Lorna Tracy is a co-editor of *Stand* magazine. In 1981, Virago published her story collection, *Amateur Passions*. Recently her stories have appeared in *Iron, Panurge, Bête Noire, The Cuirt Journal* and *New Writing 5*.

John Tusa, former Managing Director of the BBC World Service, was born in Czechoslovakia and came to England in 1939. He joined the BBC in 1960 and worked as a journalist on radio and television. In 1983 he was the Royal Television Society's TV Journalist of the Year and in 1984 won the BAFTA's Richard Dimbleby Award. He is Managing Director of the Barbican Centre.

Marina Warner is a novelist, historian and critic. Her most recent fictions are *Indigo* (1992) and the collection of short stories, *The Mermaids in the Basement*. Her non-fiction includes *Alone of All Her Sex, Monuments and Maidens* and *From The Beast and the Blonde*. In 1994 she gave the BBC Reith Lectures on the theme, *Managing Monsters: Six Myths of Our Time*.

John Hartley Williams teaches English at the Free University of Berlin. His first collection, *Hidden Identities* (1982), was followed by *Bright River Yonder* (1987), containing the poem with which he won the Arvon International Poetry Competition in 1983. Subsequently, he has published *Cornerless People* (1990), *Double* (1994) and *Ignoble Sentiments* (1995). *Teach Yourself Poetry*, written with Matthew Sweeney, and *Canada*, a new book of poems, will appear in 1997.